DEVIL'S OWN DAY

A SPY DEVILS THRILLER

JOE GOLDBERG

JOE GOLDBERG BOOKS

NOTE

All statements of fact, opinion, or analysis expressed are those of the author and do not reflect the official positions or views of the Central Intelligence Agency (CIA) or any other U.S. Government agency. Nothing in the contents should be construed as asserting or implying U.S. Government authentication of information or CIA endorsement of the author's views. This material has been reviewed by the CIA to prevent disclosure of classified information. This does not constitute an official release of CIA information.

First Electronic Edition: November 2023

978-1-7364745-7-0

First Print Edition: November 2023

978-1-7364745-8-7

First Hardcover Edition: November 2023

978-1-7364745-9-4

Cover by Damonza.com

Printed in the United States of America

✿ Created with Vellum

To my family, friends, and fans

FOREWORD: FROM BRIDGER ONCE MORE

I'm a lucky guy.

I've worked in my peculiar way for the United States to protect it from its enemies. We have made a difference. I'm proud of that.

I know our story is written as fiction. But truth is stranger than fiction, as I told you in the foreword to the first book. It felt strange to inform anyone about our truth—our peculiar way of defending the country. You don't have to believe the Spy Devils exist. That is irrelevant. What is relevant to me is your awareness that individuals and groups are doing the hard things to protect our country. One is my group. The Spy Devils.

I'm a lucky guy.

I've built close relationships and surrounded myself with people I trust and who trust me with their lives. Together we formed a unique bond to accomplish critical, impossible tasks. We are not superheroes with special powers...although Imp might think he is. We are just people, slugging it out, day-to-day, because that is what we do.

I begrudgingly agreed to let Joe write these books, the *Spy Devils Series* as he calls it, as my way to let you know more about us. I need to know a few people are aware of us, what we do, and why. Call it whatever you want. Ego? Validation? A pat on the back? Stupid? Arrogant?

I wanted people to know about Demon, Imp, Snake, Beatrice, Milton…and Beast. These people have real names, lives, desires, wants, and all the rest. We are not perfect people, as you have read. Like many who serve our country, we do the hard things when asked.

I haven't asked Joe how many books have been sold. I don't really care. He told me anyway—"a few." Perfect. Those "few" know about us, and that's enough. That was the goal.

I've changed in four years. Reading about yourself can do that.

Change permeates this book.

The fact that I am writing my *third* book foreword is an example of that change.

Lena has everything to do with my growing, learning, and adapting. I now deal with moral and ethical issues across the work/life spectrum, something I have never spent time on before. I don't shrug any action off as "we are good, they are bad," and move on.

Time has changed me. These books had to be written *now*. Who knows what will happen *then*? Isn't that true about everything? I don't know if there will be more. I'm certain Joe has plenty of material if he needs it.

At the very least, I hope the stories entertained you.

Time will tell.

Bridger
November 2023

PREFACE

On April 6th and 7th, 1862, more than 100,000 Union and Confederate soldiers engaged in one of the bloodiest battles ever fought on American soil near a small, log-cabin church in west Tennessee named after the Hebrew word for peace.

Shiloh.

Late on the first evening, after twelve straight hours of fighting, Brigadier General William Tecumseh Sherman arrived at the headquarters of his friend and commanding officer, General Ulysses S. Grant. Sherman found Grant—broken sword and all—chewing on a soggy cigar in the rain, which had begun soaking the battlefield.

"Well, Grant," said Sherman, "we've had the devil's own day, haven't we?"

"Yes," Grant replied. "Lick 'em tomorrow, though."

By the end of the fight, more than 23,000 soldiers were dead, the most of any key battle to that point of the war.

1

KILL THE DEVIL

Abaddon Ranch, West Texas Hill Country

Death was near. It had its eyes on his men advancing on the ranch.

He felt death's eyes on him, too.

All due to the ego-driven stubbornness of a drug lord.

Courtesy of the Devil.

Colonel Roberto Rocha froze when he heard the *zip-thwack* followed by the *splish* of a bullet entering and then exiting a head. Warm blood droplets carried by the cool wind splattered on his thick mustache and unshaven cheeks. He waited. Then the sound came—the *thud* of a body hitting the ground.

Mierda.

He wiped the blood off with the sleeve of his camouflage night uniform.

Rocha looked down at Julio, who, until a few seconds ago, had been his loyal aide and brother-in-law. Now, sections of his head were missing.

Death had arrived. My sister will hate me.

Despite the chaos, he took a moment to admire the blanket of stars above him. The December breeze brought whiffs of sage, moist dirt, gunpowder, and Julio's blood.

Then he watched the star-like flashes from the dozens of guns firing in the distance. Sharp cracks of gunfire followed. Panicked voices screamed through his communication headset. The critical element of surprise was gone.

It will only get worse.

He warned the boss that he needed more planning time, especially after being told who he was against.

"Bridger? The Devil? Are you sure?" he said, with a suddenly dry mouth.

"Yes," Vincente Ramirez said. "And his Spy Devils. I need every one of them dead."

The leader of Mexico's notorious *Cártel de Jalisco Nueva Generación* (CJNG) sat on a couch inside one of his hideaway homes in Guadalajara. His black eyes were glued to a soccer match on a massive television fixed to the wall.

¡Dios mío!

"Many have tried and failed to capture or kill the Devil," he said. Rocha's lower teeth chewed on his mustache.

"You will not fail. Kill the Devil, his Spy Devils, and anyone in your way."

"But—" Vincente's head jerked, and the angry glower on his face informed Rocha the discussion was over. "Yes, El Hombre."

Vincente stood and put his hands on Rocha's shoulders. Vincente's fingers dug painfully into the soft flesh above his collarbone. Dark, unblinking eyes drilled directly at his eyes. Rocha concentrated on them rather than his pain. Rocha had proven his bravery dozens of times in battle. Still, the CJNG leader scared him to death.

"I have confidence in you. You have never failed me," Vincente said in a cold whisper. "Use all your resources. The Devil *must* die."

Another moment passed then Vincente released Rocha from his grip.

"Yes. I understand," Rocha said as he left.

Colonel Roberto Rocha was an experienced former Mexican Army officer. He gathered his kill teams from across the southern border and major cities of the United States. Their normal function was to protect the drugs, weapons, and humans the cartel trafficked across the United States.

He knew the success of this kind of commando operation required a well-trained force. Despite having over forty men, as ruthless as they were individually, trying to put them together as an assault force without proper training was foolish.

I have no choice. Orders.

Rocha did have a handful of elite ex-soldiers under his command. They had resigned with Rocha from their dangerous, low-paying army jobs chasing and fighting cartels. When Vincente offered him a very lucrative position in the CJNG, he accepted and took his men with him. Rocha hated to waste them on this mission.

Following Vincente's orders, he devised his attack plan working with the annoying Chinese intelligence officer who *had* provided surprisingly good intelligence on the ranch and surrounding terrain. He had hoped that, combined with the element of surprise and his professional soldiers, it would be enough to avoid disaster.

Now surprise is lost.

"Forward, move forward," he commanded the driver as he got into the passenger seat of his black Ford F-150. His team jumped into the back of the truck and started toward the ranch.

Gunfire pops pierced the darkness. Then he heard a distant *thump* like he had hundreds of times during his career.

He watched the lead vehicle explode, tumble end-over-end in the air, and break into pieces. Rocha ignored the burning wreckage illuminating the darkness as they sped by. The air was now thick with the smells of burning rubber, gasoline, and gunpowder.

Rocha gripped his pistol with a steady hand as bullets clanged off the vehicle. The truck lurched forward, swerving by a barricade and dodging the mangled bodies of his men scattered in every direction. His blood heated with rage at the waste.

Rocha felt the vehicle shake. He saw a massive detonation and a flash on the far side of the burning house.

Claymores. They have claymores.

"Who is in the field? Report!" Despite being trained to be calm and project leadership in battle, his frantic shouts betrayed anger and anxiety.

"We—" a man started to say, then Rocha heard the *rat-a-tat-tat* of machine guns and the flash of more explosions.

"Are you there?" He whipped his head toward the driver, who fixed his eyes on the chaos he was driving toward. "We will go to the front. Truck 2. Go to the far side. Truck 3. Go to the back."

When the vehicles reached the battered and burning house, Rocha's remaining men jumped out and scurried to their positions.

Rocha pushed his door open and hopped out. He pulled a rocket-propelled grenade man-portable launcher from his truck, aimed at the house, and fired. Rocha felt the ground rumble through the soles of his boots. Feeling a small degree of satisfaction, he took out another grenade and fired. His feeling of elation evaporated when he heard jet engines roaring.

How did they not disable the plane? I told them to do that first.

He ran around the back and saw the plane going vertical into the sky. Anger mixed with dejection as he surveyed the bodies scattered on the runway. When his phone rang, his jaw clenched. He knew who it was. Rocha toggled his headset to the phone connection. It connected with a beep.

"What is the status? Are they dead?" Vincente asked.

Rocha turned toward the house and took a few steps. He had survived. He had cheated death.

"The ranch was heavily defended as I said it would be. Many men are dead."

"Is the Devil dead?"

"I am not sure. A plane escaped—"

"*¡Corra!*" a soldier shouted as he sprinted by a confused Rocha. Then he understood.

Despite being only twenty feet from the house when it exploded, his mind had time to comprehend what had happened…

But how?

It didn't matter *how*.

He had been lured to his death by the Devil.

2

WHAT ABOUT ME?

Guadalajara, Mexico

"Rocha? Rocha? Are you there?" Vincente shouted into his phone, sending clouds of spit onto his well-worn brown leather couch.

When he was sure there would not be an answer, he disconnected the call and dropped the phone on the couch next to him.

He leaned back, inhaling the smells of the eggs, beans, chorizo, and tortillas cooking in the kitchen of his safe house in Tlajomulco, a city south of Guadalajara. Every few days, Vincente rotated his location among a collection of villas across the state of Jalisco in central-western Mexico, but he liked this one the best.

Morning light leaked through narrow slits in the closed bullet-proof blinds. He ground his rough palms into his eyes. It was not how he had hoped the day would start.

Rocha is dead. Unless Bridger is dead, we have failed.

Bridger and the Spy Devils had often exposed CJNG's financial operations and personnel on social media. It was an inconvenience, but Vincente played the long game.

I may lose millions in revenue, and many men will be lost or die, but I do not care.

"I will make a billion dollars this year," he said aloud as if hearing it made the losses less painful.

He had accepted attacks as the cost of doing business. His cartel operation grew daily to feed the seemingly insatiable American drug appetite. He had planned to expand his business until Bridger's recent meddling in Europe. Bridger had destroyed Vincente's multi-billion-dollar deal with Charlie Ho, the mastermind behind the Chinese cartel known as "The Enterprise."

Vincente sat forward and clenched his hands into fists, cursing himself for being taken in by the charismatic Charlie Ho. Ho's grand strategy to take over synthetic drug production, supply, and distribution in parts of Europe and the billions it would deliver was too tempting to turn down. Months of planning. Millions invested. Gone in a few days at the hands of the Devil.

Ho had allowed it. Vincente knew the Chinese cartel leader had underestimated Bridger—despite Vincente's warnings.

Ho is lucky he is in prison, or he would be dead.

Vincente stood and walked out of his first-floor bedroom into the dim hallway. A few steps brought him into a small kitchen. Mia, a dark-haired prostitute wearing only black shorts, stood over the stove, holding a pan and flipping fried eggs in crackling butter. Besides being a favorite of his security team, Mia was an excellent cook.

"Buenos días, Mia."

"Good morning," Mia replied. She scooped up Vincente's eggs and slipped them onto a plate. She added beans and tortillas and handed the plate to him. He lifted it to his nose and smelled the steaming food.

"Gracias." He smiled and nodded politely at the young pretty woman. "Do not burn yourself."

She giggled as he left.

As he ate breakfast on his couch, he tried to forget his recent string of failures—more failures than he had endured in years.

He ripped a tortilla, dipped in the beans, and stuffed it into his mouth.

I am "El Hombre." I am the man. I do not accept defeat. I am never humiliated.

He picked up his remote and mindlessly flipped from one *fútbol* match to another. It was his favorite benefit of having wealth. He could afford every satellite channel worldwide that carried soccer.

When Vincente's phone rang, his mouth curled into something resembling a smile after reading the name on the caller ID.

"This man cannot be killed," he told the former Chinese assassin as he answered.

"He...he...he is *not* dead?" Li Chu stammered.

"No, but Colonel Rocha is." Vincente stopped pushing the buttons, pausing on a channel carrying a match he cared nothing about.

"What happened to all your men?"

"I expect they are all dead."

"My information on the location was correct," Li Chu said. Vincente sensed a wave of fear in the voice.

"Yes." Already bored with the poor soccer play on the screen, he shoved a forkful of eggs into his mouth. He repeated that until his plate was empty.

"He was there," Li Chu said more as a hope than a statement of fact.

"He escaped." Vincente picked up the remote and started scrolling again.

"What do you mean? How is that possible?"

"Does it matter?" Vincente let out a loud burp.

"How could...the American authorities will search the ranch."

"They do not know anything." Frustrated with the lack of anything to distract him from the conversation with the irritating man, Vincente tossed the remote on the couch. It bounced off and clattered to the tile floor.

"What are you going to do?" Li Chu asked.

"He will come for me. If not before, certainly now." He turned toward the door and shouted. "¡Diego!"

The door opened, and a giant man stepped in. His tattooed bald head scraped the top of the frame. He wore jeans and a faded black leather vest lined in metal studs. Leather bands wrapped around his wrists. Leather gloves with fingers cut out covered his hands.

"We are leaving." The giant man grunted, nodded, and turned to leave. "Wait."

"What about me?" Vincente had forgotten about Li Chu until he heard the worried voice.

"Good question. What about you?"

Vincente abruptly ended the call. He picked the remote up off the floor and started scrolling again. Then his phone beeped, signaling a text had arrived. After reading it, he rotated his head toward the hulking man still standing at the door.

"Diego. Do you have any people left in Texas?"

"A few," replied a voice as deep as a well.

"Killers?"

"Yes," he said.

"Good. Call them."

Vincente looked at the TV one last time, then jammed his thumb on the power button. "Tell them to get to Austin immediately. There are people there that I need to die."

3

THERE ARE SURVIVORS

Santa Fe, New Mexico

Bridger's West Texas Hill Country ranch was destroyed.

Trowbridge Hall, Bridger, the Devil, leader of the Spy Devils, had named his sanctuary Abaddon, a biblical term for "Place of Destruction."

Well, that name turned out to be prophetic, he thought.

Few knew of its location and its ownership was a maze of untraceable dummy companies.

A river and tributaries crisscrossed 2,698 acres of pasture, brush, woods, and flat to rolling to hilly terrain. Located between Austin and El Paso, the former corporate retreat provided hunting, hiking, riding, and fishing. Access to the location was only by a private dead-end road or air, so it had a runway and hanger for his planes and helicopters.

A 6,200-square-foot main house sat prominently on a hill. Inside had been eight bedrooms, five baths, a workout room, a modern open kitchen, bars, and vaulted ceilings. Outside were an equestrian center, stables, corral, barns, wilderness cabins, stocked ponds, a shooting range, and abundant wildlife and livestock.

He would miss his ranch, especially the custom-built golf course made of replicas of the world's greatest par-3 holes. It was his solitude inside his solitude, but now law enforcement and others were investigating it as a crime scene.

Bridger had installed sophisticated defensive and communication systems, just in case, hoping they would never be needed. Remote machine guns. Barricades. Explosives and an armory. They used them all just hours ago when the ranch was raided in the middle of the night.

The Spy Devils barely escaped on his plane.

Before the attack, he planned to retire. That was why he asked everyone to come to the ranch. He thought he could put the Spy Devils on hold, maybe even disband them. Then, he would build a life with Lena.

Then they were attacked. He didn't know by whom, but retirement would have to wait. Now, he was on a mission to find who attacked the ranch and kill them.

Exhausted, filthy, and still in shock, they arrived at Bridger's New Mexico ranch outside Santa Fe that morning. He knew the adrenalin of the battle would wear off and be replaced by the reality of their situation. Bridger told everyone to clean up, rest, and gather later that afternoon.

The sprawling eight-bedroom stone ranch house was located south of Santa Fe between the Sangre de Cristo Mountains and the Galisteo Basin. Large windows offered breathtaking panoramic views of the five hundred acres of open range, grasslands, and trails. Scattered across the land were a caretaker's house and four more bungalows. A single road led to the ranch. It had a helicopter pad, a rifle range, off-road vehicles, trails, and a barn with horses.

Bridger sat at the end of a large rectangular natural stone table on the patio at the back of the house. The blue limestone patio was decorated in earth tones, stone, and wood, and the table, heavy chairs, and benches sat under globes that pushed out yellow light. Various foods were on another table in the outdoor cooking area and bar at one end of the patio.

Wood pillars held up the wood-beamed and stucco overhang. The arched stained-glass windows of Bridger's private library were on the wall behind him. A huge open stone fireplace warmed the area from the late afternoon chill.

Bridger focused on Lena's dark brown eyes. He gazed at her long, dark, straight hair, olive skin, and warm smile. He caught a whiff of Chanel No. 5.

In addition to being a master chef and restaurant owner, Lena Hamed had been the niece of the notorious terrorist bomb maker called Specter. She had spent her adult life protecting him, which included informing the CIA about his work. As fate would have it, her CIA contact was the legendary case officer May Currier—Bridger's mother.

Eventually, her uncle and Bridger's mentor, Wes Henslow, were killed when Specter exploded a suicide vest laced with radioactive material. As tragic as it was for them, Bridger and Lena understood both men knew they had reached the end of their interconnected lives.

Through fate, shared grief, and an immediate attraction, Bridger and Lena bonded.

"How many of these do you have?" Lena asked as she sat admiring the view of the flower and statue garden.

"Ranches? One. Maybe two or three. I think. I've got other places. Around… somewhere." He shrugged his shoulders and smiled.

"What's next?" she asked, returning his thoughts to their present situation.

"You mean what's next for us, I hope, or what's next for them?" He gestured toward the house behind him where the Spy Devils were resting and recovering inside.

"Yes," she answered.

"For us…um…I think I'd like there to be an *us*."

He recognized his mistake immediately, but even that was too late.

"You think?" Her deep dark tired eyes never blinked as she stared at him. She was dressed entirely in black. A light black sweater over a black T-shirt. Black slacks.

"I mean...I mean—" he took her hand. "There is an *us*. I just need to—"

"Nice digs," Snake interrupted as he limped onto the patio. Fresh bandages covered his hands and forehead. Dressed in jeans and a tight short-sleeved polo that strained against his massive biceps, he was early for the meeting Bridger had called for that afternoon.

He filled a mug with coffee, grabbed a bagel, and lowered his obviously aching body onto a chair. As he guzzled the hot beverage from the mug in one hand, he tugged at his sleeves with the other—a nervous habit he developed as an undercover police detective on the streets of New York City.

He would still be there, Bridger figured, if it wasn't for the bullet that pierced his knee. Bridger recruited the former law enforcement officer as a Spy Devil soon after.

"Not a real bagel," Snake said, shaking his head as he chewed on a large bite. He set it on the table. "Not at all."

Snake was on his third cup of coffee when Demon arrived. Bridger saw that his oldest friend looked even worse than Snake. A kaleidoscope of blues, blacks, and purples ran diagonally across his face. A blood-stained bandage was wrapped around his head—a swollen left eye. His crew-cut gray hair needed brushing.

"Hmmph," he grunted to no one.

"You look like shit," Snake said.

Demon grunted again in reply.

Bridger knew the leather-tough man who had been by his side since childhood was somewhere in his seventies. A former Marine and CIA special operations warrior, Demon had trained, mentored, and protected Bridger all his life. It was part of Trowbridge Hall's development since birth, proscribed by his mother for his eventual mission to create and lead the Spy Devils.

Demon wore his usual black pullover jacket and jeans. Bridger saw his most prized possession holstered to his hip—a Kimber 1911. He knew a Ka-Bar knife would be in the sheath attached to the back of his belt. A rusty pair of pliers used to motivate people to cooperate during interrogation would be in his back pocket.

"What a shitshow," Demon said as he filled a large ceramic mug with coffee. He ignored the food and sat across from Bridger on the table's far side.

Bridger nodded as he watched an exhausted-looking May exit onto the patio. She brushed her hand over his shoulder as she walked by. She sat next to Lena.

"How are you feeling, May?" Lena asked as she reached out and took her thin hand. They had bonded in Amsterdam while being held and tortured by Li Chu, the Chinese assassin. Bridger was certain May had divulged the ranch's location while drugged during the interrogation.

Li Chu. Your time will come.

"Fine, Lena. Thank you," May said as she patted Lena's hand.

Bridger could tell she was not fine.

A wrinkled hand held her sweater closed around her thin frame. Her normally statuesque presence was stooped and weak.

May Currier Hall's legendary, many-decades-long career had been predicated on her tough, no-nonsense, expert case officer skills. She had sliced her way through the male-dominated CIA culture with a fierce dedication to duty and extraordinary espionage skills.

Foreseeing a world requiring unconventional intelligence operations, the Spy Devils had been her vision. Bridger had been born, trained, and educated to fulfill that vision.

His father, Stanley Hall, an early tech pioneer, died when he was seven. Bridger always kept a golf ball marker in his pocket—a gift from his father before he was killed in a car crash.

Bridger, assisted by Demon, assembled the Spy Devils and sent them on missions against terrorists, criminals, and other enemies of the United States. Their primary weapons were posting short "news" videos on TikTok, Instagram, Telegram, and other Spy Devils global social media and internet outlets. The Spy Devils' effectiveness and status grew as new social media outlets were created.

They had become a world-famous covert action team. The dichotomy was not lost on Bridger. He knew that irritated intelligence 'traditionalists' who thought all operations should be run inside the walls of the CIA '*like the good old days.*'

Either through training or genetics, Bridger possessed the unique skills and characteristics to lead the covert action team. Since he was a boy, he had been guided in understanding espionage, tradecraft, weapons, self-defense, and more. He was Wharton and Oxford educated.

He was forty years old, nearly six feet tall, with sandy hair, almost hazel eyes, and features that allowed him to morph into invisibility, making him difficult to remember. He had a few days of beard on his face. He wore jeans, a polo, and a denim jacket.

"What's the plan?" May asked, looking at Bridger with bags under her eyes.

"Good question," Demon said.

Bridger was contemplating an answer when a limping Angel, the newest Spy Devil, and his wife, Janelle, arrived.

"Good morning, everyone," Janelle said. They replied as the couple stopped to get coffee for Janelle and a Diet Coke for Angel before they sat at the table.

Bridger liked Angel. The man had a feel for people and was a great researcher. Bridger liked Janelle and considered her a Spy Devil, too. Her journalism background gave her the same sense of networking and nose for information collection as her husband.

Bridger had thought they could use a few days relaxing at the Texas ranch without their young son James.

Instead, they were forced to fight for their lives. Never again.

Beatrice and Milton silently and slowly shuffled onto the patio, holding hands. Bridger regretted the danger he put the engaged couple through—an engagement they had announced only hours before the attack.

Beatrice's toughness, street smarts, short dark hair, and wide dark eyes often raised comparisons to Audrey Hepburn. Her multiple skills as an actress and makeup artist were vital to the team. Recently turning thirty, Milton had a Charlie Brown aura—loveably, shy, withdrawn. In some ways, it was how he dealt with being a genius mad scientist. It didn't help that he was short and skinny, with thinning hair and a ruddy complexion.

Each was sporting first-aid somewhere on their body. Milton's arm was in a sling. Like the rest, he had some cuts on his face and hands. Beatrice was favoring her right side as she walked. They followed the same pattern as their teammates by getting some coffee then sitting silently at the table.

Bridger shook his head. The silence from Beatrice, who was always friendly and greeted people whenever she saw them, hurt his ears.

"Oh, man. Coffee! Food!" Imp said as he arrived late with a laptop under his arm. He slid it on an open place at the table, then beelined for the coffee. He filled a mug and piled food on his plate.

Imp, a twenty-something whiz-kid, provided computer and technical support unmatched. Sarcastic and borderline arrogant, his eyes were perpetually bloodshot behind thick tortoise shell-framed glasses.

Imp sat, slathered cream cheese on a bagel, and started eating it voraciously, oblivious to the others watching him shovel the food into his mouth. "Great bagel," he said.

He glanced up and looked at his colleagues looking at him. "What?"

"You aren't hurt?" Snake asked, ignoring Imp's comment.

"Nope," he replied, taking another bite with cream cheese-coated lips.

"Not a scratch?" Beatrice asked.

"Not a scratch. Clean living, I guess. You guys should try it. Nice digs." Imp waved the last bit of the bagel in the air and popped it into his mouth.

Bridger looked around the table at his battered Spy Devils.

"Okay. First...thank you..." Bridger felt the emotion bubble from his chest to his tightening face. He rubbed his hand over his face as he bit the inside of his mouth to keep the emotion from streaming out.

They looked away from Bridger in a mix of shock and discomfort at his emotional display.

The sound of heaters hummed and hissed.

After an agonizingly long minute, Bridger took a deep breath and continued. "Everyone. I've made a few decisions. First decision—" he looked at Angel and Janelle "—you are done."

Puzzled looks followed a moment of silence.

"What?" Angel asked.

"You go home to your kid. I will not let you get in harm's way again."

"Forget that," Angel said.

"I'm not firing you. Work from home. No debate." He turned to Milton and Beatrice before Angel could respond. "Now, you guys."

"We are all in," Beatrice said, gripping Milton's arm. "We can be married *and* still be Spy Devils."

"Are you sure? I am not even sure what we are doing yet. So, go start a family."

"We've discussed it," Milton said, his Alabama accent accentuated by fatigue.

Beatrice stood, walked behind Bridger, bent down, and wrapped her arms around him. She finished her hug with a kiss on his cheek. "You are the best, you know that."

Bridger bit his lip as the moment stirred his emotions again. His thoughts drifted to the one Spy Devil not around the table. Beast was killed a year ago during an operation in Ukraine.

"This is getting too mushy," Imp said as he stopped gorging on food and flipped open his ever-present laptop. "If anyone is interested, I have been monitoring Austin law enforcement feeds, local news, bloggers, etc."

The fire crackled and a breeze sent a whiff of smoke across the patio.

Bridger's eyes snapped up.

"What do you have?" Bridger asked.

"I've had 'The Unemployables' monitoring the Texas Rangers, FBI, Homeland, and more local jurisdictions than you can name," Imp reported, referencing his misfit network of hacking experts. "Pretty much they say it was the Mexican cartels—" they looked at Imp "—the one lead by that cartel guy we dicked in Europe."

"Vincente Ramirez. Jalisco cartel," Angel said.

"Can we just kill him...just because?" Demon asked in a low growl.

"I second that," Snake added as he chugged the last drops of his coffee.

Imp ignored them.

"Beyond that, they don't have much yet," he said. "As one might expect, there is nothing on the ranch ownership. They are hunting for it, but no way, Jose. I buried that one deeper than the ocean. I also got access to the video they have collected."

Imp punched some buttons and rotated his laptop so most of them could see.

Birds chirping and the wind blowing filled their silence as they watched the images on Imp's massive laptop.

Bridger's eyes widened as he surveyed the remains of Abaddon Ranch. Cameras panned randomly across the landscape, showing dozens of uniformed law enforcement and medical personnel—many with large yellow block lettering across the back of their jackets. They were milling around the crime scene's burnt timbers and debris piles. Police cars, ambulances, fire trucks, SWAT trucks, television satellite trucks, and other emergency vehicles were lined up in rows like a used car lot.

Some uniformed officers were sticking colored and numbered flags in the ground marking the location of evidence—or a body. Others were taking pictures, typing on iPads, or drinking coffee.

"I think that's the library," Bridger said with some sense of loss. Up in his bedroom in Santa Fe was the now-mangled first edition copy of *Casino Royale* he managed to save. The rest of his collection, including a complete set of James Bond first edition books that had been a gift from Wes Henslow—sent after he died—were destroyed.

"This is sad," May said.

"Yes, it is," Beatrice said. Others concurred.

"Maybe I can...I don't know...cheer you up?" Imp spun the laptop back and started to type.

"What?"

His face fixated on the screen.

"I was checking the medical examiner's emails. Then checked the hospital...Dell something." He looked up. "There are survivors."

4

OLD-FASHIONED TRICKS

Austin, Texas

L i Chu checked his watch.
8 a.m. The ranch attack was just over four hours ago.
He should be exhausted, considering he had not slept in two days thinking about the impending attack—and Bridger. His neck and ear burn scars started itching, and his damaged left arm began to throb—wounds suffered during his encounter with Bridger in Ukraine.

Li Chu felt frequent jolts of excitement and adrenalin rushes of anticipation in the days leading up to the attack.

Knowing revenge against Bridger and the Spy Devils was imminent stimulated his mind and body. He received the opposite jolt when he called Vincente hours ago and was informed the cartel assassins and soldiers had likely missed Bridger and that Rocha was dead.

My Dragon Fire team could have done this in their sleep. We had a plan. What could go wrong?

Li Chu arrived in Austin—a nice city—five days before the attack to assist Colonel Rocha as ordered by Vincente Ramirez. Rocha seemed more than competent during the raid planning sessions. He was a professional soldier who exuded strength and experience. Li Chu could see the man had caused and seen his share of death.

Li Chu provided Colonel Rocha with satellite images and plans on the ranch provided by Chinese intelligence.

While a handful of men casually patrolled outside the house, Rocha and Li Chu stood examining the satellite images and aerial photos of the ranch tacked to a wall in the living room of the empty house. Next to those were typological and other maps of the area surrounding the ranch. Weather reports. Maps marking intrusion points and escape routes—mostly south to Mexico and west to CJNG strongholds in California.

"The ranch will be heavily defended. Bridger will make certain of that," Li Chu said during one of several midnight meetings at the secluded house in the desert west of the city. "I suggest a small team, maybe a few, infiltrating the perimeter. Anything larger will be spotted and give them time to react."

"I tend to agree with you, but we must use more men and firepower," Rocha told Li Chu.

"Why?"

Rocha should know better.

It was obvious to Li Chu. After all, before his appointment to lead Dragon Fire, Li Chu was an officer in China's People's Liberation Army, the PLA.

Then Li Chu understood. The leader of the CJNG, Vincente Ramirez, was demanding it.

Just like China. Those who don't know anything think they do.

It had been five years since Captain Zhen Jingping, Second Department, PLA General Staff Headquarters, Military Intelligence Department, was asked by then Deputy Minister of State Security Chen to create an assassination team. The mission was to track and remove individuals worldwide who opposed their policies.

When Captain Zhen accepted, he became Li Chu, the leader of a hand-picked kidnap and kill team codenamed Dragon Fire. It worked fine until Bridger and the Spy Devils somehow located, exposed, and killed them. Li Chu then discovered that Chen, who had become MSS leader, was a double agent for the CIA.

Chen has caused all my pain.

The years had been hard for Li Chu. He retained his dark eyes, flat face, small nose, and wide cheekbones. His stocky frame had narrowed. His left ear, arm, and side of his head were disfigured from being too close to an explosion orchestrated by Bridger in Ukraine.

After the ranch attack plans were set, Li Chu had no role to play. He waited impatiently for the moment he could gloat over Bridger's dead body. It would not happen now. Vincente's meddling in the raid's planning had led to the deaths of Rocha and the rest of his teams—and Bridger's escape.

In the hours since the attack, Li Chu stayed inside his furnished one-bedroom ground-level rent-by-the-day Airbnb in a nice apartment complex in a quiet South Austin neighborhood.

Painted in an obnoxious mixture of bright white and shades of dull reds, the apartment had a small living area furnished with a hard, uncomfortable black modular sectional. A cheap black two-tiered coffee table was on a shaggy beige rug. An off-brand TV was on a black stand. The galley kitchen contained a Keurig one-cup pot, a few mismatched dishes, utensils, glasses, and a "Don't Mess With Texas" red, white, and blue coffee mug.

Worn-out electric guitars hung from every wall next to rows of cheap-looking black and white pencil sketches of dog faces inside cheap black picture frames.

A little dining area had a cheap black table matching the other furniture color and quality. A floor-to-ceiling window on the table's far side provided a decent view of the complex and let in a reasonable amount of light. A sliding door was next to the window and led to a small concrete patio. Another door led out to the main access hallway.

He felt the chill of the December morning and wore an overpriced burnt orange University of Texas hoodie he bought at a convenience store nearby. He closely watched reports of the attack that were beginning to trickle into the local Austin online and television news.

"A shootout somewhere west of Austin. Massive emergency

response. Dozens are believed dead. Remote ranch. Gangs or cartels or both."

Video and images were appearing on social media.

It will take at least a few days before the American authorities determine what happened. That will give Vincente time to clean up loose ends, like me.

When Li Chu made the deal to hand over the address and intelligence on the ranch, Vincente had made it clear that it was a temporary truce to eliminate a common enemy.

It would be soon. Li Chu was ready.

Li Chu knew the CJNG would move on him no matter the outcome of the ranch attack, but he now clearly saw Bridger's next move.

I know where he will be. He will want to talk to survivors before the CJNG kills them.

Li Chu had seen the red Charger sitting in the parking lot the last two days. The same four men were inside, reeking with the look of a cartel sicario. Tattooed. Ugly. Mean.

Li Chu heard soft metal clicking sounds. Someone was jiggling the knob on the door to the hallway.

Finding me didn't take long, but I wasn't trying to hide.

Despite being in the apartment for only a few hectic days, it was enough time to set up cheap but effective sensors and a few rudimentary traps on the doors and windows.

The knob jiggled again.

Li Chu removed his shoes, tipped-toed over, and flattened his back against the wall next to the door. He pointed his pistol with his functional right arm and hand and waited for the door to crack open. When the sliver of a face peered through, Li Chu sent a bullet through the eye at point-blank range. The body fell back into the hall as blood splattered the doorframe.

Li Chu heard screams behind him. He lowered, spun, and pointed his weapon toward the metal-framed, sliding glass door to the patio. He saw a man lying outside with his arm pointed up and against the door. Dead from electrocution. Li Chu had stripped a lamp cord and tied the exposed wires around the handle. He plugged the other end into the nearest socket.

Sometimes old-fashioned tricks were more effective since modern-day killers were too reliant on high-tech gizmos.

They never see those coming.

He hurried over to the glass patio door and peered out in time to see a man running to the red Charger. Li Chu watched the car speed away as he slid the door open. It didn't matter where the car was going. He had placed a tracker in the wheel well during the night.

Li Chu looked down at the dead man at his feet and put two bullets into his head. He squeezed a third bullet into his chest because it made him feel better.

Distant sirens blared. He had to leave and find a place to think like Bridger. Li Chu took the weapons from the dead CJNG men, stuffed them in a large canvas bag, put on his shoes, and left the apartment.

Later that day, he watched the news on a TV bolted to a wall in a tacky western-themed diner. Reporters fighting a cold wind stood as close as allowed to the ranch, getting images and drone footage of an emergency with what seemed like hundreds of emergency vehicles.

The reporters wondered about the survivor's identity and condition while they were cared for "at Dell Seton."

The hospital.

Li Chu paid his bill and left the diner. It was time to take matters into his own hands.

5

THE STREETS OF AUSTIN

Austin, Texas

A t 2:30 the next morning, yellow-hued light glowed through the many glass walls of Dell Seton Medical Center at The University of Texas in Austin onto the sidewalks and streets at the northwest corner of 15th and Red River streets. Being a Level 1 regional trauma facility, ambulances constantly arrived with flashing red lights, and patients came and went, even during the middle of the night.

The few survivors of what the frenzied media had already labeled "The Hill Country Massacre" were taken to the hospital complex. A few police stood outside under the glow of the lights from the glass entrance doors. Local and national news trucks, their satellite masts still deployed upward in case of a breaking news moment, were parked outside.

"The Hill Country Massacre" survivors were divided into two groups by the attending doctors. Two critical patients who survived hours of surgery were inside the secured area of the intensive care unit, the ICU. Recently renovated rooms lined brown-toned hallways that radiated from a central nursing station. Doctors and nurses sat at work-stations behind a high wooden counter. The air was cool, and beeps and dings seemed to come from every direction.

A Travis County Deputy Sheriff sitting outside the nurses' station monitored the two men through a glass wall.

Four more survivors, suffering from non-life-threatening gunshot or shrapnel wounds, were being guarded by a single officer in two rooms on the floor below.

Walking out of the elevator, two CJNG assassins, acting as if they belonged there, rolled a janitor cart covered in spray bottles, towels, gloves, and trash bags through the entrance and onto the ICU floor.

The issues at Dell Seton, as with most care facilities, were chronic staffing shortages, strained ICU resources, staff morale, and the attention and time they could spend with each patient. Some rooms were always empty and stripped of their contents for use elsewhere.

Perhaps that was why the nurses did not notice that the usual jani-torial team was not working that night.

Since they carried the proper hospital identification, no one commented on the replacement's tattoo-covered wrists and necks protruding from under their salmon-colored janitorial uniforms. The nurses were unaware the usual team was dead and twisted into a closet in the hospital's basement.

"Where are Hector and José?" asked Jane, an exhausted-looking nurse wearing a dark blue uniform. She looked up from behind her screen in the cluttered central nurses' station.

"*Família*," one said in a heavy Mexican accent as he tried to ignore her. He reached for his industrial broom and started to sweep.

"Both of them?"

The man nodded.

"I don't recognize you," she said. The men froze where they were. She stood and looked at them. "Do you know what to do?" She looked at them again.

They nodded.

"Well. Don't disturb the patients. Be quiet and stay out of the way." She turned back to her screen.

They looked at each other, then around the ICU.

"Wait," a deep voice commanded.

The men froze again as the Travis County Deputy Sheriff stepped in front of them. Over six feet with a close-cropped military haircut, he was dressed in standard-issue dark pants and brown shirt. A gold star badge was pinned above his left breast pocket. Large chevron-shaped departmental patches were on each shoulder. A radio microphone was attached to his shirt. A wide bulky leather belt fitted with a gun, Taser, handcuffs, radio unit, and other equipment was buckled around his waist.

VAN ALLEN was embroidered in white above his right breast pocket.

He looked at each ID badge, glanced at their faces, then checked again.

"Okay," he said.

They hurried by the officer.

A monitor was on a wall above the files, computers, and medical gear. Divided by horizontal lines by room number, each line indicated the patient's name, health status, and the nurse on duty.

One assassin did a quick nod of his head toward a room. They walked down the hall, looking into the rooms through the large glass walls that provided the ability to monitor the patients from the hallway. When they reached the room of the first target, he was in bed with oxygen masks, IV bottles, monitors, and other leads and tubes coming from his bandaged body.

They pretended to work as they glanced through the large windows. While one cleaned, the other removed a hypodermic needle from the cart and moved toward the patient. With gloved hands, he stuck the needle into the man's arm and pushed the plunger just enough to send 4mg of fentanyl into his body—more than enough to be a lethal dose.

They had one minute to get to the other man before respiratory depression rapidly reduced the amount of oxygen to the first man's brain. The nurses would try Naloxone, but it would be too late. The nurses would never suspect a drug overdose. The men would die due to cardiac arrest or severe anaphylactic reactions.

The minute the assassins administered the drug to the second survivor and were leaving the ICU, alarm bells started ringing and beeping began behind them. They pushed the elevator button to move to the floor below.

Imp's news of ranch attack survivors set the Spy Devils in motion.

Bridger had one of the travel agencies within his Spy Devils support network book a private plane and cars under the name of another of his legitimate businesses. Hours later, they landed at Austin-Bergstrom International Airport.

Imp hacked into the Dell Seton Medical Center computer systems, adding Bridger and Demon to the security access roster. Milton fashioned ID badges and swipe cards, now clipped to their lab coats. Snake and Imp were parked in the garage near the sky bridge that connected it to the hospital. Beatrice was with Milton in another car parked a few blocks south of the hospital complex.

At 2:45 a.m., Bridger breathed in the cool and refreshing air as he and Demon walked toward the entrance of Dell Seton. They maneuvered past a few onlookers, reporters, and police and then through the glass doors.

They moved toward a bank of elevators and examined a digital department directory on the wall by the doors indicating on which floor hospital services were located.

"Sixth floor?" Bridger asked, scanning the display.

"I already told you that," Imp replied into his ear.

During the brief elevator ride, Bridger took out his Devil Stick. Invented by Milton, the Devil Stick was a multi-purpose telescoping baton that shot a homemade paralyzing agent on one setting, acted as a stun baton on another, and shot small Taser-like dart electrodes on a third.

Demon reached toward his back pocket to retrieve his trusty rusty pliers.

"I don't suppose...?" Demon asked, holding them out and ready like a gun.

"If they don't talk, you can have them," Bridger said without hesitation.

Demon grabbed Bridger by the arm. A soft ding announcing the arrival of the elevator echoed off the floors.

"Are you shitting me?" He smiled with excitement.

"No. I hope you don't have to, but I want answers. If they don't give it up willingly, I could care less what happens to them."

"Hell, yeah! That's the Devil I have missed!"

Bridger stumbled a step forward when Demon slapped his back.

Seeing his old friend actually...well...*happy*...was what Bridger had hoped for. The last few years had been hard. Grueling. Exhausting. Painful. Bridger saw the stress and natural passage of time had slowed Demon's seventy-plus-year-old body and mind.

We need a win.

When the elevator doors opened on the ICU floor, they saw the security doors to the medical unit were open. Shouting from down the hall made it clear something was wrong. When they entered the ICU, the nurse's station was abandoned.

"What the hell is this?" Demon asked.

"Come on." Bridger stepped toward the noise.

Bridger and Demon joined a policeman peering into a room where chaos reigned.

"What's the status?" Bridger asked Van Allen as he conjured his best doctor's voice.

Van Allen glanced at the two men who appeared next to him. Bridger saw worry on his face.

"You tell me, Doc," Van Allen replied with as much interest as someone watching concrete dry.

"Doesn't look good," was his professional diagnosis.

Hospital staff dressed in a spectrum of colored scrubs surrounded a bed, feverously attending to someone in distress. The electronic whirl of an AED powering up was followed by a shout of "clear" and then the thump of electricity being discharged into a body. They all paused and looked at a monitor, and then the cry of "again" echoed out the door.

"Son of a bitch." Demon pocketed his pliers.

"Let's go."

Travis County Deputy Sheriff Sammy Calvin sat with his head back, trying not to doze too deeply. That was hard, as the hospital was morgue quiet.

Fellow deputies had jokingly informed Sammy that overnight hospital security duty was the lowest of the low, but it *could* have one benefit. Nurses. To offset the boredom and fight sleep, he hoped to get glimpses of nurses in their sexy scrubs and imagine what they had on underneath. Even that was a wasted effort.

He hadn't seen any kind of human at his end of the long hall in over an hour.

Why did Van Allen get to hang with the ICU nurses?

One end of the fifth-floor hall was isolated for a reason. Non-critical prisoners were held there when more medical attention was needed than the sheriff's office could provide. The four patients found at the ranch who fit that category were in two rooms off a small corridor to the left at the end of the hall.

Since their injuries were relatively minor, they were scheduled for transport to the Sheriff's Department's facility later that morning.

"Six hours," Sammy whispered to himself. Then he noticed two men in janitor uniforms roll a janitor cart out of the elevator.

Sammy saw them look left, right, and then down the wide wood-lined halls. Then one pointed, and they turned toward him.

No one had said anything about janitors, but he thought cleaning the place up at night made sense.

Sammy's newly honed law enforcement self-preservation alarm bells started clanging in his head. His heart started racing. As they got closer, Sammy was certain something was off with these guys. Something about their looks and behavior told Sammy these men were not janitors.

They swaggered by the rooms and moved directly toward him. As they neared, he saw the tattoos on their arms and necks. Sammy could recognize gang members and drug dealers even as a relative rookie.

"Stop," Sammy said when they were within twenty feet. His left hand raised as he placed his right on his pistol.

Without hesitation, one of the men pulled a pistol from under his shirt and fired. Sammy heard the *pop-pop-pop* of the suppressed weapon and felt the stings in his chest. He had never been shot. He was surprised at the feeling spreading through him. Warm, then cold.

He dropped back onto his chair, slipped off to the side, and left red streaks on the wall as he slid to the floor.

The assassins strode past Sammy and turned left. The rooms were across the short hall from each other. Each killer opened a door and moved into a room. Inside, the sleeping men had no chance to defend themselves when the end of the suppressor was pushed into their chest.

Pop. Pop. Pop. Pop. Both men in one room were dead.

In the other room, after the first man was killed as planned, his roommate stirred, and opened his eyes. The assassin moved to him, grabbed him by the mouth, and forced his head down. The man struggled to no avail. The assassin put the bullets into his chest.

Pop. Pop.

Demon followed Bridger as he moved to the window wall of the next ICU room, where a similar life-saving scene was unfolding. A minute later, the med staff stopped their frantic effort. They tugged down their masks and stood looking at their dead patient and each other.

"Both of them. Dead. Sort of suspicious to me," Demon whispered.

"Right."

Bridger walked back to the nurses' station and looked at the board. He glanced down the hall and then back at the board.

"Imp. Where are the other ones?"

"Fifth floor."

"Let's go," he said to Demon.

"What's goin' on?" Snake asked.

"Hang on." Bridger pointed and walked to the security door. "Stairs." He pulled the handle, but the door didn't budge. He swiped his card. It beeped open.

They rushed into the stairwell and down to the fifth floor. They had a clear view of the entire hall when they opened the door leading to the hallway. Bridger knew right away that they were too late. They ran to where Deputy Sheriff Calvin lay dead. Then they turned and looked in each room.

"Son of a bitch! Every time!" Demon yelled, oozing frustration at being denied his chance to interrogate the men.

"Let's get out of here. We have to find who killed these guys." They turned away from the carnage and walked back in the direction they had come.

"You know who sent them?" Demon asked.

"Who do you think? Vincente. When we get the killer or killers, you can make sure they confirm that—whether they want to or not."

"Hell, yes!"

6

IT'S LI CHU

Austin, Texas

The quiet hospital came alive as Bridger and Demon anxiously stood at the elevator doors. Hospital staff in their uniforms and patients in gowns appeared in the hallway, looking dazed, confused, and panicked.

"What's happening?" Imp asked. "Emergency calls popping like firecrackers."

"Someone got here first," Bridger announced. He immediately pushed the button for the first floor. "They are all dead."

"Then you should be leaving. Security is heading in your direction."

The warning was too late. A pudgy, short man and a tall, slender woman dressed in hospital security uniforms came running around the corner.

Bridger quickly pressed the elevator button a few more times.

"Everyone, back to your rooms. Shelter in place," they shouted.

"What's up?" Bridger asked just as the elevator door dinged open.

"Excuse us, Doc. Don't get on that," the short man said, panting hard as he inserted a key into the elevator control panel with shaking hands. The elevator doors closed.

"Emergency. Gunshots," the woman said. Unlike her partner, she was calm and in control. "We are locking down the hospital," she added. "All elevators and stairwells are locked. Please find a location to shelter on this floor."

Bridger glanced down the hall to see how many people had yet to obey their command. It was empty.

"Shit. I hate to do this," Bridger said, shrugging as he looked at Demon. "Excuse me."

When the guards turned toward him, Bridger pulled out his Devil Stick and sprayed them with a low dose of gas.

They caught the guards as they collapsed and lowered them safely to the floor.

"Sorry," Bridger said. Demon snatched the key card and reset the elevator. It dinged as the doors opened, and they stepped on. "Snake, we are coming down now, then out the entrance at street level—in a hurry."

"Gotcha. Watch out, though. I can see from here that it's becoming a busy spot."

When the doors opened, they stepped out into the chaos of a mass evacuation.

"Why is this elevator not locked?" a uniformed security guard shouted as he moved to Bridger and Demon. "Doctors. Please leave. Follow these officers," he said, ushering Bridger and Demon into the line.

Security guards waving flashlights were herding a stream of scared people out the doors. Some evacuees used canes. Others were being pushed in wheelchairs. Others just scampered outside where emergency vehicles were gathering, with their blinding lights flashing and blinking, turning night into day.

The TV news trucks had roared to life. The rumble of their generators combined with the shouts of police, sirens of emergency vehicles, and screams of people.

Bridger and Demon did as they were told and joined the crowd spilling onto the street. A few policemen were hustling people away from the door.

When they were outside, the chill air hit Bridger, sending shivers through his body.

Bridger and Demon kept with the crowd until they could zigzag between some ambulances toward the garage. Snake had moved the SUV out of the garage and waited for Bridger to hustle into the passenger seat while Demon got into the back next to Imp.

"Someone tell me something," Bridger said as they got in.

"I've got something," Imp said. "Two really ugly guys that remind me of Demon are leaving the service entrance on the north side by the emergency entrance."

"I'm going to kill him," Demon said as he pulled his Kimber 1911 from his belt holster.

"Beatrice—" Bridger said, ignoring the banter.

"Already moving."

Sirens wailed from seemingly every direction.

"Slow and steady. Don't look suspicious. No one gets arrested for anything."

"They went right," Imp reported.

"We are looking. We have to be close," Milton drawled. "There! There they are. It looks like there is a beater parked up there that they might be headed for. Yep, they are getting in. Want us to intercept?"

"No. Follow them," Bridger said. "Stay on them. We are—" Bridger saw police and emergency vehicles arrive from all locations in his side mirror.

"Okay. We are on Trinity heading north."

A beat-to-hell Chevy Cavalier came fast from the left toward the junction of the two roads. It spun into the path of the assassin's beater, which braked and swerved to the side of the street ten feet short of the Cavalier.

"What the hell? Another car cut them off!" Beatrice shouted.

"What? Beatrice?"

Gunshots came from the Cavalier, riddling the assassins. Then a man exited the Cavalier, walked to the other driver's window, and fired in. When he turned back to his car, the light from the streetlight hit his face.

"We are stopped. What? Oh, my god. I think…I think it is Li Chu."

"What? What? Are you sure?"

"Yes…and he just shot…shot the killers. We are…let me…see… Trinity and San Jacinto. Just south of the university. Should we move in?"

Li Chu?

"No. What is he doing?"

"He is reaching into his car. He has a rifle. He…he is coming toward us. He is aiming."

"Get away. Get out of there!"

Milton didn't hesitate. He jammed the gear into reverse and floored the accelerator. The tires spun, found their grip on the road, and shot the car straight back just as the rifle flashed.

Tings of bullets striking metal echoed around them as they ducked behind the dash. A spiderweb of cracks appeared when a bullet grazed the top of the windshield.

Milton looked over his shoulder as he turned the car hard out of the direct line of fire.

Li Chu stopped, looked around, and then back at Spy Devil's car. He lowered his rifle, ran to his car, and jumped in.

"He's taking off," Beatrice said, looking out the shattered rear window.

Snake skidded the SUV to a stop next to Milton and Beatrice's car. Bridger jumped out, scanning the bullet holes and broken windows as Milton and Beatrice exited.

Red and blue emergency lights started flashing off the buildings.

"Milton. Toast that car, then get over here," Bridger said.

Milton dropped a small grenade-sized object from his bag on the car's seat. He followed Beatrice into the SUV.

"Thirty seconds," he said to Bridger. "Give or take."

"Hey. A guy is stumbling down the street," Snake said, looking back at the beater car idling in the middle of the street.

"Get him!" Police cars seemed to be all around them. "Fast."

Demon and Snake jumped out and sprinted to the man limping and groaning as he held his side.

"If he falls, let him," Demon said. "I don't want to get blood on my shirt."

"Gotcha," Snake replied.

"Help me," the injured man rasped through bloodied lips.

"Shut up," Demon said, sending a fist into his face. The man dropped like a tree. Snake dragged him by his feet to the back of the SUV. They lifted him and tossed him in through the open back hatch.

Snake hit the accelerator, wheeled their SUV around, and drove casually past a flood of emergency vehicles onto I-35 South. A spark of light appeared in the mirror as the white phosphorus incendiary device Milton planted in the car ignited.

Inside the SUV, it was silent except for the team's heavy breathing. Bridger looked behind him and saw the unmistakable numb look of stress. He had seen it after the ranch attack.

"Another shitshow plan," Demon said in a monotone. "Just like the ranch."

He wasn't wrong.

The interrogation of the wounded CJNG assassin proved helpful.

Demon dropped the moaning man to the ground and leaned him against a tree in a secluded field south of Austin, just off the I-35. He was bleeding from his left side around his waist and shoulder. Snake thought it was not fatal if he got treated "pretty soon," so questioning was quick.

"I have my med kit with me," Snake offered.

"Don't waste supplies." Demon gave the man's left leg a few taps. With a groan, a sweating pale face looked up at Demon. "He looks okay to me. He won't look so good in a few minutes." Demon pulled his pliers from his back pocket.

The rest of the Spy Devils sat around the man, drinking water and eating energy bars.

"I could use some BBQ. We *are* in Austin after all," Imp said as he stretched out on a patch of grass.

"Can I get started?" Demon asked Bridger with a grin, his pliers up and ready in his hand.

"Hang on," Bridger said. He knelt to stare into the man's eyes. "Hey, buddy. We are in a hurry. So, you need to talk. If not, in about thirty seconds, that man there will do really—I mean really— painful things to you with those pliers you will never forget—if you survive."

Bridger stood.

The man looked up and saw Demon, grinning the grin of evil. He heard a metallic clicking nearby.

"My name...my name is...Rico," he sputtered.

"Son of a bitch," Demon snarled at Bridger. "You broke your promise."

"Keep going, Rico," Bridger said as he suppressed a laugh.

Rico worked for the Austin branch of the CJNG cartel. He and his dead friend Paulo had orders to kill the men in the hospital. Their orders came from Diego. Yes, he works for El Hombre. No, he didn't know much about anything else. Yes, he knew about the attack on the ranch. He was near, in reserve, but was never called up. He saw the explosion. Colonel Rocha was in charge. Yes, Rocha worked for El Hombre.

Bridger's questioning was completed in five minutes. Then Rico passed out.

"Now what?"

"We drop Rico off outside the closest urgent care. Then whoever wants to can join me in Mexico."

Where we have to kill the most dangerous cartel leader in the world.

7

THE STREETS OF GUADALAJARA

Guadalajara, Jalisco State, Mexico

Locals and tourists were enjoying the blue skies and warm afternoon along the Calle Francisco Madero. Trees dotted the sidewalks. Parked cars on both sides of the narrow street constricted traffic, effectively making it a one-way street. Muted earth tones interspersed with light greens and reds decorated the buildings like a box of melted crayons.

People strolled and zigzagged until the road opened onto Parque Expiatorio, a wide stone plaza. Its main attraction was a raised circular fountain surrounded by a series of concentric steps. Trees grew from planters that also served as benches. Towering spires rose above them from the Parroquia El Expiatorio del Santísimo Sacramento. The historic church was a popular attraction, given its famed stained glass and Italian mosaics.

The air smelled of gas and exhaust fumes.

Without a thought, the pedestrians on Calle Francisco Madero passed a mobile phone shop where metal bars covered windows, doors, and a graffiti-covered façade. Conspicuous security cameras were bolted to the walls above the door.

One man stopped before reaching the church and entered the shop.

Antonio, the shop owner, looked up when he heard the bells *tink* above the shop door. He tried to look through the grimy two-way mirror built into the plaster wall of his cluttered office. It was pointless. Stacks of paper and boxes obscured the view into the sales area. He checked his watch and then the security feeds from the six cameras on the large flat-screen monitor screwed into the wall above his desk. The images showed all angles of the brightly lit, twenty-by-twenty-foot shop.

He saw the man shuffle across the sales floor to the glass display case. He placed his hands on the scratched and smudged glass top. He stared at a menagerie of phones haphazardly placed inside the locked case.

Dusty mobile phone accessories—covers, lanyards, bling of all colors—were randomly jammed onto pegs in the walls to the left and right of the door.

Antonio did not recognize him, but his shop had few customers, and none were regular shoppers. The person wore a baggy short-sleeve shirt with a faded picture of the legendary footballer Hugo Sánchez on the front. Tight and worn jeans and sandals. His hair was spiked blonde and stood out in every direction. Patches of stubble were scattered across his chin and cheeks.

Antonio stood, put his right hand on the Colt Python 357 Magnum tucked into his belt, and walked to the doorway. He turned left to the sales area a few steps down the dim hall through a curtain.

When Antonio walked toward the counter, the man rubbed his fingers on the top of the case, leaving smug marks behind.

"Stop that."

The man looked up, said nothing, and then continued running his fingers along the glass.

"Stop that," he repeated.

Antonio was about to grab the man's hand, wrench his arm out of its socket, and then toss him onto the street when the stranger snatched

Antonio's arm at the wrist, stopping it a few inches above the display case.

"Hello, Antonio," the man said as he stood straight up. Bluish hazel eyes sparkled at the confused shop owner. "I'm in town. I thought I would drop by. See how business is going."

There was something familiar in the voice, but it didn't match the face. He fixated on it, trying to look past the spikey blonde hair and through the stubble.

"*¡Dios mío!*" Antonio tried to step back, but Bridger kept a firm grip on his wrist. "Dear god! Bridger?"

"Hey, buddy? How are you doing?"

"You...you are...alive...?" Antonio asked with a mix of fear and disbelief.

"Um. Obviously? But—" Bridger put his finger over his smiling lips "—*shhhhhh*. Let's keep this between you and me. Okay?" He tightened his grip.

Antonio's eyes were fixed on Bridger. He winched as the pain shot up his arm.

"Yes. Yes, of course."

"Gun," Bridger nodded toward the weapon.

"Oh, yes." Antonio reached across with his left hand, tugged it from his belt, and set it on the glass countertop.

"Cool beans," Bridger said as he released Antonio's wrist.

Rubbing the red marks on his arm, Antonia looked around over Bridger's shoulder toward the door. "Where is...where—"

"Who?" Bridger smiled.

"Your man?"

"My...*man*?" Bridger looked around. "Oh. Demon."

"Yes. Him. Is he—? Antonio looked through the sculpted iron-works that protected the windows and doors.

"Son of a bitch. I'm coming anyway. I smell a *rato*." Demon's snarling voice entered Bridger's ear through his earbud.

"No..." Bridger mumbled, trying to stop his friend.

"What?" Antonio asked, looking confused.

"Right here, jackass." The bell jiggled. A sneering Demon saun-
tered through and moved toward Antonio.

"How is Ramon?" Demon taunted.

Antonio hastily stepped away from the approaching Spy Devil.

"Ramon? Not well, I heard, still. He has not been seen for many
months...since..."

"Smart man—for an idiot," Demon said.

A stout man with a watermelon-sized head and a face even his
mother would reject appeared from behind the hallway curtain. He
took a protective stance between Antonio and Demon, his bulky
muscular arms flexed at his sides. Veins pulsated blue across his head
and neck.

"This is Ramon's replacement. Momo."

"Momo?" Demon looked at Bridger and laughed.

Momo tensed his body and clenched his hands into fists, trying to
show he wasn't afraid of Demon. But the darting around of his eyes
betrayed his actual fear.

"I don't want to turn any more of your guys into salad," Demon
said to Antonio, whose face drained of color, leaving it pale like a
shroud. "I got nothing against...Bobo?"

Over the years, Bridger had been a good client for Antonio's business of providing intel on the Mexican government and other groups.
He had always fulfilled Bridger's requirements, and, in return, Bridger
always paid on time and with a generous premium to keep the transac-
tions private. Yes, there had been a... small...misunderstanding once
about the quality of some intel and the potential of a leak within Antonio's information collection empire.

When it was discovered that Antonio's man Ramon was involved,
the Demon Devil visited him. What happened to Ramon is only whispered about among his network, like a child's ghost story.

"Back off, Demon." Bridger walked around the counter and put a
hand on Antonio's shoulder. Momo started to move, but Demon
stepped forward, and Momo stopped.

"Listen, Antonio," Bridger continued. "I am not here to cause trouble. We have been friends for a long time. Years. I sent you some funds

to make it up about Ramon. Right? I am sure you bought lots of gizmos with that."

"*Sí.* Thank you." Antonio felt his body relax, and he managed a smile.

"*Bien.* I need information. Special information. And we all know Antonio has the best."

"And you are right." His body straightened as Bridger's comment had the desired positive impact. "What do you need?"

"Downstairs." Bridger looked at him.

"Of course."

Demon saw the Colt on the counter, reached over, picked it up, and stuffed it in his belt. Antonio frowned but didn't offer any resistance or complain about losing his weapon.

Antonio locked the shop door and flipped the sign to *CERRADO.* He walked down the hall until they reached the door. Antonio entered a code into a keypad. A click followed beeps. The door opened to a narrow set of rickety wooden steps leading into a shadowy basement. Antonio when first. Then Bridger and Demon. Momo closed the door behind them.

They descended into a dim, underground cavern that was longer and wider than the shop above, with a ceiling barely more than six feet high. The low mumbling of voices hung in the air, which was cooled by humming fans and air conditioners trying to beat the heat and humidity caused by people and computers crammed into an insufficiently ventilated space.

"How is the snooping business?" Bridger peered over a worker's shoulder and looked at a screen.

"Very good."

Antonio waved his arms around, indicating the crowded space. He politely took Bridger by the arm, smiled, and led him away from the workstation.

"The money helped?"

"Yes."

"I have seventy transcribers that rotate," Antonio said with pride. "They are divided by federal and state government, law enforcement and police organizations, military, cartel, individuals of interest, and others," Antonio said, pointing to signs hanging from the ceiling above each section of cubicles. "Each person has a computer, digital equipment, and an oversized LCD screen."

He directed Bridger's gaze to the transcribers wearing padded headsets typing and talking into microphones. As they did, sentences scrolled across their screens.

"They are well paid. With benefits." Antonio beamed.

Antonio walked down a narrow aisle between the workstations and pointed to a gap in the far foundation that opened to another basement. More transcribers sat under more signs. "I have had to make more space to accommodate demand."

"And sell to people like me."

"Yes. However, the new digital encryptions have required quite an outlay for new machines and experts. Very expensive."

"You raised your rates."

Antonio smiled like he had won the lottery.

"I am a businessman, after all."

"Yes, you are." Bridger walked deeper into the room as Antonio proudly surveyed his growing enterprise.

"What is it you need? I assume the Devil does not return from the dead and visit me just for old times."

"Vincente Ramirez."

Antonio stopped walking, turned, and looked at Bridger with wide eyes.

"A very bad man. You do not want to be near him."

"He started it."

"They are the ones who attacked you?" Antonio rubbed his chin with a quivering hand.

"I'd like to find out. Do you have anything?" This time, Bridger waved his arm around and then pointed at a cardboard sign with CJNG printed on it, hanging on a few inches of string taped to the ceiling above the worker's heads.

Antonio's lips pursed and flicked left and right as he pointed to the sign.

"They are evil people. You should leave them alone."

Bridger stared at him. "Perhaps, but let's see what you have."

Antonio went to an unoccupied workstation with multiple screens and sat. With a glance of embarrassment, he pulled some glasses from his pocket and put them on. Then he logged in.

"I am not as young as I used to be." He typed away as his eyes scanned the screens—darting from one to another.

Bridger waited with Demon, who was staring at Momo, who stared back.

"I have something." Antonio continued, "These transcripts are from just before you pretended to be dead. I am assuming that is good?"

"Yes."

"I will translate from Spanish to English."

"I can read it." Bridger moved in closer.

VR: Are you sure?

UKN (A?): Very sure. Can you do it?"

VR: This is very dangerous for me if it were to go wrong. And dangerous for you too.

UKN (A?): I am not worried. The information is correct. When will you go?'

VR: Soon

"What does "A" mean?" Bridger asked.

"*Asiático*. Asian sound. My teams are good with dialects."

Antonio looked at Demon and then back to Bridger.

"We need to find Ramirez," Bridger said like a general giving a command.

"Very difficult. His attack on your ranch in the United States has caused quite an issue. The military is after him. He is thought to be hiding in the mountains with his army. When he is not, he is moving from city to city. Every day. They are better equipped than the police. Better equipped than me."

"Do you know any way to get to him?"

Antonio thought for a moment. "Perhaps. I can call you?"

"I'll wait." Bridger didn't move.

Antonio unhappily rolled his head, stood, and walked to the pod of people under the CJNG sign.

"You trust him? Do you remember Marwan?" Demon said, referencing their contact in Libya who betrayed the Spy Devils to Libyan Intelligence. He was killed by the Spy Devils when they placed bomb in an ambulance he was driving.

Bridger was initially silent, then looked at Antonio working with his translators. "Yes. Mostly."

After ten minutes, Antonio came back.

"I have it. It is something, I hope," he said, proudly handing Bridger a piece of paper.

"Good." Bridger looked at it and then sighed.

"What?" Demon asked.

"This isn't going to be easy."

"So? When was that ever an issue with you?"

"Let's do it." Bridger looked at Demon and nodded.

They all proceeded back up the stairs and into the shop.

Momo and Antonio stood by the counter as Bridger dialed his phone.

"Snake. We are going to need everything." He listened to Snake's reply. "Yes.

Everything."

8

EL PUERCO GRANDE

Puerto Vallarta, Jalisco State, Mexico

L a Leche, a popular upscale restaurant where affluent locals mingled with wealthy tourists, was one block from the beaches on the corner of Pablo Picasso and Blvd Francisco Medina Ascencio—a palm tree-lined four-lane divided highway running near the coast through town. All around, over-dressed tourists out to enjoy the famous resort nightlife. Casually clad expatriates and locals strolled along the promenades and beaches bursting with late-night fun.

Floodlights splashed on the swirling black design of La Leche's otherwise stark-white exterior, creating a minimalist monochromatic white atmosphere-themed spot. White milk bottles lining floor-to-ceiling white shelves served as the main decoration. White chairs. Tables. Floors. Staff uniforms.

The Spy Devils had surveilled Emilio López, a CJNG strongman, around town for three days.

Antonio's information on CJNG operations led Bridger to López, a senior CJNG member known as *El Puerco Grande—The Big Pig.* Currently, he served as the cartel's comandante in the famous resort town. López was with Vincente as he led the CJNG viciously to the top of the Mexican drug cartel pyramid. His appetite for violence and cruelty shocked even the leaders of the other cartels.

López also happened to be Vincente's cousin.

Vincente Ramirez had put *El Puerco Grande* in charge of infiltrating the economy of the resort town by intimidating and taxing legitimate businesses to launder money for the cartel and run its extortion rackets. He made it possible for the cartel to use the renowned tourist destination as a strategic stronghold for money laundering, drug trafficking, extortion, kidnappings, and assassinations.

If anyone wanted to open a new business in the beach destination, they were required to get López's permission and pay regular fees to the CJNG. Bribes and threats, backed by kidnappings and videoed murders released to the public, provided the fear the cartel needed for unfettered use of the port. The renowned tourist destination was a hub for trafficking fentanyl and other deadly drugs bound for the United States.

López had made the port an integral part of the supply chain, receiving shipments of precursor chemicals and fentanyl analogs from China.

None of the tourists who visited Puerto Vallarta knew CJNG drug cash was being laundered through the nightclubs, bars, and restaurants where they spent their fun-filled vacations. They also did not realize that many of the boisterous people eating next to them were members of the most brutal cartel in Mexico.

What López didn't know was the Spy Devils were after him.

Snake, Demon, and Bridger were parked in a 'seen-better-days' Ford Explorer they discovered in a yard on the outskirts of Guadalajara. Stuck under the bent windshield wiper had been a jagged piece of cardboard proclaiming in thick black marker *"En Venta* 35000"— around two thousand U.S. dollars.

After some obligatory cultural haggling, Bridger paid Álvaro, an industrious teenager who showed promise as an entrepreneur, seventeen hundred dollars. Bridger put the remaining three hundred in Álvaro's hand and whispered "*Silencio.*"

A reasonable price, Bridger thought, *and good enough for what we need.*

"Imp, what do you see?" Bridger asked as he sat in the car outside the restaurant.

The window mechanism squeaked as Bridger rolled it down to let in the warm, humid breeze and let out the musty interior smell they had yet to identify. The breeze brought the smells of the ocean, thick vegetation, and marijuana mixed with the smells of food vendors cooking all varieties of seasoned meats and tortillas. Salsa music boomed from the beach resorts.

Imp had easily hacked into the restaurant's computer and security systems. They knew López had a reservation for that evening and, once he arrived, they could watch him on the security cameras.

"I've got eyes on him. I'm patching the security feed to your phones. He is the big guy at the end of the table, stuffing his fat face with some fancy food. Speaking of food, I could use a burger," Imp said from the Morningstar, the Spy Devil yacht moored nearby in the Marina Nuevo Vallarta.

Beatrice and Milton were with Imp, focusing their attention on watching López. The large man was sitting at the end of a long table overflowing with dirty plates, champagne bottles, and glasses. A dozen smiling, overdressed, drunk friends sat with him.

"Looks like he is having a grand time," Beatrice said. "Hours to go, it looks like."

"When he is done, that will change for the much—*much*—worse," Milton said, somewhat out of character for the usually mild-mannered man.

"Wow. Milton. You are a madman," Imp joked.

"Put Milton in a cage," Snake added.

"These creeps are all the same," Demon said. "Big ego jackass letting his guard down on his home turf. And Milton is right. They think nothing will happen here, that they own the place. I hate them."

"Listen. Puerto Vallarta is safe overall and a good place for a cartel takeover. Every tourist's wallet is stuffed with cash and credit cards eager to fill cartel bank accounts. The last thing they want is violence," Bridger said.

"Still only the two security guys," Snake said. "Plus the drivers."

"Snake. Give it to us again."

"Right. Once he leaves here, he will head for La Strana. He hangs in the nightclub in a booth with a bunch of cronies. Drinking every-thing. Drugs and prostitutes a plenty. The usual."

"Sounds like fun. Can I change teams?" Imp asked.

Demon's low growl rumbled through the comms system.

Snake continued.

"He can stay there for pretty much the entire night. Then he drags his ass back to one of the five apartments he uses. The Romantic Zone. Marinas. Other neighborhoods, but all upscale."

"Aren't we a little short-staffed to be going after a guy like this?" Imp asked. "I mean. They have the firepower of an army. We have—well—little sticks and flying whirlies. No offense, Milton."

"None taken, I think."

"As stated previously in reply to the same critique, normally we could involve some of my friends in the Mexican police and National Guard. National Defense. But not this time. I don't know who we can trust," Bridger said.

They are right, but we have to go on offense.

"I would like to voice my concern that we are in a cartel-controlled town, working in cartel-controlled businesses, trying to grab the cartel's leader, who is surrounded by who knows how many awful cartel guys," Imp said.

"So?"

"Just being the voice of reason…given current events."

"More like the voice of a chicken shit," Snake said.

"We are moving kind of fast, aren't we?" Demon asked.

"Maybe. Any other thoughts?" Bridger asked.

There was silence, and that told Bridger all he needed to know—what he already knew.

The events in Amsterdam, followed by the fight for their lives at the ranch, had frayed the fabric that made the Spy Devils dangerous. Their confidence, the swagger that made them so effective, had been beaten down. They survived multiple blows but suffered deep bruises to their physical and mental health.

Even Demon had been affected. The recent death of his old friend Wes Henslow and Beast's death the previous year in Ukraine had aged the old warrior.

What made his hand-picked team of covert specialists so compelling was its ability to think and act as one organism. As assembled, the group needed to act and react at a high level, under tremendous stress, all the time. Any decline in their abilities—even his—meant mistakes were likely, and Bridger hated mistakes.

They could be deadly.

Beast's death had proven that. Whatever led to the ranch attack proved it.

Combined with Bridger's innate intuition, their capabilities created a potent weapon many had felt over the years. His intuition had never let him down, so he always listened to it.

His intuition was screaming for him to abort. He forced the doubts away—but he couldn't shake it—this was different. He had admitted as much to Lena.

Lena.

Bridger sat back, rested his head against the door, and closed his eyes, knowing sleep might bring nightmares.

"He's on the move," Snake said three hours later.

Bridger checked his watch. It was just after midnight.

"Okay, everyone. Wake up."

"Are you sure we can do this?" Snake asked. "Seems like science fiction or something,"

"Stay in your lane, big guy," Imp said.

The images on their devices showed an overhead shot of López laughing, backslapping, hugging, kissing, and firmly handshaking goodbye to his guests as he exited the restaurant in the warm night air.

"He sure is playing the role of Mr. Big Man cartel comandante, isn't he?" Beatrice asked.

"Not for long," Bridger replied.

The valet had López's Tesla waiting. A Chevy Suburban, driven by one of his security team, pulled up behind it.

Staggering toward his car, they watched him hand the valet a wad of cash. The valet bowed and nodded his appreciation in return. López sat behind the wheel as the valet closed the door behind him. The security men got in their Chevy and followed the Tesla into traffic.

"The Devilbot is up," Beatrice said.

"Reminder, we have no time to waste. The club is just down the street," Snake said.

"Don't worry, y'all. We're ready. Just tell us when," Milton said. "At least traffic is a little lighter."

"Here they are," Snake said as the Tesla and Chevy sped by them.

"Imp, tell me you have the connection," Bridger said as he focused on the bright taillights moving quickly away.

"Signal connected. Strong and lovely, just like me."

"Dear lord," Beatrice said, shaking her head as she looked at Imp across the table in the lounge of the *Morningstar*.

"I'm going to kill him—I swear," Demon said.

It was his standard reply to his love/hate relationship with the young computer genius. Imp, for his part, purposely did what he could to annoy Demon to distraction.

"Focus," Bridger said tersely, like a scolding teacher.

Bridger usually appreciated the levity he had come to expect from his team. In true warrior fashion, they used humor, sarcasm, and mindless banter to, in a sense, keep sane. An inner defense against the constant stress and danger of being a Spy Devil. Bridger called it the *M*A*S*H Effect* since the doctors and nurses in that television show and movie used it to survive.

Focus. No mistakes.

"They are pulling up," Bridger announced as the Tesla and Chevy Suburban arrived outside the popular nightclub.

The Strana was buzzing with nightlife. The exterior of the hotspot for epic partying and dancing was lit bright with whites and soft fuchsia hues, creating a waterfall pattern against the walls. Eardrum-exploding electronic dance music blared from speakers.

Under a wide white awning over the front entrance and sidewalk, women twitched with anticipation, sporting their best 'barely there' tight dresses and wearing fake Ferragamo shoes not made for dancing. Fit, manicured young men, mixed with a few wishful older pudgy men, peacocked around them wearing the tightest jeans and untucked and partially buttoned floral shirts.

Snake drove past them as López slowed to turn right into a small access-controlled VIP parking area next to the club.

"Now!" Bridge said.

Imp pushed some keys on his laptop, sending the precise commands to hack the Tesla. Milton took control of the Tesla's self-driving and digitally controlled systems using the car's WiFi. López's car suddenly started to jerk, then seemingly uncontrolled, it pulled out and accelerated into traffic.

"Chase car time," Beatrice said as she smoothly stroked the keyboard of her laptop to take control of the Chevy's electronic systems. "Engine and locks."

The huge Suburban rolled to a stop.

The Devilbot image showed a confused driver trying to turn the wheel and randomly pushing buttons. He appeared to scream at the security man in the passenger seat as that man shouted at him, trying to take the wheel. In the back, another screaming guard frantically tried to unlock his door—banging his shoulder against it with all his force.

"I think I will turn the heater on—full blast," Beatrice announced like she was doing the trapped men a favor.

"You are a cruel person. I love that about you," Milton said with his eyes still on his computer as he controlled all of the Tesla's systems.

López grabbed the wheel with wide, terrified eyes. This section of Fransciso Medina Ascnesio was straight and widened where two access lanes that provided entry and parallel parking to the shops had been added in each direction. Milton directed López's car onto the outer access road.

López's body stiffened. Jamming his head against the headrest, he braced for impact as the Tesla approached the intersection. All around him were the hotels and shops of the Canto del Sol Plaza Beach and Tennis Resort where Snake had pulled over.

"Right here," Bridger said.

Milton hit a button, locking the braking system on the right side of the car. The Tesla skidded hard and fish-tailed over the low concrete median, clipping a light pole and a taxi parked with a driver inside waiting for a late night/early morning fare.

Bridger and Demon were already out of their car and running to the Tesla. They were dressed in Sinaloa cartel camo and torn jeans, dark tactical vests, balaclava or cloth covering their mouths, dark glasses, and baseball hats. Pistols were in low-ride holsters, AK-47s at the ready.

The taxi driver was out and already screaming about the damage to his car when Demon charged at him and sent him to the ground with a fist to the unsuspecting man's jaw.

"Unlock him."

Milton unlocked the Tesla's door, and Bridger flung it open. The stunned El Puerco was recovering from the shock when he saw the men approaching his car. He needed his gun, but it had flown onto the floor.

Bridger tapped his shoulder with a Devil Stick set to stun. The man shrieked and shook as volts of electricity traversed his nervous system. Demon came around the car, opened the door, reached in, grabbed the man by the hair, and pulled him out and onto the ground.

Police sirens started wailing close by.

"Let's go, you fat pig!"

Demon gassed López, then Snake helped drag and toss him into the back of the Explorer.

Snake pulled the SUV away seconds before the police arrived.

9

LOS RAMBLASES

Puerta Vallarta, Jalisco State, Mexico

"I supposed you are going to play nice with this guy and bat your beautiful blue eyes or mesmerize him with your sexy, soft voice—and *poof!*—he turns on *el jeffe grande*?" Demon said.

"Are my eyes blue? Do I have beautiful eyes and a sexy voice?" Bridger asked Snake, who was driving them through the city's side streets to a location he had scouted where they could interrogate the man in the trunk.

"Sorry, you aren't my type."

"What *is* your type, big fella?" Imp asked through the comms system. "Does it identify as human?"

Snake flashed a "kill him" look over his shoulder at Demon, which Bridger noticed.

From the darkness of the back seat, Demon absent-mindedly *clink-clinked* the rusty pliers, a sign that he was anxious.

"You didn't answer my question," Demon said.

"You are right. I didn't."

"Son of a bitch. Are we there yet?"

"Yes. We are," Snake announced.

Once they had López, Snake angled south, then east away from the ocean, passing middle-class multiple-family homes terraced into palm tree-decorated hillsides, shops, and markets.

Suddenly, the road narrowed and then transitioned from worn cobblestones to gravel. They were entering the Ramblases section of the city—a place tourists never saw. When the middle class started migrating to the western neighborhood, working-class locals moved to the hilly, unpaved roads and dim, sporadically lit streets that marked the beginning of the Sierra Madre Mountains.

As they ascended, the headlights illuminated the sides of the road, reflecting off better-kept homes interspersed among make-shift fences and corrugated steel-roofed homes where decorated ironworks covered windows and doors. Overhanging trees and brush scraped the SUV as Snake maneuvered in a series of lefts and rights past laundry hanging from wires spanning trees and past small boats, pickup trucks, and tires —some buried into the crumbling hills in a feeble attempt to protect anything from scraping against protruding rocks.

When they arrived at the remote location he found the day before, Snake pulled the Ford off the road under a crumbling, tree-covered concrete area outside a house undergoing extensive renovation.

"Nice location," Bridger said, getting out of the vehicle and looking over the city. "Good view of the skyline of the city. Mountains to the west and north. Good idea to renovate." He turned to watch Snake and Demon drag López into the house.

"Milton. Beatrice. Anything?"

Milton had kept a Devilbot over the vehicle from the moment they left La Leche. Beatrice had one monitoring the Ramblases area.

"No surveillance detected en route," Milton replied.

"Your area has been quiet," Beatrice said next.

"Okay. Let's do this," Bridger said. "Keep alert. This needs to go fast and clean so we can get out fast and clean."

"Hi, honey," Bridger said, looking into López's glassy eyes while gently tapping him on the cheek with the palm of his hand. "My name is Bridger."

The man was suspended by his feet from a rafter like a punching bag. The thick, rough rope around his feet was attached to a hook bolted into an exposed rafter. He was wrapped from his shoulders to his legs in duct tape. It took considerable tape to restrain his round belly, which had flopped toward his chest. Only his hands were exposed, and they stuck out like gills on a hooked fish.

The home's interior was deep into a demolition phase. Debris filled most rooms. Thin lists of light came through the gaps in tarp-covered windows. It had a simple floor plan. Front door and entrance area that opened to a living room. A kitchen on the other side beyond a half wall. A hall led to a back sunroom. A second story was in the process of being added.

A lack of airflow made it oppressively humid in the house. The smells of paint, plaster, wet dirt, and body odor hung in the air.

"You okay?" Bridger placed his hand on López's hip and pushed.

Lucky for López, he was not a tall man. A foot of clearance between his head and the concrete living room floor provided enough space as he metronomed back and forth to the creaking sound of the rope.

Rage and fear lasered from his wide eyes—angry muffled *mmmm-mmmm...hmmmmmmms* leaked from under the duct tape over his mouth. Drool bubbled from the corners of his mouth and trickled over his red cheeks. It mixed with the sweat avalanching down his body, over his face, nose, and eyes, then covered his forehead until it splattered on the floor like oil from a hot pan.

When he wriggled to free himself, he changed the angle of momentum, sending himself into a wobbly spin on a new axis like a dying top.

"You want to talk?" Bridger asked as he gave López a few slight pushes like a kid on a swing.

"Geez." Demon's voice came across the dimly lit room.

Rage sounds increased.

"Mmmmmmmmm...hmmmmmmm."

His attempts to break free of the tape sent the rope twisting until it wound tight. Then the spinning stopped, just enough for the rope to collect its energy, then uncoil the other way, sending López's into an even faster spin.

"You know, this reminds me of when I went marlin fishing off the Florida coast. It was a gorgeous day, and I spent hours trying to reel that massive beast in. It fought to the death. You know I did... Nah, forget it."

Bridger grabbed López's around the legs, stopping his swing with a jolt. He bent over, bringing his face to López's level. The bound man's eyes looked at Bridger with undiluted rage.

"Grumm...mmmmm..."

"A couple of questions, Mr. Pig. One chance. First." Bridger tore the tape from López's mouth with an unpleasant *rip,* causing the man to scream as chunks of his lips and cheeks tore off with the sticky tape. Blood started to flow down and mixed with the sweat rolling over his eyes and forehead. "Where is El Hombre?"

Bridger stared at him, waiting for an answer. López smacked his raw and swollen lips like a fish gasping for air.

"I will kill you!" the man managed to roar, sending blood streams toward Bridger, who backed away.

Bridger watched López violently shake and wiggle, trying to free himself. Blood tossed left and right like a radiating lawn sprinkler. Bridger grabbed the hulking man by his shoulders, lifted him out and up on an angle as far as he could, and then let him go with a shove.

López gargled an impressive litany of swear words in Spanish— some Bridger had never heard before—as his body swung high to the other side, then back, like a pendulum. As his momentum started to ebb, he began an uncontrolled spiral.

"Stop him," Bridger finally said to Demon. Demon waited for López to swing by, then sent a kick into his midsection on the return. With an *ooph* from López, as the air escaped his lungs, sweat and blood splashed off him. Demon's blow worked, stopping most of his momentum.

"Let's try this again." Bridger bent down and held a phone in front of López's face. "What is the code of your phone?" No answer.

Bridger turned and headed for the door.

"Okay. He is all yours," he said as he passed Demon. "Got your knife? Make sure you cut off a finger or two in case we may need to unlock the phone."

"What? Really?" Demon whipped his scratched and worn Ka-Bar from its sheath on his belt. "Hell, yes."

"Not too noisy. We don't want to wake the neighbors." Bridger's voice was as serious as a graveyard. He had hoped López would make it easy, but then again, he hoped he wouldn't. Either way, he *would* find Vincente.

"Hell, yes." Demon's arm whipped from behind his back to display the worn and razor-sharp six-inch blade of his Ka-Bar Marine Corp knife.

"51415," López whimpered, his eyes wide with terror.

"Really?" Bridger tried the code. He nodded to Demon. "That works."

"Son of a bitch." Demon shoved his Ka-Bar back into the sheath.

"Want to answer the question now?"

López's eyes flashed at Demon, but he remained silent.

"He is all yours."

"Finally." Demon yanked out his pliers from his pocket with his other hand, hiked up to López, then bent over and brandished the weapons in front of López's face.

"Hi. I got some news for you. I don't like pork." Demon beamed a big, toothy smile. "The question is, where is Ramirez? Please, do me a favor. Hang on for a little bit before you answer. I need the practice." He looked up at a Bridger who was shaking his head and rolling his eyes.

"Don't kill him."

"Stay in your damn lane."

With a chuckle, Bridger joined Snake outside, where he stood on sentry duty atop a five-foot-high mound of dirt, rocks, and construction debris where the access road ended just at the crest of the steep hill a dozen yards from the house. His eyes scanned down the lane—an AR-15 with an under-barrel 40mm grenade launcher at the ready.

"All quiet?" Bridger asked from below.

"So far."

Bridger's chest throbbed, and a tingling sensation like static electricity started in his shoulders and traversed up his neck. He shook and tensed his body, but the sensations remained. He knew what it meant.

Warning. Danger.

He discovered his clairvoyant tendencies to sense danger and the environment around him as a child and developed it as a weapon ever since. He learned not to ignore it when it sounded an alarm. It was trustworthy and almost always accurate. It had saved him and his team countless times over the years. Although he wanted to, he would not ignore it now.

"Milton. Anything there?"

"Not yet. Lots of people milling around—given how late…or early it is," a voice responded with a tinge of fatigue.

"Stay alert…everyone."

Bridger looked at his watch. It was just after 3 a.m. They had hours before sunrise. He knew the search for López would be fast and furious once the security guards escaped from their Beatrice-sealed car. He knew it would take a while for the CJNG to find them, but he'd rather not be found. Speed mattered now.

We need to hurry.

"Son of a bitch," Demon said as he walked out of the house, shoulders slumped, shaking his head.

"You done already?"

"Yep," he said as he returned his knife to its sheath.

"Wait," Bridger said in alarm. "You didn't kill him, did you?"

"No. I didn't touch the fat oinker." Demon looked forlorn as he stuffed his pliers into his back pocket. "I was about to work on his fingers when he started babbling like a teenager. He was more than willing to say they were behind the attack on the ranch and that the El Hombre was on the move. Being hunted by the army and all like we already know. They are supposed to talk later today about coming to Michoacán—to a location yet to be disclosed."

"Really?" Bridger folded his arms and dug his toe into the dirt.

"What are you thinking?"

He paced a few steps, then stopped.

"This is too easy," Bridger said as he stared across the dark hills of Los Ramblases toward the glimmering lights of Puerto Vallarta.

"Easy? Why?"

"When I mentioned who I was, he didn't act surprised at all, like he was expecting it, and now talks without putting up a fight."

"I think you had him pretty nervous after jerking him around on that rope."

"That was nothing. This is a tough man. Perhaps the toughest. Even after you sliced him like a kabob, I wasn't sure he would talk."

"Antonio?" Demon asked.

"I don't know."

Bridger shoved his hands into his pocket and took a few slow steps toward the lane.

"Everyone! Look out for—" Beatrice shouted into their earbuds before he could finish his warning.

"Vehicles are coming up the road. They look like those CJNG armored trucks. Wait. What? Milton says there is a proximity ping on the Devilbot we have above you."

Their heads snapped back as their eyes scanned the star-filled sky. Bridger lowered his head and shook it.

Trap. I've led us into a trap. Again.

10

EL HOMBRE

Puerta Vallarta, Jalisco State, Mexico

B ridger heard the first rumble of the vehicles coming up the
lane.
   "You guys get out of there!" he shouted.
   "What?" Imp asked. "What did you say?"
   "Go. Get off the boat!" There was a second of delay, which was too
much for Bridger. "Now!"
   "We're moving. We're moving!" Milton yelled in panic.
   "We're moving too." Bridger looked at Demon and Snake. If Beat-
rice was right, up-armored CJNG trunks were appearing over the crest
of the lane. He pointed to the Explorer. "Let's get the bag. I've had
enough of these guys."
   "Hell, yeah."
   They sprinted to the Explorer, opened the rear hatch, and pulled out
a large, long, heavy canvas bag. They quickly unzipped the bag and
reached in.
   They each took out a body armor loadout tactical vest and secured

it around their torso. Bridger and Demon grabbed their AR-15/grenade launcher weapons as Snake clipped a holstered Sig Sauer to his belt and stuffed extra clips into pockets.

Demon found clips for his 1911 and did the same.

As headlight glow grew brighter from down the lane, a flash mushroomed in the harbor, briefly illuminating the entire resort. Another explosion followed. As flames rose to illuminate the dark sky, booms rumbled from the direction of the explosions and echoed into the hills of Los Ramblases.

Bridger, followed by the other two men, scrambled up the pile of construction debris. Bridger spun to look at the fires burning in the harbor's direction. The sounds of distant sirens and honks of car alarms echoed across the resort and off the hillsides around them.

"Milton!" he shouted. No answer came from through his earbud. "Beatrice!" Still no answer. "Imp!" Wide-eyed with worry, he looked at Demon and Snake. Their jaws were set tight as the same concern registered on their faces.

A whirly noise came from above them, followed by the *thunk* of something metallic hitting the top of the Explorer. Whatever it was bounced off the roof and landed on the ground with a *thud*. Snake scurried down the mound and ran toward the SUV.

"Devilbot," he shouted with shock in his voice.

"Holy hell," Demon said.

The ground started to shake from the deep revving of powerful engines. Then, the imposing camo-painted trunks accelerated over the access road's crest.

"Blast them."

Each man pumped grenades at the headlights, sending a flash and ear-shattering booms across the neighborhood that easily had to be heard in the downtown area. Lights started to appear in the houses on the hill, as well as screams, dogs barking, and still-distant sirens.

The first CJNG vehicle's heavy armor required a half dozen grenades, but it finally exploded in a mushroom of flame, sending burning debris arching in every direction like fireworks. Men dressed in full military uniforms—helmets, weapons, equipment— ran from

the exploding vehicle, hoping to escape secondary explosions from the munitions inside. Some of them were on fire themselves.

The Spy Devils unleashed a continual barrage from their AR-15s toward the burning truck, dropping anything silhouetted against the backdrop of flames.

The air was thick with smoke, the smell of Comp5 explosives, and the burning CJNG vehicle and men.

"More behind us, coming up the road." Snake was looking below them where the road weaved up to their location. Headlights reflected enough light to reveal two massive, armored trucks creeping up the narrow incline. "Those are the Toyotas. Heavy armor and weapons."

"These guys are a damned army," Demon said as he pointed his AR-15 down the hill. Bridger saw the unmistakable and absurd expression of joy on his friend's face.

"We can't drive out," Snake said, shouting over the cracks of gunfire. "The road is blocked. We have to get down this hill."

Bridger did a quick assessment of their position. At the foot of the slope, lining the road, were homes constructed of stone, bricks, and wood—most with metal roofs. Many had fenced animal pens. Goats and chickens.

"Let's go."

As Bridger turned to the hill, Demon grabbed his arm. "Hang on." He turned to Snake. "You got any incendiaries in there?"

Snake rummaged in the bag, pulled out a canister, and flipped it to Demon.

Snake lobbed a few grenades at the new threat, stopping the trucks on the road below. Several men jumped out, firing wildly up the hill. Bullets pinged off rocks and thumped off dirt around the mound— more bullets whizzed by over their heads.

Bridger and Snake rained more grenades on the trucks and men on the road at the bottom of the hill. The multiple explosions shook everything on the hillside.

"Roast pig," Demon said, flinging his seventy-year-old body over the hill.

Bridger watched Demon run toward the front of the house, ready to pull the pin on the incendiary hand grenade.

"Demon. The trucks!" Bridger shouted as he turned back to see Demon prepare to pull the grenade's pin and toss it into the house. Bridger pointed at the road.

Demon stopped and looked at Bridger and then back at the house. He rotated, pulled the pin, and tossed it with all his might down the road. White blinding flashes exploded in front of the men sprinting up from the vehicles blocked by the burning wreckage.

Demon scrambled over the mound as the shrieks and the cracking of burning trees came from behind him.

"This is fun," he said with a grin as he sucked air between his teeth.

"Hey. What about the others?" Snake asked, looking toward the harbor where the flames were subsiding.

Bridger clenched his jaw and gripped his weapon.

"Let's go."

By controlling the high ground, Bridger, Snake, and Demon pummeled the vehicles below with grenades and bursts from their AR-15s. They saw some CJNG men take cover and return fire. Some shot with precision while others shot wildly in any direction, hitting a few of the homes, which started to burn.

Screams came from inside many houses. In the flickering fires illuminating the road, Bridger watched frightened men, women, and children run out of their homes in confusion, panic, and terror. Their bodies jerked, dropped, or were blown apart by the cartel forces, cutting them down at close range with machine guns.

"What the hell?" Demon shouted from his covered position behind the mound. He looked at Bridger. In the glow of the fires, Bridger could see Demon's face covered in sweat and dirt. Streaks of blood trickled off his cheek and chin from unseen wounds. "I've had enough of this!"

Demon jumped up, threw himself over the mound, and started to partially skid, partially run down the hill, seeking cover from a squat house at the bottom of the slope.

"Demon!" Bridger shouted. "Crap."

What the hell? Are you trying to die today?

Bridger jumped up and released grenades to cover Demon's mad scramble down the hill. The view was obscured by smoke and dust, so Snake burst rounds at the areas where he last saw the men.

During his sixty-foot charge down the sloping hill, Demon dodged, fell over, or slammed into brush, rocks, sporadic coconut palms, and conifer trees. He slid into an animal pen, ran, and leaped over a fence and around the road.

Three bloodied CJNG men staggered from around a truck, firing at Demon, who fired back, dropping two before his clicks signaled his magazine was empty. He dropped the AR-15, pulled out this 1911, and marched up to the last man standing and swaying in the road. Demon pointed the pistol at the cartel man's face and fired. His head snapped, and he fell like a tree to the ground.

This is going to hurt a little, Bridger thought.

Bridger started to slide down the hill mostly on his feet, using his hands to keep from falling. His right foot caught on a rock, and he tumbled the remaining twenty feet, crashing into an animal pen with a *thud.* He bounced and rolled into something soft. Bridger looked up and found himself face-to-face with a bleating goat.

"Sorry," Bridger said to the goat as Snake arrived behind him.

"You okay?" Snake asked.

Bridger winced as he stood, testing his ankle to determine if he could stand. He sniffed, looked at the ground, rubbed his fingers together, and sniffed some gunk on his hands. He wiped them on his pants.

"Don't tell anyone."

"I won't have to, but a shower wouldn't hurt."

Bridger nodded, and they ran to the road.

Demon was standing among the flames of burning trucks and houses.

"We should get the hell out of here," Demon said, panting with a smile on his bloody and dirty face. Two more bodies were on the ground behind him.

"Good idea."

Bridger looked toward the harbor and started jogging as best he could, wincing with each step.

Demon and Snake followed him.

"Something smells like shit," Demon said. He sniffed toward Bridger. "What happened to you?"

"He fell on a goat," Snake said matter-of-factly.

"Okay. Makes sense," Demon said.

Bridger's face and hands stung from scratches, every muscle in his leg ached, and his ankle was going numb. He rummaged in his pocket and was relieved he had not lost either phone during his tumble down the hill. He dialed his phone and waited for an answer. It didn't come. Sirens blared not too far away, and from their vantage point on the hill, they witnessed the flashing lights of emergency vehicles snaking through the roads leading to the neighborhood.

"We need a car."

It was hard to be inconspicuous among the frightened Los Ramblases residents who were yelling and running away from the battle around them. In the chaos, Snake stopped by a battered and rusty Dodge Caravan parked outside a dark house.

"No one home," he said.

Snake pried open the hood and searched in the near darkness for the wires he needed to jump the ignition. Bridger panted and groaned as he pulled open the passenger door and wiggled onto the seat, his muscles tightening with each move. Demon swiftly yanked open the sliding side door, got in, and closed it with a bang behind him.

The engine sparked a few times and then Snake found the correct wires, sputtering the Dodge to life. He slammed the hood down, hopped behind the steering wheel, and started the Dodge down the road.

"Open a window, somebody, please," Demon said, sniffing the already dank air in the van, made worse by the odors radiating off Bridger's clothes.

Bridger pushed the power button control for the window, but nothing happened. He clicked it back and forth a few more times with the same result.

"Great," Demon said.

Snake slowly maneuvered the Dodge down the narrow road. It was hard enough in daylight, but the tight space and the van only having one working headlight made the journey infinitely more difficult and hazardous.

An unfamiliar ringing came from Bridger's jeans. He ignored the stings on his knuckles as he fished López's phone from the front pocket of his jeans. He entered 51415 with a slimy finger.

"Hey, El Hombre. I was expecting your call," Bridger said.

"Bridger. Nice to talk to you."

If Vincente was surprised, Bridger didn't detect it in his voice.

The situation was spiraling out of his control. He was battling for his team's survival against a killer cartel leader. They were on the man's home turf, with few weapons, less leverage, and dwindling options.

We've been in worse situations.

11

MARINA NUEVO VALLARTA

Puerto Vallarta, Jalisco State, Mexico

By the time Bridgers's voice screamed into their ears to get off the yacht, Beatrice, Milton, and Imp were already on the move.

"Let's go!" Beatrice shouted as she started to shut down her Devilbot controller. She looked across the dark water from the main aft deck of the *Morningstar*.

It had been a pleasant, albeit stressful, evening. A light breeze barely rippled across the water. Lights from the modern resort living communities glimmered as the three Spy Devils monitored the operation against López from the rear of the Spy Devil superyacht.

The massive Palmer Johnson Sport Yacht 210 was a recent addition to Bridger's fleet, taken from a Ukrainian oligarch after they exposed and shut down his arms trafficking deals with the Chinese, which included the theft of some technology from a U.S. company.

Given the option between working for the crazed oligarch or

Bridger and the Spy Devils, Captain Andre and the crew of four defected to Bridger's side.

The yacht was moored to a dock in the Nuevo Vallarta Channel, in the waters of Marina Nuevo Vallarta, where the Bay of Banderas hooked north three miles from downtown Puerta Vallarta. Surrounded by planned communities, resorts, and golf courses, *The Morningstar*'s commander, Captain Andre, suggested the marina as a less crowded alternative to the more popular Marina Puerto Vallarta and its proximity to endless tourists and festivities.

"You have got to be kidding," Imp said with little concern when the call to escape came. He begrudgingly closed his laptop and reached for a chilled glass filled with the latest pour from the margarita pitcher. "I had plans to hit the pool—"

"The Devilbot is getting a proximity alert," Milton said as he rose from the couch and looked above them into the dark sky. Beatrice did, too. Then they looked at each other in realization.

"Jump!"

"What?" Imp was puzzled as the ordinarily stoic Milton scurried by him and scrambled down the steps to the pool deck.

"Come on!" Milton yelled.

"Go, idiot," Beatrice yelled at Imp incredulously.

"No way—"

She shoved Imp to the side of the lounge and kept pushing until one mighty shove in his back sent him flopping awkwardly into the dark water with a loud *kerplunk*. She dove in immediately.

An instant after they entered the cool water of the bay, the radar and antennas at the boat's mast exploded and flashed like a sparkler. Seconds later, the deck where they had been sitting became a ball of flame and blasting yacht chunks. Flaming pieces of cushions, deck, and other debris became searing, deadly projectiles as they shot out in every direction.

The explosives dropped from the CJNG drones were not large enough to sink the vessel, but fire was spreading across the decks, and a hole in the deck to the stern risked igniting the two fuel diesel fuel tanks.

Lights flicked on from most windows of the resort hotels lining the marina's edge, sending more light over the turmoil in the water below.

"Beatrice! Beatrice!" Milton shouted as he splashed and bobbed in the water illuminated by the fires quickly consuming the *Morningstar*.

"Here!" Beatrice swam over with rapid but controlled strokes. When she reached him, they hugged and kissed. An explosion from the burning yacht made them sidestroke away farther into the channel. Then they stopped and looked at each other as the same thought came to them.

"Imp!" They rotated around in the water frantically. They waited for a response. When all they could hear was the snapping and crackling of the burning boat, they separated, listened, took a few more strokes, and shouted.

"Imp!" Nothing. They kept repeating the process.

A weak *"hel—elp"* came from the somewhere.

"Imp!" Beatrice cried out as she took in a mouthful of water. Choking and gagging, she made several powerful strokes in the direction of the weak cry. She stopped and listened, then saw Imp's head barely above the waterline just ten feet away.

"Milton! Here. Over here!" Beatrice shouted. "Dear lord," she said softly when she reached Imp and saw his pale face and almost-shut eyes.

She leaned back and wrapped her left arm across Imp's chest. She floated on her back and she used her right arm to paddle away from the flames as fast as possible. When she reached what she hoped was a safe distance, she shouted again for Milton as loud as she dared. Emergency vehicles and boats approached the listing *Morningstar* near where they were treading water.

Milton dog-paddled over and grabbed Imp's left arm. Beatrice took the other.

"Over there," Milton pointed and splashed in a direction across the marina.

Sucking in water and fighting to keep Imp and themselves afloat, they swam as best they could to a low stretch of ground they had seen from the *Morningstar*.

During the tiring ten-minute struggle, Imp wheezed and moaned with every stroke. Exhausted, they desperately grabbed at slimy rocks and soggy roots protruding from the edge of the several-foot-high rocky shoreline. They took a few seconds, panting and resting, to gather any remaining strength, then hauled him over the steep, craggy incline.

Beatrice stood above them as Milton did his best to get Imp's arms within her grasp. Milton struggled to get close to Beatrice, and when he did, Imp's hands slipped from hers. Each attempt only brought more frustration and desperation and sapped the strength from their aching muscles.

Mustering their final energy reserves in what they feared was their last attempt, Beatrice pulled with all her might and managed to pull Imp up as Milton pushed from below. Safely on dry ground, they rolled onto their backs, exhausted and gasping for air.

"We...have...to...move," Milton sputtered as water droplets flew from his mouth.

Beatrice rolled onto an elbow, then forced herself to her knees. She crawled over, tore off Imp's soaked shirt, and wiped blood from his wound. Beatrice uncovered a gapping three-inch gash that ran on an angle from below his ribcage to his waist. She could not tell how deep it went, but the continual flow of blood was a bad sign.

"He's breathing, but—" she looked at Milton, who instantly registered the concern washing across her face. Milton unbuttoned the baby-blue Tommy Bahama shirt Beatrice bought him, removed it, and applied pressure to Imp's wound.

"A piece of something from the explosion hit him...and look at his head, too," Beatrice said.

Beatrice surveyed the one-hundred-foot-wide thumb of land that served as a breakwater protecting buildings directly across from the marina entrance. On it were a few trees and brush. About three hundred feet from the tip toward land were more trees and parking for the golf course and adventure park.

Light reflecting off the water illuminated a welt on the left side of his head near his ear. "He must have hit the boat on the way down."

"He needs a doctor," Milton said, standing to get a better view of their surroundings. "We need to talk to Bridger, but I lost my phone in the boat."

"Me, too."

They checked Imp's pockets, but his phone was gone, too.

"The fire is out," Milton said, looking back at the boat.

"I wonder if Captain Andre and the rest..." she let her words taper off.

"I don't see how, but those boats are looking for survivors," Milton said as he watched small crafts swinging searchlights across the water's surface. "We have to go."

"Trees." Beatrice pointed toward where their thumb of land broadened into roads and structures.

Milton put his tired arms under Imp's shoulders and folded his hands across his chest, locking his fingers. Beatrice grabbed his ankles. They groaned in fatigue as they stood. Imp let out a howl.

"*Shhhhh!*" Beatrice said. "It is all right, Imp. We're getting you some help."

He let out another, softer moan.

They made slow, staggered progress, finding that they had to set their wounded Spy Devil colleague down several times to rest their weary bodies.

"Imp...I wish I knew his name. Calling him Imp at a time like this sounds...ridiculous," Beatrice grunted.

"Jer—e—my," Imp panted between gulps of air. "I hurt."

They looked at each other and then at him.

"It's okay, Jeremy—it will be fine."

Their muscles burned to numbness by the time they reached the protection of the trees. They did their best to set Imp down softly on scruffy grass. They heard the sirens whirling across the water and saw the emergency lights flashing. The smell of salt water filled their noses. Beatrice checked Imp.

"He's passed out but is alive."

A row of military vehicles swerved from the street into the parking lot next to the trees. They accelerated across the lot, crashed over some speed barriers, and veered between the trees and the three Spy Devils. When they slammed on their brakes, they kicked up dust and dirt that reflected in the near-blinding lights shining on the crouching, exhausted people.

Squares of metal plates were welded in patches to the exterior of the vehicles, looking like someone had bent a checkerboard down the middle with their knee. Slits were cut into the metal that covered the windows. In two-foot increments, gun barrels poked out of circular holes in the exterior armor.

The heavy doors of the vehicle flew open, and a dozen men in full military gear jumped out. They sprinted to encircle the three Devils.

Beatrice picked up a rock, stood, and raised it over her head, ready to fling at anyone who came close. Milton looked around, but all he could find was a pile of dead palm leaves.

"Let's come here for our honeymoon," Milton said in a moment of dry humor.

"You are such a romantic," Beatrice said, keeping her body turned and ready for an attack. "Cartel," she added, looking as a man sporting slacks and a polo rather than military gear, exited one car. Two men in full combat gear fell in behind. Seemingly without a care, the man strolled with total confidence to the Spy Devils. Beatrice cocked her arm.

"Please," he said softly as he held his palm toward Beatrice. "Your man is injured."

The man walked by her, stopped, and looked down at Imp like a father over his frightened child. The man turned and spoke to a few soldiers behind him, who jumped from the line and knelt by Imp.

"Hands off him!" Milton shouted, trying to get between Imp and CJNG soldiers, as one pointed his rifle directly into Milton's face. Milton froze.

"Get away." Beatrice lunged forward and swung her rock, hitting one soldier on the side of his helmet without effect. She tried to shove him, but he stood firm like a mountain. He pushed her back, sending her sprawling onto the dirt and gravel. That motivated Milton, who jumped the soldier, but he grabbed Milton and tossed him to the ground like a rag doll.

"Please, please. Everyone. Do not worry, my friends." The man in the polo shirt held out his hand. "Let my men care for your friend. He looks seriously injured." The men got to work on Imp. One ran to the truck and came back with a medical kit. They ripped open an IV bag and stuck a needle into his arm. Bandages were applied to his stomach and head.

Milton and Beatrice watched Imp receive the critical medical attention he needed.

"My name is Vincente Ramirez. I am sometimes called *El Hombre*. I need to talk to your leader."

"We lost our phones." Beatrice stood and walked to face the man.

Vincente reached into his back pocket, took out a phone, and dialed.

Bridger heard the ring, pulled out the phone, and entered the security code López gave him.

"López? Is this you?" Vincente asked, then listened.

"Hey, El Hombre. I was expecting your call," Bridger said as their van rumbling down the hill.

"Bridger. Nice to talk to you."

"You missed killing me—again. Hey, if you see fires, that is your men cooking too well done, just like at my ranch. This never gets boring. Keep trying."

"Since you are alive, we should talk."

"About what?" Bridger asked as calmly as he could.

"Whether I skin your people while you listen, or—" Vincente said.

"Or what?" Bridger interrupted, taking a breath, knowing what was coming but hoping it wasn't.

"Or if the Devil agrees to start working for me."

12

EL HOMBRE

Puerta Vallarta, Jalisco State, Mexico

B ridger heard the first rumble of the vehicles coming up the
lane.

"You guys get out of there!" he shouted.

"What?" Imp asked. "What did you say?"

"Go. Get off the boat!" There was a second of delay, which was too
much for Bridger. "Now!"

"We're moving. We're moving!" Milton yelled in panic.

"We're moving too." Bridger looked at Demon and Snake. If Beatrice was right, up-armored CJNG trunks were appearing over the crest
of the lane. He pointed to the Explorer. "Let's get the bag. I've had
enough of these guys."

"Hell, yeah."

They sprinted to the Explorer, opened the rear hatch, and pulled out
a large, long, heavy canvas bag. They quickly unzipped the bag and
reached in.

They each took out a body armor loadout tactical vest and secured

it around their torso. Bridger and Demon grabbed their AR-15/grenade launcher weapons as Snake clipped a holstered Sig Sauer to his belt and stuffed extra clips into pockets.

Demon found clips for his 1911 and did the same.

As headlight glow grew brighter from down the lane, a flash mushroomed in the harbor, briefly illuminating the entire resort. Another explosion followed. As flames rose to illuminate the dark sky, booms rumbled from the direction of the explosions and echoed into the hills of Los Ramblases.

Bridger, followed by the other two men, scrambled up the pile of construction debris. Bridger spun to look at the fires burning in the harbor's direction. The sounds of distant sirens and honks of car alarms echoed across the resort and off the hillsides around them.

"Milton!" he shouted. No answer came from through his earbud. "Beatrice!" Still no answer. "Imp!" Wide-eyed with worry, he looked at Demon and Snake. Their jaws were set tight as the same concern registered on their faces.

A whirly noise came from above them, followed by the *thunk* of something metallic hitting the top of the Explorer. Whatever it was bounced off the roof and landed on the ground with a *thud*. Snake scurried down the mound and ran toward the SUV.

"Devilbot," he shouted with shock in his voice.

"Holy hell," Demon said.

The ground started to shake from the deep revving of powerful engines. Then, the imposing camo-painted trunks accelerated over the access road's crest.

"Blast them."

Each man pumped grenades at the headlights, sending a flash and ear-shattering booms across the neighborhood that easily had to be heard in the downtown area. Lights started to appear in the houses on the hill, as well as screams, dogs barking, and still-distant sirens.

The first CJNG vehicle's heavy armor required a half dozen grenades, but it finally exploded in a mushroom of flame, sending burning debris arching in every direction like fireworks. Men dressed in full military uniforms—helmets, weapons, equipment— ran from

the exploding vehicle, hoping to escape secondary explosions from the munitions inside. Some of them were on fire themselves.

The Spy Devils unleashed a continual barrage from their AR-15s toward the burning truck, dropping anything silhouetted against the backdrop of flames.

The air was thick with smoke, the smell of Comp5 explosives, and the burning CJNG vehicle and men.

"More behind us, coming up the road." Snake was looking below them where the road weaved up to their location. Headlights reflected enough light to reveal two massive, armored trucks creeping up the narrow incline. "Those are the Toyotas. Heavy armor and weapons."

"These guys are a damned army," Demon said as he pointed his AR-15 down the hill. Bridger saw the unmistakable and absurd expression of joy on his friend's face.

"We can't drive out," Snake said, shouting over the cracks of gunfire. "The road is blocked. We have to get down this hill."

Bridger did a quick assessment of their position. At the foot of the slope, lining the road, were homes constructed of stone, bricks, and wood—most with metal roofs. Many had fenced animal pens. Goats and chickens.

"Let's go."

As Bridger turned to the hill, Demon grabbed his arm. "Hang on." He turned to Snake. "You got any incendiaries in there?"

Snake rummaged in the bag, pulled out a canister, and flipped it to Demon.

Snake lobbed a few grenades at the new threat, stopping the trucks on the road below. Several men jumped out, firing wildly up the hill. Bullets pinged off rocks and thumped off dirt around the mound— more bullets whizzed by over their heads.

Bridger and Snake rained more grenades on the trucks and men on the road at the bottom of the hill. The multiple explosions shook everything on the hillside.

"Roast pig," Demon said, flinging his seventy-year-old body over the hill.

Bridger watched Demon run toward the front of the house, ready to pull the pin on the incendiary hand grenade.

"Demon. The trucks!" Bridger shouted as he turned back to see Demon prepare to pull the grenade's pin and toss it into the house. Bridger pointed at the road.

Demon stopped and looked at Bridger and then back at the house. He rotated, pulled the pin, and tossed it with all his might down the road. White blinding flashes exploded in front of the men sprinting up from the vehicles blocked by the burning wreckage.

Demon scrambled over the mound as the shrieks and the cracking of burning trees came from behind him.

"This is fun," he said with a grin as he sucked air between his teeth.

"Hey. What about the others?" Snake asked, looking toward the harbor where the flames were subsiding.

Bridger clenched his jaw and gripped his weapon.

"Let's go."

By controlling the high ground, Bridger, Snake, and Demon pummeled the vehicles below with grenades and bursts from their AR-15s. They saw some CJNG men take cover and return fire. Some shot with precision while others shot wildly in any direction, hitting a few of the homes, which started to burn.

Screams came from inside many houses. In the flickering fires illuminating the road, Bridger watched frightened men, women, and children run out of their homes in confusion, panic, and terror. Their bodies jerked, dropped, or were blown apart by the cartel forces, cutting them down at close range with machine guns.

"What the hell?" Demon shouted from his covered position behind the mound. He looked at Bridger. In the glow of the fires, Bridger could see Demon's face covered in sweat and dirt. Streaks of blood trickled off his cheek and chin from unseen wounds. "I've had enough of this!"

Demon jumped up, threw himself over the mound, and started to partially skid, partially run down the hill, seeking cover from a squat house at the bottom of the slope.

"Demon!" Bridger shouted. "Crap."

What the hell? Are you trying to die today?

Bridger jumped up and released grenades to cover Demon's mad scramble down the hill. The view was obscured by smoke and dust, so Snake burst rounds at the areas where he last saw the men.

During his sixty-foot charge down the sloping hill, Demon dodged, fell over, or slammed into brush, rocks, sporadic coconut palms, and conifer trees. He slid into an animal pen, ran, and leaped over a fence and around the road.

Three bloodied CJNG men staggered from around a truck, firing at Demon, who fired back, dropping two before his clicks signaled his magazine was empty. He dropped the AR-15, pulled out this 1911, and marched up to the last man standing and swaying in the road. Demon pointed the pistol at the cartel man's face and fired. His head snapped, and he fell like a tree to the ground.

This is going to hurt a little, Bridger thought.

Bridger started to slide down the hill mostly on his feet, using his hands to keep from falling. His right foot caught on a rock, and he tumbled the remaining twenty feet, crashing into an animal pen with a *thud.* He bounced and rolled into something soft. Bridger looked up and found himself face-to-face with a bleating goat.

"Sorry," Bridger said to the goat as Snake arrived behind him.

"You okay?" Snake asked.

Bridger winced as he stood, testing his ankle to determine if he could stand. He sniffed, looked at the ground, rubbed his fingers together, and sniffed some gunk on his hands. He wiped them on his pants.

"Don't tell anyone."

"I won't have to, but a shower wouldn't hurt."

Bridger nodded, and they ran to the road.

Demon was standing among the flames of burning trucks and houses.

"We should get the hell out of here," Demon said, panting with a smile on his bloody and dirty face. Two more bodies were on the ground behind him.

"Good idea."

Bridger looked toward the harbor and started jogging as best he could, wincing with each step.

Demon and Snake followed him.

"Something smells like shit," Demon said. He sniffed toward Bridger. "What happened to you?"

"He fell on a goat," Snake said matter-of-factly.

"Okay. Makes sense," Demon said.

Bridger's face and hands stung from scratches, every muscle in his leg ached, and his ankle was going numb. He rummaged in his pocket and was relieved he had not lost either phone during his tumble down the hill. He dialed his phone and waited for an answer. It didn't come. Sirens blared not too far away, and from their vantage point on the hill, they witnessed the flashing lights of emergency vehicles snaking through the roads leading to the neighborhood.

"We need a car."

It was hard to be inconspicuous among the frightened Los Ramblases residents who were yelling and running away from the battle around them. In the chaos, Snake stopped by a battered and rusty Dodge Caravan parked outside a dark house.

"No one home," he said.

Snake pried open the hood and searched in the near darkness for the wires he needed to jump the ignition. Bridger panted and groaned as he pulled open the passenger door and wiggled onto the seat, his muscles tightening with each move. Demon swiftly yanked open the sliding side door, got in, and closed it with a bang behind him.

The engine sparked a few times and then Snake found the correct wires, sputtering the Dodge to life. He slammed the hood down, hopped behind the steering wheel, and started the Dodge down the road.

"Open a window, somebody, please," Demon said, sniffing the already dank air in the van, made worse by the odors radiating off Bridger's clothes.

Bridger pushed the power button control for the window, but nothing happened. He clicked it back and forth a few more times with the same result.

"Great," Demon said.

Snake slowly maneuvered the Dodge down the narrow road. It was hard enough in daylight, but the tight space and the van only having one working headlight made the journey infinitely more difficult and hazardous.

An unfamiliar ringing came from Bridger's jeans. He ignored the stings on his knuckles as he fished López's phone from the front pocket of his jeans. He entered 51415 with a slimy finger.

"Hey, El Hombre. I was expecting your call," Bridger said.

"Bridger. Nice to talk to you."

If Vincente was surprised, Bridger didn't detect it in his voice.

The situation was spiraling out of his control. He was battling for his team's survival against a killer cartel leader. They were on the man's home turf, with few weapons, less leverage, and dwindling options.

We've been in worse situations.

13

UN PACTO CON EL DIABLO

Puerto Vallarta, Jalisco State, Mexico

"Why would I work for you?" Bridger shouted into the phone as he jammed a finger in the opposite ear to help him hear over the ear-splitting clatter of the van.

"I have a pretty lady… Beatrice and…what is your name…ah yes, and Milton," Bridger heard Vincente say. "They are not too damaged. The other? Imp? He is suffering a serious wound. My medics are attending to him."

"I have a doctor on call in Mexico City. I can have him—" Bridger started to say.

"That is unnecessary. I own a hospital here. He will get the best of care."

Bridger paused, took a slow breath in, and released it even slower. He then informed Demon and Snake of the condition of their teammates.

Demon leaned forward and shouted to the phone, "You hurt them, and I will skin *you*." Then he turned to Snake. "Get this thing moving."

The condition of the Dodge Caravan that Snake had stolen was two levels below a piece of junk. It needed a functional suspension, so it bounced and rolled like a boat on rough seas. It lacked a muffler, sending deafening booms and choking exhaust fumes into the Dodge. Snake jammed his foot down, and the van rattled as it resisted accelerating, but it finally gave in and moved slightly faster.

"As I said, I would like to discuss something important with you," Vincente said. "Tonight."

"Me too. Let's do it. Where are you?"

There was a moment of muffed words, then Beatrice's weak and frightened voice came and told them where they were.

"Hurry. Imp needs a doctor."

Beatrice is as tough as they come. I've never heard her like this.

Twenty minutes later, the bald Caravan tires skidded as Snake swung the van into the parking lot. In front of them were heavily armored vehicles—trucks that looked like they had been created in Dr. Frankenstein's laboratory.

More men than Bridger could count, outfitted in the same combat uniforms worn by the men in the battle in Los Ramblases, pointed myriad weapons at them.

Snake stopped the van short.

One armed man moved toward them.

"Drop your weapons. Out!"

"We've got this," Bridger said.

"We do?" Snake asked.

They got out, tossing their AR-15s and pistols to the ground.

The CJNG man watched and reached out to take the pistol holstered on Demon's belt.

"I ain't letting no one take this," Demon said, taking out his prized Kimber 1911. He held it up so they could witness him ejecting the magazine and emptying the chamber. "Understand?"

The man stopped when a police car's lights flashed. The car stopped blocking the entrance to the lot. The policeman peered through the windows scrutinizing the activity and, when he saw the CJNG group, waved, and then sped away.

Vincente walked from the shadows.

"Bridger. We meet."

Bridger ignored him.

"Beatrice?"

"Here." In the headlights of the CJNG trucks, he saw Beatrice and Milton sitting and watching men kneeling over Imp.

Ignoring the men who tensed and prodded their weapons in their direction, Bridger, Demon, and Snake moved past the cartel men to where his people huddled on the ground. Two men with medical equipment were tending to Imp. A stretcher rested on the ground next to him.

"Your people need attention," Vincente said, raising his hand toward his men.

"His wound is serious, but not fatal, but immediate treatment is needed. His head wound is not as significant," one medic said.

"This...sucks," Imp grunted.

"How are you, Imp?" Bridger said as he knelt.

"I...have...ache," Imp slurred as lamplight reflected off his glazed eyes. He grabbed Bridger's hand. "Jelly Bean. Call Jelly Bean."

"Kid is losing it," Demon said.

"I get it, Imp." Bridger patted his hand, signaling understanding that Bridge needed to contact Jelly Bean, one of Imp's 'The Unemployables,' if he needed tech support.

"He is going to my hospital," Vincente said from behind Bridger.

"The hell he is." In a swift move, Demon spun toward the cartel leader and lifted his arms, fists balled.

"Stop it, Demon." Bridger reached over, placed his hand on Demon's arm, and gently pushed them down.

"You...care." Imp's head was turned toward Demon, and then he closed his eyes.

"Shut up," Demon growled, but not as menacingly as usual.

Bridger could see flood lights illuminating his still smoldering yacht across the marina.

"Captain Andre and the crew?" Bridger asked Beatrice.

"I don't know, but..." Her voice trailed off.

Bridger nodded.

Dead or alive I will take care of them and their families.

Bridger waved to Vincente, who indicated his medics should continue helping Imp. They carefully placed Imp on the stretcher, and then a couple of men lifted it, carried it to an ambulance, slid him in, and closed the door.

"You can go to the hospital later. First, we must talk."

As the ambulance pulled away, Vincente moved closer to Bridger.

"We have mutual enemies."

"Really? Who?"

"I think we can help each other." Vincente tried to place his hand on Bridger's shoulder but Bridger swatted it away. Vincente recoiled, preparing to strike back, but he stopped and smiled.

"First, we must agree. We can make a deal."

"*Un pacto con el Diablo.* I am all for that." Bridger smiled.

Vincente smiled.

"Yes, *un pacto con el Diablo.* A deal with the Devil."

"This isn't the first time I've dealt with one of the worst people in the world," Bridger said.

Just the first time I've had to make a deal to keep us from being slaughtered.

But he knew that didn't mean they were safe.

Not even close.

14

EL HOMBRE

Puerta Vallarta, Jalisco State, Mexico

B ridger heard the first rumble of the vehicles coming up the lane.

"You guys get out of there!" he shouted.

"What?" Imp asked. "What did you say?"

"Go. Get off the boat!" There was a second of delay, which was too much for Bridger. "Now!"

"We're moving. We're moving!" Milton yelled in panic.

"We're moving too." Bridger looked at Demon and Snake. If Beatrice was right, up-armored CJNG trunks were appearing over the crest of the lane. He pointed to the Explorer. "Let's get the bag. I've had enough of these guys."

"Hell, yeah."

They sprinted to the Explorer, opened the rear hatch, and pulled out a large, long, heavy canvas bag. They quickly unzipped the bag and reached in.

They each took out a body armor loadout tactical vest and secured

it around their torso. Bridger and Demon grabbed their AR-15/grenade launcher weapons as Snake clipped a holstered Sig Sauer to his belt and stuffed extra clips into pockets.

Demon found clips for his 1911 and did the same.

As headlight glow grew brighter from down the lane, a flash mushroomed in the harbor, briefly illuminating the entire resort. Another explosion followed. As flames rose to illuminate the dark sky, booms rumbled from the direction of the explosions and echoed into the hills of Los Ramblases.

Bridger, followed by the other two men, scrambled up the pile of construction debris. Bridger spun to look at the fires burning in the harbor's direction. The sounds of distant sirens and honks of car alarms echoed across the resort and off the hillsides around them.

"Milton!" he shouted. No answer came from through his earbud. "Beatrice!" Still no answer. "Imp!" Wide-eyed with worry, he looked at Demon and Snake. Their jaws were set tight as the same concern registered on their faces.

A whirly noise came from above them, followed by the *thunk* of something metallic hitting the top of the Explorer. Whatever it was bounced off the roof and landed on the ground with a *thud*. Snake scurried down the mound and ran toward the SUV.

"Devilbot," he shouted with shock in his voice.

"Holy hell," Demon said.

The ground started to shake from the deep revving of powerful engines. Then, the imposing camo-painted trunks accelerated over the access road's crest.

"Blast them."

Each man pumped grenades at the headlights, sending a flash and ear-shattering booms across the neighborhood that easily had to be heard in the downtown area. Lights started to appear in the houses on the hill, as well as screams, dogs barking, and still-distant sirens.

The first CJNG vehicle's heavy armor required a half dozen grenades, but it finally exploded in a mushroom of flame, sending burning debris arching in every direction like fireworks. Men dressed in full military uniforms—helmets, weapons, equipment— ran from

the exploding vehicle, hoping to escape secondary explosions from the munitions inside. Some of them were on fire themselves.

The Spy Devils unleashed a continual barrage from their AR-15s toward the burning truck, dropping anything silhouetted against the backdrop of flames.

The air was thick with smoke, the smell of Comp5 explosives, and the burning CJNG vehicle and men.

"More behind us, coming up the road." Snake was looking below them where the road weaved up to their location. Headlights reflected enough light to reveal two massive, armored trucks creeping up the narrow incline. "Those are the Toyotas. Heavy armor and weapons."

"These guys are a damned army," Demon said as he pointed his AR-15 down the hill. Bridger saw the unmistakable and absurd expression of joy on his friend's face.

"We can't drive out," Snake said, shouting over the cracks of gunfire. "The road is blocked. We have to get down this hill."

Bridger did a quick assessment of their position. At the foot of the slope, lining the road, were homes constructed of stone, bricks, and wood—most with metal roofs. Many had fenced animal pens. Goats and chickens.

"Let's go."

As Bridger turned to the hill, Demon grabbed his arm. "Hang on." He turned to Snake. "You got any incendiaries in there?"

Snake rummaged in the bag, pulled out a canister, and flipped it to Demon.

Snake lobbed a few grenades at the new threat, stopping the trucks on the road below. Several men jumped out, firing wildly up the hill. Bullets pinged off rocks and thumped off dirt around the mound— more bullets whizzed by over their heads.

Bridger and Snake rained more grenades on the trucks and men on the road at the bottom of the hill. The multiple explosions shook everything on the hillside.

"Roast pig," Demon said, flinging his seventy-year-old body over the hill.

Bridger watched Demon run toward the front of the house, ready to pull the pin on the incendiary hand grenade.

"Demon. The trucks!" Bridger shouted as he turned back to see Demon prepare to pull the grenade's pin and toss it into the house. Bridger pointed at the road.

Demon stopped and looked at Bridger and then back at the house. He rotated, pulled the pin, and tossed it with all his might down the road. White blinding flashes exploded in front of the men sprinting up from the vehicles blocked by the burning wreckage.

Demon scrambled over the mound as the shrieks and the cracking of burning trees came from behind him.

"This is fun," he said with a grin as he sucked air between his teeth.

"Hey. What about the others?" Snake asked, looking toward the harbor where the flames were subsiding.

Bridger clenched his jaw and gripped his weapon.

"Let's go."

By controlling the high ground, Bridger, Snake, and Demon pummeled the vehicles below with grenades and bursts from their AR-15s. They saw some CJNG men take cover and return fire. Some shot with precision while others shot wildly in any direction, hitting a few of the homes, which started to burn.

Screams came from inside many houses. In the flickering fires illuminating the road, Bridger watched frightened men, women, and children run out of their homes in confusion, panic, and terror. Their bodies jerked, dropped, or were blown apart by the cartel forces, cutting them down at close range with machine guns.

"What the hell?" Demon shouted from his covered position behind the mound. He looked at Bridger. In the glow of the fires, Bridger could see Demon's face covered in sweat and dirt. Streaks of blood trickled off his cheek and chin from unseen wounds. "I've had enough of this!"

Demon jumped up, threw himself over the mound, and started to partially skid, partially run down the hill, seeking cover from a squat house at the bottom of the slope.

"Demon!" Bridger shouted. "Crap."

What the hell? Are you trying to die today?

Bridger jumped up and released grenades to cover Demon's mad scramble down the hill. The view was obscured by smoke and dust, so Snake burst rounds at the areas where he last saw the men.

During his sixty-foot charge down the sloping hill, Demon dodged, fell over, or slammed into brush, rocks, sporadic coconut palms, and conifer trees. He slid into an animal pen, ran, and leaped over a fence and around the road.

Three bloodied CJNG men staggered from around a truck, firing at Demon, who fired back, dropping two before his clicks signaled his magazine was empty. He dropped the AR-15, pulled out this 1911, and marched up to the last man standing and swaying in the road. Demon pointed the pistol at the cartel man's face and fired. His head snapped, and he fell like a tree to the ground.

This is going to hurt a little, Bridger thought.

Bridger started to slide down the hill mostly on his feet, using his hands to keep from falling. His right foot caught on a rock, and he tumbled the remaining twenty feet, crashing into an animal pen with a *thud.* He bounced and rolled into something soft. Bridger looked up and found himself face-to-face with a bleating goat.

"Sorry," Bridger said to the goat as Snake arrived behind him.

"You okay?" Snake asked.

Bridger winced as he stood, testing his ankle to determine if he could stand. He sniffed, looked at the ground, rubbed his fingers together, and sniffed some gunk on his hands. He wiped them on his pants.

"Don't tell anyone."

"I won't have to, but a shower wouldn't hurt."

Bridger nodded, and they ran to the road.

Demon was standing among the flames of burning trucks and houses.

"We should get the hell out of here," Demon said, panting with a smile on his bloody and dirty face. Two more bodies were on the ground behind him.

"Good idea."

Bridger looked toward the harbor and started jogging as best he could, wincing with each step.

Demon and Snake followed him.

"Something smells like shit," Demon said. He sniffed toward Bridger. "What happened to you?'

"He fell on a goat," Snake said matter-of-factly.

"Okay. Makes sense," Demon said.

Bridger's face and hands stung from scratches, every muscle in his leg ached, and his ankle was going numb. He rummaged in his pocket and was relieved he had not lost either phone during his tumble down the hill. He dialed his phone and waited for an answer. It didn't come. Sirens blared not too far away, and from their vantage point on the hill, they witnessed the flashing lights of emergency vehicles snaking through the roads leading to the neighborhood.

"We need a car."

It was hard to be inconspicuous among the frightened Los Ramblases residents who were yelling and running away from the battle around them. In the chaos, Snake stopped by a battered and rusty Dodge Caravan parked outside a dark house.

"No one home," he said.

Snake pried open the hood and searched in the near darkness for the wires he needed to jump the ignition. Bridger panted and groaned as he pulled open the passenger door and wiggled onto the seat, his muscles tightening with each move. Demon swiftly yanked open the sliding side door, got in, and closed it with a bang behind him.

The engine sparked a few times and then Snake found the correct wires, sputtering the Dodge to life. He slammed the hood down, hopped behind the steering wheel, and started the Dodge down the road.

"Open a window, somebody, please," Demon said, sniffing the already dank air in the van, made worse by the odors radiating off Bridger's clothes.

Bridger pushed the power button control for the window, but nothing happened. He clicked it back and forth a few more times with the same result.

"Great," Demon said.

Snake slowly maneuvered the Dodge down the narrow road. It was hard enough in daylight, but the tight space and the van only having one working headlight made the journey infinitely more difficult and hazardous.

An unfamiliar ringing came from Bridger's jeans. He ignored the stings on his knuckles as he fished López's phone from the front pocket of his jeans. He entered 51415 with a slimy finger.

"Hey, El Hombre. I was expecting your call," Bridger said.

"Bridger. Nice to talk to you."

If Vincente was surprised, Bridger didn't detect it in his voice.

The situation was spiraling out of his control. He was battling for his team's survival against a killer cartel leader. They were on the man's home turf, with few weapons, less leverage, and dwindling options.

We've been in worse situations.

15

HE WAS A PATRIOT

Purcellville, Virginia

W es Henslow had the most secure funeral anyone had ever attended.
To get within a quarter mile of St. Peter's Church in rural Purcellville, Virginia, northwest of Washington D.C., you had to be on a pre-approved CIA security office list. Local police and Loudoun County Sheriff patrol cars were positioned at off-ramps of Highway 7 and along the route to the church.

Helicopters noisily cruised above the area on overwatch.

A line of black limousines and SUVs slowly advanced as uniformed deputies checked the list and approved occupants of the cars to proceed to the crowded parking areas demarcated around the church.

"Tight security," May Currier said as she looked out the window in the backseat of their government-supplied town car.

"It's Wes. What would you expect?" CIA Deputy Director of Operations Max Hawkins replied from the seat beside her. "The man spent his life hunting terrorists, drug traffickers, arms dealers, and depots of all types. This is a target-rich environment for an attack."

"I see a lot of FBI jackets."

"In case there are some party crashers," Hawkins said with seriousness.

May knew what Hawkins was thinking and who he was looking for.

May scanned the people—many with canes, using walkers, or in wheelchairs—proceeding toward the church. They wore ill-fitting or bespoke suits, military uniforms, or flight jackets covered in patches.

She recognized every face. Gray-haired men and women who represented the history and foundation of the CIA—for good and bad at every level of the intelligence profession. They were legends whose names were utterly unknown to the public. People who defended American foreign policy based on the core need to make the USA a safer place and keep it the preeminent country in the world.

Wes Henslow was the legend of all legends in the world of intelligence.

"He was a patriot," May said. "He would hate the attention to his bones."

Wes had been her boss, mentor, friend, and the person who had helped develop her son Trowbridge, more than anyone, into the man he had become. It was all part of the plan they had devised years ago to make a group to counter future threats to the USA no others foresaw.

That group had become the Spy Devils, led by her son, Trowbridge "Bridger" Hall.

That morning, they had stopped at CIA headquarters, where, despite her pleas to Hawkins not to, he had arranged a retirement ceremony for her, the now ex-Senior Advisor, Special Projects to the Deputy Director of Operations.

In the Director's Dining Room on the 7th floor, she nodded, shook hands, greeted well-wishers, and snacked on hors d'oeuvres with more people than expected. It was an enjoyable time with people she had spent all her life with. She was grateful Hawkins ignored her pleas.

"Come on. I want to show you something," Hawkins said as he took May by the elbow when it was over.

"We have to get to the funeral," she said, checking her watch.

"We will. We are going outside. It's chilly." May took her dark wool coat and scarf from him.

They silently walked out the glass front doors of the Old Headquarters Building into a gray Northern Virginia winter day. They went down the steps and turned left down the sidewalk. May tightened the scarf around her neck and stuffed her hands into her pockets, wondering where Hawkins was taking her.

On their left, they passed the statue of Nathan Hale, a copy of the original at Yale, the patriot's alma mater. On their right was the auditorium, known by Agency employees as the "Bubble" for its shiny dome shape.

"Here." Hawkins stopped and pointed to the ground.

May looked down to see a small bronze plaque. Raised lettering read "In Memory of Wes Henslow. Patriot."

May blinked away the tears chilling in her eyes.

"It's the only memorial of its kind on campus. We will plant a tree here in spring."

They stood silently, looking at the plaque as the cold wind blew.

"A crab apple?" May asked.

"Of course."

"I want to talk to Bridger," Hawkins told her, his breath vaporing into the cold air.

She had been waiting for this and wondered why it had taken so long.

"You do?" she asked through tight lips as she turned away from him.

"He committed a crime, May." Hawkins's voice was firm and laced with a lethal dose of the anger she had experienced many times before.

"He should not have attacked you. I asked him to apologize, but I am only his mother," she said jokingly.

"I don't believe that social media garbage for a second. He wasn't killed in the ranch attack. That's for all the clickbait-loving, reality TV-watching, brain-sucking morons."

The mysterious status of Bridger and the Spy Devils had flooded social media and, to some degree, the regular press. Although a covert group in operation, the Spy Devils' existence was not a secret, given that the group had used social media as a weapon throughout the years to expose their targets. They had gathered a cult following across most social media platforms and with academics, journalists, law enforcement, and intel organizations.

May had prepared for the question. She looked back with blinking, moist eyes, and a convincing look of grief made possible by her turn into the wind and letting the cold air sting her eyes until they watered.

"What do you want me to say, Max? He is my son."

"It doesn't matter. He is lucky I haven't issued a warrant for his arrest yet."

You are lucky he didn't do something worse than pushing you around.

She thought his face was getting redder from the chilly breeze, but she decided it was Hawkins's renowned anger.

"If he were alive, he would certainly be seeking revenge, something like what just happened in Mexico," he said, his eyes staring at her from the corner of his eyes.

She let the breeze fill the seconds of silence. Then she looked at her watch.

"We should go, Max. You can't be late."

Their town car reached the front of the line of cars arriving at the funeral, where a deputy grasping a clipboard in gloved hands stood with one raised. The driver rolled down the window and spoke to the deputy. He nodded and stepped toward the rear windows, which the driver remotely lowered.

"Good day, Madam. Sir," the deputy said with a slight southern accent as he stuck his face through the window. "Names, please."

"Hawkins. Max. Max Hawkins."

Deputy T. WOODS was embroidered in block white letters on his vest. He ran his pen down the list on his clipboard. He then flipped the first page up, crinkling it over the top of the clipboard, and examined the second page. His face wrinkled.

"Hawkins?"

"Yes. Hawkins," Max said with growing irritation.

Woods flipped the first page back and started his scan of the names again. Then he stopped.

"Ah, here it is. Hawkins." He scratched it off.

Woods looked at May.

"Name." Woods' broad smile and dark eyes with wrinkles at the corners peered at May's face from just a few feet away.

May looked closely at Deputy Sherriff Woods. He wore a black uniform sporting a fully equipped tactical vest and belt. A radio was clipped to his shoulder. He looked around 50, with wavey dark hair with a bit of gray around the temples—a little round around the waist.

"May Currier," she said as she suppressed a smile.

He glanced at the list then back at her.

"Here is it. Thank you." Wood's eyebrows flicked up, then he stepped back and waved the car into the parking area.

Oh Bridger. I knew you would be here.

Every pew in the church was filled. Some people were standing along the walls. Heads turned when May Currier walked in wearing a tasteful dark dress and followed her until she sat on a pew near the front, stoically observing those around her.

Wes's family was there. Two sons and their spouses. Five grand-children. An ex-wife.

On the altar were items to memorialize Wes. What remained of his body was contaminated with radiation and had been safely disposed of in Amsterdam. Beside a gold-framed photo of a smiling Henslow was a bottle of Chivas Regal and a cigar humidor. An American flag folded inside a mahogany triangle display box. Books and certificates and mementos.

One book caught May's attention. It was frayed and dirty. She tried to get a better look at it, but the service began.

May patted Hawkins's leg when an unnamed staffer concluded softly singing *God Bless America.*

Hawkins stood and walked to the front, filling every inch of his black suit with his massive frame.

"I will keep this short because Wes would hate this attention." Soft chuckles. "He hated many things, including me, most of the time." A few more laughs echoed off the marble walls. "Wes never met a terrorist or, even more broadly, an enemy of the United States, he didn't hate, which is probably why he was hated as much in return. He didn't care. He would say, '*We are the United States of America. We do what we need to do. If you don't like it, too damn bad.*' He lived that right up to his last terrorist-hunting moments."

May smiled, recalling how often she had heard him say this to anyone. It was why the politicians on the Hill hated him.

"Wes, do you want everyone to think you're a shit?"

"I am a shit."

That attitude was a primary reason he was forced into retirement, which only afforded him more time to pursue his nemesis, Specter, the master bomb maker. That pursuit eventually led to the showdown in Amsterdam, where they both died...*what? Just weeks ago?*

When the service concluded, May stood and looked for Deputy Woods. She found him standing against the back wall. He winked at her, turned, and walked out the church side door.

May walked up to the alter and saw a tattered copy of Casino Royale by Ian Fleming. She looked inside. It was a first edition and signed by the author.

"How did I do?" Hawkins asked as he came up next to her.

"Great, just great," May said as she took Hawkins's arm.

They moved to the reception in the impressively large church fellowship hall in the basement. By some gray-haired guests who knew their history, May was viewed like a grieving widow—since she was the person closest to Wes—including his family, who left right after the ceremony. In some ways, she felt like it, too. Hawkins knew this and tried to keep the conversation upbeat, but these people only had one thing in common.

Espionage.

They ate finger foods, small-talked, and reminisced about *the old days back when the Agency was good.*

Do you remember, May? Wes and you lived by the mantra—mission over means.

They don't make them like Wes anymore, am I right?

They are just a bunch of resume-building kids now. Three years and out. No dedication.

And on it went.

Old intelligence officers talking to old intelligence officers was like the fountain of youth, so they spent hours laughing, whispering, and re-living. When the last guest cleared out, May and Hawkins stood in the chill, silently waiting for the town car.

"Bridger didn't show. That is too bad. Too much law enforcement, I guess."

May kept silent.

"Tell him I don't forgive him, but I get it. I don't want to put your son in jail, but we need to come to…an understanding. Make it happen, May."

"Trowbridge is a big boy. He can do what he wants and deal with the consequences."

Hawkins let out a *hmmph* and shoved his massive, gloved hands deeper into his tent-sized overcoat as their car arrived.

The driver opened the door for May, then ran around to open it for Hawkins, who did not wait. He saw something on his seat and flicked it over as he sat. The driver closed the door behind him.

She allowed him to tug off his gloves, waiting for him to notice the card. When he did, he snatched it and stared at a red "S" with horns. He flipped it to the other side, knowing what was written there.

Greetings from the Devil.

16

SERVE THE PEOPLE

Beijing, People's Republic of China

"Those are significant losses, Vice Minister Sun," Chen said to the man sitting across the desk from him. Chen didn't consider himself a violent man, but something in the smug face of Chen's number two—MSS Vice Minister Sun—needed to be slapped.

"Yes. First, it was our assets in Boston. Kansas. Los Angeles. Chicago. Now, the FBI has broken our networks in New York City. They are accused of many crimes, but espionage is the most significant," Sun told Chen during their weekly meeting.

The meetings always took place inside Chen's official home office within the tall red walls and gates of historic Zhongnanhai, the former imperial garden in the Imperial City adjacent to the Forbidden City. Chen's apartments were compact but ornate. His small office, consisting of a functional desk, couch, and visitors' chairs, had a view of Nanhai Lake.

By having the meetings within the power center of the Chinese

Communist Party (CCP), Chen was reminding the ego- and purpose-of-mission-driven Sun of his lower position within their professional and personal hierarchy.

He had to. Sun was China's proven master of counterespionage.

Chen sat back and sipped tea and let Sun continue his briefing.

"Our assets had built an extensive network for over ten years, reporting on the anti-China activists and human rights leaders across the United States. All our access and influence are in danger, it is apparent," Sun said. "Not to mention the ability to collect on other topics of importance to China. The subversive pro-democracy Hong Kong elements. Taiwanese independence. Uyghur and Tibet activists."

"Is there any explanation for this? These officers and their assets have been in place for years."

"There can be only one of three reasons," Vice Minister Sun said, eyeing Chen. "Either our people suddenly became lazy or brought suspicion upon themselves. Maybe. Doubtful. Two, the FBI suddenly became more effective in its counterintelligence capabilities. That is even more doubtful. Three. We have a traitor."

Sun let the powerful words hang in the incense-laced air.

Chen knew Sun was right. Someone was a traitor. A high-ranking officer *had* provided the CIA with the names of MSS officials on American college campuses. Chinese agents were being arrested or suspected because of that person's betrayal.

That person was Chen.

Chen knew that Sun Jingwei, the 57-year-old Vice Minister of State Security, was dangerous and a threat to Chen's future. Genius-level smart with night-black eyes, a square chin, and an infectious smile—and ruthless in this pursuit of spies.

A true believer in communist party politics, Sun rapidly moved up the ranks, gaining favor within the Xi Jinping faction and playing a role in Xi's powerplay to become president. The president appointed Sun to leadership positions with the MSS, which vaulted higher as he displayed remarkable skills at hunting, exposing, and capturing foreign agents and the Chinese nationals who spied for them against China.

He despised traitors. Once he had a suspicion one existed, he would not stop.

"These activities were only known by a few at the highest levels," Chen said. "I have seen the messages regarding our MSS officers being arrested from Bureau 18."

"Yes. The United States Operations Bureau has moved to protect our assets that might be in danger next. But the Americans still are making arrests."

"So, the traitor is inside Bureau 18? It is their American operations that are being exposed."

Sun smiled back.

"Perhaps. Perhaps not," Sun said from the uncomfortable leather high-back chair in Chen's office.

Chen tapped his fingers on his desktop, slowly stood, picked up his teacup, and strolled to the windows of his Zhongnanhai office and residence. The courtyards and fountains looked gray and cold on the cold Beijing morning.

The CIA will get me killed, Chen thought.

Chapel and the CIA promised Chen's information would be used sparingly and strategically. They had done neither. And now Chen was in peril. Chen held his emotions in check, seeing the thrill of the hunt in the country's top spy catcher's eyes.

"Then you should find this person immediately," Chen said, turning to Sun.

Sun's eyes were on him, and it took all Chen's concentration not to get up and run. Instead, Chen used his years of experience to remain calm. He registered an appropriate look of concern and control.

I will not be next.

"What do you think, Vice-Minister?" Chen asked, looking out the window.

"I know the president is not pleased with the damage this is causing our reputation. The United States Congress will do everything it can to harm us...the fools they are."

"I am aware of that! I do not need you to tell me what needs to be done." Chen sipped his tea. "If it is a high official, then *all* senior MSS officials must restate their loyalty to the president and the Communist Party and adhere to directions set by the National Security Commission. They must all study the president's political thoughts on national security work."

As Sun nodded, a trace of a smile froze to his face.

"Plus, we need to remind our officials of infiltration tactics and espionage by foreign actors. If we have insiders colluding with foreign intelligence agencies to conduct anti-China activities, we must have all eyes looking."

"That is a good plan. Remind them they *'serve the people'* and the Middle Kingdom," Chen said, quoting the most used slogan of the communist party.

What is your actual plan, Sun?

"I fear this high-ranking official will know how to cover his actions," Sun said.

"Why is that?"

"He will know we are searching. Time is short."

"You have my full support in every way." Chen stood.

"Thank you, sir." Sun stood also and prepared to leave.

"I would appreciate updates—daily. Written reports will suffice," Chen said.

Sun paused.

"Yes, of course."

"Good day, Vice Minister Sun."

When it opened, Chen walked Sun to the door where Sun's guard was waiting on the other side.

"Please, again, keep me informed on your progress."

"Yes, Minister."

When they were out of sight, Chen nodded at Wu, his placid-faced guard and driver standing outside his door, and then closed it. Chen rested his head on the doorframe and let out a long breath. Then another.

Sun is suspicious. I feel it. I know it.

Had Sun told the president of his suspicions? Had Li Chu made good on his threat to contact Foreign Minister Yi's office about Chen?

Wu had not been ordered to handcuff and arrest him, which was a good sign—but they could at any time.

Something had to be done. He had to prepare.

Chen went back and sat at his desk.

He moved papers, pens, and desk clutter to expose the wood top. He pressed down hard with both hands until the decorative herringbone pattern section in the middle of the desktop clicked. An almost imperceptible separation appeared around the square section. He pressed again on a small segment of the pattern.

The foot square panel of the top released without making a sound.

Chen reached in and slid out his CIA-supplied computer tablet. Whenever he used it, he considered the technology a work of art. It looked like any tablet, except this was layered with partitioned hard drives and encryption. It had tampering and wipe functionality, among other detection-avoidance capabilities. If he weren't working with the CIA, he would have given it to the MSS Bureau 13 for technological evaluation and reproduction.

Sun was feared for his counterespionage prowess but, as MSS minister, Chen possessed the most dangerous weapon in all of China.

Since the formation of the People's Republic of China, perhaps before, the leader of the country had gathered any information to intimidate, blackmail, or influence potential rivals, foreign leaders, citizens, diplomats, journalists, businesses, citizens—anyone anywhere—that might threaten the leader's power.

The files were known as the Dossier. The president owned the Dossier, but the head of security was the collector and caretaker. The threat of exposing the contents was a deterrent that kept most from speaking or acting against the leader.

It was the ultimate deterrent.

Chen pulled a palm-sized ultra-secure portable flash drive developed by the technology bureau of the MSS from its hiding place. Inside it were millions of categorized and stored digitized entries. Chen did not use "the cloud" since the MSS could roam freely there undetected.

He looked at the gray titanium shell, knowing his name was inside.

As was Sun's. As was everyone's—except the leader, who wiped his information from the Dossier as had all his predecessors.

Chen assumed Sun wanted it. Every leader of the CCP did.

Chen put the drive into a small backpack. Then he accessed and copied his computer files containing the names of the U.S. intelligence community and American officials passing intelligence to China and the names of Chinese spies operating in the U.S. He copied intelligence with sensitive information about China's special weapons programs.

He loaded all the files on his CIA tablet, stuffed it all back into the secure area of the desk, and resealed it.

He took his cup of tea and looked out the window as the sun tried to penetrate the gray clouds over Beijing. He thought of May and how he wanted to speak with his former CIA contact.

With the tablet's secure communication system, May Currier and Chen rarely met over the years. When May had messaged through the tablet that she was retiring, she tried to reassure him but, over the years, only May had protected him above all else.

I want to talk to May.

"Everything will be fine. Chapel will be your connection."

"To whom?"

"Hawkins."

He knew right then that he was on his own.

Hawkins wasn't May.

Sun didn't believe it, but he knew it. He could feel it. He just couldn't prove it—yet.

Chen is the traitor.

It was an unconscionable level of treachery. Horrifying. Outrageous. Sickening.

He was eager to alert the president and get approval to arrest Chen, but utilizing his renowned patience was critical now.

In the meantime, he would increase the surveillance on Chen, which would be problematic. Chen's loyal sources inside the government would alert him to anything unusual. The man was a professional intelligence officer who could not easily be fooled.

And Chen had the Dossier. If he felt threatened, he would expose Sun's many transgressions to save himself.

Sun would not allow that to happen to him. If it came to that, the answer was simple. Chen would have to die like anyone else who stood in his way. If all went as planned, that would happen soon.

Very soon.

17

BEIJING DUCK

Beijing, People's Republic of China

C hen tossed and turned all night.
Every hour, he awoke in a cold sweat from visions of armed security police breaking down his door. Shouting, "Traitor!" Glimpses of being locked in a pitch-black room. Flashes of torture. He was looking down at his bloodied face. Looking down at the rifle barrels pointed at him before they tightened the blindfold around his eyes. The sound of firing squad guns cracking woke him.

I've recruited dozens of spies over the years. So, this is what it is like from the other side.

Chen stared at the ceiling, letting his overactive mind recall his rise through the octopus-armed bureaucracy of the MSS and how it led to this moment.

He gasped and jumped when the phone *beeped.*

Chen rubbed his eyes and blinked. He swung his legs over the side of the bed. He didn't need to hurry. He knew who it was. Only one person had this number. He answered and waited.

"I think we need each other more than you realize." Li Chu's voice was soft.

Chen contemplated what Li Chu was implying.

"Oh? Why is that?"

"Really, Minister? I do not have time. Please give me what I want, when and where I want it. Do you want me to inform Foreign Minister Yi, who will tell Sun you are a traitor?"

I needed you to be silenced. I'm tired of giving in to your threats....

"What do you need?"

"I need money, cover, and travel documents, and other operational needs."

It was the same list every time he called. Rather than expose him, Li Chu, to his credit, was using his knowledge to leverage Chen and the MSS—unconditionally—to help Li Chu find and kill Bridger. This culminated in Chen providing satellite imagery to help Li Chu's plan to raid Bridger's ranch and kill Bridger—to kill May's son.

"I will get you what you need."

"Thank you, Minister. I am sorry for waking you."

Chen put down the phone.

Chen put on slippers and a robe, got up, and checked the security monitor. No one was there.

Still, he could not shake the feeling that his time was running out.

The CIA's Chen operation ran through American businessman Danforth Chapel.

May had established Danny Chapel's cover with the MSS years ago to benefit Chen's status. The influential American businessman supported the President of China's economic and political initiatives. The business relationship between the MSS and the Chapel Group had proven valuable to both sides, practically and covertly.

Many in the CCP leadership were skeptical of Chapel. They did not like an American presence so deep into China's government and foreign policy—but it was Danforth Chapel. The keeper of secrets.

They could not debate the professional quality of his work to act on their behalf in the constant stream of domestic and international crises.

In an emergency, it was Chapel whom Chen would contact.

Chen rested his head back on the cushion, letting Wu worry about the chronically stalled Beijing traffic.

The distance to Quanjude Roast Duck Restaurant in Qianmen was short, less than a mile, but Beijing traffic made even that drive an ordeal.

He spotted the surveillance cars performing a hiding-in-plain-sight pattern. The first car pulled out immediately after they exited Zhongnanhai. Two more cars weaved in and out of traffic to take its place. The message was clear.

Sun thinks it is me but he doesn't know. He knows the Dossier is a danger, so if he pushes me too far, all it should take is a meeting with the president—usually.

If Chen released the contents of the Dossier regarding Sun, it might relieve Chen of the problem, but he would have one of equal concern. The president would disapprove of Chen's unilateral use of the information. Chen would be removed and disappear.

Could Chen do a controlled leak? Use a friendly newspaper in Taiwan to publish the story? He could, but again, the president could become suspicious and ask why Chen wanted Sun removed. Was it because he *was* the traitor?

Chen knew the president would just as quickly get rid of Sun and Chen rather than deal with a war between the security service leaders.

Getting a message regarding his plans to Chapel tonight was dangerous but critical. With Sun on his tail, Chen's decision was made for him.

The original Quanjude was always packed with tourists looking to try the variations of the classic Peking Duck offered by the most famous duck restaurant. Government officials dined there, having the advantage of immediate seating in a more secluded area of the large open dining area.

When he finally arrived, thirty minutes late, early in Chinese meeting terms, he was escorted directly through the VIP entrance of the brightly lit ornate Chinese temple exterior. The two-story interior was as decorated with traditional Chinese motifs as was the outside.

Inside were white tablecloth-covered tables lined in perfect rows where white-jacketed carvers sporting white chef hats manned the duck carving stations. Large lamps hung from the ceiling. Smells of cooked duck and vegetables. The clinking of silverware was everywhere, like the roar of the guest's voices.

As Minister of the MSS, Chen also knew which rooms did not have listening devices or cameras installed. Two waiting guards started escorting Chen to his reserved room when a smiling Sun appeared from between groups of tourists.

"Hello, Minister Chen. It is a welcome surprise to see you," Sun said with a slight bow, then extended his hand, which Chen shook.

You aren't surprised at all, are you, Sun? Chen thought.

He felt his stomach start to cramp. In less than an instant, the constant pressure that developed behind his right eye built up like a rice cooker until he thought it would pop out. He had to blink to stop the tears of pain from running down his cheek.

"Vice Minister Sun, I did not know you were a fan of duck." His wire-rimmed glasses slid down his nose from the moisture, and he used both hands to reset them.

"I am. You are here to meet with your friend, Mr. Chapel."

"Yes, I am. It is good to see you," Chen said as he moved past Sun to the room.

"I would like to greet him also." Sun followed.

They found Chapel sipping wine at a table set for two. When Chen and Sun entered, Chapel set his glass down and stood.

"Hello, Mr. Chapel," Chen said with a slight bow, then held out his hand.

Chapel stood, bowed, and held out his hand.

"Hello, Minister Chen."

Chapel's face displayed no surprise or concern as Sun approached.

"Vice Minister Sun, what a welcomed surprise. It is so good to see you," Chapel said warmly as he shook Sun's hands with both of his own. "Are you joining us for dinner?" He looked at Sun. "Waiter, please set the table for—"

"No. No, thank you. It is totally by chance. I am here with other guests, but I understood you might be here and hoped I could greet you properly."

"Very well then. It is good to see you." Chapel shook his hand again.

"Minister." Sun let his smile widen on his handsome face as he turned and left.

A stone-faced waiter pulled out Chen's chair, and he sat. The guards took positions just outside in the noisy dining hall. Chapel casually took out his phone and placed it on the table as he switched on the white noise generator and an electronic signal detector. Chen looked at him and then put a phone next to Chapel's.

"Would you like some wine, Minister? I have a Syrah. I find the tannins not as linear as pinot noir when accompanying the rich greasiness of the duck."

"Yes, please, thank you."

The waiter poured, and Chen flipped his hand, signaling that the glass was full enough and that he should leave.

Chen decoded Chapel's facial expression as *"What the hell is going on?"*

"It is good to see you, Minister. I am glad I could make this meeting. I hope all is well."

"As expected, there are always difficulties, plus I am not feeling well lately."

Chapel nodded.

"I hope it is nothing serious?" Chapel's eyes looked over Chen's shoulder to the noisy main hall where Sun was eating.

"Perhaps." Chen upped the signal.

Chapel sipped his wine. "Well, please let me know if there is anything I can do."

Chapel took another sip and watched the chef prepare the duck. They watched and discussed how to prepare the roast duck and the types of sauce needed. Sides of vegetables arrived with a plate of their famous quick-fried duck hearts.

I need to take the risk. Now is the time.

"How is your...former business colleague?" Chen used his fingers to pick up pieces of chopped crispy duck skin. He sucked them from between his fingers.

"She is well."

"Tell her I miss her." Chen licked more duck juice off his fingers.

Chapel emptied the last drops of wine from the bottle and ordered another.

"I will."

"Tell her I would like to see her again someday." Chen interrupted, dipping a fired duck heart in a bowl of spicy mustard sauce and eating it. He smiled through his thin lips.

Given the circumstances, Chen relayed his messages to Chapel as clearly as possible.

I am in danger. The CIA promised to protect me. Call May.

18

ENCRYPTED CALL

Over the Pacific

D anforth Chapel drove directly to the airport, boarded his private plane, and popped antacids. He liked duck, but it sometimes didn't like him, and the tannins in the Syrah weren't mixing well with it.

As his jet flew east over the Pacific Ocean en route to Hawaii, he dialed a number using his NSA-modified secure Signal app.

"Yes. I met him." Pause. "Yes. It transferred perfectly." Pause. "Yes. I am heading back now." Pause. "Max, you should know..." Pause. "He is worried about his situation." Chapel listened. "No, nothing imminent, but he said." Pause. "Yes. That is what he said." Pause. "No. I didn't see anything myself, but—" Pause. "He is quite experienced and able to ascertain if there is something to be concerned about, don't you think?" Pause. "I am not sure. Paranoia? Did he make a mistake? Li Chu is an issue that–." Pause. "Really? That's good to hear. But as it is—" Silence. "Hello? Max?"

Idiot.

Chapel dialed another encrypted call and hit speaker.

"Yes?" The tired voice brought out May Currier's New England accent.

"May? Did I wake you?"

"Yes. What do you want, Danny?"

"I saw your boy."

"Oh? You saw Trowbridge?"

"No, I mean your boy in Beijing."

"Oh, that one." There was a static-filled pause. "I'm retired, and you should not be telling me anything…officially. I should hang up."

Chapel knew she wouldn't.

"He says he doesn't feel well."

More seconds of static-crackling silence

"Shit. Did he say that? *He doesn't feel well?*"

"Yep…doesn't feel well…lately."

Chapel didn't say anything more—he didn't have to.

"Shit. Do you know why that is?"

"Even a pro like him can only handle so much pressure. And some, surprisingly, can't handle much of the double life. Chen might be one of those."

"You think he is cracking?"

"He asked to see you."

"No, he didn't."

"Tell her I miss her."

"Shit." May took a breath and rolled a little on the couch where she had fallen asleep.

"Oh. And Vice Minister Sun happened to show up at our meeting."

"Sun? Double shit. What do you think?"

"I've seen the *look*, May. You worked years to get him to where he is. Chen getting blown would be catastrophic. You know that." He paused. "He said he *wasn't feeling well.* Sun shows up. If he isn't blown, it is coming."

"Hawkins?"

"He knows but thinks it will be okay."

"Triple shit. Any mention of…the files?"

"No, come on, May." He paused. "He is counting on you."

"Danny, I'm retired—"

"May. I'm too tired for that. This is Chen—your once-in-a-career operation decades in the making. May Currier doesn't retire or walk away from anything. Not Chen. Not then. Not now. Not Ukraine. Not Amsterdam. Not the Spy Devils. And she certainly doesn't hand it to Hawkins and wipe her hands of it."

He did not tell her about eliminating Chen's other concern. She didn't need to get involved.

"Contact him…before it's too late."

May set her phone down and looked at the ceiling of her living room. Blinking a few more times to clear her eyes, she stood and stretched. She walked through the living room to the kitchen of her Great Falls, Virginia home, west of Washington, D.C.

She decided a warm pot of tea would help her think. She contemplated Chapel's call while waiting for the kettle to whistle in her kitchen.

He doesn't feel well.

A simple code they had established years ago as an alert.

Danny was not a fool. If Chen used it to raise the alarm about his situation, then Chen was seriously in danger. The man was no fool either.

Tell her I miss her.

The kettle whistled, and she poured the steaming hot water into a tall ceramic mug with a filter filled with loose tea leaves. She put a lid on it to let it steep as she carried it to her study. She sat on the couch, looking at the lovely clear sky of the December day. May could make out some waves on the Potomac River in the distance through trees bending in the wind.

Chen had collected and provided the CIA and U.S. intelligence community with outstanding intel over the years. The knowledge that the Minister of MSS was a CIA asset was held in the strictest Special

Access Program security protocols. Inside the intel community, no more than ten people knew.

The best strategy for Chen was to get out. It was over. Why risk it?

Hawkins might see his best strategy as letting Chen go dormant—at least for a year. Limit Chapel's interaction and expect that if Chen came out now, he would come with the files.

That would take some fortitude from Hawkins, who would press to squeeze all the intel he could out of Chen. *But the Dossier.* The Dossier files were Chen's hole card. As long as he had them, he could dictate terms. If he wanted out, he would find a way.

May's Signal app rang on her phone, and she checked the ID. She sighed and sipped her tea. It wasn't ready.

"What is it? Speak, Max."

"Our friend in China."

She watched a ball of leaves blow across her veranda.

"Yes? What about him?"

"I don't suppose you have heard from him."

"Heard from him? Why would I hear from him? Is there something wrong?"

"No, nothing."

"Then why are you calling asking if I have heard from him if there isn't anything wrong?"

The chain yanking gave May some pleasure.

I hear you squirming, Max. A sharp little poke between your eyes couldn't hurt.

"Come on, Max. What is it?" She knew it hurt when his reply was delayed a microsecond too long.

"Have you heard from Chapel?" he asked.

"No." She lied. "Is there a problem?" she asked sharply. "Is he in danger?"

"Chapel seems concerned."

No shit.

"If there is even a chance Chen is about to be arrested, you are obligated to get him out." He paused too long for her. "Max, we are obligated."

"I don't know. I want to be sure."

"Max, you have to shut him down. Shut him down, now."

Are you listening?

"Yes, that is the right thing to do...then there are the files...if we just cut it all off for some time, say a year."

They listened to each other in silence.

"Screw the files, Max. Do the right thing. What do you want? Chen's safety? More intel? The files?"

"Goodbye, May. When you see your son, say hello. I would love to talk to him."

May set her phone down.

You son of a bitch. People are going to die.

She walked to her bookshelves and moved a few to the side. Reaching in, something went *click*. A two-foot shelf section detached on one end and swung out an inch.

She pulled out a tablet and powered it up. The highly encrypted device was a digital cryptographic version of the old one-time pad where only a single-use pre-shared key could decipher the message. Her tablet and Chen's were the only ones with the random independent keys needed.

Once he logged into his system, the message would download directly to his tablet.

Then, he would know what to do.

If Chapel got the message right, the CIA need to act now. If Chen listened, it might work out. If Hawkins did the right thing, it might work out.

If not, then I will make it right.

She sat back at her window and tested her tea. It was perfect.

19

HUDSON YARDS

New York City, New York

The cheerful colors of the season reflected off every surface along 34th Street, brightening an otherwise gray and cloudy afternoon.

From everywhere, the same songs of the holiday season played. Car tires rolling over pavement made wet by an overnight two-inch snow *splished* with the city's usual continuous chorus of sounds—honking cars, sirens, people yelling, dogs barking.

"This is nice," Lena said as she pulled up on her Patagonia coat zipper, closing it as far as she could to her neck. A tug on her wool scarf protected the remaining exposed neck from the chilly breeze funneling between the buildings. Earmuffs over her long black hair covered her ears. Her arm locked around Bridger's, slowing him down whenever he tried to quicken their pace.

Frustrated New Yorkers weaved and sliced around them like slalom skiers maneuvering an Olympic downhill course, sometimes grazing into the couple as if they were flags.

"Yes, it is nice, but this is New York," Bridger informed her politely as he dug his hands into his leather bomber jacket. A back fedora was tucked tight on this head. "Everyone here walks with a purpose, which means fast and forward. If we go too slow, we will be mowed over like we're peddling a bicycle in the middle of a highway. Understood?"

"Yes, but I meant it was nice being with you," she said. Bridger didn't feel guilty for interpreting her comment the way he did. He didn't want to get mowed over.

After Bridger's deal with Vincente saved them, Bridger's plane landed at Teterboro Airport in Jersey. A car was waiting to drive him to his 35th-floor Hudson Yards penthouse in the city.

I am going to fulfill that deal to avoid the most vicious cartel in the world making me and everything I have ever touched disappear.

Bridger made the deal as a last resort to get the Spy Devils out of Mexico alive.

After he did, Imp received the immediate critical medical attention Vincente promised and was now at Mount Sinai with Demon, surprisingly acting as his guard dog. Angel and Janelle were safe at home with their son. Snake was visiting relatives and friends in the boroughs. Beatrice and Milton were wedding shopping in Manhattan.

I had hoped they would move on from this. Get away. Start a life.

The respite gave Bridger a chance to spend time with Lena.

As they strolled, Bridger glanced at the reflection in the window of a passing store. The two men were still lagging fifteen feet behind on the opposite side of the street. He assumed the other two were ahead to take up shadowing the couple.

"I'm so glad I am here. Quite spontaneous for the mysterious Bridger."

He heard the familiar *ding* of a Salvation Army bell, then saw the bell ringer in her Salvation Army uniform, standing by the red tripod holding a white sign with a red shield above it and a red bucket below.

"I am loaded with spontaneity—as long as it is planned. I'll show you." He quickly veered on an angle to avoid pedestrians and angled over to the bucket. He removed two hundred dollars from his wallet, folded them, and stuffed the bills into the narrow slot.

"Merry Christmas," the smiling woman said, her cheeks rosy-red from the cold and wind.

"Same to you," he said as he turned to Lena. "See?"

As he spoke, he scanned the street over her shoulder. The two trailers had stopped at a store pretending to window shop. He could see them mumbling into their comms system, warning the other team members.

Lena grabbed him by the arm, and they resumed their walk to the slippery crunch of gray slush under their boots.

Bridger knew the surveillance he detected since they left the penthouse was from Chapel. First, only Chapel had the power and access to locate Bridger's NYC hideaway—or he just asked May. Second, the teams trailing them weren't very good.

Freelancers. They won't have any connection to Chapel.

The call from Chapel came as Bridger and the Spy Devils were on the plane escaping Mexico.

"Li Chu," Chapel said.

"What about him?" Bridger asked, irritated. He wanted to sleep all the way to New York.

"You *know* what about him. No one likes him. Certainly, that includes you."

"You called to tell me the obvious?" Bridger yawned loudly into Chapel's ear. "Why are you calling me, Chapel? What do you want?"

"He is in New York, fortuitously."

"So?"

"I saved you in Amsterdam, remember? He had May...and *Lena*." He emphasized her name, hoping to get under Bridger's skin. "You called, begging for help. I got you the intel from Chen in time to save all of you. Remember? You made a deal. Time to pay up."

"Begging? I was trying to avoid lots of us getting shot by a highly motivated former Chinese assassin."

Bridger grimaced in the frustrating realization that Chapel had him by the horns. Chapel *had* come through in an impossible situation after

Li Chu captured May and Lena and tortured them. Bridger leveraged the details of Li Chu's family by threatening his parents and sister. The sister was a professional violin player based in New York, which would explain why he was in town.

"What do you want?" he asked, defeated.

"You know what I want. I will send you the information."

The call was over.

Walking down 34th street and as they crossed 9th street, Bridger pointed at a Deli restaurant among a row of four eateries, including a Subway and a bakery, a block from Penn Station and Madison Square Garden.

"Let's go in here."

In block gold letters above the door was a sign that read *DINER*.

The interior was thirty degrees warmer and much brighter than outside. The smells of a working kitchen hit them in the face. Like many of its peers, the diner was deep, narrow, and decorated with bright red and white tiles. Two- and four-top tables and wire chairs were spaced too close along the window, counter, and the wall to the kitchen.

They took a table for two by a window—Bridger insisted—but as far away from the door as they could—at Lena's insistence. They peeled out of their coats and other warm weather gear and sat.

"This reminds me a little of Lena's."

Lena's Café, a breakfast and sandwich shop in a trendy area of Amsterdam, was a popular spot for locals and tourists, making its chef and owner, Lena Hamed, also quite popular.

The waiter brought water, and they ordered chicken noodle soup. They sat silently, listening to "White Christmas" play from the speakers recessed into the tin ceiling.

"You don't need to do it anymore," Lena said from out of nowhere.

"What?" He knew what she meant, but he let the comment hang there to give him time.

"I know you think you have to do, but do you?" Her expression was honest—not emotional or pleading.

Bridger took her hands and looked at her.

"Yes, I do."

Two piping hot bowls of soup arrived, along with hunks of sour-dough bread and butter. She took a spoonful of chicken and broth and tasted it. She made an approving look and tried some more, smacking her lips and tongue.

"Rotisserie Chicken. Garlic. Fennel. Coriander. Celery seeds. With cavatelli pasta. Interesting." She saw Bridger smiling at her. "I'm good at my job, too."

"You are, but I taste rosemary and herbes de Provence."

Lena looked at him, then ate some more. Her mouth waggled, then she looked at him with an expression that confirmed he was right. She tired the bread and smiled again. "Excellent. Has to be made here."

"I'm glad."

Bridger looked casually out the window. The men were still there, milling around, trying to look like they had a reason to be there. He resisted jumping up, running outside, and confronting them.

"Let things go."

"Let things go? After what happened in Texas? And to May? Can you tell me you are letting Li Chu get away with your uncle's death?"

He saw the pain in her eyes as he reminded her of the moments in Amsterdam and her agony caused by Li Chu.

"I...I don't know...I am willing to try if you try, too."

"I can't do that. Not yet. I have made promises to...well...about everyone. I have to see it through. Then—"

"I need to return to my restaurant," she said abruptly. He did not detect anger, but he clearly sensed her disappointment.

Bridger looked at her.

"You should...go...yes...go," he told her, although he didn't mean a word of it.

Stay. I want you to stay. Can't you tell?

"Are you sure?" she asked.

No. Not at all.

"You can go as long as you come back."

She touched his face and looked into his eyes.

"You *could* come with me," she said. She set the spoon by the soup bowl and took his hands in hers. "Remember. Forgive. It is the deal I hope the Devil makes."

When they were done, they retraced their steps back to his penthouse. The surveillance followed. He didn't care.

They talked, laughed, and made love all night. In the morning, his limo would take Lena to the airport. It worried him to have her out from under his cover in case something happened. He would have to discuss security and other precautions.

After an emotional goodbye, Bridger went to the 35th floor and sent a secure text to the team.

It's on. Tonight.

20

NOT DEAD

New York City, New York

Sipping a Coke from an ice-filled glass, Li Chu sat in a corner with his back to the wall of the pizzeria frequented by his sister and the other chamber orchestra members.

"You are coming with us. Have a little fun," she said after each concert. She was petite. Dark hair and eyes. A few years younger than him.

Li Chu tried to decline the nightly offers, but she would grab his good right arm in both of hers and pull him along.

"You enjoy yourselves. You don't need me to spoil your fun," he would always say.

She refused to take "no" for an answer.

Li Chu didn't mind at first. He was not in New York to have fun. He was protecting her from Bridger.

Bridger knew all about my family—that she played violin and was in New York during December playing concerts. Only Chen, the traitor working for the CIA, could have been provided that information.

To protect her, he had to endure being disgusted by everything he saw, smelled, and touched inside the pizzeria. The interior was decorated in obnoxious checkerboard patterns. Black, white, and red tiles covered the floors, walls, and ceiling.

Dozens of wide, thin, stinking pizzas were stacked on shelves inside the glass display case that ran wall-to-wall. The air was putrid with the smells of the ingredients cooking inside ovens that endlessly spat out pizzas. The heat was stifling.

Li Chu's stomach quivered as he watched his sister and her friends eat. Two slices. Folded. Grease dripping.

Disgusting.

At 1 a.m., Li Chu convinced his sister he was tired—which he was —and left. He took a taxi to Brooklyn and had it drop him off blocks from his apartment. From there, he walked an SDR through the dark, tree-lined neighborhood until he reached his apartment.

He checked the motion detector app on his phone that connected to the sensors inside the apartment. All green. Li Chu waved a fob over a sensor, unlocking the building's exterior door. He took the elevator up to his too-expensive one-bedroom apartment on the third floor.

A glance at the nearly invisible strip of tape placed just above the floor across the door jam showed the door had not been opened. He unlocked the door and stepped into the dark main living area.

The hardwood floors creaked beneath his weight. Dim orange streaks of streetlight glowed through the curtains of the two floor-to-ceiling windows on the opposite wall beyond the L-shaped living room and kitchen. Li Chu stopped and then slowly closed the door behind him. He stood for a moment to let his eyes adjust, then reached his hand into a coat he had hung on a hook by the door.

He felt around, but what he was looking for was gone.

"It isn't there. I took it." A familiar and unwelcome voice came from the patch of darkness. It chilled his bones and blood like he had been dropped in a tub of ice water.

Li Chu took a small step to his left toward the alcove that was listed as a "home office" by the relator and where he had some of his bags—and a spare pistol.

"Won't find that one there either," Bridger said.

Although the room was small, he could not determine where Bridger was. Li Chu's eyes darted diagonally across the living room to the L-shaped sofa and table. Then at the small kitchen.

He took a small step toward the kitchen, where he had had another weapon taped under the table.

"Forget the one under the table." Bridger stepped out of the shadows. "I'm unarmed." He raised his hands and showed them into a streak of light so Li Chu could see that Bridger was not holding a gun. "We need to talk." He sat on the couch.

Li Chu put his hand in his pocket and gripped the knife.

Cautiously, Li Chu sat on the end of the couch the farthest from Bridger. He looked around the room. Then out the windows.

"It's cold. Did you pay your heating bill?"

"Are you alone?" Li Chu asked, regaining the composure that made him the leader of the Dragon Fire assassins.

"It is just me," Bridger said, but Demon's growl wafted disturbingly through the dim room. "Well, and Demon."

Li Chu jumped up and took a defensive stance toward where he thought he heard Demon's voice. His eyes darted left and right, knife out and at the ready.

"Relax, idiot," Demon said from somewhere. "And toss over the knife."

Li Chu twitched and thought momentarily, then folded the blade and dropped it on the floor. He sat back on the couch again.

"Why...why are you here? I assume it is to kill me."

"I didn't say that. If I wanted you dead, you would be by now. Sit," Bridger commanded.

Li Chu hesitated and then sat.

"Then what is this about?" Li Chu looked around at Demon, who had appeared and looked ready to split Li Chu's skull like a melon at any moment.

"Despite my better judgment, I have been convinced to make a deal with you."

"Deal?" Li Chu asked after a moment. "You made a deal to kill me?"

"Vincente Ramirez." Bridger let the name chill Li Chu like a slushie drink from the gas station.

"The Devil is an assassin for Vincente Ramirez?"

"That hurts. Speaking of hurt, he really—I mean *really*—wants you and the others dead. I am supposed to bring him a part of your body as proof. I won't tell you which one."

"You threatened my family. My sister."

Bridger let out a loud rush of air.

"You threatened and tortured some of us." Bridger glared at him and let the words take their time to fill the room. "Lena, you remember? She says I should...*forgive you*...and move on," he said, forcing his mouth to form the words.

"She does not want to harm me for what I did?"

"I asked her that. All I know is that this is her idea. I didn't *really* have anything against you until Amsterdam, even after our explosive little first meeting after you ambushed me in Ukraine. That was business."

"I'm going to puke," Demon said.

"You are responsible for killing my men in Dragon Fire and...for... this." He pointed to his arm. "Information provided by the traitor. Chen."

Bridger didn't answer at first. Then, he spoke in a more conciliatory tone.

"We both have enemies, so walking away is a good idea. Right now. Believe me. I'm going to try. Let's give it a try for both of our sakes. *Zhìzuò yǔ móguǐ de jiāoyì.*"

"Make a deal with the Devil," Li Chu said, looking off to nowhere.

"Take the deal, jerkoff," Demon advised.

Bridger reached his hand out to Li Chu.

Li Chu didn't take it at first, but Bridger held it there, unwavering. A moment later, Li Chu finally took it.

"This will not work, you are aware," Li Chu said.

"I actually agree with the jerkoff on this one," Demon said.

"I hope you are wrong." Bridger looked at Demon and then Li Chu. "Just go away, for both of our sakes. Here." Bridger stood and then reached into his coat pocket. He stepped around the table and handed Li Chu a mobile phone. "Our hotline, like our government's. Use only in an emergency. Call the number. They will take a message, and I will call you back."

They left Li Chu alone in the room.

After an SDR to be sure the surveillance they lost earlier had not located them, Demon peeled off and headed for the hospital to check on Imp's status. Bridger returned to his Hudson Yards penthouse, where he sat looking out his window across the city, sipping some wine, and thinking about the life changes he was starting...trying to start.

Li Chu is right. It isn't going to work. But I will try.

Bridger was exhausted and hoped draining his third glass of red wine was enough to keep the nightmares away. His phone rang as he climbed the wide, curving stairs to the second-level master bedroom.

"Did you meet with Mr. Li Chu?" Chapel asked in the arrogant tone Bridger had learned to tolerate. He was not in the mood to deal with Chapel.

"Yes."

"And?"

He placed his Devil Stick by his bed and sat with his back against the headboard.

"We had a lovely conversation."

"*Conversation?* Is he—"

"Alive? Yes. He is alive."

"Not dead?"

Bridger enjoyed jerking Chapel's chain.

"No, that is the opposite of alive."

"Why is he...*alive?* I believe we had—"

"I'm forgiving him."

"What?"

"Look up forgiveness, if you can, Chapel."

Silence.

Then, the connection clicked dead.

Bridger resisted the urge to call Lena. Instead, he sent a text that read: *Forgiveness granted.*

21

SILENT NIGHT

New York City, New York

The next evening, the obnoxious checkboard patterns surrounded Li Chu again as he sat in the pizzeria with his sister and her cohorts.

The smells and heat also surrounded him and the zombie American who rushed in, sputtered a few words, scanned a card, grabbed a paper containing the slimy, limp tomato-sauce-covered dough, and ran out. The entire transaction lasted less than a minute.

The endless brain-melting Christmas music kept blasting through the small shop.

Finally, he decided to try a slice and, to his surprise, he liked it. He had a second slice.

The deal with Bridger and all its complexities flooded his thoughts. Li Chu was re-considering the idea of a truce with Bridger—he was his sworn enemy.

Bridger had killed his team and ruined his career. He had scarred and maimed him.

And I am just to let that be the end of it? It is a mistake.

The phone from Bridger was in his pocket. Would he ever use it? Since the ambush in his apartment last night, he decided to carry his pistol.

A bell tinkled when the door opened. Cool air rushed into the oppressively hot restaurant. When Li Chu saw the man, he instinctively went on alert—he wasn't exactly sure why, but he had.

Despite the space being a sauna, the man did not remove his coat or stocking hat. He sat at a table so Li Chu could not see his face directly —a wall partially obscured his view—but not enough to prevent Li Chu from seeing the earbud just below the man's stocking hat. An inch of a wire was exposed before disappearing beneath the man's collar.

His personal phone vibrated on the table. An alert came up, signaling activity in his apartment. He had enough time to open the app and see gray figures move into view of one of the micro cameras he had hidden in the apartment.

Bridger? No. He had already proven he could evade my alarms.

Li Chi rose and put on his puffy ski coat. It was a knock-off name brand that was very warm, which was good since Li Chu hated the cold. Cold fueled his hate of the frigid family pig farm back in China. Another advantage of the coat was it was big and baggy enough to store his knife, suppressed pistol, and a few phones.

He tugged on his bulky fur-lined capped with ear flaps. Adding the scarf around his neck, his face was as protected as it could be from being recognized by the extensive camera system monitoring the streets of NYC.

"I must go," he told his sister.

The bell jiggled behind him as he exited the restaurant into the cold night air. The sidewalks and streets were relatively quiet, which was good, he thought, since that would change in seconds.

Outside, he moved behind the door, lower than the condensation line on the windows. He pulled out his serrated pocketknife and let the spring asset open the high-carbon stainless blade with titanium coating —a sharp and effective killing tool.

The door opened with the sound of the jingling bell. The man paused just on the inside of the door. "Silent Night" flowed out the door and into the night air.

A hand clutching a gun came first, and then the man stepped onto the sidewalk. Li Chu came from behind the door and neatly slid the 3.5-inch blade into his exposed neck just below the jaw, slightly forward of the ear. He didn't wait to witness the blood spurt out. He knew both the carotid artery and jugular vein were now severed. The man collapsed like a marionette cut free of its strings.

Li Chu heard screams coming from inside the pizzeria as he dropped the knife on the sidewalk. It hit with a wet *clunk*.

He didn't hesitate.

The muscle memory of a trained assassin took over as he went into hyper-sensitive alert mode. Li Chu wanted to be on offense. His instincts took in his surroundings like a sponge absorbs water. They said to turn left toward the nearest corner.

Li Chu reached into his jacket, pulled out this pistol, and raised it chest high.

His left arm was better but not well enough to help support a two-handed firing position.

There should be at least one more person on foot. That is where the second man will be.

His instincts proved correct. A man eerily dressed the same as the man Li Chu just killed popped from around the corner. Streetlights clearly showed the gloved hand holding a pistol.

Li Chu calmly put two bullets into the man's face without breaking stride as people on the sidewalk screamed and scattered.

He saw the lights of a sedan parked on the other side of the cross-street flick on. It pulled out and accelerated toward him. Li Chu kept walking toward the car, stepping to the corner and firing twice into the driver's windshield. The sedan jerked slightly to the left as it rolled into the intersection.

Brakes and skidding-tire sounds were followed by the *bam* of a cab T-boning into the side of the car. More skidding was followed by the crashing of glass and the awful hissing, signifying a car accident. A few screams echoed off the buildings.

Li Chu turned around and walked down the sidewalk away from the corner, the pizzeria, and his sister. He stopped two long New York blocks from the chaos but could still see the flashing emergency lights bouncing down the street off the wet pavement.

He took out his phone and checked the security app once more. He could not see outlines of the men in the apartment, but he knew they were there. He opened the keyboard screen and dialed.

The image on the security app flashed and went black as the small amounts of C-4 placed inside the apartment exploded.

Danny Chapel rubbed his eyes. The news couldn't have been any worse. All dead. The target was alive.

He picked up a wine glass and gulped some chianti. He refilled it and gulped that down, also.

Chapel always considered himself one of those "I plan to die at my desk" or "die in the saddle" types. Retirement had never entered his mind. Tonight, after receiving the news, serious consideration began.

This is a disaster. Bridger, you ass. If you had done what I asked... now? Disaster.

First, he called Hawkins, who, as Chapel expected, went ape, rambled instructions to Chapel, and then hung up.

May didn't answer her phone, so he left a message in her Signal app.

He walked across the library in his Long Island home to a book-shelf left of the fireplace. A fire crackled and radiated comforting heat to his cold bones. He swiped away a panel decorated as books to expose a shoebox-sized metal door. There were no discernable buttons, handles, or knobs. Placing his right palm in the middle of the door, a green light appeared under his hand, then a beep followed. He repeated the action with his left palm.

The door clicked open and slid to the side. Chapel rummaged around until he found what he was looking for. He pulled out an enve-lope with a red stripe diagonal across the front. After unplugging the power cord from an electrical outlet built inside the safe, he pulled out the tablet computer.

He closed the safe and carried the envelope and tablet to his chair.

He powered up the tablet and set it on the table. He ripped open the envelope and pulled out a card.

A second later, he sent Chen a message that would determine if he lived or died.

22

NORWEGIAN SALMON

New York City, New York

L ike a German train, the nightmares arrived right on schedule. Three in the morning—on the dot.

The themes would vary, but they always had images of tortured faces. Beast. Lena. May. Wes. Eyes looking at him for answers. Then the sounds came. Screams. Explosions. Gunfire.

With those came the terror, the sweats, the racing heart, and the deep feeling of vulnerability. So, when the nightmares arrived again, the full force of the stress hit him. He knew what was going on. He hoped he was wrong.

When did I start to hope?

Bridger was exhausted, as one might expect for an insomniac managing his complicated life-and-death career and missing the woman he loved.

So, he got up and looked out the window.

The view from the Hudson Yards penthouse was spectacular. It was a "sunrise and sunset" condo. He could watch the Manhattan sunrise on one side and the sunset on the other. Watching black-shadowed buildings silhouetted below streaks of pinkish-purple clouds against a blue sky can be spectacular.

It was December—in New York City. His terror-induced sweat dried in the chilled air. He shivered.

He liked the condo, but he loved and missed his West Texas Hill Country ranch. Mainly, his designer golf course replicating the world's most famous par-3s. It was gone with the ranch. As was his favorite set of golf clubs. That really pissed him off.

His Foresight Sports GC Quad SIG12 Golf Simulator installed in his penthouse gym had served as a backup. He pulled out the driver of the set of Calloways he kept at the condo. In the pocket of his sweatpants, he felt the golf ball marker—a gift from his father before he died that started his son's passion for golf.

He swung hard. Then harder. One ball after another. In rhythm. The sweat started to roll.

Swack. Bend. Tee it up. Stand. Swack. Bend. Repeat.

In a few minutes, he knew it was a waste of time. After a few more lousy swings on the 16th at Firestone—"The Monster"—he frustratedly dropped his driver on the faux grass.

He turned away from the window in disappointment and checked the time.

Just after four.

"What's the use?"

Bridger plucked a towel off a shelf, walked to his kitchen, and flipped on the TV. As he started peeling a banana, he paid little attention to early morning news detailing another shooting. Then they switched to a story on an explosion at an apartment in Brooklyn that was suspected to be some kind of gas leak.

Bridger's head spun faster than a figure skater when he heard the address.

What the hell?

Then his phone rang.

"Jelly Bean? You are up early."

"Up from what?'

"Sleep?"

"Huh?" He heard smacking and sticky chewing.

With Imp still recovering, Bridger had been working through Jelly Bean to utilize the services of "The Unemployables"—Imp's virtual team of computer misfits that collectively comprised a powerful cyber and hacking force.

"Sleep," he repeated to silence. "Don't you...why did you call, Jelly Bean?"

"Yeah. Rancid Penguin is monitoring the board. That number called."

Bridger heard a wrapper crinkle and then chewing. Bridger knew she was popping a mouthful of her namesake candy.

"Okay. Thanks for calling, and please tell...Rancid Penguin... thanks."

"Why?"

"Get some sleep, Jelly Bean."

"What? Why?"

He pushed the red button.

Then Bridger called Li Chu. He didn't answer.

———

Danny Chapel was famous. A man of wealth and power. And the quintessential New Yorker. He loved a good bagel, so breakfast always meant a lox and bagel platter—usually at historic Russ & Daughters.

Many excellent little bistros were near his headquarters on 5th Avenue, between 52nd and 53rd, but the crosstown traffic was worth the effort to savor his favorite breakfast. It was loud and noisy—an atmosphere only a New Yorker could appreciate.

He sat in his reserved booth toward the back under historical black and white photos of the eatery's history. He flipped the pages of the New York Times in his manicured hands.

Dressed in his expensive bespoke suits and custom shoes, in any other city but New York, he would get odd looks. He was sporting a perfectly cut for his full head of gray hair. A Rolex Submariner clipped to his wrist. If a person wasn't sure they were looking at the great Danforth Chapel, he could be identified by his trademarked flamboyant, colorful silk tie.

Two of Chapel's security team sat at the counter drinking coffee and munching on pastries. The others were outside in the car.

A waiter in a white-waisted smock approached and set a phone on Chapel's table.

Chapel looked up.

It rang immediately.

"I'm coming. Tell your tin soldiers to stand down."

The line went dead before he could reply. Chapel put the phone down and scanned the entrance at the far end of the restaurant.

Bridger came from behind him and sat at the chair across the table.

"What the hell were you thinking, Chapel?"

"Bridger," Chapel said with annoyance and relief as he saw him men rapidly talk into sleeve-mics as they hopped off their stools.

From nowhere, Demon blocked their path.

"Hey, Ugly and Uglier. Sit down."

"It's okay, Ryan," Chapel said as they were about to jump Demon. They stopped, glowered at Demon, and sat.

"Good little puppies. Eat your treats." Demon faked a smile and kept his eyes on the men as he moved to a position near Bridger's table.

"You are an idiot," Bridger said as he snatched half of a toasted bagel stuffed with salmon and cream cheese. "Hiring freelancers. What did you expect would happen?"

"I expected a better outcome, and don't blame me. You were supposed to...solve...the Li Chu situation." Chapel waved his knife in the air dismissively.

"I decided that I didn't want to. I'm on the forgiveness trail." He smiled and flipped his eyebrows as he savored the salmon. "This is good salmon. Norwegian smoked?"

Chapel nodded as he watched Bridger pick a wad of salmon from the bagel sandwich and flick it into his mouth.

"Admirable, if even possible. Your action—or lack of action—is one big disaster. Isn't getting Li Chu what you have been dreaming of?" He slid his plate closer to him when Bridger glanced at the other half of Chapel's breakfast.

"We had a deal to go our separate ways. Bygones and all that." Bridger shook his head. "Not anymore, I bet."

"A deal. Give me a break. He has been trying to kill you and the Spy Devils for years. And what he did to May *and* Lena in Amsterdam. *And* what he did to Wes. I would think there would not be a moment of hesitation to kill him. I never imagined you would make a deal with him."

"And not to mention what removing him would mean to Chen's cover."

Chapel took his bagel off the plate before Bridger could take another bite.

"Your mother worked very hard on that operation—for years. Li Chu can ruin all of it."

"Chen is Hawkins's issue. Anything happens—it happens on his watch."

"Yes. Quite," Chapel said as he finished chewing. "Speaking of Hawkins, he wants to talk to you. Face to face." He took his napkin and wiped the corners of his mouth.

"I am sure he does. They would probably love to lock me away. Good luck with that."

Chapel leaned forward.

"Listen, Bridger. Lena is a nice woman. Smart. Extraordinary. But on this, she should not be affecting your judgment."

"Back off, Chapel." Bridger's eyes burned at Chapel with the kind of fire that would make the Mona Lisa blink.

"Doesn't she want Li Chu dead for what he did to her uncle?"

Bridger kept silent.

"She does, doesn't she?"

Chapel took a bite of what remained of his bagel, ensuring his tie and pants were clear of any falling debris, as he watched Bridger decide how to respond.

Chapel took the napkin and rubbed his hands hard like he needed to get to the next layer of skin.

"Have you heard from May?" Chapel asked.

"No."

"You should call her. Seek some motherly advice." Chapel stood. "Goodbye, Bridger. Now that you have decided to stay out of things... stay out of things."

As he left the restaurant, Chapel signaled to his men, who were already taking positions in front and behind him.

Bridger watched Chapel leave, then looked down at the empty plates. He wanted to order some of that delicious salmon, but his phone rang.

An "M" appeared on the caller ID. He rolled his eyes and then ignored it.

"You going to answer that?" Demon asked as he sat in Chapel's chair.

"No."

It rang again. Bridger let out a sigh and answered.

"Hang on." He placed his hand over the phone.

"Order me that salmon," he whispered to Demon.

"I'm not your butler."

Bridger looked with wide, pleading eyes.

"Son of a bitch." Demon got up and walked to the counter.

Bridger removed his hand from the phone.

"What?"

"Are you done with Chapel?" May asked.

"Yes." He pivoted in his chair, searching the restaurant for his mother.

"Don't look around expecting to see me."

"I'm not," he said, turning back, feeling caught like a child with his hand in the cookie jar.

"I need your help."

"Let me guess. China."

"Yes," she said.

"I figure Chapel failing to kill Li Chu in New York must have prompted new urgency, considering Li Chu had the proverbial gun at his head."

"Chapel did what?"

"You don't know? Didn't he call you? Watch TV much? You *are* retired."

"Wait. Let me check my messages." May was back in less than a minute. He could imagine her face melting, and then he heard her utter, "Oh my god" and "What?"

"My message from him said it is your fault."

"Really? Chapel asked me to kill Li Chu. I declined."

"Bastard. I mean Danny, not you, sort of. You know the danger Li Chu is and what he has done—to all of us."

"Yep, but Lena said I should forgive."

"She said that?"

"I don't think she would cry if Li Chu was killed—by someone else."

"Like by Danny."

"Do you think a failed ambush in the middle of NYC might seem a little desperate?"

"Bridger. You know what I think?"

"Yes, and I don't want any part of it.

"Too bad."

23

ESCAPE ROOM

Naperville, Illinois

ngel sat with James on the floor of the child's room, trying unsuccessfully to piece together the Lego pirate ship he bought for his son at an airport shop. He flipped the colorful little booklet filled with impossible-to-decipher pictures, wondering if the little thingie he needed next was supposed to be beige or white. He stirred the mound of plastic pieces until he found one that looked right. Angel triumphantly handed it to his son.

"Here."

The boy took it but shook his head, causing James's long blond bangs to cascade over his eyes.

"No. Not that one," the eight-year-old said as he dropped it on the pile. It hit with a *clink*.

Frustrated, Angel swept the hair off his son's face and snatched the booklet again.

"Someone is at the door," the tinny digital voice proclaimed from his Google Assistant.

"Google. What time is it?" he asked.

"It is seven-thirty-two p.m.," the female voice proclaimed.

"Who is it, Daddy?" James asked as he snapped a porthole cover onto the pirate ship hull.

He clicked the app on his phone to open and view the camera feed from his video doorbell. Two large, clean-shaven, thick-necked men wearing bulky overcoats against the cold evening, stood patiently, staring blankly at the door.

"Who is it, Daddy?" James repeated.

They rang again. He rose and moved out the door of the second-story bedroom. Holding her phone, Janelle was waiting for him at the bottom of the stairs. In her other hand, she held a mini-Devil Stick Bridger had gifted her.

"Peter?" she asked, more puzzled than worried.

His body shuddered as his foggy mind thought went back over a year ago to another instance when strangers came to his house at night. That time, the security officer from Kirkland, his former employer, had come to kill him.

After that, Angel improved the defenses in his home in a western suburb of Chicago. He had reinforced all the interior and exterior doors and windows and installed a complete security system. The master bedroom closet was turned into an escape room with a steel sliding door, monitors, emergency kits, and a shotgun.

"Who is it?" Angel asked into his mobile doorbell app.

"FBI. Here to see Peter Schaefer."

"About what?"

"Please open the door, and we can explain."

"FBI?" Janelle asked, looking at her husband with the panicked but protective fierceness of a lioness as she put a robe over the Walter Payton Bears football jersey she used as pajamas.

"Go upstairs. Get James and go into the safe room."

Angel waited until he heard the faint *thud* and *click* of the escape room door latching.

The bell rang again. Then, the app flashed a warning of movement on the rear patio. Angel clicked on that camera in time to see dark figures flash by. Then, a warning buzz came from the garage sensor.

"I'm on my way," he said as calmly as possible into the phone. As he walked, he sent out a quick text to Bridger.

FBI here.

He checked for a reply. It had not come by the time he reached the door.

When he opened it, the non-smiling faces were waiting.

"Hello. My name is Special Agent Roy," said the taller of the two eerily similarly-looking men.

"I am Special Agent Rogers," said the shorter man.

They each flipped open and held a small black leather case containing their FBI credentials. Each had a small gold badge with "FBI" in large blue letters on the top half. A signature and color photo, roughly passport size, were on the lower half of the credential.

"Really? Agents Roy and Rogers?" Angel said mockingly. "Where are Dale Evans and Trigger?" He exaggerated, peering over their shoulders.

Roy grabbed Angel's arm and took the phone out of his hand while Rogers clutched the other arm like a vice. They pulled him off the porch and toward an idling car.

"What the hell?" Angel shouted. "Janelle!"

Agent Roy wheeled and buried his fist into Angel's stomach. His legs gave out as the air rushed from his lungs like air from a balloon.

"Are you armed?" Rogers asked.

"*Aggf,*" was all the air Angel could muster in his lungs to reply.

They stopped. Angel felt the grip on his arm tighten to the point it started to tingle. Rogers reached into his coat, pulled out a wand, and waved it around Angel.

"Nothing," he declared.

Roy dumped Angel's phone into a cloth bag and zipped it shut.

They bent Angel at the waist into the back of the sedan, and one man shoved a bag over Angel's head.

They zip-tied his hands together in his lap. He heard car doors slam and felt the car accelerate away from his home and family.

Angel did not know where they were, but he estimated they had driven for an hour—*or was it less, or maybe more*—to reach the destination. Every time he tried to wipe the sweat from his stinging eyes, a hand swatted his hands down. He could not control his shaking legs. He needed to urinate badly.

His captors were silent during the entire ride, and Angel knew they were uninterested in answering his questions.

They only responded when Angel said he had to pee desperately.

"You will have to wait." Angel recognized Roy's voice coming from the driver's seat.

"It had better be soon, or this car will need to be cleaned."

With some satisfaction, Angel felt Agent Rogers slightly move away beside him.

The hood stayed on when they arrived—wherever they were. They yanked him out of the car, guided him up some steps, through a door, then down flights of stairs.

The building's interior was warm. Their footsteps clicked on a hard floor, and the HVAC system rumbled above. The lights were bright enough to cause a faint glare through the hood. He heard doors open and close and then muffled voices echoing from somewhere.

Where am I? Who would want me? What will they do?

"How about you take this hood off, Hopalong?" he asked. Roy and Rogers tightened their already tight grips around his arms as they jerked him forward.

"No," they said simultaneously.

Angel heard a door open in front of him. He was shoved through and then pushed onto a chair.

The zip ties were cut, and then there was the clink of a metal chain, the cold feel of metal around his wrists, and a *click* that told him he was handcuffed into position. His body started shaking again.

Angel heard the men leave and the door lock.

Then nothing. He sat in the darkness of his hood. The sweat rolled again in the overheated room. He turned his head to position his ears in different directions, thinking he might hear more than the hum of the hot air flowing in and the buzz of lights.

He waited, and as each minute passed, paranoia and fear took increasing control over his thoughts.

Have I been forgotten? What will happen to Janelle and James? Are they safe?

Angel was startled when he finally heard the door lock click and open.

"Oh, my goodness," a deep voice said.

Angel heard something plop onto the table and felt large, rough hands pull the hood off his head. He sucked in a long deep breath of fresh air.

"I am so sorry, Peter. I ordered them to remove the hood and *not* lock you up. I am so sorry."

Angel blinked, and then once his eyes adjusted, he saw a mountain-sized man sitting there. Despite the heat in the room, the sweat on his body turned cold. He recognized Max Hawkins immediately.

Angel's heart beat faster than a hummingbird's wings. He knew nothing good would come from this—for him.

Hawkins pulled out a ring jammed with keys and fumbled to find the right one. Once he had, he unlocked the handcuffs. Angel wiped the sweat from his face and rubbed his wrists. His sweatshirt was soaked.

"You must be thirsty." Hawkins looked at a mirror on a wall. "Get some water for Peter right now."

Angel looked around the room. He was curiously pleased that it was like he had imagined. Square. 15x15. White walls, floor, and low ceiling. Nothing besides the metal table and two chairs. The red light on the camera above the door was on. A sizeable built-in mirror took up a large portion of the wall to his right. It was the two-way mirror he had seen thousands of times in police television shows and movies.

"Peter. I am Max Hawkins, Deputy Director of Operations for the Central Intelligence Agency."

"Yes, sir. Hello."

"Peter, I am sure you are wondering what is going on. I will get to that, but first, will you answer a few questions for me? Okay?"

"Sure," Peter said, trying to sound confident, but his heart was beating like a drum.

Hawkins opened a leather folder on the table and looked at it.

"You had a brief career at the Agency."

"Yes."

"You were quite a star in your class, but you left—" Hawkins looked at the folder again. "Family issues."

"My mother died, and my father was…sick."

"Yes, I see, Alzheimer's Disease. Nasty. You did the right thing. Then you went to Kirkwood. Your father had worked there. You went to their corporate intelligence office. Did well, until the nasty situation in Ukraine when they unceremoniously let you go."

"There is more to it than that. I actually quit."

"Yes, I spoke to Danforth Chapel about that." Angel looked up at the mention of the powerful man who manipulated him during the quest in Ukraine to find technology stolen from Kirkwood. "That is where you encountered Bridger and the Spy Devils. Events unfolded, oligarchs, Li Chu, etc., and you became a Spy Devil. I believe they call you…Angel."

Peter Schaefer, AKA Angel, tried not to react again but failed.

"Don't look shocked, Peter. You will find there is very little I do not know. Except—" Hawkins rested his elbows on the table and leaned in toward Angel.

"Where is Bridger, Peter?"

"Bridger is dead." Angel's lower lip pushed out to try to control the emotion tightening his face.

"Really? Bridger dead?"

"He was killed in the attack."

"The attack? I don't think so."

Angel hesitated.

"He was in the ops center. He sent us all ahead. Then he radioed us to leave. We rejected that, of course. Demon wanted to get him, but…Bridger said not to. He was injured. We took off, and then everything exploded." Everything he said was true.

Hawkins looked at a file containing photos of the ranch.

"Where is the body?"

Angel looked at the aerial photos of the destroyed ranch house.

"Buried." He pointed. "Deep in the tunnel from the ranch to the hanger. He is dead, okay?" Now, he was lying.

"Well, you are lying Peter. He has been in New York with Chapel. Also, you sent the text *FBI here* to an untraceable number—Bridger's untraceable number."

Angel did not answer.

"Oh, and if you are wondering, that text didn't go through, so he didn't get it."

Angel looked away.

"So, Peter, here is the situation. You are in a little trouble, and I don't want you to be in trouble, given you are a family man." Hawkins pulled some color photos of Peter, Janelle, and James at different locations from the folder. The park. The mall. At a restaurant. "Everything I know indicates you are a decent guy. You got caught up in the Bridger web of manipulation. So, here you are."

"I haven't done anything wrong."

"I guess that depends on the definitions of wrong when the FBI and district attorney investigate. There are a lot of dead people in Texas that need to be investigated. We don't know yet your involvement with that. Oh, and there is—" Hawkins went to the file again "—the mysterious disappearance of a Mr. Benton, a security guard from your former employer Kirkwood." Hawkins looked up. "Did you know him?"

"Yes."

"Do you know anything about his being missing?"

Angel again flashed back to the night when his home was invaded. The noises in the dark. The sound of a body falling. Benton collapsed in his hallway. Demon picked up the body and said, *"Greetings from the Devil,"* as he carried the body to who knew where.

Angel kept silent.

"It is called accessory, Peter."

Hawkins stood and walked around the table behind Peter.

"You see, Peter, I know he is alive. I think you know where he is or where he is going to be. Peter, you should consider your family when I ask you this next question. Because, you see, if you do what I ask, you can walk away. If you decide to protect him...then well...the future of you, your lovely wife Janelle, and your adorable son James will take a drastic turn for the worse. Indictments. Trial. Prison?"

Hawkins walked around to the table and leaned on it toward Peter. An odd combination of understanding and malice layered the next sentences he spoke.

Peter nodded.

"Great." Hawkins leaned in toward Peter even further. "When I call, you will tell me where I can find Bridger—or else."

24

CALL BRIDGER

Amsterdam, Netherlands

The men entered the restaurant just before closing and sat at the table by the door. They were out of place among the usual clientele that visited her popular little café, aptly named *Lena's*.

Young men. Less than six feet tall. Dark hair cut short. Black leather jacket. Dark pants and shirts. The tattoos on their wrists and arms were visible when they moved. They spoke Spanish, but it was different than what she had learned and spoke with her guests from Spain. They watched her as she moved about the restaurant, cleaning and prepping for the next day.

Something in their dark, intimidating eyes made her feel like she was a fat, unprotected sheep, and they were wolves.

Lena was sure she had seen these two men earlier in the day. Was it as she walked to pick up some flowers for her popular restaurant? At the fish market? She was sure she spotted them other times while walking along the streets.

I have seen the two men before—more than once. What did Bridger tell me about that... Once was random. Twice was a coincidence. Three times meant you were being followed.

Surprisingly, she didn't feel as panicked as she had expected.

Since her return to her restaurant sanctuary a few days earlier, she had been fighting a morass of discomfort and restlessness. She did not feel the same happiness greeting customers or seeing their satisfaction when they ate her food. Amsterdam felt a little less like home.

When she slept, her bed was empty.

Her...anger? Disappointment? Whatever she felt about Bridger and their "relationship" had not subsided some since her return. She had to concentrate to pick up her routine, but it wasn't easy.

She knew he wanted a life with her. She wanted a different life for him—she knew he wanted it, too, or she would not have brought it up.

But, not so deep down in her heart, she *wanted* Bridger to make Li Chu pay for killing her uncle. Bridger wanted him for that and many reasons—not the least of which was the death of Wes Henslow.

She realized she was still traumatized by what Li Chu had done to her. Her emotions collided with rational and irrational thoughts. Compassion. Revenge. Tenderness. Retaliation. Sadness. Concern. Vengeance. Grief. Love.

And more.

Bridger made her feel safe despite all the danger, death, *and destruction.*

She could recognize the danger now. These men meant danger to her and the staff.

When the bell above the door *clinked* as it closed behind the other guest, the men looked at each other.

"Please go to the kitchen," she whispered into the ear of Annika, the server.

She looked at Lena as she picked up a gray rubber tray for the dirty dishes. "The table needs to be serviced," she said.

The men stood.

"Go, now. Tell the others to stay there."

Annika saw the look in Lena's eyes and followed her gaze to the men.

She stiffened. She looked at Lena again, turned, and hurried to the back of the restaurant.

Lena had been attacked in her own home already. When Li Chu's men broke into her apartment on the floor above the restaurant, she was drugged, taken to a storage container in a warehouse in the city, and tortured.

Not this time.

Lena turned her back to the men, but she saw them look cautiously around in a reflection from a picture frame.

She reached into a pocket in her long, high-waisted corduroy skirt as the adrenalin rush caused her to shiver under her long-sleeve black turtleneck sweater.

She pulled out the mini-Devil Stick Bridger had given her before she left.

"Just in case," he told her, using the phrase she had heard him utter dozens of times.

Her hands shook as she fumbled with the controller, trying to remember the simple instructions he had given her.

"Too little, not much happens. Too much, they die."

She could sense the men creeping closer and heard them mumble. Chairs scrapped the floor as they moved them out of the way. She spun around and looked at them, making the most threatening face she could. They smirked as if they were amused or bored, reached under their jackets, and pulled long-bladed, sharp-looking knives.

Lena willed herself not to freeze. Instead, she aimed the mini-Devil Stick at their faces and thumbed the release button. She sprayed their faces like she was painting a wall. Back and forth. Then she quickly backed away, remembering that he told her to avoid the spray.

She heard their coughing and choking and watched as they clawed their eyes. Their faces turned a bright red, and then they staggered back, tripping over tables and chairs. Suddenly, they seized up and fell to the floor like anvils dropped from a plane.

Thud. Thunk.

Screams came from the kitchen. She whirled around, holding the weapon in front of her, and saw her staff looking wide-eyed at her and the men on the floor.

"Call the police." They didn't move. Lena took a moment to slow her rapid breathing. "Now!" she shouted.

Her hands were now shaking so violently she dropped the Devil Stick.

Tink.

She clenched and unclenched her hands as she reached into her pocket, pulled out her phone, hit a button, and spoke.

"Call Bridger."

"What are you doing? What was that all about?" Bridger shouted into his phone.

"Stay calm. They had orders not to harm her. Just scare her—which they did." The calm voice of Vincente Ramirez annoyed Bridger.

In a life built on being in control, Bridger found it challenging to control the rage he felt. He could barely speak the words through the tightness in his throat. "They didn't have the chance to harm her, and now they are enjoying the hospitality of the Amsterdam metro police."

Vincente laughed. It wasn't the phony laugh of the evil adversary from television and movies. It was the laugh of a person running the most violent drug operations in the world. A "not a care in the world" laugh.

"Your Lena is resourceful." Hearing him say her name made Bridger's stomach churn like a cement mixture.

"She is. They will be in jail for a while," Bridger said.

"Who? I have forgotten them already. See how easy it is? That's life in this business. Yes, and regarding business, I hope *you* haven't forgotten the deal you made with me?"

Bridger looked out his penthouse window and tried his breathing exercises. Slow in. Hold. Slower out. "I haven't forgotten. I will get to it. It just isn't the right time yet."

"I think you think I am a fool. Do you think that?" Vincente asked pleasantly like he was teaching a college course on cartel leadership dynamics. "Do you think I am the cliché cartel psychopath from books or movies? Bridger, you know me better than that. I am a businessman."

"Honestly, Vin, I don't care about you at all. I mean, I *really* don't care. I have things to do. But I do know one thing. If you try to harm Lena or anyone I know again—"

"Save your threats. You are alive because I said you can live. You made a deal for your life. That was a good business decision for both of us. I expect…the *Di-ab-lo*…to keep his word."

"When this is over," Bridger hung up.

That Vincente had targeted her was not unexpected. Bridger had had a feeling—a feeling he *hoped* was wrong. It wasn't—of course. He was glad he had given her Devil Stick and thankful she had the bravery to use it.

But I slipped up and put her in danger.

The woman he was in love with had been attacked. She had been attacked because she was too close to him. The cycle continued of the people nearest him ending up in danger, near death, or dead.

Bridger now knew what he wanted in his future and what he had to do.

25

RABBIT

Beijing, China

C hen sat in his Zhongnanhai apartment, reviewing the final details of his escape plan. He had activated the needed resources. Untraceable bank accounts and safe houses he had established over the years were ready.

If this goes well, I will be free by the end of the day. If not, I am dead.

Living in Zhongnanhai was an honor and a perk of leadership. But it was, in reality, a beautiful cage used to watch anyone in power who might threaten the president. It kept his enemies and potential rivals close. The only way in or out was through the few exits guarded by security forces that reported only to the president.

But I have found a way.

Chen put the CIA-provided thumb drive containing the Dossier and other intel he had collected into an envelope and then stuffed it into his coat pocket. If anyone other than him tried to access its contents, he had been told the device would simply cease functioning.

I hope they are not lying, but aren't we all spies and liars?
This thought amused Chen as he powered down his CIA-provided tablet and placed it in one of his backpack getaway bags. One contained personal items, a change of clothes, and various identification documents. The other was filled with money, gold, and diamonds. After ensuring his pistol was loaded, he dropped it in his bag. He kept a knife in his pocket.

Chen had only killed two men in his intelligence career. The guard in Helsinki. The boat captain in Malaysia. *Sometimes it had to be done.* He would kill his third or more today if needed for him to escape.

Chen closed his eyes briefly, calmed his nerves, and summoned Wu, his bodyguard and driver.

"I must go to the airport immediately to attend an unplanned priority meeting," Chen told Wu, a tall, thin man with an imperturbable smile. "Be back in five minutes."

When Wu left, Chen's race for freedom officially began. He knew more than anyone the mental and physical punishments that awaited him if captured. His nightmare would become a reality as expert torturers ask him in a pleasant, fear-inducing voice to confess as they beat, twisted, drilled, burned, or sliced pieces off him. Chen had ordered the same abuses on many people.

It was one reason he decided to work with the Americans. The injustice of the Chinese system. The treatment of its people...of his own family.

When Chen's car pulled up outside his Zhongnanhai home, Wu held the car door open. Chen got in and placed the backpacks on the seat next to him.

"Take the tunnel."

Over the decades, several tunnels were built from Zhongnanhai to strategic locations. The hospital. The Great Hall. Out of Beijing entirely. They also served as locations to use in the event of an uprising —like Tiananmen in 1989.

The tunnel Chen was in had a modern four-lane, lighted highway that went directly to the airport where his plane was waiting to take him out of China. Hopefully, he would have time before they discovered his destination and sent an MSS hit team to meet him.

These moments required all the intelligence and espionage skills he had honed during his decades-long career. More than anything, he needed emotional control. And, for the moment, he still had the formidable power of the Chinese Minister of Security at his disposal and planned to use that until the end.

Wu was wholly dedicated to him and was still protecting him from danger. That would change when he realized Chen's plans. Then Chen would put a bullet in him.

It had only been twelve hours since the tablet May Currier had supplied him pinged with the one word he hoped never to see —*RABBIT.*

Chen was blown or soon would be. He had to run fast like a rabbit.

The exfiltration protocol required him to confirm receipt of the codeword.

Chen weighed the stakes and risked sending May secure texts. Her response confirmed he was in danger and couldn't depend on anyone but May.

M: Did you receive the code?
C: Yes. What happened?
M: Attempts to stop LC failed.

Was Li Chu still alive? CIA incompetence.

C: Option 4
M: No! Please follow protocols for your safety.
C: Option 4
M: You are sure?
C: Yes.
M: When?
C: Now.
M: I'm not ready.
C: Leaving now.

M: I will meet you.

As the bright tunnel lights rushed by, he thought of the operational actions launched and in play after the RABBIT code was sent.

The actions I am now ignoring for my survival.

If all was going as planned, Chen knew Frank Timmer, the CIA Beijing Chief of Station, whom Chen considered slightly better than many Americans he worked with, should have received a FLASH cable from Hawkins. Timmer, one of the few who had been read into the Special Access Program security protocols for Chen, would brief his deputy and, together, they would handle the dangerous exfiltration of the MSS Minister.

Chen had the address of the CIA safe house in the Changping northern outer suburb of Beijing, where they were supposed to meet in the event of a life-threatening emergency. When he arrived at the house, after an extensive SDR, the task would have been to assess which option *they thought* was the safest and quickest way to get *him* out of the country.

The preferred option was to get on a plane and fly out.

Disappearing into the massive interior of the country was on the table. That would utilize a series of friendly assets to get him to Thailand or the Philippines—less obvious destinations than Taiwan, South Korea, or Australia.

If it was game over and Chen was the most wanted man in China, the extreme exfiltration method would have to be used. Sedating him, strapping him into a climate-controlled, anti-scanning lined, pressurized shipping container—more like a large box. It would be placed on a plane or ship, whichever was the fastest way to safety.

All of those mean I would be at the mercy of the CIA. That is no option.

As his car sped toward the airport, that safe house got further behind him with each passing minute. The tinted windows helped him scan the area for security forces waiting for him. He exhaled a long breath when he saw nothing unusual as his official car sped through security gates and drove directly to his plane.

Chen had established the pattern with airport authorities and security that he preferred to board from the tarmac rather than from within the terminal itself.

Wu stopped the car, hustled out, and opened Chen's door. Chen stood and looked around one more time. No vehicles were speeding his way. No teams of special police were running toward him, shouting with guns pointed at him. But he did know that a web of surveillance cameras was detailing his every move.

Just a few more minutes. Let me be on my way.

He let Wu carry his bags up the steps and into the aircraft. When Chen turned to go down the aisle to his seat, he first saw the bodyguard.

Then he saw the grinning, dangerous face of Foreign Minister Yi.

The call Sun answered from Foreign Minister Yi was as gratifying as it was shocking. He was right. *Chen was the traitor.*

At first, Sun did not comprehend the convoluted story that Foreign Minister Yi was re-telling.

"Li Chu. Li Chu is the key. You know Li Chu?"

"I recognize the name. The Dragon Fire team failure."

"It was Chen who caused the failure."

"Of his own initiative?"

"Yes. Li Chu has several examples of Chen spying for the CIA."

Yi summarized what Li Chu told him, including his connection to Danforth Chapel, May his CIA handler, and her connection to Bridger and the Spy Devils.

"Bridger? The Spy Devils? Is he certain?" Sun asked.

"He is certain."

"The Spy Devils," Sun said softly, shaking his head. "Why is Li Chu telling you this now?"

"Revenge."

"I can understand that. Minister. Here is what you are going to do..."

26

NEED TO IMPROVISE

Beijing, China

"Greetings, Minister," Yi said. "Please sit."

Chen saw Yi keep his eyes on him as he raised his hand toward the seat facing him.

Chen sat.

"Leave the bags, Wu. Go outside while I talk to the Minister."

Wu did as he was told.

At that moment, Chaihong, the one flight attendant onboard, approached with a pleasant smile and bright eyes. She did a quick combination bow and curtsey in her dark-blue form-fitting uniform with a hat pinned to her bobbed black hair.

"Hello, Ministers. May I offer you something, gentlemen?"

"Hello again, Chaihong. Yes, I will have the usual," Chen said.

"Of course." She looked at Yi and waited.

"Water," he said in a voice that sounded as if he needed a drink.

"Yes."

She walked toward the front of the plane managed by the 34th division of the People's Liberation Army Air Force for air transportation of senior government officials. Chen was provided this Boeing 737-300 for his travel and missions.

The customized interior was divided into three sections. The forward VIP area where they sat was similar to First Class on commercial airliners but retrofitted with three rows of two large seats separated by the center aisle. The middle section had conference tables, private bedrooms, and office suites. The rear area had seats for other passengers and the galley. Each flight had 1-3 flight attendants, depending on the number of passengers.

Yi's face looked serious, reminding Chen of the look of a man about to checkmate his opponent in Xiangqi, the popular board game similar to Western chess that Chinese children learned. Chen noticed Yi was alone—which was telling. Through a window, he saw Yi's bodyguard outside talking to Wu.

Worse, his already fragile plan was now delayed. Yi had to go, one way or another.

He felt the pistol under his coat and moved his hand closer.

"How might I help you?" Chen asked, wanting to know what was going on.

They were both dressed in white shirts, dark trousers, and the short gray casual windbreakers favored by the president—with its costly zipper compared to the more ideologically correct common buttons.

Compared to Chen, Yi was a giant. He was a tall, powerful man with broad shoulders who stood and sat ramrod straight. Dark hair, slightly graying on the sides. Round wire-rimmed glasses.

"Minister Yi. What is this about?"

"I have spoken to Li Chu."

Here it is. May was right. Li Chu made good on his threat. They missed Li Chu, and he made good on his threat—American incompetence.

Chen made a puzzled face and sat forward.

"Li Chu? Really? Why did he contact you?"

"You know why, Minister."

"No. I do not—" Chen sat back, playing the innocent man as much as he could, even though they both knew he wasn't.

"You are a CIA spy," Yi interrupted. His tongue pushed out his cheeks and lips, flicking around inside his mouth. "This Li Chu detailed your relationship with the Americans—suspicious and damning information. I think it is true."

Chen's resolve slightly buckled, but he recovered when he heard the word every Chinese person feared spoken about them.

Suspicious.

Chen didn't answer at first. He always liked Yi, but Yi was a CCP believer. A doctrine-follower. A sycophant of the president—like Sun.

Chen set his bag down and sat.

"Why are you *really* here?" Chen asked, trying to take the offensive. "Li Chu is a failure and a liar. He hates me for some delusional reason."

"He says you provided information to the CIA and the infamous Spy Devils, which was a direct cause of the death of dozens of MSS officers and incalculable damage to foreign policy initiatives for my ministry."

"So, you are blaming your failures on imaginary ramblings of—"

"Please, Chen. Don't embarrass yourself. Do not deny that May Currier of the CIA recruited you."

Chen did not react.

Chaihong arrived with the water, which Yi emptied with a steady hand. She handed Chen a glass of champagne.

"You are investigating me? You should be careful when you make accusations against me."

"Danforth Chapel, the American, is your point of contact. Please do not say you do not know him since you met him recently."

Is this Sun's doing, or is Yi making his own play?

"I do not deny that. You have met him, too. Are you a spy?" Chen looked at Yi with his lips a narrow line from cheek to cheek.

"I want it," Yi said without further explanation. Chen knew what he meant, but he wanted to hear Yi ask as part of what the foreign minister thought was a negotiation. Yi didn't know that this wasn't a negotiation at all.

It had become a recruitment.

"You are already a member of the Standing Committee. The former Ambassador to the United States."

"True. I still want the Dossier."

"The what?" Chen asked as if he had no idea what Yi was talking about.

"Please, Minister. I know you have the file. Everyone does. I want it. *Now*."

"You want information that can be used against your rivals."

"I want to make the right kind of friends and keep the enemies away—like all of us.

"And in return, you will not tell anyone about...your suspicions about me. Perhaps you will not give the file to Sun. That is who sent you here, correct? Why didn't he come? Maybe it is because he wants to hide behind you in case you fail, or I decide to use the Dossier to prove you are a criminal."

Yi sat back and smiled after Chen's bombardment of questions and comments.

"I have no intention of giving this file to Sun."

The plane's engines started. The spinning and high-pitched sound filled the 737.

"You think he will just let you defy him? He will kill you and not think one extra second about you. I thought you were smarter, Yi—coming here all alone. Thinking you could outmaneuver both me and Sun."

"Please, Chen."

I am running out of time.

"Sun knows, and he thinks—as do I— that the president would be interested in knowing how you have committed serious crimes, Yi," Chen said. "I am sure the courts will determine that you have caused a heavy loss to the interests of the people and the Middle Kingdom. *Serve the People?* You serve yourself and your criminal family."

"I do not know—" Yi started to speak, but Chen cut him off.

"Please, don't. I have all the intelligence to put you in front of a firing squad or get you hanged. What is the amount you took, Yi? My sources say 117 million yuan in bribes. That is seventeen million dollars in foreign accounts. Switzerland. Cyprus. Virgin Islands. I have the numbers in case you want to doubt me."

"What...what..." Yi stammered. "At least I am not a traitor!"

"We are ready, sir." The voice of the pilot came over the intercom.

Chaihong returned, took the empty glasses, and handed Chen another glass bubbling with champagne and water for Yi.

"Chaihong, please tell Yuze we will leave momentarily," Chen said to the attendant. "But leave the door open for a moment and—" Chen handed her one of the bags Wu had set beside him. "This is for all of you."

She nodded and walked toward the front of the plane.

With that last payment, there was nothing to do except go forward with Option 4. May was right. It was dangerous. He had resources and had prepared in the event of a plane escape scenario.

Plus, Chen knew people and how to manipulate people.

Chen had spotted the pilots, Yuze and Lim, as potentially valuable assets several years ago. As much as they seemed to enjoy ferrying Chinese leaders around the world on a moment's notice, for most it was a dead-end job. No promotions. No better homes or schools for Lim's children. No excitement. Chen provided support and filled the natural gaps in their lives.

When Yuze started dating Chaihong, Chen helped them with getaways and perks they would not usually receive. Slowly, they began to depend on Chen's generosity. And gradually, he recruited them all. He found what it would take for them to help him leave and for them to keep quiet and never return.

Money and the chance to leave China. Chen could make that happen. Inside that bag, they would find the last thick bundle of one-hundred-dollar bills and diamonds in a white envelope.

Chen looked at Yi. He leaned back in his seat. He could tell Yi was shaken. Chen pulled his gun from his pocket and rested it on his lap, pointing in Yi's direction.

"What are you doing?" Yi started to stand, terror in his eyes.

"When Li Chu threatened to tell you about me over the months, I decided to review your file entry. Interesting."

"There is nothing—"

"There is much, Yi. In 2005, you were head of the Beijing Municipal Public Security Bureau, then Vice Minister of Public Security, Ambassador, and Minister of Foreign Affairs. How many serious crimes and how much evidence did you conceal involving crimes committed by your brother Fu? Bending the law for personal gains."

"I-I-I...you—" The blinking was faster than a strobe light.

"You will get the death penalty, but perhaps you can avoid it. They may give you a lenient sentence if you confess all your crimes and return the money. Then you will spend the rest of your life in prison or disappear."

"You will be right next to me. I will make sure of that."

"Have you told anyone of your suspicions about me?" Chen asked.

"Sun knows," Yi replied.

"So you have said. That is why I...*we*... must leave."

"W—we?" Yi's expression sent his eyebrows down and his jaw up, squishing wrinkles around his nose.

Chen checked his watch. The anxiety and adrenalin rush mixed, sending his heart beating again like a rabbit. Yi forced Chen's hand, so he needed to improvise.

"I do not have time for you or Sun. I am not normally violent, but today—" he raised his pistol.

Yi's face flashed panic and turned pale.

"We are both in a situation. There is one more option, and you, as a diplomat and negotiator, know what it is."

Yi's eyes looked around the plane. Chen watched Yi's large frame tense as he contemplated his position, then twitch when he realized the solution Chen was offering.

"My wife. My son," Yi said. "I cannot."

"Yes, you can. In fact, it is your best option."

Chen knew that Yi's resolve would dissolve once he had time to think.

He would make a break for the door.

Chen needed to go. Delaying even momentarily now was too risky. He needed to get into the air, and the easiest way was to kill Yi. The hard way was to blackmail him.

Chen chose to try the hard way—as long as it was quick.

"Your family is in danger either way. You probably have a few days before they realize what has happened. During that time, you might be able to arrange for your family to leave the country before the MSS takes them and forces them to tell where you are."

"But they don't know anything!"

The engines were spinning fast now.

"That is irrelevant." Chen could not hold back a sardonic, thin-lipped smile.

Yi jumped from the seat when his phone rang. He stood holding it, looking down at Chen, who still pointed the gun at him.

"Sit. I assume that is Sun. Answer it." Yi hesitated. "Now. Please," Chen said politely.

"This is Yi," he said, then listened. "Yes, you were right. He is right here. With a gun. Yes." Yi handed the phone to Chen.

Chen took it, sat back, and rested the gun on his lap as he placed the phone to his ear.

Chen looked at Yi.

"I turned down the offer. I am leaving, Sun." Chen glanced at his watch.

"You are not going anywhere," Sun said with a lack of menace Chen found worrisome. "All airports and border crossings are alerted."

"Goodbye, Sun. Please leave me alone, or I will release *your* Dossier information. That would be career-ending."

He ended the call, dropped it on the floor, stood, and smashed it under his heel.

"Time is up. Let's begin."

Chen looked out the window then walked toward the front door. Sun must have called the guards instantly. They looked wide-eyed at the plane. Chen saw them look at each other, pull their weapons, and run toward the plane.

Chen stepped back down the aisle and waited. Yi's bodyguard ran through the door first, gun out, head on a swivel. Wu came next. They spun when they spotted him standing in the aisle a few rows back.

The first of Chen's bullets punctured their heads. They bounced off seats and spiraled to the floor without even a grunt. Chen added two more shots into each body—because that was what all MSS officers were trained to do.

Chaihong's scream brought Lim, the co-pilot, out of the cockpit. He froze at the sight of the bodies and the sounds of Chaihong weeping.

"Thirty seconds. Close the door and leave." Chen waved his gun in his direction. "No one knows your destination."

Chen reached into Wu's pocket and took a pair of handcuffs from the coat of his dead bodyguard. He liked Wu. Over the years, Chen purposely helped Wu's family get better housing and jobs. Wu had been loyal until he entered the plane to arrest him.

He hurried back to Yi, who was standing and staring, horrified at the bloodshed.

"You killed them."

"Obviously. Did you think we could take them with us? Or I could take you?"

Chen grabbed Yi's wrist and slapped the handcuff around it. Before he could react, Chen snapped the other cuff around the support of the armrest.

"What? What is this?"

"I decided you are too much trouble."

"Where are you going? Where is this plane going? Where are you going to do now?" The questions came fast and staccato.

Chen picked up his backpack and walked toward the front. Stepping over the bodies crumpled across the aisle, he gave Chaihong the stern look of a father instructing his child.

"Keys." He dropped them in her shaking hand.

"What—" Yi rattled his arm and tried to stand. He couldn't.

"Don't free him. No matter what."

He felt terrible as he walked out the plane's door, knowing there was a good chance that all aboard that plane would be dead by the end of the day.

27

CALL THE SPY DEVILS

Macau, Special Administrative Region, China

Mmiay's mirrored aviator glasses shielded her eyes from the bright sun of a cloudless blue Macau sky. It was a mildly cool and breezy 68 degrees. The ephemeral smell of money and flowers wafted in the air.

For May, Macau smelled like the first—albeit a majorly dangerous—'

step toward freedom for her asset, Chen. It also meant she was back in the field.

Sure, she had only been officially retired for a few weeks. And sure, she was in Amsterdam recently handling Lena as a source reporting on Specter, Lena's terrorist uncle. That had led to Lena and her being captured and tortured—and the death of her most beloved friend, Wes Henslow.

This time, she was free from any *official* encumberment. Now, she was interfering with the Agency's most important intelligence source —which might be a felony.

Hawkins could arrest her. He wouldn't.

Not much ever worried May during her long and illustrious career.

She had roamed behind the Iron Curtain early in her career, chipping away at the Soviet Union and Berlin Wall until they fell. She spent many eventful stays in less-than-pleasant basements courtesy of the East German Intelligence Service, STASI. Then she worked the "*stans*." Then Beirut during the middle of a civil war. Marcos in the Philippines. Noriega in Panama. She stood in Tiananmen Square with hundreds of thousands of freedom-seeking Chinese. She hunted terrorists around the world with Wes Henslow.

Every continent—wherever she was needed.

But that was then. This was now.

Now, she was facilitating her most significant recruitment to defect from China and run from the CIA.

To accomplish this, she needed Trowbridge, which she knew would be problematic.

"Where are you?" May asked after calling his secure phone.

"On my way to Australia. Why?"

"Australia? Why? Are you on vacation? Is Lena with you?"

"Okay, let me do this. Yes. No comment. No. She might meet me somewhere around there when I am done. Did I get it all?"

May's once hibernating maternal instinct was awakening. Her outer shell was cracking open, albeit slightly, like a pistachio. She sensed it more when Trowbridge was not with Lena. He truly missed her.

"I know Demon is there. How about the rest of the Devils?"

"Aren't we inquisitive? Maybe I don't want to tell you."

"Is there ever a moment you are not insufferable?'

"No, but I will answer because I am wonderful. Most of the rest are with me. Angel is on my *'no-fly because you are married and have a family'* list. Imp is functioning, and despite my plans to have him recuperate in New Mexico, he is here sleeping on a couch."

"Well, it was a nice thought."

"I agree."

"And humble."

"It is hard to be humble when you are as great as I am." She knew

Bridger thought his banter, as annoying as it might seem, was his way of telling her that he…well…cared in some way.

"What about Milton and Beatrice?"

"I told them to stay. Didn't work. Want to talk to them?"

"No," she said, suppressing a laugh. "Are they ever getting married?"

"We were thinking Hawaii on the way back, maybe. I'll make sure you get an invitation."

"So, you are on a mission."

"Why are you calling?" Bridger used the juvenile 'answer a question with a question' deflection technique—and she knew it. He didn't want to tell her why they were there.

"You need to go to Macau. Now. It's Chen…and Li Chu."

Crackles of the international call mixed with jet engines and jet cabin airflow were all that May heard for a moment. She knew Bridger was analyzing a variety of paths forward, but he would need more details prior to choosing a direction.

"Talk to me," Bridger said.

May told Bridger everything that had taken place.

"He doesn't want to be taken by the CIA?" Bridger asked. "Why not?"

"He doesn't want to be under Hawkins's control."

"I can understand that."

"I thought you, of all people, would appreciate that."

"What about Chapel's New York screw-up? I'm sure Hawkins is thrilled."

"It is a disaster. Which is why I need your help saving Chen."

"Why would I do that?"

"Because I am your mother, and I am asking?"

"Try again," Bridger said—no laugh from her this time.

"Trowbridge."

More jet engines. Crackles. Whooshing air.

"Where is he now?" he asked finally.

May checked her tablet, but there were no messages from Chen.

"I don't know. The last pings from the embedded GPS came from the Beijing Airport. Since it can't be turned off, he must have it in a Faraday Bag. But Option 4 means he is heading for Macau."

"Where The Enterprise is based," Bridger said, referencing the illegal Chinese drug triad, one of the largest in the world. He had dealt with its previous leader, Charlie Ho, in Europe.

"Yes."

"As luck would have it—both bad and good—The Enterprise is related to our trip to Australia—but that can be postponed. Do you and Chen have a plan?"

"Yes. I call it 'Call the Spy Devils.'"

CIA Headquarters, Langley, Virginia

"What the hell is going on? Can someone...anyone...*please* give me an idea of what the hell is going on?" Hawkins shouted at the image of Beijing Station Chief Frank Timmer on the secure video connection within the DDO conference room. "Run this rolling ball of crap at me again."

The eyes of the two analysts at the table wandered around the rectangular room. Although it had been remodeled sometime within the last decade, the CIA's tradition and history reverberated invisibly inside the room.

Muted colors. One brown-paneled wall. A high-resolution map. Digital clocks set to different times. London. Beijing. Tel Aviv. Berlin. A massive screen. A kitchen area had been added in the remodel. Black-framed 8x10 headshots of previous DDOs were nailed to one wall—a mixture of black & white and color. Hawkins would not let his photo be hung until he was gone. He was superstitious.

"We initiated the location extraction protocols as instructed. We covered the safe house. He never showed. We are, quietly, of course, tapping any sources who might know anything."

"And?"

Timmer was a career region case officer and China specialist who had done everything possible in his twenty-year career to get to the job he coveted. Chief of Station, Beijing. Now that he had it, he wanted to keep it.

"They don't know anything. Did Chen receive the signal?" Timmer could not completely hide the *cover your ass* squeaky mouse sounds in his voice.

"It was sent, for fuck's sake," Hawkins let his frustration pressure valve out. "He confirmed receipt. That was the last we heard from him."

Hawkins inhaled and then looked at a ginger-haired woman in her late twenties sitting to his left.

"You're Dawn, right?"

"Yes," she said.

"What do you have?"

Dawn opened a legal-sized pale-blue hard-cover folder.

"There has been a significant increase in MSS activity around their headquarters and Zhongnanhai," she read. "Security was also heightened at Beijing International and the MSS are there also."

"The airport?"

"Yes—"

Timmer cut Dawn off.

"Station contacts indicate a government plane left before the MSS arrived at the airport."

"Really? Don't you think that might be intel worth sharing earlier, Frank?"

Timmer adjusted his body in his chair but remained silent.

May? Is this you? Hawkins wondered.

He took out his phone and dialed. He waited. He dropped it on the table with a clack when it wasn't answered.

Hawkins stood and walked to the kitchen area of the room. He selected a cookie that, for most, would be labeled 'jumbo' but, in Max's colossal hand, looked the size of a quarter. He ate it in two bites and chews. He snatched one more. It was gone by the time he was back in his chair.

May. You just couldn't stay away.

Hawkins pushed another button on his phone. This one, he knew, would be answered. Chapel always answered.

"Max?"

"Danny, have you heard from Chen?"

"No. Why would you ask? I sent the message as instructed. I wouldn't expect him to contact me. I am not aware of any specifics, but I expect it is against whatever protocols are in place. Am I wrong?"

"No. You are not wrong."

"So, I assume there is an issue."

"Yes."

Hawkins snapped his fingers, looked at Dawn, and pointed to the basket of cookies. She didn't move. He snapped again. If looks could kill, Hawkins would be dead. He looked at Ed, the man sitting across from Dawn, and snapped. Ed stood immediately.

"I will fill you in later, but cancel any future trips to China," Hawkins warned.

"Ever?"

"Forever."

"Oh, that is costly. LC, I assume? We knew it was coming. It's good that I am on my way to a profitable engagement in Nigeria. Keep me posted, will you?"

"Yes. Happy travels, Danny."

Hawkins set his phone down when the call ended. Chapel worked for years with May on the Chen recruitment. Hawkins had told Chapel it was risky. To his reputation. Business. And maybe his life. Chapel never blinked. Years later, his prediction was reality. But Danny was a big boy and a patriot who knew what he was getting into.

Hawkins looked at Dawn.

"Anything regarding Vice Minister Sun?"

Dawn flipped through the pages.

Ed placed the entire basket in front of Max, who took a cookie but made no symbol of gratitude.

"He has not been seen," Dawn said, her eyes darting disgust at Ed.

"What about Foreign Minister Yi?" Hawkins asked.

An expression of surprise covered her face.

"Yes. Yes, sir." She flipped a few pages.

"He missed a meeting today with the South African ambassador. He has not been seen," Timmer said.

Dawn looked at Hawkins.

"No further info."

"Do we know where this mystery plane is headed?

"No one is sure," Ed said.

"Do we, the CIA, know anything?"

Hawkins focused on the monitor displaying the map zoomed into eastern China and the countries in the region—South Korea. Japan. Taiwan. "Have all stations within flying distance of the plane alerted to look for it or any unusual MSS activity."

"We are already getting reports of Chinese intel officers acting strange. Seoul. Tokyo. Manila," Dawn said.

"He wouldn't go to Taiwan, would he?" Timmer asked.

"I hope not. That would mean war."

"Speaking of war, the Pentagon just issued a communication. China has alerted its carrier task force in the region," Ed said, staring at an open laptop and typing. "Jets are being scrambled from the carrier group in the Philippines Sea."

"Fantastic. We are starting World War III. Congratulations, everybody."

Hawkins stood suddenly and hurried to the monitor. He stopped a few feet away, hands clasped behind his back, staring at the display.

Jets and carriers. May. Do you know what you are doing?

28

THE GREEN SCREEN

MSS Headquarters, Beijing, China

For hours, Sun sat in the MSS operations center watching the oval blip move across the concentric circles and green glow of the radar—indicating the location of the Boeing 737.

The fact that the plane had left at all was Sun's mistake. Another mistake. Sun thought...hoped...Chen would see he was trapped, listen to Yi, and turn himself in. Chen knew he would be interrogated. Through the years, Sun considered Chen to be, at his core, a man of common sense, therefore understanding that attempting to escape was pointless.

But Chen had leverage. He had the Dossier. Sun needed time to think. So, he let him leave.

The plane was heading south over international waters over the Bashi Channel between Taiwan and the Philippines. That meant Manila was the probable destination. The Philippines was of high strategic interest to China. A large contingent of MSS officers were stationed there. He could order them to meet the plane, arrest anyone onboard, or kill them there.

Currently, no one knew exactly what was causing the alerts—just that it was important and coming from the top of the government. After briefing the president in person, Sun was put in total command of the search for Yi and Chen—a clue to the uninformed that this was a counterespionage situation.

Every resource of the MSS and any other element of the government—including the military—was at Sun's disposal to find the missing officials before the Americans did. Sun convinced the president to keep knowledge of the situation under tight secrecy. The need to do something was overwhelming.

Sun suspected Chen of being involved with the Americans for several reasons. His impressive list of fantastic intelligence operational successes during his career. His relationship with the American Chapel. The increased intel failures that started when he was Vice Minister— Dragon Fire being the most damaging. The sudden discovery of established influence networks in the USA that began when he became a minister.

But Yi? Sun never suspected Yi, and that bothered him.

Could he have been working with Chen all this time? Was this a plan to escape together? Was he taken or killed by Chen? How could I miss Yi?

Sun's identity, reputation, and status were built on a career of meticulously assembling an unsurpassed counterespionage organization that had killed or imprisoned dozens of CIA sources over the last decade. He took pride in his ability to hobble the U.S. spying operations. Some in the myriad technical departments would claim they hacked the CIA's covert communications system—he would counter that dismantling the CIA network was years in the making.

He knew China's success in breaching the CIA resulted from their careless tradecraft. They were traveling the same routes to the same meeting points. Meeting sources at restaurants where the MSS had planted listening devices—where didn't the MSS have listening devices?

Stupid Americans...stupid me. If I did miss Yi, the president must never know.

Chen could not be allowed any opportunity to give the CIA the Dossier—assuming he hadn't already—which was a reasonable assumption given the leverage having it afforded.

That plane cannot land...so....

If Sun could not get the Dossier—then no one could. The president may be upset, but Sun knew him to be a reasonable man. Keeping it out of the hands of the CIA was paramount. When Sun accomplished this, his objective—becoming the Minister of the MSS—would still be intact.

He looked again at the blip on the green screen. That plane had to come down.

———

Two J-15 fighters, carrying PL-10 air-to-air missiles under their wings, were ten kilometers above and behind the 737. The pilots were prepared to launch them and were waiting for permission to fire.

Permission arrived at the People's Liberation Army Navy Eastern Theater Command and was passed to the Shangdong Carrier Task Force. The flotilla of the carrier and two destroyers was returning from a security patrol around Taiwan, which included passing through the Taiwan Strait into the Western Pacific. Its destination was its home port in Hainan.

The flotilla's arrival would be delayed a few hours.

The orders to shoot down the airplane were transmitted through the strictest communication channels. The two J-15s were launched to intercept the Boeing 737.

Only seconds after Sun told the military commanders to fire, one of the J-15s sent a PL-10 toward the unsuspecting passengers in the ill-fated plane. Sun sat alone in the massive MSS Operations Center and watched one of the three green dots on his radar vanish.

In the blink of a green dot disappearing, Sun knew Yi, Chen, and the flight crew were dead. He could imagine the burning plane debris falling thousands of feet into the ocean, along with the Dossier.

Did Chen and Yi see the missiles coming? Did they feel shame as they were ripped apart and fell?

It didn't matter. His problems were solved.

Sun knew the international condemnation would be swift and tax China's already tarnished reputation.

The press would flock to the area and show countless hours of water and perhaps some parts of the plane. The United Nations might waste time by assembling the Security Council. After politically motivated speeches with clever made-for-the-press sentences to maximize traditional and social media reach, China's ambassador would repeat the CCP-approved narrative.

Uyghur terrorists, pro-Taiwan nationalists, or remnants of Hong Kong's pro-democracy movement hijacked the plane—Sun was tired and could not recall which group they had selected as the foil in their cover story.

Whichever it was, they had announced they would crash the hijacked plane into Yulin Naval Base in Hainan...or some other location decided upon by the CCP Central Propaganda Department. Subsidiary units and independent entities would have hacked into any social media sites of these groups with misinformation laying blame on them.

Any rational person would know it was all a lie and wonder what was happening, but there was nothing anyone could or would do. It would be old news or the stuff for conspiracy theorists in a week.

Sun stood and stretched his tired body. Then he realized the feeling of victory was absent from his brain and nervous system. Experience had taught him that meant only one thing—something was wrong.

His aide walked into the room.

"A message for you, sir." He handed Sun a slip of paper.

I sent you a video file.

Sun's head slid back like he had been smacked in the forehead with a tree branch. He reread it and flipped it over to look at the back. Nothing. He flipped back and then looked to the aide.

"Who is this from?"

"I do not know, sir. It arrived on the private lines reserved for the Minister. As acting minister, you have access to them. I have the video ready on your office computer."

"Good. Thank you."

When Sun arrived at his office, he sat at his desk and found the file. He opened it.

The video was security footage taken at the Beijing airport. A remarkably clear clip showed Chen getting off the 737 carrying a backpack and a bag and walking toward the VIP terminal. Non-continuous cuts from various cameras followed Chen zigzagging through the terminal and then eventually out another door. The next clip showed Chen boarding a private jet. It rolled away and out of view of the camera.

The short message attached to the video told Sun what he wanted to know.

He picked up a phone and pushed one button to reach the director of the Third Bureau, the Hong Kong, Macau, and Taiwan Bureau, responsible for all intelligence and security operations in these areas.

"Place every resource in your area on alert. I'll be there in four hours."

29

MAN OF THE WORLD

Macau, Special Administrative Region, China

Ay's call gave Bridger time first to divert his Gulfstream 650 to Manilla. From there, Milton, Beatrice, and Snake would travel to Macau separately, which Bridger thought better than arousing suspicion by all arriving together. Imp's health was improving, but he was still recovering, so he stayed onboard the jet with Demon and Bridger.

Travel into Macau was easy since it did not require a tourist visa. That allowed Milton, Beatrice, and Snake to quickly arrange flights through a Spy Devil-dedicated travel agency within Bridger's more extensive covert support network. There was not enough time for them to arrive from different locations and dates. They would get to Macau at about the same time.

Bridger sat pondering the situation from the back of his ultra-high-speed, long-range jet. Configured to seat eighteen, his jet had crew quarters and a galley forward, a dining/conference group area, single seats, couches, and an entertainment credenza in the midsection. Aft was a divided compartment with a sofa and two chairs opposite a desk, and a sleeping area.

If Chen was on the run, and Li Chu was the cause, then there was a better than decent chance Sun knew the Spy Devils were in play.

"Macau. Are we going to Macau? Blackjack, baby," Imp said, finally awake and reclining on a couch watching the 42-inch TV. He flinched then grimaced as he tried to raise his hand to fist-bump the nearest person—Demon, across the aisle in a recliner.

"We should have left you in Mexico and let the cartel bastards deal with you," Demon growled, ignoring the raised fist. "Hey. Shit-for-brains."

"What?" Imp asked.

"No, the other shit-for-brains." Demon nodded over his shoulder to the small aft office/bedroom where Bridger was sitting, noodling on a notepad. He looked up, dropped his notepad, stood, stretched, and walked into the main cabin.

"What?" Bridger asked as he stood next to Demon's recliner.

"What's the plan?"

That is a good question.

"I informed Gilchrist we are on our way."

"And what did that old criminal say?"

"His men will meet Chen when he arrives, then come get us when we arrive."

"He is bringing toys?"

Bridger looked at Demon, knowing precisely what he meant.

"The toy store will be full."

Demon beamed a smile through his scruffy face.

"Well, that's a start."

Chen's private charter Citation Mustang landed at Macau International Airport, located on the eastern tip of Taipa Island, at the mouth of the Pearl River. It was near the coast of the South China Sea, sixty kilometers southwest of Hong Kong—seven from the city center.

Tourists flocked by the thousands to "The Las Vegas of Asia," a haven for festivals, sporting events, theater performances, and—of course—gambling in the massive hotels and resorts. It was an excellent location to temporarily hide and use as a jumping-off point—if he could.

Having rented the plane using a throwaway alias with funds from one of his many hidden bank accounts, Chen peered out the windows of the light jet as it rolled to a stop on the tarmac area reserved for small private jets. He expected to see an ocean of black vehicles, police, and MSS security waiting to arrest him.

They should be. Did I get away?

He stuck his head out the jet's door when the charter company ground crew opened it and pulled out the airstairs.

"I will wait here. Someone is coming to get me," he told the man dressed in gray overalls, a baseball cap, and a lime green reflective vest, after he helped fold out the airstairs. He nodded and waved at the transport waiting to ferry him to the main terminal.

They drove away.

Chen had his gun. He had decided on the trip that if they were waiting for him, he would not cooperate.

Defiance during interrogation was his last opportunity to rebel against the regime. Perhaps he would "disappear" to avoid the embarrassment and the media asking, "Where is Minister Chen?" questions, then obediently reappear months later at some obscure event.

An interrogation by Sun was not something he looked forward to. Then Chen remembered what May had said.

"Call the Spy Devils."

Chen reached into his backpack and pulled out his CIA-supplied tablet. He powered it up and entered the necessary codes to access the secure area. Trying to recall the information he needed, he typed quickly. When he was done, he sent the message and stuffed the tablet in his bag. He would wait to destroy it until the last moment. Perhaps he would make it to the safe house.

If captured, he would give them an incorrect access code which would cause the electronics to self-destruct.

He looked up to see a black sedan pull around the end of the terminal, drive across the fifty yards of tarmac, and then stop at the foot of the steps to the plane. A medium-sized man dressed in a black suit with a cap exited the passenger side. The similarly dressed driver got out and moved toward Chen.

Chen clutched his backpack and stepped out to descend the steps.

"Sir," the sedan driver said, moving up the steps and reaching out to take Chen's bags.

"No, thank you," Chen said.

The other man waited with his hand resting on the now-open passenger door.

Chen looked when he saw a white cargo van with tinted windows suddenly speeding along the same route taken moments ago by the sedan. Over the airport's noise, he heard wheels screech and saw black puffs of rubber swirl into the air as it skidded to a hard stop beside the sedan. Chen stepped back as the van's side door violently slid open with a *thunk.*

Three men with balaclavas over their heads sprung out, shooting pistols.

They've found me.

The sedan driver reached for a weapon under his jacket but he was too slow. When a half dozen bullets entered his gut, he shook and staggered his last steps before bouncing off the car and falling.

The man who arrived with the driver had his weapon out and was firing rapidly, but on the cramped stairs, he couldn't get his footing or a good aim before a portion of his head above his left ear disappeared. His upper body twisted as his lower body motor functions mechanically tried to find balance on the narrow stairs. They failed, and he collapsed and slid uncontrolled down a few steps until he crumpled in a red heap between the railings at the bottom.

Chen froze when he felt the pieces of the man's head sticking to his face and tasted blood on his lip.

Go. Run. Get in the airplane. Close the door.

Chen's shocked brain convinced his body to turn and climb the narrow steps, but his bags got stuck in the railing. Screaming and jerking his arms, he panicked when he couldn't free himself. He screamed again when he saw an attacker leap over the dead body blocking the steps. Chen grabbed the railing, hoping to hoist himself into the airplane.

Then, an unimaginable pain, like his muscles were exploding, seized his entire body. Chen shook, dropped his backpack, and fell back toward the man jamming a Taser into his back. The man scrambled back to let Chen crash onto the metal steps.

Am I dead? he wondered as they carried him and his bag to the waiting van.

Forty seconds after the attack began, the van door slammed shut and sped away.

Bridger looked out his window at the spectacle of lights flashing from emergency vehicles as the G650 rolled toward the private terminal.

"We're being diverted to a different gate," Alan, the pilot, announced over the intercom.

"Uh oh," Imp said, looking through his window.

Demon looked at Bridger who had grabbed his phone, but it rang before he could dial it.

"Gilchrist. What the—?"

"I am deeply regretful, Bridger," a baritone voice said steadily. "They took your man."

"What happened?" Bridger cranked his head, keeping an angle as best as possible on the action.

"They killed my men. Shot. The authorities are not happy about the use of weapons."

Bridger noted that his friend sounded more disturbed by letting Bridger down than he was about the death of two of his men.

"I'm sorry, Gilchrist. Any idea who did it?" Bridger's mind was already working on the suspects. It was a list with three names.

"I will find out by the end of the day, I swear, by the sun and moon of Portugal, my beloved ancestral home. I swear it!"

Bridger knew his old friend meant it.

"Portugal now?"

Gilchrist was a man of the world—meaning no one knew where he came from, a mystery he fed whenever he used his signature "I swear" expression by changing the country of his ancestry on each occasion. He used his size, bravery, loyalty, resourcefulness, and boisterous personality to his advantage as he corkscrewed worldwide, joining causes he felt were *"on the side of the blessed angels of—"* whatever country he was from that day.

Gilchrist seemed to know everybody. Sometimes for free, most times for a hefty fee, he supplied weapons, intelligence, operational and logistical support, and access. Whatever was needed, he magically could make happen.

That was how he met Bridger and became an essential cog in the global Spy Devils network. He had come to the team's aid in numerous precarious situations without hesitation. In the last decade, Gilchrist focused his talents on Asia—*"where it was the most profitable."*

Gilchrist was cold-blooded. Deadly. Greedy. Loyal. Large. Loud.

"Your cars and all requested equipment await you outside the airport terminal. I have extra men there, too."

Bridger ended the call.

Once they had made it through the airport terminal, Gilchrist and his men were waiting outside the airport in black Cadillac SUVs, as promised. Bridger and Demon got in the first SUV with Gilchrist. Imp, moving slowly, was helped into the second vehicle by Gilchrist's men, who also loaded the luggage.

They pulled out from the Macau International Airport and headed toward the quaint Taipa Village section of Macau, a popular spot for tourists and expats.

"I am happy you called, Bridger, my old friend," Gilchrist said, sticking out his massive hairy hand from the front passenger seat, his deep voice echoing inside the luxury vehicle.

"Hello, Gilchrist," Bridger said from the seat behind the driver, shaking the hand as his was enveloped.

Gilchrist flipped up his bushy mud-brown eyebrows, exposing equally dark pupils set into yellowish eyeballs.

"And my very dear friend, the famous Demon." A smile appeared on his broad, tanned face. He rotated to grasp Demon's hand.

"Gilchrist. Cause any wars lately?"

A hearty, deep laugh now ricocheted in the car, and then the smile disappeared from his face.

"No, but I am now at war with whoever killed my men. They will die, I swear by the sun and moon of Greece, my beloved ancestral homeland."

"Count me in," Demon said.

"Your mother is waiting," Gilchrist said twenty minutes later as they turned off the bridge into Taipa Village. Portuguese and Chinese influences mixed to create modern Macau in this historical and cultural heritage area.

The SUVs pulled through open iron gates into an upscale series of duplexes near Taipa Central Park. Bridger, Demon, and Imp, carrying his laptop case, followed Gilchrist down a path through palms and other plants to the open door of the safe house, where May was waiting in a yellow sundress with arms crossed.

"Oh, Trowbridge," she said as he hugged him. "Demon." She hugged him, too. She saw Imp doing his best to keep up. "Imp. How are you?" She patted his shoulder.

"Hungry, thank you." Imp went to the refrigerator and opened it. "It's empty," he said, flipping it closed and nervously looking around to decide what to do next.

"They shot down the plane!"

"What plane?"

"The plane Chen was *supposed* to be on."

She told them the news as they walked into a bright, modern living room with a wall of glass that looked across a garden court. The furniture was sparse. A couch. Some cushioned chairs around a coffee table. Kitchen table and chairs.

Bridger looked in his Signal mail app. A synopsis and current news report were waiting in his inbox courtesy of Angel. Bridger read it as Demon and Imp looked over his shoulder.

"Sons of bitches," Demon said, sitting down at the kitchen table.

"Who was on the plane?"

"A flight crew …and sources indicate…Foreign Minister Yi."

Bridger stopped his search and walked to May. He felt for the white and blue golf marker kept in his pocket. He took it out and rolled it in his hand. Bridger saw her eyes looking at his hand and then at his eyes.

Right, May. I have a 'tell' sometimes with this thing that your husband, my father, gave me. It helps me think. That's it.

"Yi? They shot Yi out of the sky. Why?" he asked.

"I think it was a mistake. They really want Chen. Dead or alive, it seems now."

Bridger walked back to the refrigerator.

"Still empty," Imp announced.

Bridger ignored him, opened it, and looked in. With a firm flick of his wrist, he slammed it shut. Bridger frowned at Imp, who looked back with an "I told you so" grin.

"Have you heard from Chen?" Bridger asked as he rubbed the marker with his thumb.

"Not since he told me he was doing Option 4 this morning."

"Option 4?" Demon asked, absent-mindedly wiping his Ka-Bar on his leg to clean the blade.

May walked toward the kitchen table and sat by Demon.

"It is a last resort exfil plan. I was against it, but he felt better if it at least existed. It all depends on the situation. How blown is he or thinks he will be shortly? Can he use regular air transportation? If not, he ignores the *Rabbit* code to go to the CIA safe house. Gets a private jet to Macau." May looked around at the eyes staring at her. "It is the easiest place to get in and out of compared to other ports of call. Hong Kong is nearby. A boat or plane become options," she said defiantly.

"Then what?" Bridger opened and closed empty cupboards, looking for something, anything.

"Can we get something delivered?" Imp asked.

May's face soured like she had sucked on a lemon tree, then shook her head.

"Then Chen either gets out immediately or burrows into the safe house."

"I hope it has food," Imp said, trying to get comfortable on the couch.

"Then…?" Bridger put the golf ball marker back in his pocket as he sat on a cushioned chair.

"Then…we do our best. We have Gilchrist," she pointed to the man looking out the windows.

"I would be of service to you, Mayflower, of course," Gilchrist said.

"Mayflower?" Bridger asked, raising his eyebrows.

"Who do you think took him?" Demon asked.

"It's a short list."

"Sun and the MSS?" Bridger asked.

"Maybe."

"Hawkins?"

"Doubtful," May said. "But maybe?"

"Who else?"

May crossed her arms. "There is one other option."

May told him the history of Chen, Ho, and Zhang and how she used Chapel to wedge Zhang into the head of The Enterprise as a favor to Chen.

"Crazy. How's that plan working out?" Bridger asked. "You know Zhang has a Charlie Ho complex."

"Boo fucking hoo-hoo-*HO*." Bridger looked over at Demon, who crossed his legs, removed his K-Bar again from its sheath, and cleaned his fingernails. "You sure you haven't heard from your missing Chinese spy guy?"

"Well, I haven't checked in the last hour or so," May replied quickly, realizing her error.

She snatched her tablet from her large leather handbag. Tapping the screen hard, her eyes widened briefly. She sat back and then handed the device to Bridger.

"What do you think?" she asked.

Bridger looked at the screen and handed the device back.

"What do I think? I think Imp's right. This place needs food." He sat back, lacing his fingers behind his head, and closed his eyes. "Since we are here, I guess we need to rescue him."

30

A BAD VISUAL

Macau, Special Administrative Region, China

"It is impressive, is it not?" Zhang asked, standing on the balcony of the Banyan Tree Hotel's nine-hundred square foot split-level Presidential Suite, looking at the lights of the Macau skyline.

The vibrant beauty of Macau's nighttime skyline was a stunning palette of blue, lavender, gold, red, and white. Like in Las Vegas, the world's more prestigious casinos and hotels made sure the skyline and architecture attracted guests from around the world.

"Yes, it is," Sun said.

"It is cold. Let's go in," Zhang said after a few more minutes of enjoying the view.

Inside, Sun sat at a modern, burnt-copper-colored chair that was part of a large U-shaped sectional that made up the main sitting area of the Presidential Suite living room. The décor was a mix of modern and traditional Chinese with Western influences—much like Macau. An entire wall of glass provided stunning city views.

Zhang sat at his large cherry desk.

"Thank you for sending the video and message, Zhang," Sun said. "Banyan Tree Hotel Macau. I knew it meant I should come here."

"I knew you would."

Sun had arrived hours after Chen in the darkness and coolness of the Macau December evening.

"I watched the security video of Chen walking through the airport. He wasn't always on camera," Sun told Zhang. "We are interrogating airport employees, but retrieving the Dossier might be impossible now. But, perhaps with the help of your organization, there might be a chance."

"I always enjoy assisting the leader...of the MSS," Zhang said, pleased with himself.

When Ho was arrested, Zhang took over the symbiotic relationship between the Chinese cartels and the CCP that had lasted for decades. They helped each other with power and money. The cartel took care of a few dissidents in Hong Kong in exchange for lax to no import/export issues. The Minister of the MSS shared intelligence with the cartels and ran the relationship.

Built to Amazon-like precision by Charlie Ho, The Enterprise was a partnership of the five powerful Chinese triads to dominate the world's drug trade—primarily fentanyl and methamphetamines—through the supply of precursor production chemicals, control of drug-distribution networks, and money-laundering services. It was a multi-billion-dollar annual business.

Zhang had been Ho's loyal and obedient chief operating officer. Tall, thin, intelligent, and unassumingly ruthless. That was until Zhang removed Ho by secretly plotting with Minister Chen to manipulate the CIA to get Ho arrested. Despite being in prison in Australia, Ho believed he was still in command and Zhang was there to fulfill his orders.

He thinks he runs the business even after he was arrested—foolishly caught by the Spy Devils and sent to prison—good.

Immediately, Ho sent dozens of annoying orders passed through Ho's lawyer for Zhang. *Move money from one Swiss account to another. Inform a partner in Laos*. Then, somehow from prison, all day and night, came WhatsApp texts with *Ho's* strategic plans and what *Ho* wanted *Zhang* to do.

Then, more recently, short videos with Ho's smug round face, whiney voice, and haircut like he was ten years old.

Zhang's irritation was only surpassed by his anger. As COO of The Enterprise, Zhang had done all of it. He didn't need Ho to tell him anything. Nothing ever got done without Zhang.

Zhang only replied "Received" with each message.

The Enterprise is mine, Ho. I am not your caretaker. Enjoy prison.

He grinned. Then he took in a deep breath and exhaled slowly.

Underneath the fragrance of the fresh-cut flowers arranged in crystal vases dotting *his* Presidential Suite, the air carried a faint layer of stale cigarettes that had made it through the hotel's HVAC and filtering system.

What does it smell like in prison, Ho?

The hotel and casino complex was owned by a conglomerate of holding companies that owned more holding companies, which usually made the business of The Enterprise untraceable.

"We should eat," Zhang said to Sun as he reached for the phone.

"No. We should start." Sun stood and then picked up Chen's backpack.

"It is hot," was his first conscious thought. He could feel the tacky sweat on his body.

Chen's back ached like he had been kicked by a horse where the device had stunned him. His head felt as heavy as a bag of rocks as he lifted it. The effort exhausted him.

The jet engine-level ringing in his ears was slowly clearing. What he heard then was frightening—complete silence. Opening his eyes took more effort. His reward when he finally blinked away the pain was a view of darkness.

Chen knew he was sitting in a chair. He tested his arms and legs.

No movement. The fear spiraled him into a panic attack, worse than anything in his nightmares. Then he felt straps around his wrists and ankles. His arms were at his side, bound to the chair. His ankles felt connected to the front chair legs.

He started quivering as tears came into his eyes and unfiltered fear leeched from his body. Total isolation with no idea how long it would be to...whatever. After a life of controlling others, he had no control over...anything.

For the next...he didn't know how long...he performed deep breathing exercises. He controlled his brain slowly, which sent chemicals through his nervous system signaling to the rest of him to relax.

This was it. Sun had him. Or was it Zhang? Both? That would be interesting. Either way, they won't get what they are seeking.

The lights came on without warning, sending lightning bolts into his eyes. He squeezed his eyes shut, but the blaze glared through his lids as tears cascaded down his cheeks.

He heard a door open, and shadows eclipsed the searing light piercing his eyes.

"*Ni hao*, Chen."

He blinked continuously as he opened and shut his eyes until the blur came into focus.

"Hello, Sun. Zhang." Chen looked at Zhang, who didn't reply in any way.

Sun put his face near Chen's.

"I am looking forward to asking you some questions." Sun stood and paced around the small square concrete room. "Let's start with a question with the only answer that interests me. Where is the Dossier?"

Milton, Beatrice, and Snake arrived at the Macau safe house the following morning. They saw Bridger, a large man, and Demon sitting at a table covered with papers. Imp was lying on the couch munching on a bag of chips from the now well-supplied safe house.

"Hi, guys. Hungry?" Imp asked. "There's chips." He held up his bag. "And more stuff over there." He pointed to the kitchen where the counter was covered with food Gilchrist had brought.

"This is Gilchrist. Our man in Macau," Bridger announced.

"Hello, my friends," Gilchrist said, joyously shaking their hands and hugging each of them with his tree trunk-wide arms. "We shall all have fun, I swear, by the sun and moon of Canada, my beloved ancestral home."

Puzzled and bemused, they looked at each other and then at Bridger.

"You get used to him."

"When?" Demon asked.

"Get settled. Get something to eat and drink, and we can get you up to speed."

They filled their plates with meat and vegetable dim sums, egg tarts, and almond cookies and gathered around the table.

"These are detailed blueprints of the Banyan Tree complex that Gilchrist found somewhere," Bridger said. "We were working on a plan right now."

"This place is a beast," Snake said as he leaned in to get a better view. "I see...a twenty-two-story, slightly curved urban high-rise luxury hotel, mall, and casino."

Gilchrist nodded.

"Yes. Very much a trendy resort hotel. Busy all the time with hundreds or thousands of guests and tourists," he said. He dragged a thick, hairy, and surprisingly well-manicured finger over the plans, zigzagging it up, down, and across as he spoke. "Two-hundred-forty-five suites. Ten Luxury Villas. Many have pools. Cabanas. Outdoor pools. Shops. Fitness. Many restaurants. The top floors are the Presidential Suite. That is where Zhang lives and works." He sat back and crossed his arms. "A raid is impossible. Hotel and cartel security are thick like the hair on Demon's balls."

"That's a bad visual," Beatrice said as she sipped water from a bottle.

"What? How does he know?" Imp asked.

"Everyone. Shut the hell up," Demon growled at them as they laughed.

"Where would Zhang take Chen?" Bridger asked.

"Here." Gilchrist slid his finger down to several basements below the complex.

Bridger glanced at the plans, folded his arms, turned, and paced.

There is a hard way and a harder way. Not even a middle way to get Chen out. Why can't anything be easy—just once?

After ten minutes of constant pacing, Bridger stopped. They looked at him as he stared off into space.

"Got an idea?" Milton asked.

"A good idea for once?" Demon asked.

"Nope." He turned to face them. "I am walking in, then walking out. With Chen."

Momentary stunned silence was followed by laughter and then a return to silence.

"That's a good idea?" Snake asked finally.

"Trowbridge, are you sure?" May asked with more than a dab of concern.

When am I ever sure anymore?

"Imp. You and the Unemployables need to get busy. Everyone else, we have a lot to do, too."

Chen's interrogation had proved to be difficult, as Sun expected. He knew how to control conversations and manipulate the manipulators. Nothing short of coercion would break Chen.

"He is a professional and determined," Sun told Zhang after Chen refused to answer the only question Sun cared about after a full day of questioning with minimal rest.

"Where is the Dossier?" Sun showed Chen the CIA tablet. "Is it here? /I know about these—as *you* know. The technical bureau has determined that accessing the stored data or devices without the correct codes will result in the drives being erased by electronic pulses. The internal hardware will be destroyed."

"I will make this easy, Sun," Chen said. "The Dossier is not on the tablet. Neither is any other information I might have supplied the Americans."

"So, you admit you are a traitor," Sun said.

"That is not a point of inquiry, Sun," Zhang said.

Sun waved him off.

"Where is the Dossier?" Sun repeated.

After an hour of intense and coercive interrogation, they left Chen beaten, exhausted, and without the needed answers.

31

LET'S DEAL

Macau, Special Administrative District, China

B y late afternoon of the next day, the Spy Devils were ready and getting into position.

"Are you going to walk in and expect to walk out?" May asked. "It is dangerous."

"It is a dumb plan. Let's do it," Demon said as he stood next to Bridger outside the entrance to the Banyan Tree.

"Milton? Beatrice?" Bridger asked.

"We are in our room," Beatrice said. "Nice place for a honeymoon."

"Right...um...I'll be ready...I mean—" Milton added, his Alabama accent pronounced with embarrassment.

"Just stop, Honey," Beatrice's voice added softly.

"Snake?" Bridger asked.

"In the lobby. It's nice. Traditional Chinese architecture and design featuring high ceilings and red color accents," Snake said, dressed in tourist-comfortable khaki long pants and a shirt that strained at the biceps.

"What?" Imp asked.

"That's what it says in this brochure here. It *is* huge."

"Gilchrist? May?"

"We are in place, Trowbridge. I'm worried about Chen."

I'm more worried about us.

"I swear this is a good plan by the moon and sun of France…no, I hate the French…Italy, my beloved ancestral home."

"We are going in."

They strode under the large white overhang with "BANYAN TREE" in large neon-green letters glowing above it, through the glass doors, and into the lobby.

"Snake was right. This lobby is massive," Bridger said as he looked at Snake sitting off to the side in a square sitting area.

"Waste of space," Demon said. He sniffed. "Smells like a flower shop puked in here."

The lobby was buzzing with people crisscrossing the off-white shimmering marble floors. Balinese-style wood carvings typical of the Banyan Tree style adorned intricately detailed walls. Lounge areas with birdcage chairs and deep couches. Chandeliers and plush carpets. Blown-glass art and an array of other pieces accented the space.

A slight young woman wearing a tan jacket and black slacks and holding a clipboard below her golden nametag, "Mimi," greeted them as they crossed the lobby toward the reception area. She had an earbud in one ear connected to a radio clipped to her waistband.

"How may I help you, gentlemen?" she asked with a polite and warm smile.

"Yes. Hello. We would like to see Mr. Zhang."

Her head cocked, and she blinked in confusion, then surprise.

"I am sorry. Who?"

"Mr. Zhang. The owner," Bridger said with a smile that showed his white teeth.

She looked at her clipboard, then around the lobby, her neck craning, looking for someone.

"One moment, please," she smiled, raised a finger, then scampered away, mumbling with her hand to her ear.

Moments later, she reappeared behind a woman and two men. The woman, obviously in charge, wore a tan suit over a white shirt, open at the collar. A nameplate and Banyan Tree Logo were on the breast pocket of the suit. The men were also in tan jackets and black pants and were large and fit with the look of security—or cartel.

"I am the manager, Ms. Wei. How may I help you? You are looking for Mr. Zhang? I am afraid he is—"

"Tell him Bridger is here to see him."

Bridger stood on the balcony looking over the city and checked his watch. Demon kept near the door that led from the balcony to the living area. Two unconscious and bounded security men were a few feet from them on the balcony.

"Any second," Bridger said.

"They are in for a hell of a surprise...or we are dead," Demon said.

A loud *bing* echoed through the Presidential Suite, and Bridger waited to see who exited the elevator.

Four security guards came out first, spreading out low and fast and arcing their pistols around the suite's large living area. They expected to see the two visitors under the control of their guard colleagues.

"We are over here," Bridger said as he went inside from the balcony. Demon followed.

The four guards swung and pointed their pistols at Bridger, who stood smiling back at them, and Demon, who looked back with an "if looks could kill" expression. Getting the signal from his security team that it was safe to enter, Zhang and Sun stepped into the room.

"So, you are Bridger," Zhang said as he walked towards him with an extended hand.

"Hey, Zhang. Sorry about the guards." Bridger thumbed over to the men lying on the balcony. Two of the four security men ran to the balcony to check on their colleagues.

"Don't touch!" Bridger shouted.

The men stopped and looked at Zhang, who shook his head. The guards stood over their colleagues but left them untouched.

The others kept their weapons pointed at Bridger and Demon.

"You are Sun." Bridger's hand was out.

Sun hesitated, looking at Bridger like he was a zoo exhibit. Then he shook.

"The Devil," Sun smiled at what he thought was an insult or a joke.

"This is Demon." Bridger waved his hand at his colleague, who remained expressionless.

Zhang and Sun reacted to the name by flinching and taking what appeared to be half a step back. All four security men glanced at each other and around the room.

Bridger looked at Demon and shrugged.

"I think they've heard of you."

"They ain't heard nothing yet."

I'm counting on that.

Bridger surveyed the cartel leader and the MSS counterintelligence wizard. Neither was a particularly impressive-looking man, although Sun looked like a wolf—a hunter who would never give up when he got the scent. Zhang looked like an accountant.

"Shall we sit?" Zhang asked.

"I don't think there is time for that," Bridger said. "Hey Zhang, how is Ho? Heard from him lately?"

Zhang glowered at Bridger, who smiled back.

"You have to give us Chen now," Bridger continued.

They both blinked as Bridger allowed them a moment to comprehend what he said.

That's important. Really important.

"What? Why would we do that?" Sun laughed.

Suddenly, two *pops* came from the direction of the balcony. When they turned, they saw dark splotches reflected by the light across the doors. Then, the guards' bodies *thudded* against the doors and slowly slid down.

Two whirling Devilbots whizzed inside and spun toward the two remaining security men.

After a *crack* and a *crack*, they clutched their chests, staggered backward, and then fell as the 9mm bullets fired from the pods under the Devilbots struck their bodies.

Sun and Zhang stood horrified, like they had seen a zombie, as the Devilbots hovered a few feet from their heads. Demon walked over and picked up the guards' weapons. He stuffed one in his belt. The other he pointed at the still petrified Sun and Zhang.

Demon nudged Bridger.

"Hey, can I drill those other two guys?" Demon waved the gun at the first two guards, still bound and gagged on the balcony. "Maybe toss them over the side?"

"Maybe in a minute."

"Liar."

Bridger walked up to Sun and looked him in the eyes.

"Now. Let's deal."

32

BANYAN TREE MACAU

Macau, Special Administrative Region, China

"Imp. Elevator."

"What goes up—stays up." Imp's hack gave him access to elevator control systems. He locked the Presidential Suite private elevator in place on the top floor.

Wrangled by Demon, Zhang and Sun sat next to each other on the couch.

"Here's the deal," Bridger started. "You give us Chen, alive, and we leave."

"You are dead." Zhang was regaining his composure. "There is no way out for you."

"Please. Really? Oh, geez. I didn't think of that," Bridger said mockingly. "Your turn, Sun. Give me your best cliché."

Sun was silent.

"First important question that will determine your future. Is Chen alive?"

"Yes," Sun answered, puzzled.

"Second important question. Did he mention the Dossier?"

That question was answered with a room full of silence.

Bridger looked around the massive suite.

"Nice place, Zhang. You have done well. Did you tell Sun that you owe the position as the head of The Enterprise to Chen and the CIA?"

Sun looked at Bridger and then glowered at Zhang.

"Is that true?" Sun asked.

"No. No. He is a liar," Zhang replied with too much desperation.

"Sticks and stones, Zhang," Bridger said. "You don't know the story, Sun? It is classic. We need to get moving, so here is the short version. Better than a Clancy novel. Chen wanted to remove Charlie Ho, who, as you know, built The Enterprise. Chen was getting sick of Ho's demands and decided to inform on him so he could be arrested in Europe using—quite masterfully—the resources of the CIA. Well done, Zhang."

"Charlie Ho was good at building his business. I ran it. Grew it. I had nothing to do with the CIA." Zhang said.

Sun had not taken his eyes off of Zhang.

"Yeah. Right." Bridger walked over to the dead men Demon had slid into the corner. "There was a time when killing was against my rules." He turned to the men on the couch. "For you guys, I have waved that rule. Where was I?"

"Talking too much," Demon said. "Tick tock." Demon tapped his wrist with the barrel of the pistol.

"Zhang here assumed control once Ho was out of the picture—with Ho's approval. Being the grateful, big-hearted guy, Zhang plays along with Chen until the Dossier situation arises. Chen calls for help, thinking it is Zhang's opportunity to pay him back. Chen tells his buddy that he needs the cartel's protection and a plane to take him out of the country. So, what does Zhang do? He calls Sun the spy catcher."

Bridger sat down in a chair across from the couch.

"Be careful who you are friends with Sun."

"This is all very interesting but has nothing to do with—"

"It has *everything* to do with *everything*." Bridger leaned forward, placing his elbows on his knees.

"You are going to call down to wherever Chen is and have your guys take him to the lobby. Nice and public. I have a guy there. They hand Chen over, and we are gone." Bridger suddenly stood and exclaimed like he was rallying the troops, "Let's do it!"

They didn't move.

"I told you. You owe me twenty bucks," Demon said.

Bridger shrugged his shoulders.

"You want to know where the Dossier is?" Bridger asked.

Zhang slid to the edge of the couch. Sun stood with wide eyes.

"I have no clue."

Sun seemed to deflate.

"But I have something else that might interest you." Bridger turned on the flat-screen TV fixed to the wall across from the couch. "Imp."

"Sit down and watch. This is exciting. I haven't seen the final cut yet."

The screen blinked, and a red "S" with horns—the logo of the Spy Devils—appeared.

Ominous music faded in, and a close-up photo of Minister Sun appeared.

The narration began:

"Sun Jingwei is the 57-year-old Vice Minister of State Security. And he is a thief and a killer..."

"Let's skip the biography stuff. You know who you are. Imp, get to the good stuff."

The video scanned forward and then stopped.

"Ah. Here is the good part. I wish we had some popcorn. This part is from the Dossier part about you."

"Me?" Sun looked at Bridger.

"Yes. It was a surprise to me, too—a present from Chen before you took him. I'll summarize. You are as corrupt as the rest—maybe a little more. The offshore accounts total...a lot. You paved the way for the president to take power when you had his rivals arrested in Shandong. You protected his family in millions and millions worth of real estate deals. I've got to hand it to you guys and your anti-corruption campaigns. Very effective."

"That is all there is about me? Perhaps the Dossier is not so valuable." Sun said as he stood and walked to the television and pointed. "This is nothing."

"You have a point. Unimaginable corruption is a badge of honor at the highest levels of the Chinese government. But, lucky for you, there is another part. Take a seat."

Sun warily moved back to the couch and sat.

"Imp. Let it rip."

The screen flicked, and the narration began. Under it, images relevant to the voice-over appeared. Photos. Buildings. Charts. Maps. The music swelled up and down dramatically.

"It was Sun who ordered the shoot-down of the China government plane over the Bashi Channel between Taiwan and the Philippines. It was purely a Chinese leadership power play."

"The Spy Devils have learned Minister Chen, the head of China's Ministry of State Security, was expected to be on board. Lucky for Chen, he made a last-second change. That saved his life from a man who wanted Chen's job so badly he killed three flight crew members."

"Who else was on the plane? Chinese Foreign Minister Yi. If Sun murdered four people by shooting down a plane in international waters—who approved it?"

The "S" logo reappeared, "Greetings from the Devil" superimposed over the graphic. Then it faded to black.

"This is a lie," Sun shouted, his angry face filling with red blotches.

Bridger turned to shaken Sun. "You think so? It wasn't our best, but we only had a few hours. What do you think, Zhang?"

He did not answer.

"This is a lie," Sun repeated. "Who—"

"That is the question. Let me see," he checked his watch, "in five minutes. This is going global on all our extremely popular social media sites and as many others as we deem relevant. It will be sent to the major television stations and cable channels worldwide—with a press release. Going viral will not be an issue since it will also be big news that we aren't dead. The alternative is…"

"Chen."

"Exactly…and you have four minutes left."

"Don't do it, Sun. Don't give them Chen. You will never see the Dossier." Zhang said.

"Who cares about that? If the president sees this, I am done."

"Three minutes," Bridger announced. "Get ready, Imp."

"He is yours," Sun said, defeated.

"No, he isn't," Zhang stood.

"Hey, Zhang. We didn't have time to make something professional about you, but I will."

Zhang spun toward Sun.

"Sun, don't give—"

Sun punched Zhang in the throat. The man gurgled, gasped, and sucked air as he fell.

"Wow. Two minutes." He turned to Demon. "Now *you* owe me twenty."

"Don't celebrate. We don't have him yet," Demon warned.

33

BAD THINGS WILL HAPPEN

Macau, Special Administrative Region, China

The security guard opened the door and let Sun and Bridger into the room. Demon stayed in the hall of the well-lit sub-basement level. Narrow, white-walled halls seemed to radiate at right angles from the elevator. Snake was stationed by the elevator.

The smell hit them first.

Inside, Chen was still in the chair—an unconscious bag of sweat, dried vomit, urine, and blood.

Bridger glanced at Sun with total contempt.

"Release him, clean him up, and help get him outside."

When the guards were done with Chen, he was dropped—barely conscious—in a hotel wheelchair and taken up a service elevator. Bridger and Sun led the way as Snake and Demon flanked the chair.

Outside a service exit, three SUVs and a van were idling. Gilchrist and his men, carrying pistols and submachine guns at the ready, were waiting in sentry positions around the vehicles.

"I swear. You did it! We will take him to the van," Gilchrist said as he signaled some of his men to help Chen out of the chair and into the open side door of the van. When they placed him inside, Gilchrist's men jumped in and closed the door.

"Everyone here?" Bridger asked. Windows rolled down in the third SUV. The smiling faces of Imp, Beatrice, and Milton peered out. "Snake. Stay close." Snake went to the driver's seat of the SUV.

"Let's go," Demon said as he got in the back seat of the second vehicle.

Bridger turned to Sun.

"Anything goes wrong, or we have any trouble, the video gets released. So, make sure nothing happens."

Bridger got in next to Demon. Gilchrist got in the lead vehicle.

Sun watched as they disappeared into the darkness. He started shaking from the chill in the December air, fear, dehydration, and the knowledge that letting them go was a mistake, regardless of the threat of releasing the video.

It was a short drive from the hotel to the Centro Náutico de Hác-Sá sports club and beach on the shore of Zhujiang River Estuary and the South China Sea. When they arrived, the vehicles stopped at a concrete boat ramp that sloped to the dark water.

"Stay here and expect trouble," Bridger told his team as they exited the third SUV.

Two of Gilchrist's men took Chen under his arms and legs and carried him to a waiting Numarine fifty-nine-foot-long Sputnik Motor Yacht bobbling gently in the water.

The yacht pulled away from shore with Bridger, Demon, Chen, Gilchrist, and two of his men onboard. The captain gunned the engines, digging the hull into the dark water with a wide turn.

"Nice boat," Demon said, dropping onto a section of an aft L-shaped lounge sitting area.

"It is one of my businesses. Charter yachts for tourists and fisher-men. Very profitable."

"Must be helpful for the smuggling business."

Gilchrist just smiled.

"We must be careful. China's Coast Guard is much improved."

Bridger nodded as he slid glass doors open to enter a long modern eating and kitchen cabin. Windows ran the length of the area, providing a spectacular view of Macau's lights and Hong Kong's glow in the distance. He went below to the bedroom cabin. Chen was lying on a bed.

"Chen."

The man's eyes darted to Bridger. "Thank you."

"Don't thank me. Just tell me where the Dossier is."

"Lights. Aft. Approaching fast!" Gilchrist shouted from above.

Bridger lost his balance as the yacht jerked when the captain pushed the throttle, shooting the Sputnik's engines to their 28-knot max speed and steered toward the South China Sea.

Bridger spun and ran to the living area, grabbing what he could as the speeding yacht slammed into the waves. Gilchrist and his men were tossing couch cushions to the floor. They pulled up the wooden platform below. Inside were an array of weapons. AK-47s. Handguns. Grenades. RPGs.

"Give me something," Demon said, his arm out. He took an AK-47 just as the first distant sporadic sounds of gunfire snapped the darkness.

The now-armed men took cover in the aft section. Gilchrist's men scrambled up ladders to the upper level.

Bridger saw the lights of two boats approaching from Macau and sparks of light as they fired toward the Sputnik. Bullets from the pursuing boats were getting closer—a few pinged off the yacht.

"They have faster boats," Gilchrist said.

They sent a wall of bullets across the water at the boats.

"One second, please." A voice with an Alabama accent crackled among the static in Bridger's earbud. Then, an incredibly bright flash of flames briefly turned night into day. "Kamikaze drone with a thermite grenade."

The light of the other boat veered away from the explosion and wreckage of the now-burning speed boat. They watched it get smaller as the Sputnik kept its maximum speed.

"I swear by the sun and moon of my beloved...United States of America. Do not tangle with the Devil or his Spy Devils!" Gilchrist shouted. He tossed his AK-47 on a seat and went to the bar. "There is wine here. We need to drink. We should have many toasts."

"I'll drink to that," Demon said.

Thirty minutes later, the yacht approached a huge, imposing dark shape that blocked out the stars, sitting silently in their path. The yacht pulled alongside the fading red hull of the two-hundred-ton oil tanker converted to a cargo transporter named the *Mediterranean Gold*.

Bridger and Demon returned to the bedroom to get Chen, who was now sitting on the edge of the bed.

"Chen?" Bridger saw the man's bloodshot eyes looking up at him. "Dossier?"

He winced as he formed a smile with his bruised, thin lips. "It will be with a friend. Safe," he said in a soft rasping voice.

"Okay, I get it. We are leaving."

Bridger and Demon assisted Chen outside, where a winch screeched as it lowered a cargo platform to the yacht. They stepped on and stood as it ascended, squealing slowly until they reached a cargo opening on the ship's side. Some men reached out, grabbed Chen, and brought him aboard.

"This rust bucket has seen better days," Bridger said as he leaped through the opening.

"This rust bucket has saved many lives over the years," May answered as she marched up to Bridger and hugged him. He didn't resist. "Thank you, Bridger."

She turned to Demon and hugged him, which Bridger noticed was slightly longer than she did him. She released Demon and looked at them.

"Did you have any trouble?"

"Piece of cake," Bridger said.

"Cake that was dropped on the floor and stomped on," Demon added. "Besides that? A piece of cake."

"I'm not sure saving Chen was worth it," Bridger said.

"What do you mean?"

She doesn't know? He wondered.

"Um...no Dossier," Bridger said.

And?

"Oh, that. I am sure it will all work out."

She doesn't know or is ignoring the truth. Either way...

"If this...um...ship gets you to the first rendezvous, we will see you at the resort," Bridger said. He and Demon hopped back on the platform as it noisily lowered toward the yacht bobbing below them in the darkness.

"Now what?" Demon asked once they were back onboard the yacht.

Bridger held onto the rail as the yacht's engines revved.

"Well, my hope is we get away for a moment to relax and enjoy a wedding," he said as they bounced on the waves and pulled away from the massive dark outline of the ship.

"Hope? Relax? Enjoy?" Demon asked. "Give me a break. Hope is for losers. And when we try to 'get away,' only bad things happen."

Bridger looked into the darkness.

Demon is right. Bad things will happen. I can feel it.

34

PRESIDENTIAL SUITE

Abuja, Federal Capital Territory, Nigeria

C hinara Egbe checked the clock. It was 4:15 p.m.

Only one more hour.

Chinara knocked, listened, and scanned her badge at the hotel room door. She blocked the door open and started servicing the last room of her twelve-hour shift. She was tired, and her back hurt more than it should for a twenty-two-year-old. She worked long, hard days cleaning rooms at the Transcorp Hilton Hotel.

It's hard...but better than no job at all.

She grabbed her housekeeping trolly's handles and shoved the heavy cart with her body to position it by the door as she stepped in.

She looked forward to spending the evening with Sade at the pool when the shift ended. Chinara knew her precocious eight-year-old daughter was splashing around the cool water at that moment with Chinara's friend Lanre, another hotel maid. As one of the hotel's better perks, staff families were allowed to use the pool once a week.

Sade has so looked forward to this day. I cannot be late. She will want two treats from the pool grill!

Humming a Yoruba song she learned as a child from her grand-mother, she quickly stripped the bed and dumped the dirty linen in the bag attached to her trolly. She wanted to hurry the trolly to the base-ment laundry, change out of her baby-blue, short-sleeve tunic and stretchy black slacks maid uniform, and put on her swimsuit.

When she heard the explosions, she had one thought.

Sade!

Moments before, a dirty, drab-green Hilux Toyota pickup truck turned south off Aguiyi Ironsi Street and sped onto the long palm tree and flagpole-lined access road that led to the sprawling Transcorp Hilton Hotel complex.

Seconds later, the truck neared where the security station enclo-sures spanned the road, housing gates that blocked the road, both coming and going. Four men tossed grenades from the windows as they rose out of the truck bed, jumped out, and fired at dozens of cars waiting to enter the complex.

Trying to see what was happening, Chinara leaned close to a window and saw the Hilux swerve left onto the sidewalk and smash into the guard building, detonating a bomb. The explosion sent flaming debris into the trees, which caught on fire on the right side of the road. On the left, more trees ignited the storage lot filled with hotel construc-tion materials.

Chinara felt the glass shake and heard other windows facing the blast shatter in the Y-shaped ten-story hotel.

She stepped back and stood panting as terrifying and heartbreaking memories flashed of her husband, Ladi, being murdered by Boko Haram less than a year ago, leaving her a single mother. That also led to her job in Abuja. She knew she had to move. Panic turned to survival.

I must get to Sade.

Out the windows, she saw motorcycles emerge from the smoke and race up the roads, past the destruction of the guard stations, and toward the hotel entrance.

She grabbed her phone and dialed Lanre as she ran to the staff elevator.

"Hello! Chinara. Hello!" a panicked voice screamed into the phone.

The elevator door opened, and Chinara jumped in.

"Lanre! We are under attack!"

"Yes. I see men. With guns. Coming over the wall."

"Sade—" Chinara heard the beeps indicating she lost her connection.

From the southwest side of the complex, a force of twenty men with black balaclavas covering their heads and faces hopped the security walls. Dressed in full combat camouflage uniforms with ammunition belts strung over their shoulders and chest, they had their collection of machine guns up as they sprinted across the tennis and squash courts.

The elevator door opened, and Chinara sprinted toward the pool, shoved open the glass doors, and stood searching for her daughter. Then she saw Lanre crouched and clutching Sade, shielding her to her left by the Suya Grill.

"Lanre! Sade!" she yelled in panic, waving her arms to get their attention.

The attackers spread out across the hexagonal-shaped pool area, crowded with hotel guests and visitors enjoying the relief from the heat. Sun-screen-drenched guests who had been enjoying the hot summer sun on cushioned sitting areas, or sitting under large umbrellas, in the shade of the bar deck, or snacking at the Suya Grill were shot in their backs as they ran screaming.

As bullets indiscriminately hit swimmers, Chinara screamed and rushed forward, ignoring the crimson swirls mixing with the bright blue water.

Her arms were out and ready to grab and shield her daughter when she saw a bullet strike Lanre in the throat. She let go of Sade and clutched her hands on her neck. Blood squirted from between Larne's fingers, and gurgling blood bubbles came from her mouth as she fell.

"Lanre!" Chinara shouted as she looked at the lifeless eyes.

She looked at Sade, who was shaking and crying. Chinara wiped Larne's blood away from her child's traumatized face.

She snatched Sade in her arms and squeezed her tight

"Stay with me," she said, kissing her head.

Chinara turned as sirens screeched from alarms. She considered following the guests stampeding up the steps and through the doors into the hotel.

"They are leaving. We will stay here," she told her daughter with a smile as she tugged her braids. "*Shhhh*. Quiet. I will take care of you."

Inside, a few armed security guards rushed at the attackers, but they were shot as they ran, dropping onto the tile floor's high-gloss neutral brown tones. Reloading and firing as they moved, the force broke into groups toward the piano bar, reception desk, and hotel entrance. Any glass on the front doors that had not shattered by the blast was broken with the bullets fired from inside the area out to the crowded entrance drive.

One group of four men secured the elevators located across from the reception desk. They stood with guns raised, ready to shoot at anyone inside when a door opened.

Another group went back to the shattered pool. Stepping over bodies, they tossed a few grenades out the door to kill survivors and deter would-be rescuers. One grenade bounced on the concrete and rolled to within a few feet of the young woman and her child.

Chinara turned her back to the grenade and protected her daughter as best as she could with her body.

Then the grenade exploded.

Danforth Chapel heard the explosions as he enjoyed an early afternoon glass of Chianti while watching international news and business reports on the flat screen perched in the center of the ninth-floor executive lounge. For a moment, the well-dressed businesspeople and uniformed servers looked at each with motionless, puzzled faces.

It was a lounge crowded with important people. CEOs. Politicians.

State Governors. A minister or two. All were below the level of Danforth Chapel who was undoubtedly the most important and influential person in the room or staying at the hotel, and possibly the most influential person in Nigeria at that moment, including the president.

Danforth Chapel—Danny to many—had founded the appropriately named Danforth Chapel Company, the world's leading private intelligence agency. Politicians, celebrities, and world elites—good and bad —came to Chapel with embarrassing scandals when they were being blackmailed or had media issues or other crises outside their control.

As always, he was resplendent in his signature bespoke suit, dress shirt, and floral tie.

The Danforth Chapel Company had a contract to be the lead political campaign consultant to the Nigerian president, who was fighting for re-election. While Chapel put a complete campaign support team in the country—campaign management, scheduling, messaging, social media—regular visits by the man himself were part of the deal. Because of who he was, Chapel always traveled with a four-person personal security unit.

The alarms started blaring when the explosion came, followed by the crack of automatic weapons.

Then chaos struck as everyone pushed through the wide entrance at once, past the reception stand, then through the open glass doors. Some ran to their suites on the same floor. Others slammed through the stairwell doors, planning to descend the nine floors to the lobby.

The hotel staff didn't even try to calm them. Instead, they made for the back employee elevator inside the lounge kitchen.

Chapel sat forward but remained in his seat to avoid the mayhem around him. Three of his security team pushed through the crowd in less than a minute. They looked like triplets. Short dark hair. Muscles strained their blue business suits. Stump necks in open-collar white suits. Guns drawn. Heads on a swivel.

"Sir, we should go," said Marco, the lead guard. The other two guards, Vern and Barry, flanked him. As he stood, they stopped and, in unison, raised their hands to their ears. Then they glanced at each other.

"Rick says they are shooting people coming out of the elevator," Marco relayed, getting the intel from their man in the lobby.

"We can't use the elevator or go down to the lobby. The suite," Barry announced, as they clutched Chapel by his arms and hustled him from the lounge.

They went up the stairs to the Presidential Suite—Chapel's usual residence while in the capital. Once inside, they bolted the lock and swung the latch to secure the thick wooden door.

The smell of smoke, gunpowder, and scented candles flowed through the room.

"Get in the bedroom," Marco ordered.

Chapel did as he was told, acting calm, but concern and worry were on his face. Vern went with Chapel.

Chapel's large bedroom was down the corridor straight ahead. Behind a mirrored door, the bathroom was in the hall to the left.

"Not much of a lock," Vern said as he closed and locked the bedroom door behind them. "Get on the other side of the bed. On the floor."

"Is that necessary?"

Vern gave him a look of *This is my show now, so do what I damn tell you.* Chapel complied. Vern scanned the room, determining his best defense. He grabbed the end of a low sitting couch under a window and dragged it toward the narrow hallway.

"Let me help you."

Ignoring Chapel and without effort, the man picked up the couch, walked to the closed door, and ledged it against it. He did the same with part of the desk set, low table, and nightstands. He pulled out his Glock, positioned himself on his knees, and rested his arms on the desk pointed down the hall toward the door.

Chapel noticed the HVAC system was off as the heat rose in the top floor room. He stripped off his jacket, ripped off his tie, opened his collar, and rolled his sleeves.

"Do you perhaps have a spare weapon, Vern?" Chapel asked. Vern looked at Chapel. "Just in case. I am quite proficient in how to use them."

Vern reached behind his jacket, pulled out another Glock, and handed it to Chapel. Holding the pistol, Chapel retreated to his corner between the bed and windows and peaked around a curtain. He pulled out his phone, hoping to fire off texts and calls, but the mobile network was down.

Chapel looked at Vern who was crouching by the desk with his gun pointed toward the door. Chapel was scared, but somewhere deep down was a gold-rich vein of youthful excitement.

The memories came. The masterminding of coups or extracting governments being overthrown, juggling dozens of intricate intel or communications operations, saving careers, and destroying others. Now, he went to fabulous dinners and delegated responsibilities. Went on the occasional visit to important clients where his face being seen was more important than the results of his work.

Boring.

The *thump-thump* of helicopters shook the windows and rattled broken glass. Lights brighter than the sun's surface panned across the sides of the hotel, blinding Chapel with each pass. More flood lights lit up the rest of the area, along with the reds, blues, and whites from hundreds of lights atop emergency vehicles.

Chapel watched people being escorted under heavy protection away from the hotel.

He realized the booms of explosions and gunfire were more sporadic—but still came.

"I'll try again—" Vern said as he checked his radio pack on his belt. "Rick. Can you hear me? Rick. Are you there?" Vern frowned. "Nothing. It's been too long."

BOOM. BOOM.

The explosion cracked the bedroom door off the frame, followed by shouting and bursts of gunfire. Vern looked at Chapel, sweating and nervous, and pointing his borrowed pistol over the bed. His skyrocketing, medically controlled blood pressure made his head and chest feel like they would explode. Sweat tidal-waved over his body.

Suddenly, the bedroom door exploded, sending smoke and chucks of the Presidential Suite door across the bedroom. Chapel lost sight of

Vern as the force of the explosion tossed him back and as smoke and chunks of the room filled the air. He heard shots close and readied himself for death.

A flash-bang grenade blinded him, sending a screaming pain ricocheting between his ears. His temples were throbbing.

The next moments were confusing. He felt his mouth forced open, and then two or three sharp pricks punctured his cheeks and gums. Then, hands grabbed him and jerked him to his feet, but his balance was hard to find. He managed enough sense to try to resist. Then he felt a fist cave in his stomach.

"Walk," he thought he heard through his traumatized ears. He tried and failed—a few painful blows to his side motivated Chapel to try harder.

He felt the gravity change as an elevator descended. When the doors opened, through watering eyes, he discerned guns pointing at his head.

He could smell gunfire and fire. He heard panic, shouting, gunfire, and terror. He heard a thick-accented voice shout, *"Chapel. President. Security."*

Chapel's eyes started to focus, but the bright light pouring through the shattered windows across the lobby didn't help. Blinking at his captors, he saw they were tough men wearing suits so they looked like escaping guests. Their accent was Nigerian.

His legs responded better as they rushed him out of the hotel, bypassing the stream of people pushing and shoving their way to safety. His escorts didn't stop as they pushed the locals to the side who tried to assist them.

Chapel looked, attempting to warn the local officials, but his mouth and jaws felt like they were missing.

Then he felt a sting in his arm. Chapel was jerked back and away from the hotel and hustled across the large lawn. Nausea rose as his head spun with the bright flashing lights. He stumbled and welcomed the darkness as he lost consciousness.

. . .

The room was so stifling hot he was drenched in sweat. Lifting his head took effort and his eyeballs felt as heavy as bowling balls. He rubbed his hands over his wet, stubble-covered chin and then through his damp hair.

He was not restrained, which he appreciated, so he eased his legs over the edge of the platform he was lying on and looked around the room. One close-to-zero-watt light bulb provided all the light in the space.

It was a concrete square decorated—if that was the right way to consider it—with a wooden platform that doubled as a bedframe. A mattress that he thought had to be held together only by mildew.

Chapel was startled when the door opened. He watched an Asian man with a bent left arm and burn marks on his face come through. He recognized him immediately.

"Hello, Mr. Chapel. It is nice to meet you finally. My name is—"

"Yes, I know. Hello, Li Chu," Chapel said.

35
RELATIONSHIPS OF CONVENIENCE

Chad Basin, Borno State, Nigeria

"I will be direct. A man of extreme importance such as yourself should appreciate that."

Li Chu waited for Chapel to answer. It didn't come.

"Chen works for the CIA. That is not an issue of argument. Then there was the assassination attempt in New York City attempted by your men—"

Chapel painfully crossed his legs—knee over knee—one foot bounced up and down, signaling impatience—or defiance. The chronic lower spine and arthritis issues in his back spasmed. Pain flashed.

"I am sorry about New York. That was a misunderstanding."

Li Chu scratched his arm and smirked at Chapel.

"Bridger told me it was you."

"Yes, and I heard you were bosom buddies now."

Li Chu's face wrinkled, not understanding the phrase.

"Where is Chen?" Li Chu asked.

"I don't know."

The door suddenly swung open, smashing into the concrete wall with a bang as a uniformed man strode in.

"*Sannu.*"

As he entered the cell, the first Nigerian man greeted Chapel in a frightening, haunted-house baritone voice. Two armed men followed, closed the door behind them, and stood at attention on either side of the door. The man took Chapel's hands in both of his and shook firmly. They were large. Callous. Rough, like a gravel road.

"I am Yusef. This is my camp. I hope all is well with you."

"Not really. May I go?" Chapel asked.

"That is funny. I am glad the most famous Danforth Cha-*pel*—" he accented the second syllable of the name "—is a funny man."

A broad smile with caramel-colored teeth flashed, then disappeared as quickly through a scruffy, bushy beard that looked like the man had glued tarnished steel wool to his face.

Yusef looked powerful, with eyes radiating danger. A cream and black herringbone-pattern cotton shemagh tactical scarf was wrapped around his head and neck. He wore a camouflage uniform that looked new.

Chapel recognized the uniforms and patches as belonging to one of Nigeria's insurgent groups.

The other men wore similar but well-worn camouflage uniforms. AK-47s were tucked under their arms, and ammunition belts were strapped across their chests. Sidearms and knives were tucked into their belts.

"Yusef? Abu Yusef? I recognize that name. You are ISWAP. If I remember, you split off from Boko Haram and control the Lake Chad area."

The man beamed.

"Yes. You have heard of me. I am most honored. And you, Mr. Cha-*pel*, according to this man," he indicated Li Chu impatiently, standing to the side, "you are an enemy and tried to kill him."

"We need to try harder," Chapel said, hoping the ISWAP leader had a sense of humor.

Yusef walked up to Chapel, who still sat on his bed.

"You are a funny man. But! I also know you are working for the infidel president in Abuja. That makes you *my* enemy. Very, very disappointing." Yusef shook his head and slapped his hand down on Chapel's leg. He grimaced as waves of pain ripped through his body.

"Can you tell me why I am here? What do you want? Is it money? That is easy," Chapel said through gritted teeth, attempting to get some control of the situation. Chapel noticed considerably less enthusiasm in Yusef's voice as the smile dissolved into a frown.

"This Chinese convinced us that taking you would greatly benefit our war against those who are killing my people."

Chapel slowly turned toward Li Chu, sending sweat streams rolling down his stiff neck.

"I didn't know you were connected to Western African Islamic groups."

"China has a significant amount of business in Africa, as you know," Li Chu said, taking a few steps toward Yusef. It was a tight fit between the scant furniture and the five men packed into the small space. "These businesses hire private military contractors for protection. Some of these PMCs have…relations…with the militias fighting the government."

"Relationships of convenience." Chapel looked from Li Chu to Yusef.

"Profitable relationships that help fund our goals." Yusef's face flashed pride for a second, then morphed into a scowl. "Money also to help the Muslim people ignored and beaten by the infidels—the people whose money you are taking—and others who flock here for our protection. That requires money."

"Through kidnappings."

"Highly profitable."

"Arms sales."

Another smile. "Yes. Weapons are bountiful here. They are always in great need here and across the borders."

Li Chu looked at Yusef.

"I would like to begin. Time is very important," Li Chu said impatiently.

Yusef gave Li Chu a death stare, and Chapel saw Li Chu, a trained assassin, flinch. Yusef abruptly turned and stepped toward the door. He stopped and set narrow, penetrating eyes on Chapel, and then, in a moment, he smiled and walked out with his guards trailing.

"Awful man," Li Chu said when they were alone. "But to get what I want, I needed him to get to you."

"What do you want?" Chapel asked as he wiped the sweat away from his face.

"A trade. You for Chen. I informed Foreign Minister Yi of MSS counterintelligence of Chen's deceit, but I have not heard that he has been arrested. I can only assume something has happened."

Chapel looked at Li Chu.

He doesn't know about the plane. Or Yi, Sun, or Chen.

"Do you know about the plane being shot down with Yi aboard?"

"What are you talking about?"

Chapel filled him in on all the events after Li Chu outed Chen. When he was done, Li Chu leaned against the wall with his head down and arms crossed as best as he could get them. Chapel continued.

"So, you see, swapping me for Chen will not work. He is probably dead."

Li Chu kept silent in thought and then looked up. His face was blank.

"No, I don't think he is dead. The CIA would not want that and would have plans to get him from the country. And Chen...he is too smart to allow himself to be killed or caught so easily. Even when I informed Yi, I knew he would get away. No. Chen is alive."

Li Chu looked at Chapel with an expression he recognized. Determination.

"You must get Chen, or it will not end well—for you.

36

RED JUMPSUIT

Chad Basin, Borno State, Nigeria

Sitting in his windowless room had warped Chapel's sense of time. The lengthening gray stubble signaled that another day had passed since the attack on the hotel.

He was tired and needed his meds. Elusive sleep mixed with his rising blood pressure, which, combined with stress and fatigue, created constant anxiety and depression. He wanted his freedom back.

The air was thick with heat, humidity, and the fumes from the bucket in the corner that served as the bathroom. The one aspect of captivity that was passable was the food. He liked Nigerian food, and whoever was in the kitchen knew their jollof rice and how to fry plantains.

He was sure his tactical teams were readying a rescue, likely in coordination with Hawkins and the CIA Special Operations Group. Together, that was a dangerous force, but he was being held in a remote location with a highly skilled, well-armed insurgent army surrounding him.

It would be a challenging mission…and could get me killed.

Nothing much had happened since Yusef's visit besides the same conversation of Li Chu pestering him about Chen.

"You will bring me Chen."

"How am I supposed to do that?'

Repeat. Repeat.

Chapel didn't move when the metal sounds of the door unlocking screeched in the cell. As he expected, Li Chu came in, but he seemed different. Excited?

"You will tell the CIA to bring Chen in exchange for you. If they decide to attack, then you will be killed." Li Chu pulled out Chapel's phone from his pocket. "Now. Do it."

"Why don't I just give you as much money as you want and disappear? Isn't that what Bridger and you agreed to? What do you and your jihadist friends want? One, five, ten million? Just say so. I am insured."

Li Chu looked at him. "I don't want money. I want Chen."

Chapel knew people. People were his currency. What motivated them? How to manipulate them. In his singularly myopic quest, Li Chu was proving difficult to control.

"Listen, Li Chu," Chapel stood and stepped toward the man, but Li Chu motioned him to sit. Chapel stopped walking but remained standing. "You are not innocent in everything that has transpired these past few years."

Li Chu fiddled with the phone, held it out to Chapel, looked toward the door, and whispered, "These Nigerians are not reliable."

But before Chapel could take the phone, the door to the cell slammed open. Four ISWAP men came in.

Two men grabbed Chapel by the arms.

"What is this?" Li Chu stepped toward them. One ISWAP guard pushed Li Chu back, sending him flopping to the floor like a rag doll.

"Take off your clothes. Put this on," another guard said. He tossed a red jumpsuit at Chapel. Chapel's only reaction was to look at Li Chu.

The third man shoved a pistol against Chapel's temple. Chapel started shaking and uncontrollably coughing.

"Faster!" The man backhanded Chapel across the face, snapping his head to the side. They held him to keep him from falling. The man raised his hand again.

Chapel flinched but did as he was told.

Yusef stood in the doorway looking pleased.

A small man in civilian clothing came in carefully carrying a canvas bag. They held up Chapel's arms, and the small man wrapped an ammunition vest filled with plastic explosives tight around his chest. Then he rolled sticky shipping tape around Chapel until it was secure and tight from his waist to his chest. He fashioned a thick red wire over the tape around his body. The man adjusted the wires, powered on a mobile phone, placed it in the vest pocket, and nodded toward the ISWAP men.

Chapel's face turned the color of the concrete walls. His eyes were wide, and he held his breath as if even that movement would set off the suicide vest. He stared with hate at Li Chu, who was in the corner of the room witnessing them wire Chapel with the explosives.

"Why?" Li Chu asked Yusef.

"If you want anything, you must show them you will kill to get it. Now they know I am serious."

Yusef walked to Chapel, who stood motionless.

"You are a nice man—but a dead man if I don't get what I want. If your government tries to rescue you with Navy Seals as it has done before, you are blown up. You are blown up if the Nigerian government tries to attack, which they know is foolish. If they don't do what I ask in the time I ask, you are blown up."

"You...won't...kill...me." Chapel focused on each word, momentarily regaining control, before he started shaking uncontrollably.

"I don't care about you—or him." He motioned a thumb toward Li Chu. "I will get what I want." He turned to Li Chu. "He will read this." Yusef handed him a piece of paper. "You ask for whatever you want. I don't care. If he does not read this and I don't get what I want, he is blown up, and you are shot. Follow me."

Chapel now felt the barrel of a pistol press against the back of his neck, causing him to stumble forward.

"Li...Chu," Chapel managed to blurt out as he found his balance.

Li Chu looked at the note, then at Chapel as he was led out the door. He scrambled past Chapel and his guard.

"You...you can't kill him!" Li Chu shouted as he seized Yusef's arm.

In a flash, Yusef whirled, breaking Li Chu's grip and grabbing his shirt.

Li Chu suddenly felt something hard against his cheek. His eyes flicked down to see Yusef's pistol. Yusef's face was glowering inches from Li Chu's. He could smell his horrible breath and felt drops of spit hit his face as the man whispered with total menace.

"I can kill anyone I want. Anytime I want."

37

I AM ALIVE

CIA Headquarters, Langley, Virginia

H awkins heard the crows cawing in the distance and felt the cold air rush into the room through the slightly open sliding door to his balcony. He usually liked to listen to the birds. *Crows are never a good sign.*

Hawkins liked his office and used it as a sanctuary, not from the world of intelligence–which constantly came through his door, across his desk, and via his computer. It was a sanctuary from all the other crap—like the attack on the Transcorp Hilton in Abuja.

It had led the global news headlines for two days, knocking the shootdown of the Chinese plane into the *no one cares about yesterday's news* slot.

International cable, traditional broadcast, and social media replayed the story hourly with a crawl across the lower screen running non-stop for the "breaking news." Nigerian and West African newspapers ran banner headlines.

They estimated the number of dead and wounded at 60 injured and 27 dead—so far.

Hawkins hated watching drone footage of the smoldering building repeating as news people recounted the same story. The same ambulances jammed the roads. The same emergency personnel rolled the wounded and closed body bags.

3-D and AI-generated images of the area recreated as much of the attack as was known. Hotel guests were interviewed. The hotel workers. Government and police officials. Tourists. Their clips were replayed with all the rest.

Then, a day after that, ISWAP's initial statement taking credit for the attack "by the soldiers of the caliphate" was released on social media, and terrorism "experts" appeared on programs to explain the spread of jihadism in Africa.

Then, the video was posted.

It started with the monotone chanting of a prayer in Arabic.

Yusef was dressed in black robes and pants with a black headscarf wrapped around his face. Six similarly dressed, heavily armed men stood at attention behind him, holding AK-47s tight across their chests. One waved the black flag of ISIS.

In front of all of them, two hooded men dressed in red jumpsuits were on their knees. One was wearing a vest filled with explosives.

Yusef started a long monologue on the fight against the Christians and every American president since George Bush with an inexplicable ranting passage on Abraham Lincoln.

His eyes never blinked.

"Our demands will follow."

On a signal from Yusef, a heavily uniformed soldier walked from off the screen, held a gun to the side of one hooded man's head. He tipped over and rolled to the ground.

The other hooded man was visibly shaking. The dark red blood splattered across his shoulders and hood.

Hawkins jumped to his feet.

"Shit! Shit!"

"For the safe release of the other man before me on his knees, these are my demands. Release of thirty brothers from the Kuje Prison. Four million American dollars...." Yusef kept rambling until the video suddenly ended with music and the waving ISIS flag.

Moments after the video's release, Hawkins's phone pinged. Hawkins snatched it up and opened the messaging app when he saw it was a text from Chapel's phone.

I am alive. Li Chu is here. Demands Chen. ASAP. VEST. ISWAP. Deliver $$ and prisoners. No rescues. Tell May. Hurry. Please. Danny.

"Li Chu," Hawkins said aloud. "That son of a bitch needs to die."

Hawkins walked through a set of double oak doors into his conference room where experts, analysts, special ops, and lawyers jammed into every chair.

He was looking for input, but he had already run the options.

Chen for Chapel wasn't even on the table—Chen was still on the *Mediterranean Gold* with May. Considering all the options, the only group who knew most of the actors, could get into Nigeria, get past the Nigerian government, get and hand over the cash, rescue Chapel, kill Li Chu, and get out safely in a matter of days was led by the last person Hawkins wanted to ask.

Hawkins went to the kitchen area, slathered some cream cheese on a bagel, and plopped it on a plate. He added a Danish. He skipped the fruit and poured some coffee into a mug. He turned to the conference table, pulled a chair away with his tree-trunk leg, set down the plate and coffee mug, and let gravity drop him in his chair.

"I've been in contact with the board of the Chapel group and officials," he started. "They are quite upset, as you might imagine. The insurance company wants to negotiate the price. Some want a full U.S. and Nigerian military response. Others want to bypass the Nigerians totally...which isn't the worst idea."

He picked up his bagel and looked around at the crowded table and the faces on the video screen.

"Roger. Stephanie. This is your show. Start."

The man to Hawkins's right—Roger, the DI's Africa Jihadist Movement expert—brushed the bangs of his cereal bowl-style haircut out of his eyes and pushed his glasses up his nose. He pushed a button and one of the side screens changed to show a close-up of Yusef dressed in white robes and a skullcap.

"Mr. Chapel was taken by some very bad people—the Islamic State of Iraq and ash-Sham – West Africa, ISIS-WA, aka the Islamic State West Africa Province, known as ISWAP. They were a faction of Boko Haram that broke off and pledged allegiance to ISIS. Yusaf didn't think BH was jihadi enough."

"Imagine that," Hawkins said as he licked cream cheese from his fingers.

"Yusef implemented ISIS's strict interpretation of sharia and replaced the regional governments with an Islamic state."

Stephanie, the Africa expert in the Counter Terrorism Center, took her turn. She moved her laptop closer and grabbed a mouse.

"ISWAP operates primarily in northeast Nigeria. The greater Lake Chad region but, as of 2022, they spread to other regions, including in and around the capital Abuja."

"No shit. I think that intel has been confirmed, don't you?" Hawkins said, too loud for the room.

Stephanie ignored Hawkins's comment.

"Since the split, ISWAP has been on a rampage. They have overrun dozens of military bases. Killed hundreds of soldiers, if not thousands. They govern the Lake Chad region near the border with a strict interpretation of Islamic law focusing on filling gaps in governance.

"Yusef's main tactics are the entire array of insurgency options. Ambushes and coordinated ground assaults. Hit-and-runs. Assassinations. Roadside bombs. Kidnappings…obviously."

"The State Department added them to the list of Foreign Terrorist Organizations in February 2018," interjected the man on the screen within the video box labeled STATE.

"Thanks for that, Gaylord. Good to know," Stephanie said, then continued.

"Interestingly, the kidnappings have been almost exclusively aimed at aid workers, Christians, and civilians who aid the Nigerian military. The man killed in the video was a member of a religious organization who was kidnapped a month ago. Taking Chapel is big—I mean *big*—step up to the kidnapping majors."

"Kidnappings are an excellent source of revenue. They also get funding from core ISIS and local sources and through extortion," Roger said. "Their ranks have swelled to over five thousand heavily armed, experienced fighters. ISWAP has small arms, machine guns, vehicle-mounted weapons, RPGs, mines, rockets, IEDs, armored vehicles, tanks, and drones. A lot of that which they capture in their raids."

"They have a "Caliphate Cadet School" for 8 to 16-year-old kids for indoctrination and military training," Stephanie added.

"We have satellite imagery of their major force concentrations. We are certain Chapel is in their stronghold area near Lake Chad," said a uniformed man in the box on the screen labeled PENTAGON.

"Enlighten me with your knowledge."

"We have successfully used small tactical special operations units —SEAL Team 6—to free hostages. The Chapel Group has private military personnel on contract," the uniformed man said.

"So, it is decision time, people." He stood and took out his phone. "Have your recommendation when I get back," Hawkins said. He dialed as he walked out the double doors to his office. "Peter? Where is Bridger?"

38

HELLO, HAWKINS

Kapalua, Maui, Hawaii

Bridger's dreams were intense. Runaway images of faces and places of Spy Devils missions. A suffocating array of death and near death. Booms of explosions. Unrelenting gunfire. Screams and more screams.

He awoke as he did every night, gasping for air, shaking, and sweating.

Lena grabbed him and soothed him as much as possible. No sleep came to them after that. They walked to the balcony and looked across the estate.

"Why not open a restaurant here?" Bridger asked without prompting.

"Here?"

"I mean somewhere in the U.S."

She didn't answer, and a long period of silence followed.

"I like it here," Bridger said finally, as he gazed at the 180-degree west-facing panorama of the Pacific Ocean. Lena wrapped her arm around his waist and titled her head on his shoulder.

"I can see why," she sighed, "since I also see a golf course nearby."

"What? There is?" Bridger looked around in circles. "Who put that there?"

Bridger's Kapalua five-acre, 12,000-square-foot estate on the island of Maui, overlooking the Pacific Ocean and Moloka'i, had fourteen rooms, a six-bedroom main house, and a two-bedroom guest house. A guard house sat at the beginning of the long, curvy driveway, with security fencing and other more advanced protections.

That morning, they walked to the back patio and pool area, where everyone gathered for the wedding.

After the ranch attack, then Austin, Mexico, New York, and Macau, the wedding of Milton and Beatrice was one of the rare moments when they could relax together and celebrate without worrying about outside interference.

Finally.

They were all there except May, who would miss the wedding. May and Chen should be arriving in Manila soon, if they had not already. Bridger expected her to call with an update on Chen and the next phase of his escape from China.

Milton and Beatrice had asked Bridger if they could be married at the Texas ranch and if he would officiate.

"Absolutely," he said, too stunned and excited before he realized his mistake.

"We just want to get a civil ceremony as soon as possible because anything can happen." Nerves brought out Milton's Alabama accent.

"Then, when we get some time, we will have something for our families," Beatrice said. "His are in Alabama. Mine are in Indiana."

Fast didn't happen. Delay did, and Bridger felt terrible. Nothing he could say would stop them from being on every mission.

"I want to see whales and dolphins," Imp said as he took labored steps toward the tile patio to sit by the long rectangular crystal blue pool.

"Let me toss you off the cliff," Demon said as he sat in one of the thick, red-cushioned chairs surrounding a glass table in the open space between the main room and the pool.

"Who are you?" Imp asked as he gingerly walked up to Demon and sat beside him.

"Get away, rat." Demon said.

"No, I mean, you *actually* look...good...you clean up well—for a man your age."

"I will kill you someday, and everyone will thank me."

"Oh, Demon, you proved your love for me in Mexico."

"Yep," Snake said. "You did."

Demon growled.

"I saw it too," said the groom, who was shaking, pale, and swaying from one foot to the other.

"You don't look too good, buddy," Imp said to Milton. "Hey, a bit of advice. If you are thinking about taking pictures of your—you know —" Imp pointed to Milton's crotch. "Don't. I mean it. It isn't cool. Voice of experience. Just warning."

"You are charming," Janelle said as she and Angel approached them.

Angel squeezed Janelle's hand tight as he looked through the retracted glass walls opened to allow the main floor rooms a view of the ocean.

"It's true." Imp looked toward a table covered with food. "I'm hungry."

Bridger flew Luciana and Luis from Santa Fe at the bride's request. Luciana stood in her finest dress by a table covered in her favorite dishes, wringing her hands. Luis was next to her, smiling in black pants, a white shirt, and his faded Dallas Cowboys hat on his head.

Bridger took some cards from his cotton pants and rifled through them. "I don't know what to say. I'm never nervous talking to drug dealers. I wrote some stuff, but it is all gibberish." He adjusted his loose-fitting cotton floral shirt.

"I am sure you will do fine." Dressed in a draped floral gown, Lena patted his arm and smiled. "Grow up."

"It's time," Bridger announced. He moved to the middle of the space made by the open walls of the main room and pool.

"Milton," Bridger said to the groom, standing in the back of the room. "Over here." He wiggled his finger for him to stand by him.

Milton nodded and took his place. Beatrice looked stunning in her opera silk dress in pearl white with a matching silk headpiece. Milton was not quite as attractive in his brownish suit.

Beatrice took her place next to him.

Bridger cleared his throat.

"We are here to witness the joining of two people we all know, although most of you don't know their real names." Laughter. "People we have stood by in some of the worst situations and some of worst people. Now, it is our turn to stand by them in a wonderful moment."

Nods all around.

"The world is a big, strange place—today proves that."

He looked right at Lena.

"Marvin. Donna. You have your own vows...I hope!" he continued. "Turn. Face each other. Marvin, you go first."

"Marvin?" Imp tried to whisper.

The sound of a helicopter and fast-moving cars filled the air. The helicopter landed quickly on the large, manicured, sloping lawn between the house and the ocean.

"Cars are coming up the road," Demon said, having run over to look out the front of the house. He pulled his Ka-Bar from the sheath on the back of his belt.

"You brought your knife to a wedding?" Angel asked.

"Why wouldn't I?"

Bridger looked at the team. No one besides Demon was armed.

"You got guns here?" Snake looked at Bridger as he ran to the food table and picked up the cake-cutting knife. The rest looked at him for an answer. He turned to see six men in tactical gear, fully armed and pointing at the wedding party, rushing out of the helicopter. They split and started coming up the stone steps on either side of the first level.

"Yes, but not this time. Everyone stay still. No fighting. Demon, put that knife away."

"Screw that." He raised it and took a stance, preparing to fight.
"Demon."

Demon stared at Bridger, then re-sheathed his knife.

"What happened to you?"

A man sprinted toward Bridger when another voice boomed through the room.

"It's okay, Sargent," Hawkins said as he entered the room.

"Hello, Hawkins."

"Hello, Bridger."

Hawkins sent his massive fist into the side of Bridger's head without breaking stride. Bridger flew and hit the tile on his back.

Lena screamed and stepped toward Bridger, who was rolling to his elbow, trying to get up. Janelle stopped her.

"What the—" Demon started to move, but an AR-15 in his face stopped him.

"Take him, and congratulations," Hawkins said toward Beatrice and Milton. With a glance to the rest and with a momentary pause at Angel, he turned to leave.

An assault team member zip-tied Bridger's hands and used it to pull him off the tile. The others still had their weapons in ready position.

"Tell me this is one of your plans," Demon said.

Bridger's woozy, bloody face turned to Demon and the rest of the stunned Devils.

"Pentacrest."

Demon's eyes widened.

"Great. Fan-fucking-tastic."

They watched the helicopter lift off into the orange sky of the Maui sunset. When it disappeared, they stood not knowing exactly what to do.

"Pentacrest?" Lena asked with a strong voice, blinking away tears.

"Pentacrest. It means we need to wait." Demon looked at Imp. "But we are to track him and be prepared to move."

Imp pulled out his phone and punched the keyboard. He wiggled with impatience as his eyes scanned the phone, looking for the tracker in Bridger's watch.

"Got him," he announced.

Demon turned to the Spy Devils, who were waiting for him to take charge.

"Now what?" Snake asked.

He took out his 1911 and racked a bullet into the chamber.

"We wait."

39

MANILA STATION

Manila, Philippines

"We are here," May told Chen as she looked out his cabin window. "What happens next—" she turned to Chen, who was sitting motionless on his bed recovering from a severe bout of seasickness, "—is officers from the local station will come onboard and take you."

Chen looked puzzled.

"Not Hawkins?"

"No. A high-ranking CIA official in Manila would attract attention. They will take us off and get us to a secure location."

Chen did not respond.

"What's wrong?"

"It is a good plan, but I am not certain I want to be handled by low-level officers."

It had been the constant conversation topic as they transited the South China Sea. Chen's second thoughts were a common factor for a defector.

Internal voices were asking if he had done the right thing. What did the future hold? Would he have the same power and stature he had at the MSS, or would he live in a CIA safe house, only to be let out as a showpiece when needed?

Chen had some Armageddon-sized leverage—the Dossier and the intel on Chinese networks in the U.S. On the other hand, Chen did not have the intel in hand. He had mailed it to a location he would not disclose.

Sure, Chen had a head filled with the most sensitive and valuable intel on China the CIA would ever collect. But, for Hawkins, the files containing the blackmail points for all of China's government, business, academic leaders, and others were the prize.

Under the *Mediterranean Gold's* no-communication conditions, Hawkins was unaware that Chen did not have that intel on him. Chen and May knew that when he found out, Hawkins would go crazy.

"Chen, remember why we started this decades ago," she said.

He looked at her with the corners of his thin lips curved slightly upward.

"I am not having second thoughts, May. But I appreciate your concern."

"Good," May walked toward Chen and sat on the bed next to him.

Chen looked at her just in time to see her stick the needle into his thigh.

She let him fall back onto the bed seconds later.

"Gilchrist," she said loud enough to be heard in the hallway.

CIA Manila Station case officer Adel Burge watched the *Mediterranean Gold's* agonizingly slow progress across Manila Bay as it was piloted into the International Port Basin at Barangay 20. Once secured, a frenzied army of dock workers with cranes and forklifts began to offload the mountain of shipping containers in the bright afternoon sun.

A few days before, Manila Station received a series of cables directly from the DDO. They alert the station of a high-value Chinese asset, accompanied by a CIA contact, who would be on the tanker. The Station was to locate the assets and relocate them to a secure location under the strictest security. The cable concluded with:

BE ADVISED OF POTENTIAL INCREASED MSS ACTIVITY. WILL ADVISE SOONEST OF NEXT STEPS. REGARDS.

Once the cables arrived, she queried her sources at the Port of Manila to be on the lookout for anyone who might be Chinese intelligence. Even that was no small task. It was a crowded port in a crowded city. The city of Manilla plus its metro area had grown to around twenty-two million people—making it one of the most densely populated cities in the world.

Burge and other station officers witnessed MSS personnel crawling over the massive port. Countersurveillance teams were scattered around the dock and the path out of the port. They would shadow the asset to the safe house, looking for MSS tails.

The Headquarters pukes were right this time—for once. This must be big, she thought.

When the gangway was secured and the frequency of people leaving the tanker decreased sufficiently, Burge led a team of four—two case officers and two vetted Marine Regional Security Officers from the embassy—onto the ship.

Burge and the team, dressed in civilian port official clothing, descended to the crew quarters deck and the cabin identified in the cables where they would find the asset. No one answered Burge's several knocks. She slowly opened the door.

"Hello? Mr. Shi? Karen?"

The cabin was empty.

Sun watched the CIA team board the ship from a distance. This was it, although it might be too late.

Through a process of elimination, reports from the surviving speed boat, military updates, and commercial databases, Sun was confident Chen was on a cargo ship heading to Manila called the *Mediterranean Gold*. He alerted the MSS resources in the area and boarded a plane.

Once the CIA had him, easily retrieving Chen was over. After the airplane incident, Sun could not fail, especially with Bridger's damning video still hanging over his head like a guillotine. Chen had to die.

Sun looked around at the locations the snipers had chosen to cover the ship's exits. He couldn't see them—so neither could the CIA. Then, he saw a confused CIA team walk off the ship. One was on the phone as the others were scanning the port area.

Where is Chen?

In the hectic movement around the ship, no one noticed a crate with "THIS SIDE UP" and "HANDLE WITH CARE" and corresponding symbols stenciled on the sides being lowered out a hull cargo door. No one reacted to a large hairy man and a smaller person in baggy crew clothing helping load it onto a flatbed truck.

They didn't know that an unconscious Chen was strapped to a cushioned zero-gravity chair or that the crate had been modified to support safe clandestine human transport.

A puzzled Sun looked at the confused CIA officers walking away from the ship.

Then Sun's phone rang.

40

TICK. TICK. TICK

Maui, Hawaii

"Y ou don't seem surprised that we came to your place to get you. Did Peter tell you we were coming?"

Bridger laughed as he gingerly touched the lump swelling near his left eye.

"Really? You didn't get me. I got you. I was tired of your *I want Bridger,* and *I need to talk to Bridger* whining. Pathetic. I gave you a chance at Wes' funeral. Three feet away from Deputy Woods. No clue."

Red rushed to Hawkins's face as he realized he had been fooled.

"It's a crime to attack a federal officer."

A few weeks prior, after Bridger returned from Amsterdam, where his mentor Wes Henslow was killed, Hawkins had tried to take over the Spy Devils by making them part of the CIA. Bridger refused, and after Hawkins's threats, Bridger tackled the huge man and knocked him out with gas from his Milton Stick.

"Boo-hoo. I have no intention of apologizing for that. Come on,

Hawkins. You are a big boy. The only way *you* could find me would be through people you know are connected to me." Bridger's mind flashed to Amsterdam. The rescue of Lena and May from their interrogations by Li Chu. "May. No way. Chapel? Nah. That leaves Peter Schaefer, who we affectionately call Angel. He is former CIA, so you have his address."

Hawkins sat back and folded his arms across this chest, a smirk on his face.

"Go on."

"I told Angel what I expected, how he should play it, and what to say. So—hocus pocus—you showed, and here we are. By the way, threatening a man's family—especially a Spy Devil—is wrong, even for you. And there must be a few federal laws that say you can't use the FBI or other government resources to kidnap and threaten a U.S. citizen."

Bridger looked around the small white conference room. He recognized a flag and some emblems on the walls.

"Is this the Maui Coast Guard Station? Hawkins. I'm impressed. How did you pull that off? Friends in the Pentagon?"

"Shut up."

Hawkins's expression turned into a face-load of anger.

"Tell me. Were you in any way involved in the attack on the ranch?" Bridger asked. He leaned back and laced his fingers behind his head. That kept Hawkins from seeing Bridger peel off a small flesh-colored patch glued to his wrist.

"What?"

"I want to know for certain who was behind the attack. Li Chu, for sure. Ramirez, of course. Chen? You? Anyone else?"

"Screw you."

Bridger could sense that Hawkins knew more, and he also knew that Hawkins would not voluntarily hand over or trade information. "I have something much more vital to talk to you about," Hawkins snarled.

"Wait. First, I've been told to be more forgiving, and I am trying, but in your case..." Bridger shot forward, flicked his hand towards

Hawkins's, and jammed a plastic needle about the length of a finger-nail into the top of his hand.

"What the hell?" Hawkins pulled away, clutching his hand. "What was that?"

"It is an extremely lethal little toxin that we whipped up. You might be dead in about," Bridger checked his watch, "four minutes—give or take."

"What? What the—? You're lying." Hate burned out of his eyes.

"Maybe, maybe not. If I'm not lying, you are okay. If I am telling the truth, your heart will seize up, and you will be dead in the next few minutes. If you talk, I can give you the antidote. Your choice. Roll the dice, Hawkins."

Realization slowly swept across his face.

"You...are lying."

"Fine. I'll wait." Bridger sat back, folded his arms, and stared at Hawkins. "This will be entertaining."

Hawkins tensed and started to rise from his chair.

"Sit down. Time is fleeting. Tell me what you know about the ranch attack."

"You have an antidote on you?" Hawkins asked as he sat back down.

"Maybe. Maybe not." Bridger checked his watch. "It is ticking closer to three minutes. How's your hand?"

Hawkins looked at the scratch, which was burning and turning red. He scratched. Licked his lips.

"Come on, Max. You will never find it in time. No way." Bridger tapped his watch. "Tick. Tick. Tick."

"Stop this crap. I planned on getting you here and beating you to a pulp, then arrest you, but now I need you to save Chapel."

"What?"

"Li Chu is holding him hostage in Nigeria," Hawkins grabbed his wrist and looked at the time on his watch.

"Why?"

"He wants Chen." Hawkins rubbed his now-swollen hand with more force.

Bridger didn't have time to process the news about Chapel, but he needed to know.

"Best laid plans…but, the ranch. Tell me."

"For hell's sake, Bridger!" Hawkins was sweating profusely now.

"Two minutes."

"Okay. Li Chu. Ramirez. Chen. I had nothing to do with it."

Bridger sensed some deception, but glancing at his watch, he reached behind his left ear.

"Where is it? I know we put it on. At least, I think we did."

"Come on, Come on."

Hawkins was standing already, with his hands out. Fingers wiggling.

Bridger brought his hand back in a fist. Hawkins grabbed at it and forced his finger open. His hand was empty.

"Surprise! No instant death for you. Just a pepper spray concoction."

Hawkins sat, stunned. Then anger took over as his fists balled up.

"No, you don't. You got one freebie." Bridger stood and grabbed Hawkins's wrist and twisted it over and down. Hawkins collapsed. "Thanks for warning us they were coming. Oh, that's right, you didn't." Bridger twisted it a little more, then released it.

"Guards!" Hawkins yanked his hand away as a guard rushed in, weapon drawn.

"Far enough," Bridger said.

Hawkins waved the man off as he lifted himself into his chair.

"Now, what about Chapel?" Bridger asked as he sat.

Hawkins took a moment to slow his breathing and regain some composure. His eyes fixated on Bridger. Hawkins rubbed his wrist.

"You are on the verge of ruining your get-out-of-jail-free card, you smug jackass."

"It's okay. It's forgiving time," Bridger held his hand out. Hawkins wavered, then took Bridger's hand and squeezed it, tightening the pressure of his grip.

"You done with the schoolyard games?"

Bridger waited stone-faced for Hawkins to release him, which he did.

Hawkins explained the events, who was involved, and the recommended responses. Bridger watched the video of Chapel three times.

"To say Chapel is in trouble is an understatement."

"You know Yusef?"

"No," Bridger said, with a mock look of shock. "You think I would associate with low-life terrorists like him?"

"Yes."

"You win on that one."

Hawkins flexed his hand and then showed Chapel's text.

"What the hell, Hawkins?"

"Go get Chapel. Kill Li Chu this time, okay?"

"Chapel for Chen isn't an option?"

"No," Hawkins said without hesitation. "Danny knows the game. Chen and the intel are once in a generation—"

"You mean career," Bridger interjected.

"Career. Generation. Whichever makes you happy. Bottomline, Li Chu is not getting Chen."

"Why us?"

"You know why you." Hawkins glanced at his hand, which seemed to be getting better.

Hawkins's phone rang. As he listened, he stood and took a step, and stopped.

"What?" His head whipped to look at Bridger. "Find him."

After disconnecting the call, he shoved his phone into his pocket. He walked to Bridger, who sat watching the spectacle.

"What's the matter, Hawkins? Lose something?"

"Bridger. I will stomp the living crap out of you until you tell me where Chen is."

"Relax, big boy. Take a chill pill, Max. It will be okay." Bridger stood. "I wanted to keep him for a while."

"What does that mean? Where are you going?"

"First, I have a couple to marry after you ruined their wedding day. Then, we have to go save Chapel, remember? Give me a ride back. Just think, Hawkins, you just made a deal with the Devil."

41

LEGEND

Moyock, North Carolina

Demon balked when he was told no personal weapons were allowed inside the massive state-of-the-art private training center—a high-tech complex used by the U.S. military, international governments, federal, state, and local law enforcement, and private corporations.

"For hell's sake. This is a *weapons* training center. Weapons!" Demon held up his Kimber 1911. "If I don't get this back—"

The all-business female security officer at the check-in area was unphased and appeared immune to the daily dealings with testosterone-laden males.

"Relax," Bridger said, unable to keep the grin off his face as he stood with Demon and Snake. They were inside the isolated "Special Visitors" entrance, constructed to allow certain visitors to avoid using the main gate to the compound.

"Don't worry, sir," she said, smiling as she took the pistol from Demon's hand and gave him a claim ticket.

"Grrrrr," he replied, sulking as they walked between the stone pillars of the main facility.

Discrete and isolated, the campus included tactical ranges, ballistic houses, scenario facilities, ship-boarding simulators, airfields and drop zones, K9 training, a three-mile tactical driving track, classrooms, a fast rope/rappel tower, multiple explosive training ranges, a training center, lodging, and other activity centers.

"Why, again, are we here?" Demon asked.

"It was part of the deal," Bridger answered.

"Deal with who?" Snake asked, tugging his too-tight sleeves around his biceps as he looked around at the massive training facility. "Don't get me wrong. I love any place where we get to shoot and blow things up."

"Amen, brother," Demon said. "Wish I had my gun."

Only three days had passed since Bridger's confrontation with Hawkins in Hawaii.

"I've told you guys. Chapel's board insisted that their Private Security Services Unit members are part of the extraction. They are here in Moyock," Bridger said, scanning the activity in some distance training course and hearing the constant snap of gunfire, "and about every other private security contractor, it seems."

"That's right, you said that, but I don't get why you agreed. It isn't like we haven't told others who begged to tag along with us to go to hell. When did you change your mind?"

Bridger stopped—his expression was a granite wall.

"When? When four of their guys fought to the death in Nigeria trying to protect their boss against an overwhelming force."

Demon placed his hand on Bridger's shoulder.

"Okay. I'm a grumpy old idiot. I'm all in."

"Ditto," Snake said, "on everything Demon said. I've been here before. Nice place."

"Hope they know what they are doing and don't get in the way," Demon added. "This mission is hard enough."

That was almost the same line Bridger used when he had briefed the team in Hawaii.

"How are you?" Lena had asked as she wrapped her arms around Bridger's neck when he returned to his Kapalua home after his confrontation with Hawkins.

"Fine." They kissed. "Lots to do."

Before the ceremony began, Bridger gathered the team in the main living room and told them everything about the encounter with Hawkins and the mission to save Chapel. When he was done, the only sound was the waves hitting the shore.

"This mission is hard. This is volunteer only."

"What?" They all asked. "When do we start?"

Bridger called to Beatrice and Milton over the blazing stone fire pit.

"Beatrice. Milton. I'm sorry about—everything," he said.

"Sorry?" Milton asked.

"About what? Today is our wedding day. Let's do it," Beatrice said.

So they did. After Bridger pronounced the husband and wife, they celebrated by eating Luciana's food, drinking, and swapping stories. After, Bridger split the Spy Devils, and then they left on their various missions.

Angel was taken off the no-fly list and sent west with the newly married Mr. and Mrs. Milton and Beatrice to meet with May. Snake, Demon, and Imp went east with Bridger.

"What about me?" Lena asked.

"You...need to help May when she gets here." She smiled.

Endless secure calls with Hawkins and the Chapel Board of Directors occurred on the flight east to North Carolina. Imp had been sent on a "treasure hunt" trip to Chapel's headquarters in New York when they arrived.

Inside a large stone and wood building, they walked into a room that appeared to serve as a bar and a rec center. To one side, two rows of four classroom tables with two chairs each per side faced a wall with a smartboard, TV screens, and blackboard. A podium was placed to one side.

Seven tough-looking men dressed in khaki tactical pants, black shirts, and boots sat on the tables, in backward chairs, or stood talking. Each was around six feet tall. Tan. Bearded faces.

"Gentlemen," one of the men said, alerting his men of the approaching visitors.

Talking became mumbling as they watched the strangers cross the room to the podium.

One man walked up to Bridger and shook his hand. "Bridger. I'm Hawk, team leader." He turned and pointed. That's Eagle. Vulture. Buzzard. Falcon. Owl. Kestrel. Kite."

"Really cute, ladies. At least the tall guy ain't named Shorty and the fat guy Slim," Demon said.

"Who the hell are you, old man?" Eagle asked, moving toward Demon with a posture he used to convey that he was dangerous and a threat.

Demon looked down and turned his head up to show an emotionless face. He put his hands in the pocket of his jeans and strolled up to Eagle, who had three inches and at least forty pounds on Demon.

"I'm Demon, asshole," he said matter-of-factly, flashing his scruffy graying eyebrows up and down.

All talking stopped among the Chapel team.

"Demon? You...you are Demon?" Eagle asked, taking steps backward like he had just seen a ghost. The tough man had turned into a wide-eyed kid.

"You are him? For real?"

"Yeah. So what?" The attention tugged on Demon's self-defense triggers.

"I suggest backing off, Eagle," Hawk, the leader, said with a broad smile on his bearded face.

Eagle instead raised his hand out and stepped toward Demon.

"Demon, sir. This is an honor and a privilege, sir. May I shake your hand?"

"Su-re?" Demon looked confused as he took the hand and shook it.

"What's going on?" Snake asked.

Bridger shrugged.

The rest of the team encircled Demon, acting like kids trying to get a glimpse of their favorite celebrity. Words and phrases came from the awe-stuck group.

"Are you really him?" "I can't believe it." "Spy Devils." "Legend."

"I'm a rockstar," Demon said over his shoulder to Bridger and Snake as he shook hands and started to chat.

"Can I get a selfie?" Falcon asked, holding up his phone. Others did the same.

Demon looked at Bridger.

"It's up to you."

"Okay. Make it fast. We have work to do." Demon posed with each man as they approached with their phone in selfie mode. They smiled. Demon frowned.

"Who would have thought?" Snake looked at Bridger, who was enjoying the adulation his oldest friend was receiving.

"We need to get started, gentlemen," Bridger said as he checked his watch.

Hawk got his men to sit at the tables, and a Bridger took a position in front of them.

"Maybe they aren't too bad after all," a strangely beaming Demon said as he sat with Snake.

Heads turned as Roger and Stephanie, the CIA analysts, walked into the room.

"Good, you are here," Bridger said, then made the introductions.

"As you might have determined, we are going into Nigeria, killing as many ISWAP terrorists as possible, and leaving with Chapel. All of this has to happen in just a few days."

Smiles and high-fives between the team members followed that announcement. Their attention on Bridger became absolute. The air took on the heavy weight of seriousness of purpose.

"We are receiving complete cooperation from the CIA. Transportation. Up-to-date intel, including satellite imagery. Intel and reports from area experts on ISWAP and the Nigerian government. Bio rundown of Yusef and Nigerian government officials who we might run into. Roger and Stephanie are experts on our targets and will give you the latest intel."

The CIA analysts briefed the team for an hour on anything that might matter to the mission, including the latest satellite images.

"I reiterate. Their government isn't being too supportive," Roger said. "They are embarrassed as shit about the Chapel situation." Roger looked around at the fully attentive eyes.

"What's the status of releasing the prisoners?" Eagle asked.

"That's still in the negotiations, but it is a stall. They have no intention of releasing them," Stephanie said.

"I am not afraid of assaulting a Nigerian prison," Kestrel said.

"That's not in the plan." Bridger looked at Roger and Stephanie, thanked them, and asked them to leave.

When they were alone, Bridger stood before the team.

"That is what those CIA analysts know. Now I am going to tell you everything they don't know. It is beyond top secret, but if we risk our lives together, you deserve to know everything."

When Bridger was done, the mission began.

Chad Basin, Borno State, Nigeria

Li Chu was unhappy.

He was in humid and hot Africa among hundreds of jihadist terrorists.

If he had his Dragon Fire team, he would not have had to use Nigerian jihadists to complete his mission. But Bridger and his Spy Devils eliminated them—with the help of Chapel and, most certainly, Chen.

He wanted to get out.

Chapel needed to pay for his assassination attempt in New York and his support of Chen with the CIA.

And Chen needed to pay for—everything.

That meant Li Chu needed to expose Chen to destroy his value as a double agent. That meant a brutal attack on a luxury hotel to use Chapel as leverage if Chen escaped—which he knew he would. He didn't anticipate Sun shooting down a plane with Yi onboard. That was tragic—but that was all it was.

Li Chu also didn't anticipate Yusef adding prisoners and so much money to Li Chu's demands. It only worsened when Li Chu voiced his unhappiness about the situation to Yusaf.

"If you are not happy, I am sorry. You can go."

Li Chu could taste Yusef's condescending attitude.

Yusef kept Chapel's phone from Li Chu, which irritated him, as he was never updated on the status of the negotiations.

"I don't care about your feelings, except—" he grinned a toothy grin "—I have good relations with many Chinese companies who pay me not to raid their investments. I would hate to lose any support because I killed—you." Yusef looked with total disregard like Li Chu was today's garbage that needed to be tossed.

A man walked up to Yusef and handed him a note. He read it and beamed at Li Chu.

"We have a deal."

Yusef stood and started to walk away.

"Who? What? Did they mention Chen?" Li Chu shouted at his back.

He didn't receive an answer.

42

COLIN POWEL

Abuja, Federal Capital Territory, Nigeria

As the massive black Range Rover pulled through the gates of the Jabi Art and Craft market in Abuja's central district, Bridger scanned the crowd, looking for his friend.

The market consisted of a menagerie of tree-lined rows of traditional round and brown huts with thatched roofs and wooden windows. Crammed into the space were endless rows of tin, brick, or open-air shacks overflowing with pottery, trinkets, carvings, dolls, chessboards, fabrics, beads, and other dusty African motif items. Incongruously wedged among the hordes of sellers and tourists were upscale buildings housing art galleries with works of professional artists and sculptors.

When the SUV stopped, Bridger, Demon, Imp, and Snake got out and stood on the dusty concrete slab that served as a parking area. They were immediately approached by a crowd of men dressed in tight polo shirts, shorts, and flip-flops. Each man assumed a broad smile, revealing a spectrum of dental issues.

"Sir, sir," they yelled. Their hands and arms gestured, imploring the Americans to notice and choose them to escort the visitors through the sprawling village shopping area—for a fee.

"Shopping? Great. I still need to buy the happy couple a wedding present," Imp said. He walked up to Demon. "You got any money?"

"Stay with us, Imp," Snake said.

"Why?"

"We are here because Chapel was *kidnapped. Kidnapped.* Get it?" Bridger said, scanning the faces in the crowd.

"And we are being followed. We have been since the airport. Four guys," Snake added.

Imp's head scanned left and right.

"I think I will stay with you guys," Imp said, stepping closer to Demon.

"Good plan," Bridger said.

I needed the laugh.

"Colin Powel," Bridger said to the group. Frowns instantly replaced smiles when they realized they would not get any business from the new arrivals. As a group, they turned away, disappointed, and started chatting in various languages. Bridger recognized English but was rusty in identifying all the native languages. He heard Hausa, Yoruba, and Igbo for sure.

"Maybe he isn't here," Demon said. "Or they don't know him."

"Colin will be here, and they know him. Everyone knows Colin Powel."

Bridger met the young man several years ago, early in the Spy Devils' existence, while exposing Nigerian elections corruption. He had found Colin easygoing and discovered he knew everything about everyone in Nigeria, with access to seemingly every corner of Nigerian society.

"Call me Colin Powel," the Nigerian had said.

"Why?"

"It is my name."

Bridger had called Colin when he knew he was going to Nigeria and told him what he needed. Colin reassured him everything would be available.

The Chapel rescue was imminent, and negotiations were underway on when and where to swap with ISWAP before they left. By the time the Devils and the seven-man security team landed on Chapel company-supplied aircraft at Nnamdi Azikiwe International Airport, Abuja, Hawkins informed Bridge the deal was set—for the next day.

Bridger left his plane with the Asia mission Spy Devils team with instructions to check in continually on their progress. He wasn't too worried about them. Since Nigeria was an unplanned, dangerous operation, he didn't want Lena with him. There was no role for her here. With May and Gilchrist and support from 'The Unemployables,' Lena should be safe.

It should work out. Should...

When they arrived, the Chapel team made their way to their Colin Powel-supplied, guarded compound near Wuse, an upscale area across town northwest of the city. Their primary duty was to protect the suitcases full of one-hundred-dollar bills they brought on the plane and to prep for the exchange.

Bridger and the rest went to meet Colin.

"Colin. Powel." Bridger repeated the name louder while holding a twenty-dollar bill over his head. A smaller man jumped a few times and laughed, trying to snatch it from Bridger's hand. Bridger pulled it back each time with a laugh of his own.

"Please get him."

The small man sulked, turned, and jogged away.

Snake took a few steps toward a shop displaying a variety of crudely hand-made knives. The men crowded around him like they had Bridger.

"No," he said firmly.

He was at the hut when the small man returned. He rejoined the others.

Bridger handed the smiling little man the money when the familiar wide smile of Colin Powel walked up to him.

Colin looked like a fourteen-year-old kid, but Bridger thought he was in his mid-twenties—thirty, tops. He was barely five feet tall and a twig-thin one hundred pounds. He wore a green tank top and soccer shorts. Radiating genuine warmth and happiness, he took Bridger's hand and shook it with his pipe-cleaner-thin arms.

"Mr. Bridger!"

"Colin. Good to see you."

His eyes beamed at Demon.

"Mr. Demon. Are you still an evil and mean man?" he joked, giving Demon a playful jab into his midsection.

"Yes," Demon said, only partially playing along.

"Yes," Colin retraced his arm back to his narrow chest.

Bridger folded his arms and nudged Snake in his ribs. "Watch this."

"Every time we are here," Demon said with impatience. "Can we get on with this?"

"Relax, Demon. Take a second to admire his genius."

"Colin." Knowing what was coming, the little man glinted at Bridger.

"Des Moines," Bridger said.

"Capitol of the State of Iowa. The Hawkeye State. Very easy."

Puzzled, Snake looked at Bridger.

"He knows every capital of any state, country…anything. And their history."

"Really? Hey, Colin. Vanuatu," Snake said, challenging Colin.

"Port Vila. Located on the isle of Efate. Located by James Cook in 1774."

Snake slowly turned to Bridger, who grinned at a beaming Colin.

"Show's over. Colin. You have what I asked for?"

"Yes. Follow."

They followed Colin, weaving through tourists as they walked down uneven dirt rows of open open-air shops. As they walked, many shop owners waved and shouted at Colin, begging him to bring his guests to their establishment.

"We have an issue," Snake said, soon after starting to follow Colin.

"The men who are following?" Colin asked without looking back.

"Yep," Snake nodded to Bridger.

"Colin?"

"There are four of them."

Colin waved his hand toward a group of men who ran over and huddled around him. They spoke briefly, and then they scuttled away.

"Do not worry. It is taken care of," he told Bridger.

"I'm in," Snake said. Bridger nodded to Colin, who nodded back.

"Do not worry."

They entered a corrugated steel shack that served as a small bar. A few mismatched tables were randomly placed in the irregularly shaped space. A humming ceiling fan spread the dust and smells from the open window around the space.

"Jol!"

A large woman with a white peasant blouse and a sizeable flower-pattern skirt approached Colin and hugged him to her ample bosom. When she released him, she gave her visitors a critical looking over.

"Colin. Sit," Jol said, indicating the only table that could handle the four men. She returned and set sweating pint bottles of Red Star beer in front of each man.

"Twenty-five thousand Naira," Jol said, unconcerned she was over-charging for the beer.

"That's fair." Bridger handed her fifty thousand, the equivalent of around sixty-five U.S. dollars. "Keep it."

Jol smiled and stuffed the bills in her cleavage. Snake took a beer and stood by the door. He twisted the top and took a long swallow. He checked and read the label. He raised his eyebrows and took another swallow.

Bridger watched Colin caress his beer with the tips of his fingers like it was the first he had ever had. He licked his lips and took a sip. Then another. He closed his eyes as he swallowed. That large smile appeared on his face again.

"Now, Colin," Bridger said.

He smiled.

"Jol."

The woman walked over and set a thumb drive on the table. "Everything you need."

"Not everything."

"Yes. That is waiting for you." A few of Colin's men came in and motioned to him. "But first, I have gifts."

Bridger pocketed the drive and followed Colin across a few rows of shops to a tin hut. A few of Colin's men were outside guarding a door that squeaked open. Inside, four men lay motionless on the dirt floor.

Colin bent over and examined them. He knelt, grabbed one by the hair, and raised the head off the ground.

"This is Ahmed. He is an officer in the Nigerian Defense Intelligence Agency." He dropped Ahmed's head to the dirt with a *plump.* "These three men work for him." He looked at Bridger as he stood and smiled. "They will not be following you any longer."

43

WE ARE COMING

Lake Chad, Borno State, Nigeria

"Hello, Li Chu," Bridger said when the call finally connected.

"Bridger? Bridger? I…don't want you anywhere near me. Leave. Don't call me again." Once Yusef was satisfied that his deal was set, he gave Li Chu Chapel's phone to work on his negotiations for Chen.

"I have Chen," Bridger lied before Li Chu could disconnect the call.

"You are lying," Li Chu said hesitantly. "Let me speak to him."

"You are going to have to believe me."

"I must talk to him, or there is no deal."

"You have trust issues. Hang on." Bridger handed the phone to Imp, who plugged it into his laptop. He clicked a few keys on the deep-fake audio processing software.

"This is a grave mistake, Li Chu. Taking Chapel as a hostage," Chen's voice said into the phone as Imp typed.

There were seconds of silent hesitation.

"I told you I would expose your treachery, Chen."

"Another mistake," Imp typed.

Bridger unplugged the phone and took it from Imp.

"Now let me talk to Chapel."

"Wait." Li Chu had a guard unlock Chapel's cell. "They are coming with Chen," Li Chu said as he walked in.

Conditions had gradually declined for him as each day passed. Chapel was sitting on his bed, still wearing the blood-stained red jumpsuit, which reminded him of the terror of being on his knees with a gun to his head. He hadn't recovered from that. Chunks of tape were still stuck to the suit, left behind from removing the suicide vest.

His eyes were puffy from allergies to whatever was in the air, causing them to itch and water. His lungs felt like he was breathing in chunks of concrete. He had been religious in taking his medications but now he had gone days without anything. Anxiety. Depression. High blood pressure. Allergies. Prostate.

Li Chu handed Chapel the phone. A shaky hand took it and placed it to his ear.

"Hello?"

"We are coming, Danny. Hang on."

"You...took...your time."

Bridger was surprised by how weak he sounded. His voice was a whisper. He sounded sick. Bridger heard sounds over the connection.

"Chapel?"

"Bridger," Li Chu said. "Any of your tricks and Yusef will kill Chapel and then all of you."

"After that, he will kill you. We are in this together," Bridger said before he hung up.

———————

Colonel Musa of the Nigerian Defense Intelligence Agency was working late, waiting for the report from Ahmed, which was also late.

Musa knew caution was required when following the Americans Spy Devils, so he was patient.

Tomorrow was a big day.

He had taken calls from the CIA's Max Hawkins himself, who told him of the famous team's presence. The President of Nigeria called, as did the Lieutenant General of the Army, and Musa's superior, the Director of the Nigerian Defense Intelligence Agency.

"We will not release prisoners. The approved plan is for our special forces to take the place of the prisoners," his director said. "When they arrive, you will attack. Kill Yusef."

"And the Americans?"

"Do not let them get in your way," the Director said before he hung up.

He stood and stretched. His office was in the Nigerian National Defense complex—a cluster of massive primary and black-painted block buildings that looked like a child pieced together mismatching Legos. Despite his rank, the office was small, with a semi-circular desk and a few chairs for visitors. Maps of the country were hung on the walls with colored push pins dotting the image.

His mobile phone rang, and he was pleased to see "AHMED" in the caller ID.

"Ahmed, report."

"Colonel Musa?" the cheery, unfamiliar voice asked.

"Who is this?"

"Hey, buddy. I'm sorry, Ahmed cannot provide you with any information tonight. Maybe tomorrow, either," the voice said.

"What?"

"Look out your window."

Musa walked to his window and saw his four men unconscious in the parking area.

"They aren't dead. Please *don't* get in our way. Have a nice day."

Musa was already out of his office and running down the steps. He went through the exit door and ran to the men. He checked. They were alive. Musa saw a card on Ahmed's forehead. He picked it up and read…*Greetings from the Devil.*

44

LAKE CHAD

Lake Chad, Borno State, Nigeria

Bridger was still awake when Vincente's texts arrived at 4 a.m. *Why sleep when I know the dreams will wake me up?* Not sleeping was a better alternative than the nightmares coming more often and with greater intensity.

VR: I do not think you are taking me seriously.
B: Leave me alone. I made a deal. I will get to it.
VR: Australia? Were you lying?
B: There was a change in plans.
VR: Change them back.

Bridger looked out the window at the lights of Abuja. It was a busy and dangerous day. He was tired and didn't need a crazy cartel murderer telling him…anything.

VR: You remember Antonio?

A picture came next of a bruised and bloody face of Antonio.

VR: Antonio has value. I won't kill him. Yet.

Bridger knew that whatever came next would not be good for someone. The images of the dismembered body of Momo that arrived next proved him right.

VR: Unless the Chinese die, Antonio's wife, daughter, and mother are next. Then that woman Lena.\

Bridger's fingers shook as he typed.

B: I told you I would kill you.

He waited for a reply. It didn't come.

"Twenty minutes," Bridger heard Snake say through the helicopter's headphones as they flew over Lake Chad's brown and green shrub-covered terrain—ISWAP's stronghold.

"You know this, like everything else you've done lately, is going to explode," Demon shouted into the microphone.

"It is a good plan. What are you talking about?" Bridger asked from the seat next to Snake.

"We land in a terrorist lair. Hand over a few million dollars. Oh, and the Nigerian military, which you have managed to piss off, is not the most reliable group."

"Face-to-face with terrorists? Can I stay here?" Imp asked.

"No."

"That's okay. I'm going to barf anyway," he said as the helicopter swayed.

"You barf, we toss you," Hawk said.

"I like these guys," Demon said, giving the Chapel team leader a thumbs up. They were in the cabin of the green and brown camo Nigerian military Bell 412 helicopter Colin somehow procured.

A few hours before, Hawkins had called with the final agreements negotiated with the Nigerian government and ISWAP on the three demands for Chapel's release.

The money issue was resolved quickly and easily. The insurance company agreed to the four-million-dollar ransom figure. Magically, heavy duffle bags of cash were waiting on the plane for the trip to Nigeria.

From Hawkins's point of view, the Chen issue was easy to negotiate. They couldn't have him. Plus, Hawkins didn't have him.

"I assume since you don't have Chen, you are killing Li Chu?" Hawkins asked.

"Don't worry, I have that covered," Bridger told him.

"You had better. When this is over, I want Chen, or you are going to prison—if you survive," Hawkins said.

"Love you, too, Hawkins."

And I decide what is going to happen. This is my world.

The release of prisoners was a demand out of their control, which required the State Department's involvement to resolve.

"The Nigerians have agreed to let the prisoners go—although they were quite upset about their men being attacked by you," Hawkins told Bridger. "We made some significant military assistance promises, thanks to you."

"No idea what you are talking about," Bridger said.

"They are flying them up to Maiduguri and convoying to the swap point. That's at least a four-hour drive."

"You believe them? Because I don't," Bridger said.

"It is what State says they have agreed to do."

"Well, if State says so, then I will relax."

The Spy Devils and the Chapel team met in a hangar at the Abuja Airport to prepare for the mission.

"How are they able to communicate from Lake Nowhere?" Demon asked.

"Do not underestimate these guys. They have quite a sophisticated communication system," Imp said. "They have to spread their propaganda and communicate with the other jihadist groups in their *Caliphate*. Colin's research shows that they are pretty tech-savvy. Satellite, mobile phones, and IED-style drones are all the rage in the terrorist playbook."

"Impressive," Snake said.

"I hope the Chapel guys aren't trigger-happy."

"Don't worry about them," Demon said in their defense. "They are pros."

Bridger looked at him.

"Hawk. Your *main* role until we get there is to be Fort Knox." Bridger motioned at the two large, shiny diamond-plate suitcases already inside the helicopter. "If we need you to shoot someone, shoot them."

"Understood."

"So, let's go meet them," Demon said. "I mean," he gripped an AR-15, "shoot them."

From the air, the area was an extreme contrast of browns of the land and dark green dots of brush and trees—swampy dark blue water and the tans of reed beds. White and gray gulls flew over the dull colors of a checkerboard of boats floating around small islands. Black and white smoke from villages and random gatherings of people.

Bridger knew the Lake Chad basin was home to over thirty million people carving out a living of farming, herding, and fishing. A shrinking lake and widespread poverty, combined with the humanitarian crises caused by the years of extremist insurgent fighting, had displaced millions of people.

Displaced people. Humanitarian crisis.

"We're here," Snake said from the pilot seat, as he hovered before descent. He pushed a button releasing the two Devilbots Snake attached to the underside of the helicopter before they left. "Bots away."

"Imp?" Bridger asked.

"Good signal," he said from his seat in the helicopter surrounded by laptops and electronic gear. "We will control the skies."

Snake brought the Bell down in a field marked by a cloud of swirling yellow smoke. It wasn't until they were on the ground that Bridger spotted the dozens of heavily armed men standing next to several nearby vehicles.

"Keep it running," Bridger told Snake.

"I read one drone hovering. I will EW that little sucker when told," Imp informed them.

"Colin? Convoy?" Bridger asked into his comm.

"Perhaps thirty minutes out," Colin reported. "They made the switch as you said they would. I sent the video to your phone as proof," Colin said.

"Great. Thanks," Bridger replied.

The Chapel tactical team rushed out and took positions crouched around the helicopter.

A small but formidable fighting force, each wore a desert tiger-stripe uniform and carried their standard gear. An MBITR radio. Body armor. M203 grenade launcher with a half-dozen 40mm rounds. Frag grenades. Glock 19 pistol. Garmin GPS. Strobe light. Folding knife. Thuraya satellite phone. Helmet.

Bridger insisted that all the Spy Devils team wear body armor and carry a weapon. No one declined, although Imp made his case to stay in the helicopter with Snake.

"Take care of me, big fella," Imp told Snake.

"I'll be busy," Snake snapped back without a drop of humor.

Even from fifty yards, Bridger saw the seasoned ISWAP fighters, armed from head to toe with every kind of weapon, were ready to do battle.

Yusef stood tall and confident with a semi-circle of a dozen men behind him armed with AK-47s and rocket launchers. Behind them were camouflaged armored trucks with machine guns mounted.

He saw guards around Li Chu standing outside the group.

Where is Chapel? If he is dead…we are all dead.

Bridger moved forward. Demon was at his side with his weapon raised. Three members of the tactical team carried the silver cases behind them. The others flanked and approached with their guns sighted on the several dozen armed terrorists with their weapons pointed at them.

"Anything can happen. Be ready," Bridger said, realizing how nervous he was feeling. An image of Lena's face flashed in his mind. He blinked to refocus on the terrorists now just a few yards away.

"Mr. Bridger," Yusef stepped forward. Not smiling. Not frowning.

They didn't shake hands.

The kind of tension weighed down on everyone where a twig snap or a misinterpreted hand movement could lead to disaster.

"Okay. We are here. Let's get this done. I have a tee time," Bridger said.

"Where is Chen? You said you had Chen," Li Chu yelled, pushing toward Bridger and Yusef.

"Hey, Li Chu. I canceled my deal with you, and I lied about Chen." Bridger shrugged. "You shouldn't have taken Chapel."

"Kill them. Kill them." Li Chu spun and shouted at Yusef. "Give me a weapon."

Yusef watched Li Chu try to rip a rifle from a guard. The guard swung an elbow that connected with Li Chu's jaw, sending him corkscrewing to the ground.

"Can I deal with him first?" Bridger looked at Yusef for permission and then at Li Chu moaning in the dirt.

"Yes, take care of him." Bridger nodded toward Li Chu.

"Demon."

"Gladly," he said, as he pulled out his Kimber. He moved toward Li Chu who was struggling to his feet.

Oh, damn!

"Don't kill him!" Bridger shouted.

"Son of a bitch." Demon holstered his weapon, pulled a Devil Stick from his belt, and pointed it at Li Chu's face.

"No," he cried, wrapping his face into his good arm.

Demon released a cloud of spray. Li Chu choked, fell to the hard dirt again, rolled, and then was silent. Then Demon changed the stick's setting to stun mode, jammed it into Li Chu's neck, and held it there for a second. His head rattled against the hard dirt as his saliva shot everywhere like a drooling dog's.

"Oopsies," Demon said as he smiled, grabbed Li Chu by the foot, and dragged him toward the helicopter.

"I like that weapon. May I have one of those?" Yusef asked Bridger.

"No."

Bridger looked at his watch.

"You have an issue to deal with. A convoy of trucks is coming."

Yusef looked at Bridger with a puzzled expression.

"Issue? My observers confirmed that our brothers in prison were released and flown to Maiduguri. They are on their way."

"Um...well...sort of...no. You missed the double-cross part. The government replaced the truck carrying your men with one filled with Nigerian special forces. Here. Look." Bridger held up his phone and took a step forward. All the ISWAP weapons swung to point at him.

Bridger waggled the phone at Yusef, who stepped forward, took it, and watched Colin's men's video of the trucks being switched. He handed the phone back to Bridger and motioned to a man who ran over. Yusef spoke to him, then he ran off.

"We will be ready."

"You are welcome for the warning," Bridger said with his hands up in mock frustration. Yusef said nothing. "Okay, fine. Can we get Chapel...please?"

Moments later, a stoop-shouldered Chapel shuffled into view flanked by two well-armed terrorists.

When Bridger saw Chapel, he felt...pity. For better or worse, Bridger had been in a love-hate relationship with Chapel, who was an arrogant prick, but was overall a loyal arrogant prick—and he had been a good friend to May and Henslow.

That's Chapel? One of the most powerful men in the world? He's an old man.

"Bridger." Chapel fell into Bridger's arms. "Thank you."

"You stink worse than May did." Bridger patted his back, referring to when he rescued his mother in Amsterdam. "You are welcome."

"Take him to the helicopter. Li Chu, too," Bridger said.

Several Chapel team members grabbed him and gently helped him to the idling helicopter.

"My money," Yusef said, eyes gleaming at the cases.

Bridger motioned for the cases to be brought forward and set on the ground between Bridger and Yusef.

"Four million. For your troubles."

Yusef motioned for his men to take the cases.

Explosions rumbled in the distance, and all motion in the gathering stopped. A radio in an ISWAP tactical truck started to belch static and screams. A man grabbed a handset and listened. He yelled back, dropped the phone, and ran to Yusef.

"The government ambushed our troops!" Yusef shouted, seething through his teeth.

"Yes. I know it gets confusing. I'll go slow. We warned Colonel Musa—a nice guy—that I was warning you so he could ambush your ambush. Make sense?" Bridger shrugged. "Sorry."

Yusef glared at Bridger, then yelled at his troops, who advanced and formed lines, their weapons on the Americans.

"Before you revert to your base instincts and kill me, I should warn you that these cases are special. They cannot be opened without the code. If you try, they explode."

"Do you think I am a fool?"

Bridger stood still and silent at first.

"Don't set me up with lines like that. As I was saying, I have experience with these cases. So does Li Chu. You notice his scars?" Bridger thump pointed toward the cases. "Boom."

Yusef stepped back.

Bridger guessed correctly that Chapel, who knew a good thing when he saw it, had the U.S. company Kirkwood, which developed the cases, make some for him. Created to protect the Hillcrest device during their Ukraine operation, the biometrically secure case contained, among other things, a lining of C-4 and a self-destruct option. Bridger had sent Imp to New York City to retrieve the cases.

Finally, Bridger spoke. Slow and steady.

"Understand this," Bridger said, speaking slowly and steadily. "The cases can only be opened by the approved person. If not, they explode. That's what Li Chu tried. But this is your lucky day. I will set it so you are the approved person."

Yusef stood silently, and Bridger wondered if he fully understood the situation.

"Show me."

"Okay. Good." Bridger put a case flat on the ground in front of Yusef. "Look. Just punch a code into the cases. They will open." Bridger quickly placed his thumb on a pad, causing a digital screen to show a keypad. He entered the code and opened the case. Inside were neat stacks of one-hundred-dollar bills. He opened the second case filled the same way.

Yusef's eyes gleamed.

"Cool, huh?" Bridger closed the lids and pushed some buttons. Here is the code." He handed Yusef a card.

"It is ready for me?" Yusef asked.

"Yes."

As Yusef turned to his men, a distant buzzing overhead stopped. A few seconds later, the ISWAP drone crashed to the ground. Then a Devilbot buzzed down and strafed a line of ISWAP fighters, spraying gas in every direction like a sprinkler.

In seconds, ten of Yusef's men were sprawled on the ground gasping for air and rubbing their eyes. The others stood paralyzed, waiting for orders.

As Yusef comprehended what happened, the other Devilbot hovered by his head from the right side, and the first hovered joined it and pointed at the left side of his head.

"Let me do it," Demon said, with his Kimber 1911 pointing at Yusef.

"Wait. Yusef. These drones are pointing several 9mm bullets at you....in addition to Demon's 45. If you decide to do something stupid, thinking you can kill us and walk away with the cases, you will be shot in the head. Got it?" Bridger waited, then asked again. "Got it?"

"Yes," Yusef said, nodding and looking at Bridger with a facial expression worse than hatred. "I will kill you."

"If I had a nickel for everyone who...anyway, we are leaving. Snake!"

The helicopter blades started to rotate faster, sending a wave of dirt and debris at them.

Bridger and the team quickly retreated to the helicopter. The Devilbots covered their retreat. The moment Imp brought them into the helicopter, Snake jerked it up immediately, spun it, and accelerated away.

The helicopter landed at N'Djamena International Airport in less than an hour—a Chapel 737 surrounded by dozens more Chapel security men. Chapel was taken off the helicopter, put on a stretcher, and taken onto the 737.

Bridger and the Spy Devils shook hands with their team. Then, Demon and Snake carried Li Chu to a plane Bridger had ready for them.

Moments after that, they were airborne and settling in for the flight across Africa.

Bridger closed his eyes, hoping to get some uninterrupted sleep.

It didn't happen, as one thought kept him awake.

We are getting closer, but aren't done yet.

That evening, inside his heavily defended compound, Yusef looked at the cases and smiled.

Once he got over his rage, he realized the day had not been a total loss. Sure, he lost men in the ambush, but that happens. He had gotten rid of the annoying man from China. Chapel was gone, and he was four million dollars richer.

Yusef took out the card and punched in the code Bridger had given him. The cases both unlocked, which surprised Yusef. He flipped them open, stared at the money, and then ran his hands over the bills.

A beeping started from somewhere. He looked around, then looked down at the cases. On the digital screens, numbers were counting down.

3...2...1

BOOM! BOOM!

Both cases exploded, shredding Yusef and sending four million burning dollars into the air.

45

THE BOX

Manila, Philippines

S un knew his success as China's counterespionage master would not save him.

Soon, if not already, the president would notice Sun's failures.

My time is short.

He had worked closely with Chen—not aware a CIA spy was right under his nose. Sun had let him escape from Beijing. Sun ordered the plane to be shot down, bringing international condemnation to the Mainland. Sun killed the Foreign Minister. Sun allowed Chen to escape China—only because of blackmail by Bridger and his Spy Devils—which only he...and Zhang...knew. Sun did not capture Chen from the tanker in Manila. Sun's snipers did not shoot Chen.

Worst of all, Sun had not retrieved the Dossier.

The camera footage of Chen moving through the airport the day he escaped had gaps, so Sun had teams walk the route to fill them in.

When Sun realized no camera caught Chen near the post office, he shut the facility down and had every employee arrested and interrogated.

What he discovered was another disaster for Sun. A clerk confessed Chen had been paying her regularly to provide information and perform little mail-related tasks.

Mail some letters or packages under various names.

Ensure expedited departure.

Yes, he handed me a package.

I took it to the international courier service.

Yes. UPS.

Chen sent the most secret and sought-after information in China in the mail.

If he was to live through the next few days, Sun's only hope was to use his presidential authority as Acting Minister of the Ministry of State Security to kill Chen and then tell the president that the Dossier was destroyed.

He ordered APT 41, one of the many hacking organizations supported by the MSS, to immediately infiltrate the Philippines Port Authority vessel traffic management system and the operations of International Container Terminal Services—the port operator. Hundreds of port security cameras were hacked. The commercial and cargo flight systems at Ninoy Aquino International Airport and the Manila Metro Traffic Camera System were accessed.

Nine hours later, he had the data and could create scenarios and plans.

Port cameras caught a massive man and a smaller...*is that a man or woman*...and a wooden crate—maybe four feet square and three feet wide—being lowered from the tanker's side. Several men were waiting with a cargo van and loaded it. Traffic cameras tracked the truck traveling south from the port area along the R-1 to Ninoy Aquino International Airport.

Airport security cameras followed the truck as it entered the Asia International Cargo (AIC) facility—one of many businesses in the row of air freight and cargo companies on Ninoy Aquino Avenue.

AIC's flight schedules showed eight scheduled departures after the van arrived at the facility and departing within twenty-four hours. Sun considered the plausible destinations plus how long the CIA would keep a man like Chen inside a box before they removed him.

A day or two—factoring in time to clear customs.

Searching the cargo manifests showed three flights carried crates the right size, departed inside his parameters, and would arrive at their destination in a few hours.

Ho Chi Minh City? Singapore? Bangkok?

Sun dispatched MSS and support assets to cover each city's AIC plane arrivals and facilities. Sun ordered the gate camera footage to be searched and pulled the passenger lists for dozens of flights to those cities for any trace of the two people.

Sooner than expected, he was notified that a man fitting Sun's description was seen boarding a flight to Bangkok.

He directed all assets to focus on Suvarnabhumi Airport, the main Bangkok airport.

It would be four more hours before he could get to Bangkok and kill Chen.

Bangkok, Thailand

May was exhausted when she entered the AIC CIA-funded "special visitors" lounge at Amari Don Muang Airport. She immediately perked up when she saw Lena.

"It is so good to see you!" May said when she entered the room. She gripped Lena by the shoulders and held her at arm's length, grinning at her. "How does it feel to be a Spy Devil?"

"Dangerous," she said mockingly.

"Maybe not for long," May said with a wink.

"Maybe."

The lounge was equipped to serve as a rec room, bar, place to sleep, and business center.

Two wall-mounted air conditioners hummed and rattled, working hard against the usually hot and balmy Bangkok weather. A large curtain window with bright light slicing through closed blinds. Two large leather couches and matching chairs around a glass table. Large screen TV, DVD player, and sound system. There was a small bar along one wall, with a refrigerator only good for storing ice trays. A well-worn foosball table was jammed into one corner.

"Beatrice!" May gave the newlywed a tight hug she didn't release. "Congratulations. I am so sorry I missed it," May whispered into her ear. "And I am so sorry you can't enjoy it. My son is an ass."

"No apologies needed, May. And yes, he is."

"I have a gift for you."

She moved toward Milton, who was playing foosball with Angel.

"Milton!" May kissed Milton on his cheek, which instantly turned red along with the rest of his face and broad forehead.

"Hello, Angel," she said with a hug. "Janelle is—?"

"In the hotel shops."

"Good for her."

The door opened, and Gilchrist filled the room.

"I swear by the sun and moon of Thailand, my beloved ancestral home, I have never seen such a gathering. We are all here." He saw May and took her hand. "May! We made it!"

"So far, Gilchrist. Not there yet."

"Quite right. You are quite right."

"How is our package?" May asked.

"The package, as I have been informed, will arrive at any moment."

When Bridger described his plan, May was against drugging Chen and shipping him in a box.

"He deserves better," she told him.

"Once he is out of the country, if Hawkins doesn't find him first, Chen will eventually feel honor-bound to tell Hawkins the location of the Dossier. Fine, I really don't care what he does—or deserves. I'm talking to him first."

Bridger made all the arrangements with Gilchrist for moving the Human Transport Unit, the HTU, more commonly called "The Box," to Manila.

May and Gilchrist took separate flights to Thailand's capital. They each took the hour-and-a-half drive north to the AIC buildings at Don Muang International Airport—the Bangkok area's original historic airport. CIA-cleared AIC employees, who were not aware they were assisting a non-CIA operation, would ensure the crate was handled carefully and expedited through customs on both ends of the journey.

The Box would be moved to the sorting and shipping warehouse at Don Muang, where everyone—including the Spy Devils—waited.

"The hard part is over," Gilchrist said. "After, you are all on vacation."

The door opened, and a man with AIC stenciled on his sweaty shirt stepped in and nodded at Gilchrist.

"It is here," Gilchrist announced.

Everyone filed out and walked across the large warehouse crammed with ceiling-high and wall-to-wall shelves and containers. They moved down a row, then through another door into a smaller storage room. Chen's Box was there, with two of Gilchrist's men standing guard.

"Milton. Angel. Go into the warehouse and keep watch," May said. "Take your wand and comms."

They did as May asked, which gave her the satisfying, tingly sensation of being in charge of an operation once more.

"Let's get him out," she said.

May opened a side panel of the crate, displaying a panel of lights and controls. She pushed a few, and the top and side of the Box released with a hiss.

The Box was empty.

No one spoke, and nothing moved.

"Chen is missing," Gilchrist said, looking at May. "How can that be?"

May took out her phone and punched a button.

"We have a problem," May said after Bridger answered.

"What?"

"Chen isn't in the Box." It was Bridger's turn to be silent. "What do you think?" She waited. "Bridger?"

"Tell me who shows up, which I expect will be soon," he said after a moment.

"Cars coming. Pulling up in front," Angel reported. "It's Sun."

Gilchrist snapped his fingers. His men pulled out pistols from the small of their backs and took positions at the door to the sorting warehouse.

"Bridger. Sun is here. Should we—"

"Sun? Good. Don't worry. Keep me on the line."

May saw Sun move quickly into the sorting warehouse ahead of four of his men.

"What's he doing?"

"Searching," she reported as she followed Sun and his men move up and down the rows, their heads rapidly swiveling left and right.

"I want to talk to him."

"Really?"

May stepped farther into the large room and waved her hand.

"Sun. Over here," she shouted. She saw the MSS men flinch and crouch with their weapons raised and their heads bobbing up and down from behind shelves, catching quick glimpses of the room. "Bridger would like to speak with you."

Sun weaved through the stacks until he reached the door and stopped.

May stood with Gilchrist behind her and his men on either side. She motioned them to lower their weapons. She handed Sun her phone, which he took.

"Sun. Chen is gone," Bridger said.

"What do you mean? He is here, I know," Sun said as he tried to look through the door, but Gilchrist blocked his view. "The Box was empty."

"We both know who has him. The question is, what of many things does he want—or more, what are we willing to do?"

Zhang watched everything live on his computer.

The reach and relationships of The Enterprise were vast, which meant occasionally assisting foreign intelligence operations on a selected basis—including the CIA—in return for favors when needed.

Zhang unleashed the eyes of his global drug trafficking empire and sources inside MSS to provide intel and track Sun's search for Chen. When he learned their destination was the AIC freight facility in Bangkok, Zhang knew what it meant and saw it as his opportunity to get back at them all.

He flew to Manila immediately, arrived just after Sun, and formed a tight ring of surveillance around the MSS officers as they followed the truck to the airport.

Zhang ordered his people to dispose of the AIC workers in Manila before the Box was loaded onto the plane bound for Bangkok. Once they had, Zhang waited at another warehouse near the airport used by The Enterprise for its drug trafficking operations.

Zhang stood fascinated, surveying the ordinary-looking shipping container, knowing Chen was inside. It took his technicians a few minutes to determine how to open it, but when they did, it depressurized with a hiss. They found Chen unconscious and strapped in tight with an oxygen mask over his face. IVs provided fluids and drugs to both arms.

"Take him to the safe house location. We will keep him there until arrangements are made," Zhang said.

Chen was disconnected from the Box and carried to a van.

Zhang picked up his phone and dialed the number he had for Bridger.

"Bridger," Zhang said.

"I have been expecting your call, Zhang. Is Chen okay?"

"He is alive."

"Sun is not a happy man."

"Sun is too narrow-minded. He only thinks of himself. I take a broader picture. More strategic, like you perhaps?"

"Perhaps. Time to make a deal then, I assume."

"Ah, the famous deal with the Devil. Yes, I need you to do one simple act for me if you want Chen."

"What is that?"

"Kill Charlie Ho."

Zhang waited for Bridger to respond, pleased the silence meant he had surprised the man.

"Hey, Zhang, have you been in contact with Vincente?"

"No," Zhang answered, puzzled by the question. Bridger's next comment puzzled him even more.

"Well, normally, I would ask you to take a number and get in line when it comes to killing someone, but for you, I will move your request to the front."

46

BARWON PRISON

Melbourne, Australia

Dressed in a red jumpsuit designated for the worst criminals and with his hands cuffed behind his back, Charlie Ho was led from his cell in the Olearia wing of the H.M. Prison Barwon. The maximum-security facility in Victoria State was located sixty kilometers west of Melbourne, Australia. Guards a foot taller than Ho flanked him and held his elbows as he walked.

"I have no call scheduled with my lawyer," Ho said, looking from one man to another.

"You are special, I guess, Ho. Big-wig lawyer from somewhere wants to talk to you."

"I do not want to." He tried to turn.

The guards pinched their hands into Ho's arms, lifting him slightly in the air to turn him back on course.

They stopped at a thick blue metal door with a sign on the wall identifying the room: SECURE VIDEO CONFERENCE.

One guard opened the heavy door, and the other ushered Ho into the bland room. Tan, with a metal table, two chairs, and a TV screen on the wall. The guards sat Ho in a chair and locked his cuffs to a ring on the table. The other guard snatched a remote and clicked on the screen.

When they left, Ho sat silently, looking at the white screen. Then it flickered, and the face of a middle-aged gray-haired man with brown eyes appeared.

"Mr. Ho. Thank you for your time. My name is Everet Linquist. I am in the Office of the Prosecutor for the ICC."

"I do not know—" Ho looked closer at the unfamiliar face on the screen. "I have no contact with your ICC."

"True, you don't, but you probably should." The voice was not the same.

Ho froze, then turned his ear to the screen like that would help him remember why the voice sounded familiar.

"Bridger?"

"Hi! How are you holding up, Chuck?" Bridger waved. "I was happy to see you were extradited to Australia. Very convenient."

"I did not want to come to Australia. They have been trying to get me for years. Then, I was extradited from Amsterdam, made possible by our altercation there."

"Well, perhaps it is a good omen. I should apologize for double-crossing you and getting you arrested, but I won't."

Bridger had arranged for Ho to be captured in Rotterdam by INTERPOL and other organizations, which destroyed Ho's goal to corner Europe's illegal drug production and distribution with Vincente Ramirez and the CJNG.

It cost them all billions of dollars.

"I was disappointed, but you were very professional. I appreciate that," Ho said.

"Hey, Chuck, time is short, and I know you appreciate directness, so here it is. I'm here to kill you."

Ho frowned. "That might prove difficult, given my current housing." Ho impassively looked around the room.

"True, but it is important. I wouldn't be doing this if it wasn't important. Hey, you might be...I don't know...happy...that two people asked me specifically to do it. Vincent, of course. I had to make a deal to keep him from killing us. We will save that for later."

Ho leaned back with a big smile on his face and his fingers tapping the table. "Zhang, I assume, is the other?"

"We have a winner."

"It has taken him too long. Zhang is always too cautious. He can't reach me inside this facility. I assume he asked you as he has no other way to access me, so he hoped the Devil could do it? But why would you agree?"

"I had to make another deal, which is becoming a disturbing trend. Let me bring you up to date on current events."

When Bridger was done, Ho sat back, closed his eyes, and breathed deeply.

"Chen and Zhang conspired against me."

"Don't forget Chapel, Chuck. It seems that you are too annoying to deal with."

"And Li Chu. Can he not be killed?"

"Good question. Time will tell on that."

"So, how do you plan on killing me?" Ho waved his chained hands as best he could to indicate the prison. "I am in here. I am in solitary confinement, a cell they call a super-maximum area. It is designed well. Many cameras and extra guards, just for me. I don't see how that is possible, even if you tried to bribe someone. I see no other prisoners. The guards are tough. Believe me. I have made them many offers."

"We are breaking you out of there the day after tomorrow on your way to your Magistrates' Court appearance—if that is okay with you."

Ho stood as far as he could, his hands still locked to the table.

"Yes. But how?"

Bridger leaned forward.

"Here is what I need from you."

"Hello, Carl," Bridger said as he walked toward the tan man with the beaming white gap-tooth smile and dark sunglasses.

"G-day, Bridga," Carl Wallis said as he shook Bridger's hand. "How ya goin'?"

"I'm fine, Carl. Thanks for meeting on short notice. Nice view."

"Yep."

Wallis could have been a model for any Australian tourism poster. Tall. Blonde sun-bleached hair. Perfect white teeth. Muscular. He wore casual white loose-fitting cotton draw-string trousers and a funky cotton shirt covered in prints of seahorses. All he needed was a surfboard, and the cliché Australian look would be complete.

Standing in Alberts Park on a warm, clear-blue-sky day, they looked across the lake at the skyline of Melbourne.

"Beautiful day," Bridger said.

"This is Melbourne weather. Just wait a few minutes. It will change." Wallis said with a bright-white toothy grin that disappeared in a flash. "What disasta have you brought?"

"A big one, Carl. You aren't going to like it. I mean, no way. No one here is."

"Speak to me."

"This is a big ask, even for a man in your position. I need you to convince your colleagues and the rest of Australia's law enforcement organizations that what we were about to do is good."

"I don't like that sound, mate," Carl said.

Bridger stopped and looked at him.

As the Australian Federal Police Assistant Commissioner, Special Protective Command, Wallis commanded special security and intelligence operations regarding Australia's national interests at home and abroad.

"I'm breaking Charlie Ho out of Barwon."

He started walking and laughing. He slapped Bridger's back.

"No, you aren't."

"Yes. I am."

Carl stopped laughing.

"You are going to have to explain this to me, mate."

So, Bridger explained all the details he could.

"I need the spectacle and distraction of the prison break."

"You are crazy. It is never going to get approval. The PR itself would be horrible."

"Approval has nothing to do with it. If everyone goes along, just for three days, maybe four, it can be spun as the greatest intel victory ever for Australia because it will be. Here." Bridger handed him a piece of paper. "I got this from Charlie as a down payment."

Wallis took it, flipped his sunglasses to his forehead, and read. When he was done, he flipped them back over his eyes.

"He told you this?" Wallis said in amazement, waving the paper. "We have gotten nothing." Wallis looked off into space. "You are a dickhead, Bridga."

"Yeah, whatever that means, you are, too. I don't want anyone to get hurt, but I can only say I warned you if the answer is no. We have crawled too far for too long to get here, and too many lives hang on this happening."

"Give me an hour. I will give it a go."

Bridger shook Wallis' hand.

"This *is* happening."

47

PULL A PUERTO VALLARTA

Melbourne, Australia

I t had taken Bridger and his Africa team—plus Li Chu—a day to fly from Chad to Melbourne. The other group of Spy Devils made it from Manila in half that time. They met at a safe house in Point Cook, a western suburb of Melbourne, to strategize.

"We are going to pull a Puerto Vallarta," he told them.

"Um, that didn't work out too well last time," Beatrice said.

"I agree," Imp added.

"This time, it will. Imp, we need all the power and speed 'The Unemployables' can give us and more. We need access to that truck."

"I know. I know. I will see if they are awake. Wait? What am I thinking? They never sleep," he said as he pulled out his phone.

"Milton. Work with Imp. Success depends on you guys."

"Don't you fret," Milton answered, with stress pushing his Alabama accent to its highest level.

"Are we actually doing this? Getting Ho out?" Demon asked.

"We need Chen, May. Call Hawkins. He owes us. We need serious aircover," Bridger said to May.

"And why is *this* son of a bitch still alive?" Demon asked, pointing to Li Chu. "He should have a knife in his chest, a bullet hole in his head, be chopped up, and tossed in a meat grinder."

To his credit, Li Chu remained calm and defiant in his own way.

"I like it," Snake said.

Lena had not said a word when Bridger walked into the Point Cook safe house with Li Chu. She didn't have to. Her silent reaction said it all. Her face flushed pale, then turned red. Pinpoints of light reflected off the moisture filling her narrowed eyes. Much like May, she tugged on her fingers as a nervous tick.

"What is he doing here?" she finally asked Bridger, pulling him into the living area of the one-story home.

"He is part of this."

"It is just…" She couldn't finish. She sat at a little kitchen table in a nook that overlooked the newly built subdivision. Every house was nearly identical on the treeless, freshly paved street.

"You told me to forgive. Remember all that? Move on and the rest. Has something changed?" He sat across from her and took her hand.

She still didn't answer at first and kept looking out the window.

"He is here," she said.

"Oh. Is that it?" He released her hand and leaned back. "It is easy to say to someone *'forgive'* and *'move on'* until you face it. But he is here. The man who killed your uncle and my friend is over there."

Her face looked down, then up. There were no tears. Bridger saw the hate.

"You want to kill him, right?"

"Yes."

He retook her hands. She looked up at him. "There is a time and place for forgiveness. Right now, we need him."

"What? Why?" When he didn't answer, she nodded. They stood, hugged, then kissed.

"Geez, can we get on with this?' Demon asked as he came around the corner. "I didn't think there was time for that shit."

They separated, smiled, and nodded.

"Later," she said as they walked back to the main living area where they all were assembled.

"You sure we ain't going to prison ourselves for this?" Angel asked. "Janelle would be pissed if that happened."

"Nope, we are good," Bridger said. "As far as I know. Carl has to work fast to protect his people. One condition is no one can get injured. We can do that, but it has to look real. It will because it is real."

Wallis pulled a miracle and got approval for the operation at the highest levels of the Australian government. With the impossible approvals taken care of, Bridger now needed more impossible things to happen quickly and sequentially.

"Imp. This is on you now."

"We hacked into the Federal and Victorian Police. They were tough nuts to crack. Excellent cybersecurity. I should send a congratulations note." Imp was munching on a bag of Cheezels.

"Imp. Did you do it?" Bridger asked.

"We hacked Mack, the company. Get it?"

"No." Demon said.

"Imp," Bridger said impatiently.

"Here is where I prove I am a genius." He licked the cheddar cheese powder from the corn and rice snacks off his fingers. "Damn tasty snack."

"Good lord," Beatrice said.

"Volvo designed it. Understand? Volvo. The company. Their cyber-security is thinner than Demon's brain. Popped in. Popped out."

They looked at Imp.

"Yes. I got it. Background. The Victorian government spent nearly a million dollars to build, just for Ho and other dangerous prisoners—" he wiggled his fingers, making air quotes "—a customized, heavily armored Mack transport vehicle. This baby is packed with ballistic armor, individual internal cells, defense systems, and 360-degree CCTV cameras. It is all high-tech, digitally controlled everything. Digital—when will society learn?"

. . .

"Stay with it, Beatrice," Bridger said as he watched the Devilbot video feed of the three vehicles leaving the Barwon Prison complex.

"Wow, that *is* one big ugly truck," Angel said from the driver's seat of one of the Spy Devils' cars parked along the truck route. Milton and Beatrice occupied the seats behind him.

"Are you kidding? That is a great truck," Snake said from behind the wheel of the other van. Bridger and Demon were with him.

Much to their shared mutual displeasure and dissent, May and Lena were guarding Li Chu at the Point Cook safe house.

The armored Mack truck, carrying Ho locked inside a cell, exited and turned south on C704 Bacchus Marsh Road towards Geelong and the M1 Freeway to Melbourne. In front was a blue and white checked Ford Ranger Victoria Police car with a flashing blue and red emergency light bar on its roof. Another Ranger trailed behind.

The truck was huge, black, and imposing. Massive airless all-terrain tires dominated its profile. A three-inch steel roll-bar bumper was welded to the front and looked like teeth ready to chew anyone who came near. Light did not seem to penetrate the bullet-proof windows.

The two-lane country road the Mack was rumbling on ran through flat fields of browns and greens. An irregular stream of cars came from the opposite direction. Several more cars kept their distance behind the convoy and its flashing lights.

"Imp. Milton. Get ready. It's only ten kilometers to the Heales Road roundabout."

Bridger waited until the three vehicles were about to circle the roundabout's left lane.

"Now, Imp."

Imp tapped his laptop.

"Yours, Milton."

Milton used his computer to take remote control of the armored car.

The massive truck rapidly accelerated and slammed into the rear of the police Ford Ranger. The Ranger rolled off the road in a cloud of debris that was once its backend. Milton steered the Mack to completely circle the roundabout coming up behind the second police car, which had stopped.

Milton slightly accelerated again and rammed the car, sending it off the road. Milton pulled a hard left and stopped the truck just off the circle. Milton locked the driver and guard inside the front compartment and unlocked the exterior rear door and Ho's cell.

The guards inside jumped out with their rifles raised.

"Gas them," Bridger said as Snake sped their car to the crash site.

Milton accessed the vehicle defense system and released canisters of tear gas from the roof. A white hissing cloud enveloped the truck, choking the guards and Ho. Wearing gas masks, Bridger and Demon jumped from their van, grabbed Ho, and tossed him inside the van.

The show was over. They sped away.

48

DEAL COMPLETED

Melbourne, Australia

"Your pal Carl is having a rough day, Bridger," Angel said as he flipped the television channels on the TV inside the safe house. "It isn't much better on the international news channels, either."

Bridger looked at the screen. Carl was standing at a podium, giving a statement and taking questions. Scathing comments by every reporter and analyst rolled on through the country and world. Within hours, social media started creating conspiracies that the narco-traffickers had bought the Australian government.

Every denial fueled more conspiracies.

Sorry, Carl.

"Check your inbox," Bridger told Zhang when the video call connected.

"Is he dead?"

"Check your inbox."

He did and clicked on the attachment.

Ho appeared, taped to a chair, looking haggard and disheveled.

"Read this," Bridger's voice came from off-camera.

Ho looked up and blinked into the bright lights. The camera zoomed to a medium close-up.

"My name is Charlie Ho. Bridger and the Spy Devils took me. It is Wednesday."

Two gunshots thundered in the room. Charlie's body buckled as it violently tipped back with a thud.

The camera image jiggled as it was moved closer to the chair. It panned up and down from the seeping blood dripping onto the floor to Ho's still, white face. The camera turned, and Bridger's face filled the screen.

"Happy?"

The video cut to black.

"Are you happy?" Bridger asked, looking into the phone's camera.

"How can I be sure? How do I not know it isn't the theatrics you are known for?"

Bridger smiled.

"It's real."

It was Zhang's turn to smile.

"You *are* lying."

Bridger raised his hands like a gun was pointing at him.

"I give up. You win, Zhang. It was fake." Bridger panned his phone until it showed Ho again, taped to the chair. Alive.

"I am going to kill you, Zhang," Ho said, his voice was low and menacing.

"Shut up, Ho. Bridger, kill him."

"Demon," Bridger said.

Demon walked into the screen and raised his weapon to the side of Ho's head. The man was brave and just glared at the camera.

"Demon, hang on," Bridger said.

"Son of a bitch!" Demon said, lowering his pistol. "I quit."

Bridger smiled at his friend as he panned the camera back to him.

"Zhang. Killing him is a bad strategy."

"Shoot him, please, if you want Chen."

"I will get you, Zhang," Ho repeated.

"Demon. Shut him up."

Demon punched the defenseless man across the chin. Ho's head snapped, and his chin fell to his chest. Blood dripped from his mouth.

"I meant gag him!"

"Oopsies," Demon said as he walked away, rubbing his knuckles.

Once more, Bridge shook his head.

"Hear me out. We shoot him. He is dead, *duh,* and out of your business. Fine, you feel good and go on your merry way being the shitty person you are."

"So please do that."

"Wait. Wait. Hear me out. Let me finish. We hand him over. He has value—a big billion-dollar value for you. You can lock him in that dungeon under your little casino and wail on him all you want. I am sure he hasn't told you everything. *Or* you use him as a bargaining chip with partners. *Or* you sell him."

Bridger grabbed Ho by the hair and pulled his head up, showing the bleeding face of the unconscious man.

"Wouldn't you like to smack him around, just for the fun and joy of it?" Bridger released the hair. Ho's head dropped and flopped to the side.

"What do you propose?" Zhang asked, obviously considering the idea.

"A simple meet and swap. The tense kind where neither knows who is going to double-cross the other. You know…that reminds me of a time in Ibiza…well…I was with this fashion model, and we… well… never mind. You name the place. Listen, I am taking a major risk trying to get Ho on a plane and out of here to do this, so think about that. Unless you want to meet in Australia."

"No. I didn't think so."

Bridger could tell Zhang was giving the proposal consideration.

"Time is ticking here, Zhang. I have the entire law enforcement world after me."

"No. I think you should kill him."

"What?" Bridger asked, genuinely shocked. "This is a good deal."

Bridger thought for a moment. "Here it is. I am not killing Ho. You can have Chen. Do what you want, I will release Ho, and he will come after you like the plague."

Zhang's eyes rapidly blinked.

"I…will," a groggy Ho slurred.

Bridger waited silently.

"I agree," Zhang finally said.

"Good. This is a deal between us. I am not giving Ho to some lieutenant. Non-negotiable."

"Yes. Once I know you are in the air, I will send you the location. And if there are any tricks—"

"Yeah, yeah, I've heard that all before. You bad guys need better writers."

"And I want proof he is on the plane."

"It's a deal."

Vincente Ramirez watched the news in amazement, knowing it had to be Bridger and his Spy Devils who broke Ho out of the maximum-security prison. Who else could it have been?

Early the following day, the email with the video attachment appeared in his inbox as he sat in his villa outside Guadalajara.

The message with it read: *Deal completed.*

Vincente watched the video of Ho being shot with satisfaction.

Bridger sent May and Lena to the final rendezvous destination with Angel as their escort.

"If all goes well on this crazy journey, we will all be there in a day," he told Lena as he held her hand on the way to the waiting car.

"If it doesn't?" she asked.

"You get the keys to May."

"You are insufferable," May said as she squeezed Bridger's arm.

"You are," Lena said, leaning in to kiss Bridger.

He watched them drive away.

I've never had so much on the line going into a mission...personally.

It was dark by the time the Spy Devils boarded the plane. When they did, Bridger snapped a picture and sent it to Zhang as requested. Moments later, Zhang sent the location of the swap.

"Okay. Here it is," he told the team. "It is at The Palm Village, off the AH26 on Estrella, in the Makati neighborhood of Metro Manila. Figure it out. It's an eight-hour flight." Bridger checked his watch. "We reconvene in six hours to go over everything."

Hours later, they gathered around for the briefing. Morning light glowed through the windows as they approached Manila.

"Compact and a logistical nightmare," Snake said. "It is a claustrophobically narrow residential street in a residential neighborhood. It is wedged between small shops, a rainforest of trees, jungle-thick vegetation, and other fenced-in communities. The road outside is three lanes divided by an off-ramp of the Pan-Philippines highway, which runs above it, acting like a concrete ceiling and making maneuvering around pillars tight. Oh, and there is the pristine campus of the Catholic Colegio de Santa immediately next to the complex—just as a cherry on top."

Milton jumped in.

"A spider web of wires crisscrosses the street and runs along the sides of the road. Getting a Devilbot close without being noticed with the trees and buildings will be a rollercoaster ride."

"Look on the bright side. He can't send a hundred men into such a small space. That balances the odds out," Bridger said.

"Beatrice. Let me see our Ho," Bridger said as he walked to the rear cabin, where Beatrice had space to concentrate on her work.

She sat on the bed, swiftly manipulating make-up brushes over a man like a chef at a Hibachi grill. He turned to look at Bridger. The face was Ho. Underneath was Li Chu.

"It's a masterpiece. Even this close, I never would think this wasn't Ho—at least for the time we need."

"Prosthetics and make-up cover the scars on the face and ear. He is a little taller, and there is the arm. I can cover that and the bulk with baggy clothes."

Demon shuffled down the aisle to join them.

"Li Chu." The Chinese assassin looked at Bridger. "Welcome to the Spy Devils."

Li Chu's mouth, looking like Charlie Ho's, dropped open.

"Hey, shit-for-face. If you have any urge to shout, wave, or scream to warn anyone—don't." Demon reached behind him, slid his Ka-Bar from its sheath, and waved in front of Li Chu's eyes. "First, I will skin off the fake face. Then I will skin off your ugly face. Understand?"

Li Chu's eyes flicked from Bridger to Demon to Beatrice.

"He means it," Bridger said.

"Yes," Li Chu choked out through his disguise.

"Remember," Demon said as he gave the large knife one last wiggle before he put it back.

When they landed at Ninoy Aquino International Airport, Gilchrist was waiting with two SUVs outside the private jet terminal.

"They may have spotters here. Move fast to the cars."

"I swear—" Gilchrist started.

"Too early, Gilchrist," Bridger said as they piled into the cars.

Bridger took out his phone and sent a text: *We are here.*

"What are we looking at, Gilchrist?"

"As I know your Snake has told you, it is a difficult environment. Plus, the traffic," he waved out the window. "Nothing will be a secret. Zhang has eight to ten men there. Most are outside. The rest are inside with Zhang and Chen. You will not have room for error."

"It is the same way for them."

"They are here," Zhang said as he replaced his phone in his pocket. He walked to a worn, cushioned chair and sat. "Be glad, Chen."

Chen's arms and legs were zip-tied to a wooden kitchen chair. His face was swollen. His black eyes were spotted with broken blood vessels. Dried blood dripped from his freshly broken nose.

"I...am ready...to leave," he said in a nearly inaudible voice.

Through the ubiquitous reach of the MSS intelligence networks, Sun knew exactly where Zhang had taken Chen and how many men he had with him.

Sun was not a fool.

The unbelievable escape of Ho from Australia was not an accident of timing. Zhang had made some deal to swap Ho for Chen. That was impressive on its own. It also meant the Spy Devils would return to Manila—and try to leave.

It meant he had another chance to get Chen.

And he would.

MSS men blanketed the airport and the streets around Zhang's safe house.

First, he would let Bridger make the trade with Zhang. Then he would kill the Americans...kill everyone.

49

PALM VILLAGE

Manila, Philippines

"Two by the security booth at the entrance. One on the roof. One on the balcony looking up," Milton reported, looking at his Devilbot feed. "I am up several hundred feet more than normal."

Milton, Imp, and Beatrice were in the parking area of the shopping and business center adjacent to the village. As Milton controlled the drone from the car, Imp and Beatrice got out and walked toward the residential area.

It took over an hour creeping inch by inch in some of the world's worst traffic for them to reach the gated Palm Village community from the airport. It was a cluster of townhomes spaced in compact rows of parallel streets, built wall-to-wall, with two and three-story townhouses, recreational areas, businesses, and shops. Most of the occupants were professionals, affluent families, and expats.

"Okay, we are pulling in. Gilchrist?" Bridger asked into his phone.

"We will be ready," Gilchrist announced.

Bridger put away his phone as they reached the guarded entrance. Zhang's men checked their car and then waved them through.

Snake drove forward and turned left where cars were parked on the street, yards, and sidewalks on both sides. There was barely enough space to turn the vehicle onto the microscopically small stone and tile driveway of the address Zhang had given. Trees and utility posts flanked the drive.

Bridger, Demon, and Snake exited the car and looked around.

The brown and beige townhouse was two stories and looked like it had been built just small enough to avoid the overhanging trees and wires. Demon's eyes narrowed on a man standing on the second-story balcony that overhung a carport in the front of the house, pointing a MAC-10 machine gun at him.

"Stay here with our Ho," Bridger whispered to Snake.

Bridger and Demon walked to a door to the left of the carport, where two guards thoroughly searched them—Bridger first, then Demon.

"Don't touch anything you will regret," Demon rumbled.

Finding them unarmed, the other guard led them up narrow stairs.

"Even I can tell this place is ugly," Demon whispered as he followed Bridger up the stairs.

"You would know ugly," Imp said through their earbuds.

The narrow hardwood stairs creaked as they went up to the second level, scraping walls covered with pictures, mirrors, photos, and paintings. At the top, a guard waving a pistol directed them right into a living area with a mirrored wall, old gold-stripped, floor-to-ceiling curtains, Persian rugs, and a small dinette in a not-much-bigger kitchen. Beyond the kitchen were sliding glass doors to the balcony and another guard.

Also in the room were two guards with machine guns pointed at them. A half-smiling Zhang stood over a beaten Chen, tied to a chair.

"Love what you have done with the place, Zhang," Bridger said.

"Where is Ho?"

Bridger ignored him.

"How are you doing, Chen? You look—" Bridger approached him

but stopped a few feet short when the guard gripped his machine gun tighter "—awful."

Bridger wasn't sure Chen had any control of his head as it bobbed and wiggled.

"I will say, I am impressed with your ability to break Ho from prison."

"Now you see why Chuck offered me a job," Bridger said, turning to Zhang.

"He what?"

"You didn't know?" Bridger shrugged. "No matter. I turned him down and sent him to prison instead."

"Where is Ho?" Zhang asked with a tone that Bridger read as impatience and anxiety.

"In the car with my man. He will bring him in. That okay?"

Zhang nodded.

"Snake. Bring him in, mate," Bridger said in a slight Australian accent into their comms system.

Moments later, Snake led Li Chu, head down and hands cuffed in front of him, wearing way-too-baggy jeans and a sweatshirt, through the front door. The guard searched Snake, but did not bother searching Li Chu, deciding that Snake was the threat, not the handcuffed man.

"I'll help you up the stairs," Snake said, taking Li Chu by the arm. He glanced at the guard, who nodded but raised his weapon and positioned himself to watch them slowly ascend the stairs.

"I have you, Ho. Finally," Zhang said from across the room when they reached the top of the stairs and turned into the room. When Li Chu did not answer, he asked again—but there still was no answer. "Ho?"

Then, a puzzled look came over his face. He took several steps toward Li Chu, then snapped his head back to glare at Bridger.

In a blink, Snake and Demon reached under Li Chu's sweatshirt and pulled out Devil Sticks.

Demon whipped his arm high and crunched the Devil Stick down in the middle of one guard's skull. Demon tossed his Stick to Bridger and then grabbed the MAC-10 of the dead guard at his feet. He rotated to the glass balcony doors and rapidly fired through to the guard, who staggered back and fell as glass shattered in every direction.

Demon turned back to the guard at his feet, whose head was resting in a puddle of blood. He fired into his body just to be certain.

Li Chu fell to the ground as Snake grabbed another guard and tossed him like a rag doll to the bottom of the stairs, where he careened into the guard at the door. Snake bounded down the narrow passage, jumped, and landed on the arm of the tossed guard, snapping his elbow into pieces. Snake silenced his screams with a cloud of gas. The door sentry was on his feet and reaching for his weapon.

Snake fired electrodes into him at nearly point-blank range, sending him shaking to the ground. Snake walked over and gassed him. Then he heard a metallic *thump* and looked up to see the guard from the roof land on their SUV and bounce to the ground.

He looked up and saw a Devilbot hovering at roof level.

"Milton?" Snake asked.

"I made it," he said.

Beatrice and Imp had arrived at the guard hut at the entrance to the village. When the panicked guards ran out looking for the source of the gunfire, they were met with sprays of gas in their faces.

"Status?" Bridger asked.

Each Devil reported their targets down.

Bridger looked at Zhang, who was frozen in place.

"Zhang," Bridger said, his voice hovering between anger and relief. Then he jammed the Devil Stick in stun gun mode into Zhang's chest. He flew back, slamming against the mirrored wall. He left a spiderweb of cracks behind as he slid to the floor.

"Again," Demon said. Bridger looked at Demon and tapped the end of the weapon against Zhang's neck. He quaked on the floor until his body curled into the fetal position.

Bridger grabbed Li Chu by his handcuffed hands and pulled him to his feet.

"Good job, Ho," he said. "You get to live another day."

"Demon, get Chen. Snake, take Li Chu." Demon cut the ties with his Ka-Bar and helped Chen stand, but Chen fell back to the chair with a grunt.

"Move or I kill your ass," Demon said, grabbing Chen by his neck, lifting him from his chair, and shoving him to the stairs. Snake already had Li Chu down the stairs and out the door.

Bridger pulled zip-tie handcuffs from his pocket and bound Zhang's hands and feet.

"Everyone, let's get out of here."

"Carl. Go ahead," he said into his phone. The sounds of sirens, reeving engines, and squealing tires seemed to come from every direction.

"All went well, Bridga?" Carl's voice asked.

"He is waiting for you. We are leaving, mate."

"Gotcha."

Bridger scrambled down the stairs and hopped in the SUV with Snake and Demon. Snake managed to turn the large vehicle on the crowded street, smashing the sides of a few parked cars. Once pointed in the right direction, he accelerated the SUV out of the compound.

They passed armored cars and trucks with MANILA POLICE SWAT in large white letters on their sides. Inside, dozens of heavily armed police were ready to raid the townhouse. Carl had alerted them, and Bridger knew Carl Wallis was in one of the vehicles, ready to arrest Zhang and take him to Australia.

That was the deal.

50

DEVIL'S OWN DAY

Manila, Philippines

B ridger told the Spy Devils to meet at the AIC warehouse at the private terminal of Ninoy Aquino International Airport. He led Chen to the lounge when they finally arrived after another slow crawl through Manila's traffic.

"Snake, check him out," Bridger said as they laid him on a couch.

Snake did a quick examination of Chen and went to find his medical kit.

Beatrice started removing Li Chu's makeup at a table by the window.

The rest of the team collapsed into chairs.

"Well done, Li Chu," Bridger said as he watched Beatrice peel the prosthetics off his face. "Your assistance is appreciated. Did you like your first mission as a Spy Devil?"

"Release me now." He held up his hands, which were still cuffed. Bridger ignored him.

"You mean you didn't enjoy being on the winning side for once?

Look," he waved his arm around him, "we got Chen, and no one was killed—unlike your Dragon Fire."

"That was only because of him," Li Chu nodded toward where Chen lay on a couch.

"True. Ironic, huh? You just saved the guy who screwed you over. I greatly appreciate it. Hey, we're buddies again! Forgive and forget, right?" Bridger started to walk away.

"Set me free!" Li Chu shouted.

"Not yet. We still have some things to discuss," Bridger said without looking back.

"How is he, Snake?" Bridger asked as he stood over the couch where Chen was resting.

"Bad," he said as he put an IV connected to a bag of fluids into Chen's arm.

"Everyone. We will board soon, I hope, so don't get comfortable."

Bangs and shouts came from the warehouse, and then six MSS men armed with pistols rushed into the AIC lounge. Sun strolled in triumphantly behind them.

Sun did not notice that none of the Spy Devils moved or seemed interested in the appearance of the MSS team.

"Traitor," Sun said to Chen. "Bridger," Sun said, triumph in his eyes. "I can't believe you came back here. Foolish."

"Gee, Sun, I thought you would never show up," Bridger said as he rubbed his eyes. "We are exhausted and want to go, but why don't you take a moment and tell us how smart you are." Bridger sat at one of the tables.

Sun raised his eyebrows and projected a look of scorn as he sat across from Bridger.

"We have been tracking you ever since you arrived in Manila. We have the townhouse under surveillance."

"So, you saw what happened to Zhang after we left."

"Zhang is not important at this moment. I want Chen and the Dossier, but—"

"—but you can't get it because he mailed it somewhere you don't know."

Sun squirmed a little in his chair. He waved and grunted at one of his men to bring him some water.

"So, you know where?"

"Maybe." Bridger smiled at him. "Maybe not."

"I will ask Chen after we take him from you."

The man brought a glass of water, which Sun gulped down.

"All good questions, and you can ask him, just not after *you* take him. You can after we take *you*."

Sun was puzzled, but he understood what might be happening when different shouts and bangs came from the warehouse. Chairs tumbled, and objects flew as the Spy Devils moved on the MSS men. Tasers and stun guns *zapped* and *crackled*.

A grinning Gilchrist came running through the open door with a pistol in each hand. Ten of his men, all armed with rifles and pistols, followed. He looked around the room at all the downed MSS men—except Sun, who still sat across from Bridger.

"What is this? Is there nothing to do in here?" Gilchrist asked. "Where is the fun you promised?" He motioned to his men dejectedly as they secured Sun's men.

One stunned MSS man started crawling toward the gun he dropped. Demon raised his boot and stomped on the outstretched fingers. The prone man screamed and grabbed his hand with the other. Then, in a moment of survival instinct, he tried to reach out with his still-functional hand.

"Motivated guy," Demon said, raising his foot again and smashing the rest of the man's fingers. More screams as he turned onto his back, holding both hands to his chest. "Hope he doesn't play the piano," Demon said as he turned away.

"Sun. As you might have guessed by now, your presence was not unexpected."

"You will not harm me. I am a member—"

"Don't worry. I won't *harm* you. I have a nice comfy Box ready for you—only used once—by Chen."

Snake jammed the needle into Sun's neck. Sun jumped to his feet, staggered, tripped on his chair, and collapsed to the floor.

"They are all yours, Gilchrist. Have at them."

"I swear by the sun and moon of Iceland, my beloved ancestral homeland. It is always exciting when you are here, Bridger."

They shook hands. Gilchrist gave Bridger a wave as he ushered his men out the door, carrying the MSS men over their shoulders.

"Li Chu. Chen. Sun. Zhang. Ho. Putting Wallis in, and getting him out of, a jam," Demon said, looking around the disheveled room, then at his closest friend, with pride radiating from his eyes. "You sure have had the devil's own day, haven't you?"

"Yes," Bridger said, putting his hand on Demon's shoulder, "but we have a lot left to do."

51

KENTUCKY STRAIGHT BOURBON WHISKEY

Long Island, New York

C hapel fought to keep his eyes open. The dreams of his Nigerian trauma woke him sweating and shaking with fear. The screams of the man shot beside him, the vest's weight. Pills helped a little but, mostly, he paced the house, stopping when his legs were shaking too much to support him.

"How are you feeling, Danny?" Hawkins asked.

"Doing well, Max. Doing well."

He knows I am lying.

He was struggling mentally and doing his best to be "Danny Chapel," the all-powerful—always in control. Keeping up the façade meant he had to muster his strength. It was too exhausting.

Physically, he had endured the captivity without much damage. The doctors performed a complete physical examination during the plane ride home. Chapel had minor cuts and bruises and was dehydrated. He was pumped full of fluids, vitamins, and antibiotics. He started back on his daily drug regimen.

Chapel was recovering at his one-hundred-seventy-year-old Hampton mansion located on the border of the villages of Sag Harbor and North Haven, New York. "My weekend retreat," Chapel called it.

They sat in deep leather chairs in Chapel's library, gazing out the large windows at the winter scenery of the Hamptons and Sag Harbor just beyond his snow-covered lawn. In a fireplace, a fire crackled and snapped.

"You should have seen him. It was extraordinary," Chapel said.

"I am sure he was," Hawkins said from his chair beside Chapel.

"No, Bridger was cool and calm in the middle of chaos. He was surrounded by terrorists—heavily armed terrorists pointing guns at him. Li Chu and his Chen obsession. Millions of dollars in cases—"

"Millions of dollars that weren't his that he blew up."

"To save me and kill the man who took me. The man who was a living piece of shit."

How do I thank Bridger and his people who came for me—and got me out alive?

Chapel felt a shaking episode building in his shoulders. He adjusted his position in the deep brown cushions of his deep leather chair enough to make it recede just enough.

"I had never *really* seen him or the Spy Devils in action like that. Ukraine, some, but never close, and never when my life depended on him. He is unique."

"He is uncontrollable. Even May had problems."

"That's his strength."

Fearless, like I used to be.

He sipped an amber liquid from a crystal glass.

"Should you be drinking with all the meds you are on?"

"I had a choice. Increase the dosage of my medications, or—" he held up the glass with a trembling hand "—medication courtesy of Old Rip Van Winkle 25-Year-Old Kentucky Straight Bourbon Whiskey." He sipped. "I chose the latter. Fifty thousand a bottle. Interested? It is okay, but straight down the middle."

"Well, I am sure you are getting better," Max said, sipping the expensive bourbon from his glass. He looked at Chapel, raised his eyebrows, and then smiled.

"Told you," Chapel said, managing a weak smile.

I'm not getting better...but I need to look like I am.

"So, what are you going to do, Max?" Chapel pulled a thick plaid wool blanket over his lap.

"Do?"

"Do...as in...are you going to stay in the CIA?"

Hawkins sipped and shrugged.

"I don't know. I guess. Why?"

"You still don't have Chen's files. Are you going to trek out to Asia in search of some files that might be useful to some people? Is that how you want to spend your last years?"

"Wes did. With cancer, till his dying day," Hawkins said.

"Wes was a fool. A fool who was blown up."

But he knew who he was and what he wanted. I used to.

They sat in silence for minutes.

"I know Bridger feels it," Chapel said.

"What?"

"That he wants something else...to be with Lena." Chapel tried to cross his legs but thought better when he winced in pain.

"He could never stop. Demon wouldn't let him."

Chapel sipped and set his glass on the table between them.

This is the moment.

"Demon would be happy for him. Many would." Chapel picked up the drink and finished it with smacking lips. He absent-mindedly twirled the glass between his hands. "I'm thinking of retiring, too."

"You? Danforth Chapel? No chance! What happened to your mantra to die at your desk?"

"I almost died. I'm old. That was enough." Chapel changed the mood with a laugh. "I think I will let someone else do the actual dying!" Chapel slowly stood. Hawkins started to rise to help, but Chapel waved for him to stay seated. "I'm okay. The doctors say I need to move."

Chapel shuffled to a polished cherry table with a Tiffany desk lamp. He gingerly bent and opened a drawer, took out a package, closed the drawer, and walked to Hawkins. Chapel handed Hawkins the book-sized manila envelope, then went to his chair and sat with a long sigh from the exertion.

"That is something that might help *you* decide."

Hawkins looked at the postmark. UPS from China. Stunned, he looked up at Chapel, who nodded.

"Yes. It is. Consider this your last bit of intelligence collection before your...retirement. A gift from Chen and me." Chapel leaned over and tapped Hawkins on the knee. "It's time, Max."

Hawkins looked at the fire, stood, and walked toward it. He picked up a piece of wood and tossed it on the fire. Sparks flew as the wood sizzled and caught fire. He returned to his chair, took the bottle of whiskey, and poured a healthy portion into his glass.

They sat together in silence in the warmth of the fire, looking out the window at the cold scenery.

Chapel had to make big decisions about his future, and Bridger was the key.

Mauritius

"While we apologize for deceiving the public by staging the escape of Charlie Ho from Barwon Prison, after careful consideration and agreement at all levels of law enforcement, we felt it was necessary to obtain our objectives—which we did and more. In close partnership with the Government of the Philippines, we have captured our most-wanted international criminal, Zhang Gon, the head of the Chinese international crime syndicate, The Enterprise," Carl Wallis said.

"He is having a much better day," Lena said as she watched the news with May at Bridger's Mauritius compound.

"I'm glad. Carl is a good man," May said.

Carl continued.

"I will not go into details on the operations or the current status of Mr. Zhang, but the assistance of Mr. Ho was instrumental to this operation's success. Questions?"

The reporters at the press conference exploded with shouts. Digital cameras clicked in a constant staccato.

"What was in it for Ho?" Lena asked.

"Bridger said he gets out of solitary confinement at Barwon. Maybe many other niceties."

Angel appeared in the room, looking comfortable in shorts, a loose shirt, and dark glasses.

"I'm going out for supplies before they get here. Anyone interested in the sights and sounds of Port Louis?" he asked.

May checked her watch and then looked at Lena.

"No, thank you," May said.

"I'll pass," Lena added with a laugh.

"You lose. It won't take long," Angel said as he left the house. They heard the car pulling away.

"Want to walk on the beach? Look at the sunset?" May asked Lena, as she picked up her broad-rim straw hat by habit, then tossed it back on the lounge chair. "Our last chance to chat before the chaos arrives."

"Sure." Lena stood.

They walked off the gravity pool deck, onto the green manicured lawn, and barefoot onto the beach. The sun was setting, casting a glow over the blues and greens of the ocean and sky. A few stars were popping into view, but it would be a couple of hours before peak stargazing.

"I have never been to Mauritius. I am always working, but my friends have come here. Very tropical. Not as crowded as the French Riviera, they said." Lena kicked some sand up with her toes. "This is gorgeous." She looked out at the shimmering turquoise lagoon and the Indian Ocean. "How many homes does he have?"

"Several. They keep popping up," May said. "There's a golf course nearby, of course."

"Of course," Lena repeated with a smile.

They walked into the warm water and stood, letting the small waves lap against their legs. Torches began flicking at the resort beaches in the distance, preparing for the evening's tourist activities.

They had arrived at Bridger's custom-built home in Mauritius, located in the Indian Ocean east of Madagascar off the east coast of Africa, three days before. The home, in Anahita on the east coast of Mauritius, had high ceilings and large glass openings toward the pool and the sea. Six bedrooms. Open-plan, fully equipped kitchen. A dining and living area extended to the terrace and deck near the pool. Bars. Gym. Jacuzzi. Wine cellar.

"So, decision time is quickly approaching," May said.

"Decision?" Lena asked, but she knew what May meant.

"He will leave the Spy Devils, leave being Bridger—and it isn't *just* about you—so don't feel guilty about that. He has been searching for a life beyond the world I forced on him." May chuckled. "Quite the mother I am."

Lena sighed. Electronic dance music boomed from the resorts.

"You asked him to forgive Li Chu, and he did because you asked," May continued. "That tells me something."

They walked in the few inches of water trickling onto the beach and then receding.

"What do you think he will do with Li Chu?" Lena asked with a lower monotone voice.

May stopped and looked at her.

"What do you want him to do?"

Lena didn't answer.

"Let's go back. We could use a few stiff drinks before they get here."

52

RED ROSES AND YELLOW BALLOONS

Mauritius

Given the load and headwinds, the nearly 5,000-mile flight from Manila to Mauritius neared the maximum flight distance for the G650.

Arab sailors had discovered Mauritius, then shipwrecks and colonization brought the Dutch, French, and British, creating a unique culture of over a million people descended from indentured laborers, slaves, and European settlers. The nearly eight-hundred-square-mile island was sought after for its flora and fauna—which once included the now-extinct dodo.

Now tourists invaded it, and those seeking refuge from the "real world"—which is what intrigued Bridger and induced him to build there.

With Sun inside the Box taking all the space in the cargo hold, the main cabin was cramped with gear and sleeping Spy Devils. Any extra space was reserved for Al and his pilot colleagues to cover the long-distance flight.

Bridger and Demon were in luxury deep-cushioned seats near the front. They had them swiveled to look aft to face Chen and Li Chu sitting opposite them. Snake's medical care and some sleep had improved Chen's appearance and alertness. Li Chu's expression never seemed to change under his scars and patchy black three days of beard growth—controlled rage.

"What are your plans when we arrive…where are we going?" Li Chu asked. Chen looked up from dozing, also interested in the answer.

"I haven't got a clue, actually." Bridger looked at them both. "We will all chat when we get there and are rested. It is a big day."

Bridger's phone rang.

"You are a dead man," the Vincente said.

"You watch the news? I am surprised."

"I am glad that you broke our deal. I will be the one—" Vincente started to say.

"Let me stop your cliché maniacal evil narco sociopath blustering right there," Bridger cut in, "If I were you, I would hide. Hide someplace deep. I will come for you if I even *think* you are near me, anyone I know, or anyone I have forgotten I know. There won't be any deals."

Bridger hung up.

"Vincente?" Demon asked.

"Yep," he said as he glared at Li Chu and Chen. "He seemed disappointed to find Ho is still alive."

They arrived in Mauritius around midnight at Sir Seewoosagur Ramgoolam International Airport, a new state-of-the-art facility located in Plaine Magnien, thirty miles southeast of the capital city of Port Louis. Angel was waiting with two rented SUVs and a pickup truck. They caravanned the short drive north to Bridger's compound.

"I made it," Bridger said as he and Lena embraced. As she held him, the emotions and stress of the last month shook from his body. She held him tighter. "This is it, kind of," he whispered.

She released him when Li Chu entered the living area with Demon behind him. They silently looked at each other. Lena walked over and slapped him hard across his face. When he recoiled from the blow, she hit him again. Li Chu took both blows and looked back at her with a little trickle of blood seeping from his lips.

Bridger scrambled to secure her arms, but she was already walking away with a look of satisfaction.

"Feel better?"

"A little," she replied. "I need another drink." Lena walked to the bar.

Bridger saw the large highball glasses filled with a burnt orange liquid and chunks of fruit. A little pink umbrella was stuck into each glass.

"How many?" he asked.

"Lots," she replied with a tipsy-laden smirk.

"That explains it. Everyone," heads turned, "Get something to eat and a drink. Get some sleep. There are bedrooms on all three levels. The lower level has another bar, Jacuzzi—"

"Jacuzzi! I'll take downstairs," Imp said, shuffling in with a hulking bag slung over his shoulder. He saw the drinks and grabbed two. "Luciana?"

"Sorry. Not here this time. Everything is stocked and catered. But wait—"

"Cool beans," Imp said, as Bridger watched him disappear.

"Li Chu and Chen sit here." Bridger pointed to one of the long couches in the open living area. "Demon and Snake. Get our other guest."

"I got an idea. Let's drop them in the ocean," Demon said. Bridger could hear his old friend's fatigue and see it scratched across his face.

Soon we will rest, my friend, Bridger thought, ignoring the comment.

"Other guest?" May asked.

"I brought a surprise."

When Snake and Milton rolled the Box onto the pool deck, May took a spot by Bridger.

"Who is in this?" May asked as she slid open the access panel.

"Exciting, isn't it? Like a box of Cracker Jack. What's the surprise going to be?" Bridger said as he feigned exaggerated nervously, rubbing his hands together.

Snake pulled the top and end panels off when the seals were released. May looked in and did a slow turn to Bridger.

"You kidnapped Sun?"

Bridger stood by the Box as Snake removed his IVs and unstrapped him.

"I didn't exactly kidnap him. He just doesn't know he is going to defect—yet."

"Does Hawkins know?"

"No. You can tell him after Sun here makes it official."

Snake examined Sun and deemed him to be in pretty good shape.

"He needs to sleep it all off. He will be functional by tomorrow afternoon at the latest," Snake said.

"There is a room on the lower level with several beds. Strap Sun into one of them. Milton. Beatrice. Give Snake a hand, then you take the big bedroom on this level."

"Demon. There is an empty storage kind of room down that hall. Lock, tie, tape, glue, or whatever you want to do to these two." Bridger pointed to Chen and Li Chu.

"Not with him," Li Chu said.

"Hell, yes," Demon said. "Come on, soon-to-fish-food." He gripped them by the arms and shoved them down the hallway.

"Bridger! Treat Minister Chen with respect!" May said.

"No," Bridger said. "Not until we sort everything out tomorrow."

The rest of the Spy Devils took their fruit drinks and disappeared.

Bridger grabbed his bag and then looked at Lena.

They went upstairs to the master bedroom. The massive room ran most of the length of the ocean side of the top floor. A king-sized bed. A sitting room with a small library. A double-wide sliding door that led to the bathroom decorated with multi-colored mosaic tiles. A multi-person shower with glass walls and a soaking tub in the middle of the room where a person could look up at the sky through a glass dome.

An observation balcony ran the entire roof perimeter, providing a three-hundred-sixty-degree panoramic view of the island and ocean.

"I'm taking a shower," Bridger said.

"Me too," Lena replied with an upward flick of her eyebrows.

Afterward, they stood arm in arm on the balcony, wearing thick white robes and looking at the stars.

"Tomorrow," Lena said softly in the darkness, barely audible over the waves hitting the beach.

"What about it?" he asked.

"It is…well…a big day. It could be a big day for you and the others…and us."

"That is true."

"Do you know what will happen?" she asked.

"Meaning?"

He saw her bite her lip in the glow of the lights from the pool and living level below.

"You have a plan?"

"Meaning?" He waited. The palm trees just off the balcony—close enough to touch—gently swayed in the breeze.

He felt her body tense. "Li Chu," she said finally.

"Oh, him. You mean forgiveness? Is that what you want to happen tomorrow?" Bridger asked.

"It is your decision."

"What if I just say, 'fuck it' and put a hole in his head?"

"It is your decision," she repeated, "*if* you feel it is right," Lena replied.

"Oh?" He turned her toward her. "Listen, you. Don't worry. After tomorrow, it is all red roses and yellow balloons."

"I wish,and I don't believe you," she said as they kissed.

53

BLACKMAIL AND OTHER
UNPLEASANT THINGS

Mauritius

B ridger felt refreshed from his first good night of sleep in what felt like forever. Lena was not there. He got ready and then followed the combined smells of Italian, Mediterranean, and African cuisine being pushed through the house by the salty breeze of the Indian Ocean.

He found everyone in the combined living room and open pool area, gorging on a catered tropical breakfast, plates of cut fruit, pastries, and bread. They were dressed in a plethora of shorts, light shirts, hats, and sandals. The surrounding palm trees flapped and rustled with each gust of wind.

They seem to be enjoying themselves. Good. Today is the day. One way or another.

Bridger joined May and Lena, who were eating at a shady table under the overhang.

"I let you sleep," she said.

"Thanks for that." He gave her a quick kiss and then sat.

Milton and Beatrice sat by the pool at a round, umbrella-covered table. At the next table, Angel sat with Imp, who was tapping on his laptop with a pile of food piled high next to him.

"Has Chapel given the package with the Dossier to Hawkins yet?" Bridger asked, then he reached over and took the last chunk of pineapple off her plate. Juice dripped down his chin as he bit into it.

Lena stood, and Bridger watched her as she walked to the buffet.

"What?" May asked.

He rolled his eyes. "It was obvious. It was his only way to get it out. Didn't Hawkins tell you? Ask him."

May took out her phone and started to type.

Lena returned with a plate of fruit. Bridger looked at her plate. Lena stabbed his hand with a fork when he tried to pick a piece of pineapple off her plate.

"Ouch." Bridger rubbed his hand, looking at Lena, who winked.

"I love pineapple."

Bridger saw Lena's eyes follow Li Chu as Demon brought out him and Chen.

Li Chu was still in the baggy pants and sweatshirt he wore during the rescue in Manila. Chen was cooler in fresh gray pants and a short-sleeve button-down shirt that May had provided.

Both look worse for the wear. It is going to get even worse.

"It's time," Bridger announced. "Demon. Separate the buddies."

Demon steered Li Chu and Chen to separate lounge chairs between the living area and the pool. Demon stood in the shade nearby, dressed in jeans and a black shirt, with his Kimber 1911 conspicuously holstered to his belt.

Here we go. Everything has led to this. Let's light the fuse.

"Chen. You look like you could use some juice. Here," Bridger poured a pink juice into a glass and handed it to Chen. He hesitated. "It is Guava juice. Think of a combination of pears, strawberries, and mangos. You will find it is sweet and refreshing."

Chen sipped, sipped some more, then gulped it down. He wiped his mouth on his sleeve.

Bridger looked at Li Chu.

"You don't look thirsty." He turned to his team. "Let's get our business done quickly. It is the rainy season. I want to hit the beach while we can."

Snake, wearing shorts and a muscle shirt that exposed his massive biceps, arrived and guided Sun to a chair by Chen. Snake joined Demon.

Sun remained standing and took several steps from Chen.

"*Cào nǐ zǔzōng shíbā dài,*" Sun muttered to Chen, who jumped up. Demon and Snake moved toward the men.

Bridger waved them off.

"*Shǎo fèihu!*" Chen shouted back.

"Whoa, hang on there, fellas. Watch the language. There are ladies present."

"What did they say?" Beatrice asked.

"Well, Sun said—let me clean this up—insulted Chen's ancestors by telling him to...um...*Intercourse your ancestors to the 18th generation.* Very offensive. Chen responded with what we would say, like "cut the crap," but in China, it is rude."

Keep it up, guys. The fuse is burning fast.

"I guess they don't like each other," Snake said.

"What about you, Li Chu? Nothing to say?" Bridger asked, strolling to the other end of the twenty-foot-long pool.

Li Chu was silent.

"I demand to be taken to the Chinese embassy," Sun looked around. "I demand—"

"Nothing. You get to demand nothing, Sun," Bridger said as he stepped to close the distance between Sun and him. "Sit your ass down." Sun did as he was told. "I will give it to you straight. You are going to defect to the United States. Now. That's what you are going to do."

At first, Sun was silent, either from shock or misunderstanding. "What?" he said finally.

"You are staying here—Mauritius, by the way—until a CIA officer comes to take you. They will probably come from South Africa. It is the closest, don't you think?" He looked at May but didn't wait for her to respond.

"Imp."

Imp punched a few buttons, and the massive TV attached to the open space in a wall under an overhang turned on. A video started with muted sound.

"Remember that video I threatened you with in Zhang's office, exposing you as a criminal and the person responsible for the plane shootdown?" Sun's face turned red and his eyes never blinked as he watched the screen. "It was too good to waste, so we updated it with misinformation on your relationship with Chen. How you covered up knowing he was working for the CIA so you could take over the MSS. Blackmail and other unpleasant things...oh, and that now you are defecting to the United States."

"Lies!" Sun shouted.

"Yep, but I don't care and neither will anyone in China. Imp has posted it on social media across about every platform there is. Look on the bright side. You are trending—" Bridger looked at Imp.

"Number six and rising," Imp reported.

"Six is good. Let's go for number one! So, as you might expect, your colleagues in China are very interested in your whereabouts. Should we drop you at the door of the embassy like you demanded? You want to go back to Beijing and try to explain that it is all lies?"

Sun sat with his head down, hands between his legs. He started to shake.

Boom. That's one.

Bridger grabbed a chair and pulled up to face the three men. "Chen. Li Chu. It has been a long journey to get to this point."

"Can I just kill them? I'm getting hungry," Demon said. Bridger looked at Demon with an obvious *not now* look. "Okay. I get it."

"Chen. Tell us all about your role in the ranch attack." Chen's mouth opened but closed without making a sound. "Chen!" Bridger shouted.

"I...to my shame...I gave information to Li Chu."

"What?" May shouted as she stood.

"Are you that shocked, May?" Bridger asked. "You had to know, but you just couldn't think bad of your prized recruit."

Her eyes shot darts at Chen. Chen stood.

"Yes, May, it is true. I am sorry. He—" Chen pointed at Li Chu "—threatened to expose me. I could not...I was scared. I admit it." He looked at May

Boom. Boom. Two.

"And?" Bridger asked.

May walked over to Demon.

"Gun," she whispered and held out her hand. Without a thought, Demon took it out and handed it to her.

"I provided satellite images and information on...the...ranch." His voice trailed off. "I am sorry."

May flipped off the safety and racked the slide. The sound made everyone look as she walked over, raised the pistol, and pointed it at Chen's forehead from a foot away.

"May! No!" Lena said.

"May...what are you doing?" Bridger asked moving toward her. Bridger held his hand out to take the gun.

"You were going to kill my son...everyone...because you were *scared*?"

May's hand was steady and still pointed at Chen's head. Suddenly, she swung and pointed it at Sun.

"Are you coming with us or not?" She waited. "Answer me!'

Sun's eyes were flapping like a flag in a stiff wind.

"Yes. Yes!"

May swung her arm back to point at Chen.

"Ma-ay," Bridger said.

The bullet entered Chen's skull slightly above his left eye. He fell back, stiff as a tin soldier, and hit the pool with a bloody splash. Chen's blood mixed with the azure blue water, instantly darkening a patch around his bobbing body.

No one spoke or moved until Demon chimed in as he walked over and looked down at the water. "I think you'll have to get your pool cleaned," he said. He took the gun from May's hand, which she had dropped to her side. "May, I love you. Marry me."

Her pale face blushed, and then she patted Demon's arm.

"Thank you."

Bridger shook his head at Demon in annoyance, walked to May, and put his arm on her shoulder. Instead of the nervous post-trauma shaking he expected, she was calm.

"Hawkins has the Dossier. We have Sun. We didn't need him anymore," she told him with a firm voice.

"Now, who is insufferable?" he asked. He guided her to Lena, who wrapped her arm tightly around May's shoulder.

"Li Chu," Bridger said with a deliberate turn. "I'm a little conflicted on what to do here. You remember our conversation in New York?"

"I am glad she killed him," Li Chu said.

"Figured you would be. Anyway, I let you live despite everyone wanting you dead. We had a deal. I *forgave* you for all the murderous, horrific things you have done—not the least of which was torturing my mother and my…Lena. In return, you were to disappear."

"I was attacked."

"Don't blame me for that. Chapel and Hawkins approved the attack —after I let you go. I was planning on moving on. Then we had to go to Nigeria to save Chapel after we had already saved Chen."

"You should not have saved Chen."

"You might have been right about that." Bridger looked at Chen, still floating and bleeding in the pool. Bridger looked back at Lena.

"But I'll repeat it. I am conflicted about your status."

"You should all be dead. All of you!" Li Chu shouted, looking around the pool at the Spy Devils, May, and Lena. "I told Chen and the Mexican exactly where you were after torturing your mother."

"Let me kill him," Demon said, taking a step toward Li Chu. Bridger waved him off.

"At least I can take pride in ridding the world of the old senile terrorist Specter and the pathetic CIA creature…Henslow."

Bridger rose with a balled fist.

"Forgiveness revoked."

Lena walked to Demon and held her hand out. He looked at her and then May, who nodded. Demon flipped off the safety and handed her his weapon. Lena took it, and like May moments ago, she racked the slide as she walked.

Li Chu's eyes watched her, as did everyone else's—including Bridger. No one moved.

"What about forgive—" Li Chu started to say to her.

Lena fired at Li Chu until he, too, fell and splashed into the pool. She kept firing at him until the eight-round magazine was empty. She lowered her arm and watched him bleed and drift on the surface next to Chen.

"You are *definitely* going to have to get the pool cleaned now," Demon said, standing by them. Lena handed the Kimber back to Demon.

"Thank you."

"Marry her, Bridger," Demon said. "I'm asking her if you don't and May turns me down."

Bridger walked up to her and put his hands on her waist.

"What about forgiveness?" Bridger asked.

"Fuck it," she said.

54

ALWAYS CHANGING

New York City, New York
Two Weeks Later

"**B**ridger. Come in."
Chapel stood, came around his massive desk, walked up to Bridger, and held out his hand.

Amazingly, Bridger had never been to Chapel's office even once during the years the man helped May and the CIA support the Spy Devils.

Modern white leather and chrome furniture, tables, lamps, and chairs on a plush white carpet comprised one-quarter of the massive area. The wall to the left was divided among bookshelves, pictures, mementos, and awards of all kinds and languages.

Windows ran floor to ceiling and wall to wall behind the desk of his 17th-floor office overlooking Park Avenue Plaza.

"Nice digs, Chapel. You look better."

"Thank you. I am…" Chapel's voice cracked with emotion. "I…" Chapel pulled him in by the hand and hugged Bridger tight.

"Of course, Chap—Danny," Bridger said, gingerly patting the old man's back.

Chapel broke the hug and turned away so his guest couldn't see.

"Drink?"

"Diet Coke?" Bridger said.

Chapel walked to a bar along the wall of a large sitting area to the right of the double-wide oak door. He opened the refrigerator, took out a can, filled a glass with ice, and poured the beverage.

"This stuff will kill you," he said, handing the glass to Bridger.

Chapel poured a few fingers of Macallan single-malt whiskey for himself.

You don't look THAT good, Chapel.

"And that?" Bridger asked.

"Medicine. Doctor's orders." He pointed to a sitting area. "Let's sit."

Bridger took a chair. Chapel sat on the end of the couch nearest Bridger.

"I am offering you the position of Vice President and General Manager, Intelligence and Operations Division, Danforth Chapel Group."

Chapel sat back and sipped his Macallan.

Bridger sat, genuinely shocked and speechless—for a moment.

"What? Is this a joke? I don't want to—"

"Before you sputter a bunch of the Bridger banter I have heard before on why not, or—just listen. I am not retiring yet."

Chapel got another Diet Coke for Bridger and refilled his glass. He added another pour of his whiskey.

"Listen, I am not immediately pulling away from the company. I am not sure I could do that if I tried. This profession is a drug. I need help. Help me. You have an MBA and run a massive global intel operation, so you can't be too stupid."

"Thanks. I appreciate that."

"Plus, I owe you my life."

Maybe this isn't such a bad idea? Lena would love it, I think.

Chapel emptied half his glass, paused, then finished off his drink. "So?"

Bridger finished his Diet Coke, set the glass down, and stood with his hand out. "Deal."

Chapel grasped Bridger's hand with a broad smile on his face. "Fantastic."

"First, I need to borrow Hawk and his team."

"Want to go for a nosh?" Bridger asked.

"What's New York without a good nosh?" she said, grabbing her coat.

He enjoyed their new habit of strolling the sidewalks, hand in hand, on the mushy cold sidewalk from Hudson Yards to the little diner they had found during their first New York walk together.

When the waitress came, Bridger ordered a corned beef on rye. Lena selected chicken soup.

"You still like this place?" Bridger looked around the room.

Please tell me you do.

"Yes. It is quaint. The food is…New York." She smiled.

Good.

"Well, make it something else. I bought it for you. Lena's of New York." He smiled and moved his hands like he was reading a marquee. "The paperwork is all in your name. It's a done deal."

"What?" This is—" She looked at him in shock.

"Yours."

She moved to his side of the table and hugged him, and they kissed.

Her eyes started to look around the space, and he could tell she was already remodeling. Then she stopped. "What about you?"

"I'm taking a job working for Chapel. Based here, so I figured you might need a reason to stay here in New York."

The waitress came with their food. Lena sipped the soup and gave an approving nod.

"Keeping the chef?"

"I am the chef," she said, "but this *is* good." She took another spoonful.

"You are working for Chapel, I hear," a familiar voice said.

They looked up to see May, bundled to her neck in a heavy wool coat and scarf, smiling over them.

"May!" Lena jumped up, and they hugged. "Sit," Lena said, pointing to an empty seat at their table.

"Hello, Trowbridge," May said as she sat beside Lena. She tugged off her thick gloves and then placed them on the table. May unwrapped the scarf from around her neck and rubbed the wrinkled skin.

"Hello, May," he said, less annoyed at her sudden appearance and more bothered by his not sensing her presence. "Yes. I'm going to work for Chapel. Don't show up begging for a job."

"Oh, son. Don't worry. Max asked if I would help him on a few projects. I said I would."

"You are going to work with Hawkins? On purpose?"

"Don't be insufferable."

"So, things *haven't* changed."

May reached across the table and put her hand on his. Her skin felt warm and clammy on his. She put her other hand on Lena's.

"Trowbridge. Things are always changing. What about the Spy Devils? Are they done?" May asked.

He looked at them both.

"Not quite."

55

IT'S OVER

Jalisco State, Mexico
One Week Later

"Hi, honey," Bridger said, looking again at the glassy eyes of Emilio López, aka *El Puerco Grande*, The Big Pig. "Remember Us?"

Behind the rapidly blinking eyelids of the drug-induced bloodshot eyes, Bridger saw confusion transform into realization and then morph into fear when he saw Demon standing behind Bridger with a broad grin and holding his rusty pliers at his side.

Mmmmm muffled from his duct-taped mouth. Tears leaked from the corners of his eyes and tracked down into his tangled black hair.

Bridger turned to Demon.

"I think he remembers us!"

"Lucky him," Demon said with a *clink clink* of his pliers.

Soon after the CJNG attacks in the United States, a new anti-cartel operation, designated "Black Thunder," had pursued the drug cartel facilities and leadership in and around the Mexican state of Jalisco. The primary purpose was the eradication or arrest of Vincente Ramirez, aka "*El Hombre*," the leader of the drug cartel leadership.

Leading the effort were elite Mexican Marines, supported by U.S. military and Drug Enforcement Agency forces, and intelligence support assets—including the Danforth Chapel Group's new Spy Devils unit.

The Spy Devils found López hiding that morning in a cluster of dilapidated houses at the intersection of two dirt roads northeast of Puerto Vallarta in Las Palmas de Arriba. He was crouching in a hole dug in the floor of a closet in a crumbling brick and plaster room. He clutched a revolver but dropped it and raised his hands, shouting, "*No dispares!*" "Don't shoot!" when Hawk from the Chapel tactical team stuck a rifle in his face.

Now, he was hanging upside down from the exposed beam in the dirty room, which smelled like old grime, rotten wood, and fungus. The Chapel team secured the perimeter and the intersection. Milton and Beatrice hovered Devilbots overhead from inside one of the three vans. Snake was in the driver's seat. Angel was next to him, reading intel reports. Imp was sleeping in the back.

"We didn't get to finish our questioning last time we met, Mr. Pig," Bridger said as he circled López, playfully pushing him to swing him back and forth. A track appeared under his head as his hair brushed dirt from the floor.

"This is a one-question, one-answer quiz," Bridger continued. "If you answer correctly, your prize is an all-expenses-paid, thirty-year vacation in a lovely Mexican prison. A wrong answer gets you Demon —and eventually, we *will* get the right answer, and you *will* go to prison."

"Please don't talk," Demon said.

"Let me count it down," Bridger said. "Five. Four. Three. Two. One. *Buzz*. Time's up."

"Hell, yes!" Demon said, stepping toward López, who started to wriggle like a fish.

"Tlajomulco! South of Guadalajara! He is in a house! In Tlajomul-co!" López shouted.

"Son of a bitch!" Demon shouted to the wall as he turned and stuffed his pliers into the back pocket of his jeans.

"We have a winner."

———————

At 4:40 a.m., as DEA and U.S. forces waited, the elite Mexican Marines launched their assault on the two-story house in Tlajomulco. As they stormed inside the front and back doors, over a dozen well-armed CJNG guards tossed grenades and fired while retreating.

The Marines fired and cleared each room in the house—killing guards along the way. Upstairs, they found two dead in one room. In a bathroom, four women—prostitutes who doubled as cooks and maids —were screaming and crying.

After ten minutes, the Marines controlled the entire house. Eleven CJNG guards were dead.

The Marines located Ramirez's bedroom on the first floor. Inside were money, drugs, weapons, mobile phones, bags from fashionable clothing stores, cookie wrappers, and medicine, including injectable testosterone, syringes, and antibiotics.

They pounded on the wall next to the king-sized bed, where they found—as López had said—a door behind a mirror leading to a hidden passageway. A handle hidden in the light fixture opened the secret door leading to an escape tunnel.

The escape tunnel was lit and led to an access door for the city sewage system, through which Vincente had escaped with three guards. They had at least a 20-minute head start on the Marines.

When a filthy Ramirez and his three guards emerged from the drainage system manhole, they were met by the red pinpoints of the Chapel team's rifle laser sights. Behind them were more Mexican Marines.

"¡Párense!"

When the three guards raised their weapons instead of stopping, quick pops accompanied the bullets that ripped into them. Vincente stood paralyzed with fear as red dots zigzagged across his face and the body armor vest strapped to his chest.

Bridger set his Devil Stick to Taser and approached Vincente. He held it up and pointed it at Vincente's face. Bridger opened his mouth, but a witty, sarcastic comment didn't come out. He looked at Vincente, lowered his arm, turned, and walked away.

"Take him," Bridger said to the Marines.

"Like hell," Demon said. In a few quick steps, he was at Vincente. On his last step, he reared his leg back and brought it up between Vincente's legs with enough force to lift the cartel leader off the ground. Vincente let out an *oomph* as air rushed from his lungs and he collapsed.

"Now take him," Demon said.

"What was that?" Bridger asked.

"Oops," he said as his scruffy face morphed into a smile.

"Badass" and other comments, snickers, and laughs came from the Chapel team as the Marines secured Vincente with zip-ties.

Demon followed Bridger through the maze of Mexican law enforcement and emergency vehicles. They all had red and blue lights flashing in the early morning darkness. A few blocks away, there was enough light to glimpse yellow tape cordoning off the press and public from the frenzy of activity in the blocks around the house.

Bridger shivered as he felt the chill of the cool air against his sweat-soaked clothes. He felt for the golf ball marker in his pocket, ensuring it was there. Bridger stopped before he reached the Spy Devils' van, parked with side and driver's doors open, away from the chaos.

He saw Milton sitting on the floor of the van's open side door with his arm around Beatrice. Snake sat sideways in the driver's seat, looking out. Angel leaned against the side of the next van with his arms crossed, head back, and eyes closed. Imp was next to him— digging at the bottom of a potato chip bag.

"What now?" Demon asked Bridger, resting his hand on his shoulder.

Bridger took out his phone, dialed it, and put it to his ear.

"Lena?" he asked, despite knowing it was her. He waited for her to ask the question he knew was coming. It came.

"Yes, it's over."

ACKNOWLEDGMENTS

Here we are. The third book of *The Spy Devils* thrillers. Is it the last? Time will tell.

The idea for this series started in 2017—give or take—when I decided not to do a sequel to *Secret Wars: An Espionage Story.* I thought long and hard about a new book. Talked to a few people. Spewed out some drafts. Then more. Then some more.

When COVID hit, I thought the book was ready. I was impatient. It wasn't as ready as I thought. I found that out as I queried. That, coupled with the uncertainty of the publishing market, sent me to self-publish.

It has gone pretty well. Decent sales—I would like more! The books have received good reviews and some awards. I've met many authors, readers, and fans.

Thanks to all of you.

Every author I have spoken with says they want their book to be entertaining. If the book isn't entertaining, everything else they want— a bestseller, positive reviews—won't follow. Some authors seek "pure" entertainment, while others craft their stories with themes or messages.

I'm a "themer." Is that a word?

The Spy Devils thrillers have veins of a theme running through them. For *The Spy Devils,* there was an undercurrent of hope. For *Rebellious Son,* it was relationships. For *Devil's Own Day,* it is change.

Throughout the series, I sometimes started with "What do I want this character to be when the book is done, and how do I get there?" Bridger has always wanted to change his life to something beyond espionage. Each book gradually moves him in that direction. In *Devil's*

Own Day, he faces the moment when he would have to make a decision that combines all three themes.

What would he do? I wasn't sure until I got there. He made the choice. I just wrote it down.

Thank you, Bridger!

I must acknowledge some people. *Devil's Own Day* is dedicated to friends, fans, and family who have helped me with this book and in other ways along the Spy Devil's journey. Without them (and others I will forget to add because I am getting older and more forgetful... sorry), the difficult road to completing and marketing a book would be nearly impossible.

Ryan Steck—the man behind The Real Book Spy website and author of the *Lethal Range* series. Ryan has been providing me with support and guidance since I posted a photo of the first draft of *The Spy Devils*. He really cares about authors and the book industry. More than anything else, he is a good friend and person.

Eric Bishop, author of *The Body Man* series and other works. In addition to being a fine writer, Eric dedicates much of his time to supporting other authors. He seems to know everyone because I think he does know everyone! We speak often and share ideas. In simple terms, Eric is a good guy.

Scott Swanson and I have been talking about writing for years. We still do. Such an excellent author (doing horror now).

Once again, editor and fellow Hawkeye Laura Gehlin Powers displayed her skills and patience with me as she reviewed a manuscript that desperately needed her skills. Believe me. She was busy.

If you like my newsletters, website, social media posts, or giveaways, then you need to call James Abt at BTS Designs. I depend on James's patience and talent to get the word out, which he executes with total professionalism.

I like the covers of the Spy Devils books. They are bright, but more than that, if you look closely, you can see elements of the story within. Previous covers featured a silhouetted single man looking in the distance. For *Devil's Own Day*, I wanted to pay homage to the team. I had the *Band of Brothers* image in mind. The team at Damonza.com, which did all the covers, has been great.

The whole Best Thriller Books crew. Kashif Hussain, Steve Netter, Chris Miller, Derek Luedtke, David Dobiasek, adn the others. Their reviews and support to all writers and the industry are indispensable. A special shout-out to Todd Wilkins, an excellent reviewer who also did my video promo materials.

More fellow authors, including Adam Hamby. Ward Larsen. David McCloskey. Simon Gervais. Mark Greaney. Alex Shaw. Alma Katsu. Josh Hood. Steve Stratton. David Darling. I.S. Berry. Chris Hauty. Michael Frost Beckner. Terrence McCauley. Brian Andrews. Ama Adair. Jeff Clark.

I greatly appreciate the support of the members of 'Joe's Devils' and others. They are my biggest fans and provide moral support. Many are also authors. I will miss some (sorry again), but they include Mark Elliot. Jeff Circle. Michael Carlson. Nick Stoczanyn. Meenaz Lodhi. Neil Schoolnik. Daryl Delabbio. Manfred Genther. Tom Dooley. Richard Maverick. Larry Sheps. Steve Faris. Scott Haakenson. Richard Maverick. Aida Flick. Steve Thomas. Brian Simmons. John Morgan. Jared Macarin. Jeff Lawson. David Thomock. Joshua McGuoirk. John Edward Hebert. Kronos Ananthsimha. Tom Madden. Jeramie Edwards. Bryan Licsko. Jenny Jones. Paul Ekman. Donna Walton. Arlene Houk. Jeff Burrell. Peter Kolosick. Brian Collins. Alan Goldberg. Jeff Burrell. Cameron McClellan. Kevon Bozarth. Julie Watson. Jack Stewart. Jeff Clark.

I want to thank Carl Wallis, who is also a Devil. I asked him to help with dialogue for the chapter set in Australia. I didn't want to be too American and make it up from Google searches. Carl made valuable changes to the point I named the character after him.

One of the best consequences of becoming an author was having Alan Warren ask me to be a guest host for thriller writers on his podcast *The House of Mystery Radioshow* on NBC Radio. Alan is also a famous author and true crime TV star. I get to talk to and learn from an array of authors across the writing spectrum.

Podcasters like Dave Temple, of *The Thriller Zone* podcast. Glenn

Pasch, of *You're In Charge–Now What* podcast. Travis Davis of *Author Ecke*. Tim O'Brien of *Shaping Opinion*. Ben Buehler-Garcia of *American Warrior Radio*. Jack Clark of *Course of Action*. Terrence McCauley of *Spies, Lies, and Private Eyes*.

I want to give a shout-out to the amazing local libraries that have put my books on their shelves. The Wheaton Public Library. Glen Ellyn Public Library. Support your local library!

Who else should you support? Your local independent bookstore! David Hunt at Town House Books in St. Charles, Illinois, and Sandra Cararo, the owner of The Book Dragon Shop in Staunton, Virginia. Both put all my books out at their amazing stores.

Finally, as always, my (growing) family offers encouragement and patience. My wife Lynda tolerates my frustration rants and many moments of blankly looking off into space. The kids. Jessica and her husband Roger. Sarah and her future (as of this moment) husband Matt. Benjamin. As I always say, "Without you, there is nothing." It is true.

As I often say about my books, they aren't Hemingway. I hope they are good stories and that you have enjoyed them…so far!

Joe Goldberg
November 2023

ABOUT THE AUTHOR

Joe Goldberg is the award-winning and Amazon best-selling author of *Secret Wars: An Espionage Story, The Spy Devils,* and *R*ebellious Son: A Spy Devils Thriller. He has been a CIA covert action officer, corporate intelligence director, and an international political campaign consultant. He is currently a college instructor and writer. A native of Iowa, he loves cooking, the Iowa Hawkeyes, and his family. He resides in a suburb of Chicago, most likely listening to Jimmy Buffet music.

Joe can be found at: JoeGoldbergBooks.com

facebook.com/JoeGoldbergBooks
twitter.com/JoeGoldbergBook
instagram.com/JoeGoldbergBooks

ALSO BY JOE GOLDBERG

Secret Wars: An Espionage Story

The Spy Devils

Rebellious Son: A Spy Devils Thriller

Printed in the USA
CPSIA information can be obtained
at www.ICGtesting.com
LVHW010254151123
763986LV00087B/2690